A CONNECTICUT GUMSHOE

IN

King Arthur's Court

BY

RANDY MCCHARLES

A CONNECTICUT GUMSHOE

IN
King Arthur's Court

BY

RANDY MCCHARLES

TYCHE BOOKS LTD.

Published by Tyche Books Ltd.
Calgary, Alberta, Canada
www.TycheBooks.com

Cover Art & Layout by Indigo Chick Designs
Interior Layout by Ryah Deines
Editorial by M.L.D. Curelas

First Tyche Books Ltd Edition 2020
Print ISBN: 978-1-989407-23-3
Ebook ISBN: 978-1-989407-24-0

Author photograph: Leonard Halmrast

This book was funded in part by a grant from the Alberta Media Fund.

This work is dedicated to Humphrey Bogart. Though he passed away before I was born, I grew up enjoying many of his classic films such as The Maltese Falcon, The Big Sleep, and Casablanca. His onstage mannerisms set him apart from other actors and made him a role model for fictional noir detectives. Though Bogart's personal life was flawed in many ways, his film roles were an early inspiration for me to become a storyteller. It has been an honour and a privilege to invent a sham version of Sam Spade in the pages of this book.

PART 1

THE MACGUFFIN

1
A CONNECTICUT GUMSHOE

A HALF-OUNCE of molten lead whizzed past Sam Sparrow's ear, slammed through a pine crate that claimed to have once contained Sunkist oranges, then ricocheted off the graffiti-encrusted wall of an aging Food-For-Less grocery store. Yup. Just an average day in East Hartford.

Sam spit out a stale wad of Hubba Bubba Hawaiian Punch chewing gum and skulked further into the filthy alley. Slipping behind a second stack of empty produce boxes, he winced as the rubber soles of his knock-off Burberry gumshoes squeaked like traitorous mice on the damp asphalt. The noise probably wasn't enough to give his position away. Probably.

A gruff voice barked from the mouth of the alley. "You only got one bullet left, Sparrow, and there's four of us." A chorus of mocking laughter echoed between the concrete walls that lined the deserted backstreet.

Math had never been Sam's strong suit, but he knew the trouble boy was right. Once he fired off that last slug, even the questionable protection of grocery store garbage would be lost. It was at times like this that Sam really hated Hartford.

Crouching onto his haunches, Sam eased himself down until the seat of his dark-brown polyester pants rested on filthy asphalt. Even more carefully, he set his Smith & Wesson M&P semi-automatic revolver onto a relatively clean strip of cardboard. Like most ex-cops, Sam had purchased his service weapon when he left the job. You could change partners and precincts, but your weapon was a part of you.

Reaching into the left outside pocket of his tan trench coat, also a cheap Burberry knock-off, Sam pulled out a worn leather pouch held together by an equally worn strip of leather lace. Untying the kit revealed two pockets, each sealed with Velcro. Sam tore one pocket open and retrieved a matchbook and a thin box of Zig-Zag rolling papers. Opening the matchbook revealed three matches. Well, he only needed one. Drawing a slip of paper from the box, he pinched it between thumb and middle finger until it was trough-shaped.

With his free hand, Sam tore open the other pouch and drew out three pinches of Bull Durham tobacco, which he spread along the curved paper. Holding the open cigarette with four fingers, he rolled the paper back and forth, further evening the tobacco and working the curved paper into a tube. Then he licked the remaining edge of the paper and held it down until it dried.

Sam knew that these days you could buy pre-rolled paper and an injector to apply the tobacco; but he couldn't envision Humphrey Bogart using one, so neither did he. If that made him old-fashioned, he could live with it.

Another bullet smashed into some boxes a few feet away as Sam struck a match and lit one end of the cigarette. Palming his fedora off his head, he took a long drag and puffed smoke into the bowl of the hat; no sense giving the trouble boys a target. He'd been told the hat was also old-fashioned, even though every men's clothing store in the state sold them. What did people know anyway?

Cradling the cigarette between his lips, Sam tucked the paper and matches away, resealed the nearly empty tobacco pouch, and slid the kit back into his pocket. He then reached into his suit jacket pocket and pulled out a three-inch by four-inch spiral bound notebook you could buy anywhere for under a buck. It seemed as good a time as any to review his notes. Sam flipped the book open to the first page.

Hartford, Connecticut. Crowded. Dirty. Poverty rate second highest in the country. Murder rate five times the national average. The "beat", as Hartford is sometimes called, is a lousy place to live and a worse place to die.

Sam smiled. He'd written those words almost a year ago, the day he'd hung up his shingle: Sam Sparrow, PI. He figured he could script his cases and sell them to Hollywood. Be the next Raymond Chandler. That first day had been like living a dream.

The remainder of the book held blank pages; it had been an uneventful year. Until today. Working the pencil loose from the spiral, Sam scribbled one more line.

Worse still when at the hands of third-rate hatchet men in a filthy east-end alley.

Sam figured he'd hit a lot of lows in his life, lows that most decent folk never get to see. Not even in the papers. But this was the lowest. A hoarse chuckle escaped his lips. "When did I get so stupid as to let a pack of punk trouble boys sucker me down to the harbour front?"

He took another draw on the cigarette and shook his head.

The stack of crates Sam hid behind reeked of mouldy lettuce. The alley smelled almost as bad as his fleabag apartment kitchen, but he couldn't complain; if the crates had been cardboard instead of wood, he'd likely be dead right now. It was a hard thing knowing his life was at the mercy of the quality of garbage that surrounded him. But Sam had known harder things in his thirty years hustling the streets of Hartford.

A sharp crack interrupted Sam's thoughts, followed by the snick of thin wood splintering among the orange crates. Another pot shot. The punks couldn't see where he squatted among the garbage, but it was only a matter of time. Wooden crates were a poor substitute for Kevlar body armour. Sam knew they were trying to goad him into expending that last shell. Then they'd walk right up like wanna-be button men and tap him right between the eyes. On the other hand, a lucky shot could drop him just as easily.

Glancing back at his notes, Sam realized that his year-old prose read like an obituary, so he pushed the book back into his jacket pocket. His cigarette was half-gone, and he wondered if he'd be able to finish it before the trouble boys worked up enough nerve to come into the alley after him.

The only thing Sam had going for him was the bloated orb of the evening sun that oozed like sickly blood behind a cluster of skyscrapers across the river. Add the storm clouds that had watered the alley a few minutes earlier and looked to be rallying for a second round, and it might grow dark enough to sneak out the other end of the long backstreet without getting his head blown off. Unlikely, but still a chance. Of course, the trouble boys had to know that. At least two of them were probably circling around the block. Why was there never a cop around when you needed one?

Sam almost laughed out loud. Cops. Sam had walked a Hartford beat for ten years before getting kicked off the job. Like Philip Marlowe, he'd been fired for insubordination. He even had it in writing. The termination letter hung in a glass-cased wooden frame on his fleabag apartment wall, right next to his reprint theatrical poster for *The Big Sleep*.

Truth was, Sam had a habit of rubbing people the wrong way. He didn't deny it. Especially people he needed to be able to count on. His beat partners. His captain. Girlfriends. Anyone who got in Sam's face got a double helping served back to them. He couldn't stop himself. Usually, he didn't even try.

Despite having been one, or maybe because of it, Sam didn't have much respect for the police. That there were no sirens breaking the evening quiet was no surprise. Someone would show up. Eventually. They'd count corpses, collect shell casings, and open a new cold case. If the corpse was Sam Sparrow's, they'd raise a glass at McCauley's Tavern, and not in a good way. His precinct had been happy to see Sam go. They'd be even happier when he caught his own big sleep.

Even so, being a cop was all Sam knew. It had surprised no one when he got his PI license and opened a small office. He'd been in business a year, if you could call sitting in an empty office drinking Jim Beam while listening to the clock tick on the wall, business. Even if he survived the next hour, the overdue rent on his office and tenement apartment would put him out on the street. Tomorrow he could be living in these produce crates.

A loud crack interrupted Sam's thoughts. Another gunshot? No. Too loud. Too long. He looked up from the remains of his cigarette. Those clouds were getting mean. Another crack. Only now he recognized it for what it was— thunder. He watched as lightning crested across a grey

Hartford skyline followed by a third rumble. Then rain began drizzling its pitter-patter onto the garbage crates.

"Great. I'm going to die. Alone. In the rain." Sam couldn't keep a ragged smile from breaking the thin line of his lips.

Two more shots ripped into the wooden crates, reminding Sam of the scene from Chandler's *The Big Sleep* where Marlowe crouches in the rain behind Corino's sedan while Eddie Mars' watchdog takes potshots at him. Only here there'd be no gorgeous blonde waltzing in to distract the shooters so Sam could get away. Life was never as generous as the movies.

Another shot. These punks were getting antsy. Probably wanted to get their little murder tied up so they could retire to some hole-in-the-ground rumshop out of the rain. A fourth shot came from the other end of the alley, making a *thwap* sound as the slug embedded itself into an empty crate.

That's it, then. Trapped. Sam slumped back against the dirty brick wall of the grocery store and crushed out the stub of his cigarette.

A flash of lightning lit up the alley, and in the sudden brightness Sam found himself staring at his service revolver where he'd set it down, the matte black metal now slick with rain.

A horrible thought entered his mind. Though upon reflection, the thought had merit. Those trouble boys had gone to all this effort to pop him. He could take that away from them by popping himself. It's not the way he thought he'd go. It never is, though it happens often enough. But it was better than having his lights put out by some tattooed gorilla who would pimp his own mother for a hit of meth.

Lifting the semi-automatic, Sam waved it vaguely at his head. If he was going to do this, he'd have to do it right. Stick the barrel in his mouth. Hold his hand steady. Pull the trigger. It wasn't something you could do at the drop of a hat. You had to work up to it. Another bullet splintered wood near his ear. Trouble was, he didn't have time to work up to it.

"You all right, mister?"

The barrel still inches from his lips, Sam's hand froze. He looked around and saw a boy maybe ten years old sitting inside the shelter of an open wooden crate not four feet away.

"How'd I not see you there?" Sam asked. In the failing light, he couldn't make out a facial expression.

"You were gonna off yourself, weren't you?" asked the boy.

Sam didn't answer. He didn't need to.

The boy asked another question. "Is that what Bogart would do?"

Bogart? Sam lowered his hand until the gun rested in his lap. How did this kid know?

With the stealth of a cat, the boy left the shelter of his crate and slid over to sit against the wall next to Sam. Rain fell onto brown hair almost as dark as Sam's own. "Bogart would find a way out of this mess," the boy said. "He'd use that last bullet to shoot a gas can, showering those thugs with burning fuel. Or he'd find a smugglers tunnel hidden behind a dumpster."

Sam let out a sigh. "Ain't nothin' in this alley, kid. Already looked. No tunnels. No windows. No unlocked doors. Doors are all metal, by the way."

The boy sucked on his lower lip, then nodded.

"Look, kid. You go climb under that crate over there. Those trouble boys don't know you're here. I'll fire off this last round and run down the alley. It'll all be over and they'll leave. Then you can get away."

The boy rocked a bit, nodding his head. "Bogart might do that. If he had no other way." Then the boy cast him a mischievous grin. "But I know another way. A way we can both get out of here. But you'll owe me a favour."

Sam felt his face tighten into a brief smile. "Really, kid? A favour sounds cheap."

"It could be a big favour," the boy said. "It might even take a few days."

"I'd appreciate a few days," Sam answered. "Those trouble boys are only offering minutes."

The boy pressed a finger against the side of his nose. "Then you accept?"

Sam began to say, "Sure, kid," when a bolt of lightning slammed into the jumble of boxes that sheltered him and the boy. Light blinded Sam's eyes and a flash of heat dried the rain from his face. Then an electric eel slid up and down his entire body. Sam's last thought was, Damn, I bet this kid really did have a way out.

2

A VERY OLD, YOUNG LAD

SAM CRACKED HIS jaw and felt the bones rattle in all the right places. He could hear them pop, though the sound was muffled, as if a pillow had been wedged between his teeth and his ears.

He shrugged his shoulders, wriggled his toes, and clenched his hands into fists. His right hand failed to clench. It took him a moment to realize that was because his fingers were wrapped around the grip of his revolver. Why is my bean-shooter out? Then he remembered. The alley. The trouble boys. The lightning. The boy.

Sam opened his eyes.

Despite being surrounded by stone walls, Sam knew he no longer sat amidst garbage in an East Hartford backstreet. It wasn't raining for one thing. And there was a roof over his head and a floor beneath his keister. Roof and floor were also stone, though the roof offered long, wooden support beams thick as railway ties. The stone was brick and mortar, though the bricks were larger and rougher than any stonework Sam had ever seen.

"Good," said a youthful voice. "You are aware. It is about time."

Sam turned his head and squinted as sunlight from an open window partly blinded him. The boy from the alley stepped into the light and looked down at him with an expression of disapproval well beyond his years. "We have only just met and already I wonder if I chose the right man for the job."

Then, before Sam's eyes, the boy began to grow taller and more muscular. A man at the peak of life now stood before him, but continued to change, sprouting a beard and lengthening hair that soon faded from brown to salt-and-pepper grey. Age lines broke out around the man's eyes and mouth, and veins stood out on his nose. Finally, an old man in flowing blue robes the hue of new denim reached out a hand, plucked a frumpy hat from somewhere, and placed it on his head. The greybeard then leaned forward on a crooked staff that Sam hadn't noticed before.

"Well?" the old man said in a dry, almost wheezing voice. "Are you going to just sit there?"

"There are a number of things I could say right now," Sam mumbled, almost to himself. He holstered his revolver beneath his coat, climbed to his feet, and then adjusted his fedora. "I could write a book, a dozen chapters filled with all of the things I could say right now."

The old man seemed willing to wait, so Sam continued his song and dance, tugging at his coat sleeves and cracking his fingers while he tried to make sense of the situation. He soon realized, however, that sense wasn't in the cards and that he should say something, if for no other reason than to prompt the old man, who moments before had been a boy, to continue speaking.

"Outside the window there?" Sam asked. "Is that chickens clucking?"

A frown deepened across the greybeard's face. "If that is the best you can do, then I most certainly have chosen the wrong man."

Sam rubbed his ear, something he had picked up from Philip Marlowe. Maybe he had overestimated his host's patience. "Okay. How about this? Who are you?"

The old man nodded. "Better. My name is Merlin."

"Not—? Nah, it couldn't be."

Sam took a careful glance around the room. Two desks commanded opposite corners, with a ladder-back chair behind each and a pair of similar chairs in front. The desks and chairs were wood, white oak maybe, and were of utilitarian design. Perfect for their relatively stark surroundings. The only other fixture was a series of shelves along one wall loaded with baubles and knickknacks Sam had difficulty giving names to.

Then there was the window. Open. No glass. Plain cloth curtains hung to either side. Sam figured you could lift the ends and tie them together, effectively covering the window against bad weather. The barnyard sounds came from outside: chickens clucking, horseshoes against cobbles, and children laughing. Not the kind of self-conscious laugh one might hear on the streets of Hartford. More the carefree giggling one hears while watching the von Trapp youngsters on *The Sound of Music*. Sam had no idea what a real castle, where people actually lived and children actually played, might feel like, but he had a strong suspicion it might feel exactly like what he was feeling now.

"Not the Merlin from the movies?" he said finally.

"Movies?" the old man echoed. "Ah, yes. Those moving pictures people in the future find so fascinating. I have never bothered to experience one myself. Perhaps you could provide further clarification to your question?"

"Camelot? King Arthur? Knights of the Round Table?"

The old man smiled. "You have heard of us. That may help you in your task."

"Task?" Sam had a million questions, but he could spend years asking them. Getting to the heart of things was always the best course.

"You could not have forgotten already," said the old man. Merlin. "You owe me a favour for getting you out of that nasty predicament in the alley."

"Then you really are that small boy?"

Merlin harrumphed. "I would have thought that self-evident. How do you get anything done if you constantly stop and question every little thing?"

Sam let a brief smile brighten his lips. "I find it saves time in the long run if I avoid chasing false assumptions."

"If you say so," said the old man. "Now let me save you some time. I have been called away from Camelot and require you to keep an eye on things while I am gone. It should only be a few days. Normally I would not bother finding someone to fill in, but there have been odd whisperings of late. I fear that while the cat is away, the mice may decide to play."

The greybeard suddenly chortled and lifted a hand away from his staff to cover his mouth. He continued chortling behind his hand until he saw that Sam wasn't joining in, or even cracking a smile. Merlin ceased chortling, lowered his hand, and resumed his earlier frown. "Do you not see the humour of the phrase? I am the cat. Those who would cause discord are the mice."

"I get it no problem." Sam adjusted his fedora again, needing something to do with his hands. "But I've heard it a million times. It kind of loses its charm the second or third time around."

Merlin's frown deepened. "I am confident that such a play on words has never before entertained the human ear. I suppose that coming from the future gives you an advantageous perspective; perhaps such a perspective will help you with your task."

"And disadvantageous," Sam suggested. "What I know about kings and castles you could fit on a postage stamp. I'll be like a fish on land, a priest in a whorehouse, a one-legged man in a relay race."

Merlin rubbed his beard, his gaze turning inward as though deep in thought. At last he spoke. "Your mastery of sarcasm is wondrous. How it might help you, I have no idea. But I do understand you. You feel unqualified to perform the task I have set before you. You feel that if I leave Camelot, that the mice will not only play, they will eat all the cheese in the pantry, let the horses out of the barn, and drain the water from the moat. And you will be powerless to stop them."

"That's not how I would have said it," Sam said, lying; that was exactly how he would say it. "But you get the general idea."

The greybeard wagged his staff. "So what do you suggest? That I send you back to where you came from and find someone more qualified for the job?"

"I'd hate to lose the business," Sam said, which was true. He needed business. Any business. Just to pay some bills. But this was whacked. Was he really talking to Merlin? The magician? More likely he was bleeding out in that alley, a half-ounce of lead lodged somewhere in his brain. He looked the old man straight in the eye. "But that's what I would do."

"I see," said Merlin. "You do realize that those ruffians are still waiting outside that alley. If I send you back it will be to almost certain death."

Sam rubbed his ear. "Maybe I'm being too humble. I am a private detective, after all. And I spent ten years before that as a cop."

"Which," said Merlin, "is why I chose you. I have yet to discover if I chose wisely. It is perhaps fortunate for you that I have not the luxury of reconsidering my decision; I have delayed my departure as long as I dare." With those words, the old man tapped his staff on the floor and strode purposefully toward the room's open doorway.

"Just one thing," Sam said quickly.

Merlin stopped and turned toward him, a look of stern impatience marring his bearded features.

"You're a magician, or wizard, or whatever you call yourself. And I'm just an ordinary joe who you expect to do your job for you."

The marred face marred even further.

"Maybe you could work some magic. You know, to give me some kind of an edge?"

"I am astounded," said Merlin. "Not even Arthur when he was a lad demonstrated such impertinence. As I have not the leisure to discuss this with you, I shall accede you one work of magic. Ask what you wish, but be quick about it. I suggest you choose your words wisely; I am aware of the tales of djinn who offer three wishes yet make men poorer for the asking. An ill-sought wish is worse than no wish at all."

Sam couldn't have been less prepared to make a wish. The only thing he knew for sure was that the sky was not the limit. If he asked for Merlin's power, or the wisdom of the ages, or anything else that could really help him, he'd get at best a laugh and at worst returned to a filthy backstreet to die. Would that happen, anyway? When this was over, would Merlin send him back to the exact moment he had left? If he had left; this still felt like an insane dream.

The old man grunted with impatience and Sam knew exactly what he should ask for.

"Could you?" Sam asked. "Could you make it so that my gun never runs out of bullets?"

Merlin stared at him. Never in his life had Sam seen such a peculiar look on a face before.

"It happens a lot in movies," Sam explained, drawing his semi-automatic from its duty holster beneath his trench coat. "A cop with a handgun should only have ten rounds, but ends up shooting twenty or more shells before reloading. Westerns are worse, with a cowboy knocking an entire band of Indians off their horses with a six-shooter or a rifle that should only have two shots."

"I understood you the first time," Merlin said, his expression cold enough to freeze sunlight. Then the magician turned and stalked quickly out of the room, the words, "It is done," drifting as an echo in his wake.

3
A SMALL OFFICE IN A LARGE CASTLE

SAM DIDN'T FEEL any different. Turning the revolver in his hand, he sensed only quiet familiarity; no evidence of any magician's hocus-pocus. He didn't even believe in magic. He'd seen and experienced too much pain in his life to think there was room in the world for something as sanguine as magic. It was much easier to believe that he'd eaten his gun in that alley, or that the trouble boys had finally gotten off a lucky shot. Whatever was going on, he'd just have to deal with it.

Alone and unsure in a time and place that wasn't at all possible, Sam let out a deep sigh, holstered his weapon, and shrugged himself into the ladder-back chair behind the desk closest to the window. Whether or not this was all a dream, he had to take a load off.

Reaching down, he peeled his rubber gumshoes off his worn, plain toe oxfords and tossed the knock-off Burberrys beneath the desk. Then he leaned back into what he quickly realized was the most uncomfortable chair ever made. Kicking his feet up onto the desk failed to improve things. "Damn."

Back on his feet, Sam set himself a quest; this was Camelot, after all. He would find himself a seat cushion. Or die trying.

The door Merlin had left by stood open. Sam poked his head into an outer office where a single desk sat next to a closed door. Like the desks in the inner office, its surface was bare. Not so much as a coffee stain. A ladder-back chair sat behind it with four additional chairs lined up along one wall. They all looked identical to the hemorrhoid factory in what Sam guessed was now, temporarily at least, his office. In front of the row of chairs stood a short table occupied by a jug of water and several ceramic mugs. The only thing missing was a stack of year-old magazines. If Sam's office in Hartford looked half as nice, his PI business might be doing better. No sign of cushions, however.

Stepping back into the inner office, Sam studied the only other door in the place. It was a simple arrangement. A solid sheet of pine set in a wooden frame using primitive hinges. The frame was cemented into the stone wall and a simple latch mechanism held the door closed, with no lock or even a place to add a padlock. He hoped it might be a closet. Maybe it housed some towels or clothing. Anything soft would be a help.

Instead he found a tiny, windowless bedroom with a narrow cot taking up more than half the space. A small wooden chest occupied most of what remained. Though the chest was empty, the bed was made up with a heavy woollen blanket and a feather pillow.

The pillow should have been perfect, but the moment Sam set it on the chair and sat down, putting his feet back up on the desk, the feathers shifted away from the centre and he was still sitting on hard wood. He considered folding the blanket, but knew without trying that it would make the seat too high. Maybe he could rip the blanket . . .

The fall of footsteps in the outer office interrupted Sam's musings, though footsteps was maybe too polite a word. The sound was more like a garbage truck pushing a metal bin around. With a further clanking of metal and the rasp of hard cloth rubbing against more hard cloth, a robust-looking jasper appeared at the inner office doorway. He had jet black hair, stood about five foot seven, and was dressed in heavy cloth except for his boots, which were made of some kind of silver metal that clanked against the stone floor when he walked. The cloth on his chest was white emblazoned with a red cross, and he wore a red cape of the same hue that came almost to the floor. If not for the sheathed sword that attached itself somehow to his hip, Sam might have guessed this was some kind of wannabe superhero; a Superman whose tights were several sizes too large. Given his experiences of the last several minutes, however, Sam reasoned this must be a knight.

The knight grinned at Sam where he sat on a flattened pillow in Merlin's chair with his feet up on Merlin's desk. Then he spoke in a powerful, yet friendly voice. "You must be the pie the Merlin said would come. What kind of pie are you?"

"Pie?" If this wasn't a bullet-induced dream, Merlin must have worked some magic to allow him to understand whatever archaic English was spoken in Camelot. And for others to understand him. Apparently, that magic had some holes in it. "What do you mean by pie?" Sam asked.

The knight lost his grin. "A pastry. Stuffed with meat or fruit." His face reddened. "I had hoped you would clarify the magician's strange words. When the Merlin spoke of a pie who would come in his absence and defend the Kingdom against foul magicks, I knew I must have misheard. But that is also what my brother knights heard. So I thought, perhaps, there must be a third kind of pie."

"Could Merlin have said PI?" Sam asked. "I'm a Private Investigator."

The knight twitched his lips. "Truly, I have no idea of what you just said. Pie has more meaning."

"I investigate things. Solve problems. Catch cheating spouses."

"Pie continues to have more meaning."

"I do whatever Merlin did," Sam lied, having nowhere else to go.

A wide grin brightened the knight's powerful jaw. "Then you are a magician! Why did the Merlin not simply say so?"

Sam pulled an American Silver Eagle dollar coin out of his pocket, rolled it between his fingers, and then flipped it into the air where it promptly disappeared. "I'm afraid I have to do what Merlin does," Sam said, "but without magic."

The knight ceased looking for the vanished coin and his expression froze. "Without magick? Then it is true."

"What's true?" Sam asked.

"That the Merlin has lost faith in Arthur's knights to protect Camelot." The red-caped man shook his head. "My brother knights are vexed by the Merlin's lack of trust. As am I."

Sam slid his feet back to the floor and flipped his fedora onto the desk. He considered standing in hopes of setting this knight back at ease, but feared the move might be viewed as confrontational, so he remained seated. "Merlin said nothing to me about not trusting the knights." That was true, but the magician hadn't mentioned the knights at all. "I think he just wants a fresh set of eyes on things. I'm sure that by the time he gets back, I'll have accomplished nothing besides sitting in his office collecting hemorrhoids."

"Intentions count for little," said the knight. "Actions, however, speak as with a loud voice. I wish you well with your collecting of hemorrhoids." He paused. "I assume that is a species of rat. Rest assured that I hold you at no fault for the magician's doings. If you should have need of me, I am at your disposal." The knight turned to leave.

"Wait!" Sam said. Now he did stand, leaping to his feet and almost knocking over the crappy chair. "I don't know your name."

The knight's cheeks bloomed red a second time. "Apologies. I am unused to introducing myself as I am known by all in the kingdom. Sir Galahad, at your service." The man dipped his head and then strode away, his metal shoes clanking against the stone floor.

Sam stared at the empty doorway. Galahad? This place was lousy with Disney characters.

He had barely resumed collecting hemorrhoids when Sam heard the knight returning. Only it wasn't the same knight. This new jasper was of similar height, but with reddish brown hair and curls even the most self-assured woman would envy. He was built like a linebacker, with a thick neck and muscles straining against his sleeves. His tabard displayed a large black serpent on a blood-red background. A brick-like face with cruel, coal-dark eyes sneered at Sam. "You fail to impress me. Where is your sword?"

Sam rearranged his shoes on the desk and attempted to lean back with casual indifference, but the chair refused to cooperate and nearly tipped him over. He recovered by swinging his feet back to the floor and standing. Then, with an air of nonchalance he didn't feel, he leaned against the wall next to the window.

The knight watched his movements with cautious eyes, his fingers hovering near the hilt of his sword as though he expected Sam to draw a blade from thin air and challenge him.

Sam pressed two fingers to his temple and ran them back through his hair above his ear. "I don't carry a sword. Never liked them." In truth, Sam didn't know if he liked swords or not, he only knew that he had no idea how to use one.

The knight snorted. "Then what use are you? How dare the Merlin engage your assistance when Lancelot and I and our brother knights have things well in hand?"

Sam was about to say something clever and undoubtedly caustic, when the musclebound mook drew his sword. The blade was three feet of polished steel and looked like it could slice through stone. He pointed the weapon across the room at Sam's heart.

"What will you do should a vile miscreant enter this place and come at you with a sword? I daresay you are weaker than a scullery maid and bleed as easily. That odd raiment you wear offers no protection. And your coat bears no arms. You look a peasant to mine eye."

For the briefest of moments, Sam considered drawing the semi-automatic from his holster and putting a few holes into the snake on the blowhard jasper's shirt. Or, if not the shirt, one of the wooden ceiling beams; he did need to test Merlin's promise of endless bullets. But that maybe wasn't the best way to start this new gig. Would this medieval buffoon even recognize a handgun? Sam doubted it. The clever words he had suppressed might be a better comeback.

Sam glared into the knight's sinister eyes, the eyes of a killer. Yeah, the rowdy was just itching for a fight. That could go badly, for one or both of them. He figured the mook knew how to use that sword of his. Merlin might return only to mop his pet pie's blood off the floor stones. Damn. Sam had no choice but to attempt something he wasn't good at; he'd have to defuse the situation.

"Tell me," Sam said, casually crossing his arms. "Does Merlin carry a sword?"

"Of course not," growled the knight. "Your question is foolish. What need has a mighty magician of a blade?"

"Exactly," Sam said. "I'm here to do Merlin's job. Not yours."

The knight pursed his lips. "And you are also a mighty magician?"

"Not as mighty as Merlin, no." Sam picked his fedora up off the desk and spun it around one finger. "But I do have a soft hat."

"You do speak with a magician's confusing tongue," the knight admitted. That seemed as far as he would concede to Sam's claim of magic.

"Tell me," Sam said, flipping the fedora onto his head. "What should I call you?"

The rowdy ground his teeth and hammered his sword into its scabbard. "I am Sir Sagramore of the Round Table, Second of the King's Knights."

"Well that's a mouthful. Mind if I call you Saggy?"

The mook's eyes flew wide in disbelief. "I most certainly do mind! I am a knight, sir. I demand respect."

"Of course." Sam nodded his head. "I understand completely. *Sir* Saggy, then."

The rowdy reached for his sword and left his hand shaking on the pommel. "Not even the Merlin would dare speak so brazenly!"

Sam shook his head and mentally kicked himself. He really was useless at defusing situations.

"I shall keep you under the watch of mine eye," Sagramore said. "I do not believe when you say you are a magician. And I do not care for your words when you speak. Make trouble and you shall find yourself adorning the castle's dungeon, if not its gibbet."

With that, the foul knight stomped out of the office.

Well, that was something. Good cop, bad cop? Though in Sam's experience, most cops were bad. Sir Saggy would have fit right in at East Hartford PD.

Since he was standing by the window, Sam took the opportunity to poke his head outside; no easy task as the wall housing the window was almost two feet thick. His office looked to be on the second floor of what he assumed was Castle Camelot. Twisting his head from side to side, all he saw was grey stone in both directions. Immediately below the window lay a water-filled gully that he assumed was a moat but smelled like a privy. Adjacent to the moat, a gaggle of chickens pecked at grassy ground outside a stable. Several horses stood in the stable yard, along with pigs, dogs, several small children, and more chickens. Hay and manure were prevalent. It occurred to Sam that his office's proximity to a horse stable could be useful if he knew the back end of a horse from its front. Since he didn't, the building was merely a source of stink.

Beyond the stable, streets and buildings filled Sam's gaze for as far as he could see. Men dressed in loose-fitting pants and long-sleeved shirts with vests walked cobbled streets alongside women in buoyant dresses of every shape and hue imaginable. Some carried baskets on their heads or pulled small carts behind them. Two men ran through the crowd carrying a stretcher loaded with unmarked cloth sacks. The way the stretcher sagged suggested considerable weight. Children played unsupervised, chasing balls or dogs or goats. A carriage pulled by a massive horse hurried toward the castle as a driver cracked a whip and shouted for everyone in the street to clear the way. Camelot wasn't just a castle; it was a city. Sam figured he might be more at home here than he thought.

"And where, I wonder," he asked aloud, "in all this great city, can I find a men's room?"

From his search for a cushion Sam knew there was no toilet in his two-and-a-half room office. He'd have to check the castle corridors. How difficult could that be? He was a detective, dammit. If a men's room was hiding somewhere in Camelot, he would find it.

The corridor outside the office was as cold and quiet as a tomb. It was also wide, much wider than the narrow hallway of his apartment building in East Hartford. He assumed that all castle hallways must be wide if knights were going to wander around half-armoured and carrying swords. Even knowing nothing about swords, Sam could tell that they would be difficult to use in close quarters.

The first thing Sam noticed upon leaving his office, apart from the spacious quiet, was an engraved wooden sign that hung from a hook in the ceiling just outside the door. *Lancelot and Sparrow Investigations*. Lancelot again. That explained Sagramore's comment. And the second desk. It didn't explain why Merlin needed a Connecticut PI if he had the bravest and noblest knight in Arthurian legend at his disposal. And how did *Sparrow* get on the shingle so fast?

The second thing Sam noticed was a series of narrow openings in the opposite wall that ran as far as he could see in either direction and provided the only light. Sam squinted through one of the openings but saw only a distant wall. Listening, he heard a mumble of voices and a regular clang of metal hitting metal, which in this time and place could only be a hammer hitting an anvil. Castles had courtyards, didn't they?

Further along the hallway Sam found a closed door beneath another wooden sign. *Friar Tuck, Royal Herbalist.* Friar Tuck? That couldn't be right. Tuck was Robin Hood's man. Sam made a mental note to visit the friar and ask about his colourful past. Or was it colourful future?

The next shingle said, *The Camelot Crier*. The door to this office stood open and Sam saw several men and women sitting at desks madly reading slips of parchment and writing on other slips of parchment. One balding man, with no parchment in hand, occupied himself by yelling at the others about deadlines and news worth reporting.

The next several doors offered signs that baffled rather than informed. *Branwen's Ravelry. Beatrice's Brocades. Ribbons by Ygraine*. When he came to *Pendragon Jewellers*, however, Sam got the idea. His office was in the retail section for Camelot Castle's hoity-toity. Given the complete absence of hallway traffic, business must be slow.

Sam continued his journey, reading sign after sign and passing several stairwells that went up and down to who knows where. Worried that he might not find his way back, he kept to the corridor he was on but failed to find a sign that said *MEN'S ROOM*. Eventually he found a sign that said *Lancelot and Sparrow Investigations*. He had made a full circuit of the castle.

Miffed with himself, Sam went back into his office, stripped the wool blanket from the narrow bed, and folded part of it over the seat of his chair. He left the bulk of the blanket draped onto the floor. Then he sat and stared at the door. The first question he would ask the next person to visit his office, would be how to find the men's room.

Pulling his tobacco kit from his trench coat pocket, Sam tapped out a square of thin paper and pinched the few remaining flakes of Bull Durham between his fingers, flakes he could only pray that Friar Tuck next door kept in stock. He spread the inadequate quantity of tobacco as best he could along the curved paper and then rolled a cigarette, twisting the ends between thumb and forefinger. He flipped open the matchbook to find the remaining two matches. "Damn, I should have asked Merlin for smokes and matches instead of bullets."

He was about to light up when a woman waltzed through the inner office door. And what a woman. She was blonde, somewhere in her early twenties, and tall for a dame, taller than Sam by an inch or two. She wore a tan shirt almost the exact shade as her sun-bronzed skin, with a neckline that not so much plunged as settled craftily against the support of a generous bust. Her skirt was also tan and extended all the way down to her ankles. Bright brown eyes glistened with playfulness, as though she knew the effect her figure had on men but refused to acknowledge it.

"You are him," she said. "I need not even ask."

"How's that, angel?" Sam cocked a brow, hoping it made him appear rakish.

The looker let out a soft laugh. "Two things. First, the way you look at me, as though you have never seen a woman before."

Sam pulled his lips into a quick smile and immediately let it go. "I've seen plenty of women, sister. But none dressed like you. That's quite the outfit."

The blonde performed a half twirl, a partial dance meant to tease and perhaps encourage the rest of the dance. "My attire is not to your liking?"

"On the contrary," Sam said. "Folks back home would eat you up. You said there were two things. What's the second?"

The looker eased herself to the edge of the desk and leaned across it, causing her generous bust to settle onto her shirt rather than the other way around. She ran a finger up the lapel of Sam's rumpled trench coat, across to the shoulder, and down the arm. Then she stepped back. "I have never seen anyone dressed like you either."

Sam grinned. "There, you see? We have something in

common."

The blonde dish chuckled. "It is a start. I am Maid Peregrine."

"Pleased to make your acquaintance. You can call me Sam." He was about to say *Sam Sparrow,* when it occurred to him that he could have a little fun. It was too late to call himself Philip Marlowe, but he could still go for another of Bogart's alter egos. "Sam Spade." The fictional character wouldn't be invented for a thousand years, so why not borrow the name. "Tell me, Maid Peregrine, aren't you a trifle overdressed for a maid?"

The looker offered him a puzzled expression.

"To be cleaning, I mean."

The puzzled expression became more puzzled still, and then turned into a smirk. "I am not a chamber maid. *Maid* is my title. As knights are *sir* and barons are *lord.* I am the daughter of the Duke of Earl."

"Duke of Earl, you say? I've heard a song about him."

The blonde blushed. "Not a lewd song? I had hoped the bards would at least wait until he was dead before scandalizing the family."

Sam shook his head. "I couldn't tell you what the song was about, but I think your family is safe. For now, anyway. So, what do I call you?"

"My full name is Euphemia Peregrine, Maid of Earl. But you may call me Effie. I am the Merlin and Sir Lancelot's clerk. I suppose now I am yours, as well."

Sam debated whether to keep his promise regarding the men's room and decided not to. Broken promises had always been a sore point. He was reluctant to break any promise, even to himself, but it felt like the wrong time to ask his secretary such a question. Instead he said, "So where is this Lancelot fella, anyway? I've had two other knights drop by, but not the one whose name is on the door."

Effie glanced at the empty desk. "I was taking my midday respite, but Sir Lancelot is rarely in the office. If you excuse my honesty, our exalted knight is, in all probability, out chasing skirts."

"A lady's man, is he?" Sam asked.

Effie leaned over the desk, so that they were almost nose to nose. "Rumour has it he even took a shine to Lady Guinevere, despite that she is married to the King and twice Lancelot's age." The blonde straightened again. "I suspect that is why you are here. If Lancelot could do the job, the Merlin would have no need of you."

Another question Sam didn't feel comfortable asking the perky dish: what, exactly, is my job? Instead, he said, "I'm hoping that neither Lancelot nor myself are needed."

Effie laughed. "Would that not make my life boring?"

4
ENTER THE FEMME FATALE

SAM STOOD WITH his ear pressed against the closed door between the inner and outer office. He knew Effie was out there, sitting at her desk and waiting for business. If typewriters had been invented, he'd hear her pounding the keys. Of course, with no open cases she'd be typing a letter to a cousin or composing a romance novel.

To be honest, Sam had no idea what secretaries did for private eyes half the time. In movies they answered the phone, introduced clients, and ran interference against bill collectors. It hardly seemed like full-time work, though in his case, dodging bill collectors could be a full-time gig.

After a year sitting in a dingy East Hartford office, Sam Sparrow, PI, had no secretary. Or partner. It was a one-man operation with too little work for one man. And most of that work was, in fact, dodging bill collectors. Sam had only one person to blame for his situation, and that person was his father.

Sydney Sparrow had been a cop, a detective, the most decorated officer in Hartford history. Sam, like the rest of the city, had worshipped the man. Right up until Sam's twelfth birthday, when other cops in suits had shown up at his door and put dear old dad in bracelets. Right in the middle of cake. Six months of slanderous news later, the courts convicted Sydney Sparrow of accepting bribes, faking evidence, and paying off witnesses. He died in jail a few days later, beaten to death by fellow inmates.

Sam would like to believe his father had been set up, that he'd done none of the things he'd been convicted of. But the case against Sydney Sparrow was rock solid. He hadn't even tried to deny it. His own partner on the job, Tom Noonan, was chief witness against him. Rumour had it Noonan was just as guilty, but had cut a deal. One corrupt cop dead while the other flew free as a bird. Free because he'd stabbed his partner in the back. Sam couldn't decide which of the two men he hated more.

After that it seemed like every person in Sam's life had turned against him. His friends and teachers at school found him guilty by association. Shop owners watched him with vulture eyes when he needed to buy something, and had no work for him when he needed after-school employment. Girlfriends lost interest when their friends told them whose son he was.

Shortly after turning sixteen, Sam came home to find his mother packed and gone. Not even a note. Despite everything, he somehow managed to hide her absence for the next two years, thereby avoiding foster care. It hadn't been easy.

Sam liked to think that another teen would have wound up on the streets dealing drugs or stealing cars. The only thing that salvaged Sam was his refusal to become anything like his father. In fact, he'd entered the police academy right out of high school, partly because no one would hire him due to his last name, but mostly because he wanted to succeed where his father had failed. He wanted to be an honest cop.

He might even have pulled it off if he'd been able to trust anyone.

From the beginning, most of the Hartford police department only saw Sam's father when they looked at him. No one wanted to be his training officer. One partner after another requested a transfer. The precinct captain had known Sydney Sparrow and, like Sam, had trusted him before the truth came out. That trust had been broken. From day one, his co-workers had treated him like a criminal.

The police shrink said the root of Sam's problem was that no one trusted him, but that wasn't true. Yes, it was a problem, but what ultimately got Sam kicked off the job was that *he* couldn't trust *them*. Sam lost count of the number of times his locker had been sabotaged or his lunch had been poisoned. Not enough to kill him, but enough he could wish he were dead. Almost like clockwork, Central had sent him to addresses that didn't exist. Worst of all was when calls put him in a tight spot and his partner was nowhere to be found. Your partner was supposed to have your back. Not stab it. Sam's AWOL partners reminded him too much of what had happened to his father.

His response to this maliciousness hadn't been pretty. Sam learned to give as good as he got. Even so, it was his mouth more often than not that got him into trouble. He supposed that if Hartford PD hadn't thrown him out, he would have quit.

The life of a lone detective seemed tailor-made for Sam Sparrow. With no skills outside of policing, he'd purchased an investigator's license and rented a tiny office. But he couldn't bring himself to work with a partner or even hire a secretary. He knew they wouldn't be there when he needed them. Like Tom Noonan selling Sydney Sparrow up the river. Or the prison guards who were somewhere else when his father had been punched and kicked to death.

That Sam handicapped himself by avoiding the best source of his job description was the final nail in his coffin.

The one possession of Sydney Sparrow's that Sam had kept and that now hung in his dank office, was a *Maltese Falcon* movie poster from 1941. Not a reproduction, but the real deal. The one with Humphrey Bogart in a fedora holding a gun and Mary Astor as the lady in red sitting on a cushion beside him. Sam's mother had hated that poster and told him before she left that his father had named him after Sam Spade. She'd laughed when she said that Sam Spade was Dad's hero. Sam had wanted to see the movie, but his mother wouldn't allow it in the house. Even the poster wouldn't have survived if twelve-year-old Sam hadn't rolled it up and hidden it in the garage.

By the time he was sixteen Sam had lost any interest in seeing the movie. Spade was his father's hero, but Sydney Sparrow had been a crook masquerading as a cop. What kind of hero inspired a man like that? Sam had watched every other Bogart film he could find. *Casablanca. The Big Sleep. The African Queen.* Even bad ones like *The Return of Doctor X.* Sam itched to see what

Bogart would do with the role of a cynical PI but, mostly out of spite, chose not to. Instead he modelled himself on what he imagined Bogart would do, believing his imagination could create a bigger hero than the one his felonious father had admired. So far, his imagination hadn't impressed him much.

After several minutes passed without so much as the scratch of a nail file from the outer office, Sam shrugged and returned to his desk and finally lit his cigarette. He had scarcely inhaled when there came a quiet knock.

Effie cracked the door open and stuck her head inside. Then she stepped fully into the room and closed the door behind her. She looked at the lit cigarette. "I wonder if that thing will enhance your mystique or send customers fleeing out the door."

"You could smell it from out there? I only just lit it."

Effie wrinkled her nose with distaste. "Not at all. I came in to say that a woman wants to see you. Says her name is Morgan Le Fay."

"A customer?" Sam stamped the cigarette out on the desktop. He couldn't believe he was thinking this, but the last thing he wanted right now was a customer.

Effie shrugged and then grinned at him. "If not a customer then the knights have a new dress code. Do you wish to see her? I can send her away."

Sam searched for somewhere to stash his cigarette. The desk had no drawers and the only place within reach was the windowsill. He ended up pushing his fedora further to one side of the desk and sliding the crushed coffin nail under it. "No, no, no. Send her in."

Effie reopened the door. "Mr. Spade will see you now, Miss Le Fay."

Morgan Le Fay. The name seemed familiar somehow. Sam figured he must have heard it as a kid watching some Disney movie. Wasn't Morgan a man's name?

What stood framed within the doorway was definitely not a man, but a petite woman with pale, pale skin and eyes so blue they seemed almost frozen. A tiny lace hat that matched her eyes crowned raven black hair that looked like it had spent the day at the stylist. The cool dish's long, clinging dress matched her hair and was so black that Sam could barely make out where cloth ended and shadow began. Miss Le Fay's lips were red like strawberries against milk white teeth, which surprised Sam as he had never seen himself as a poet.

Belatedly, Sam stood and gestured to one of the ladder-back chairs in front of his desk. "Miss Le Fay, won't you sit down?" He noticed Effie had left the door open as she returned to the outer office.

"Thank you," Morgan Le Fay said, and brushed back her dress so as to sit without wrinkling it.

Sam noticed that the attractive young woman sat at the edge of the chair, but whether that was to facilitate a fast exit or was a more comfortable way to sit, he didn't know. He also sat, but managed to knock the blanket off his seat as he did.

Miss Le Fay politely failed to notice. "I inquired at my inn after a reliable private investigator. They mentioned you." Strawberry lips parted into a smile. "You must be skilful if you have earned a knighthood."

Sam rubbed his ear. "That would be my partner, Sir Lancelot."

The strawberries drooped with disappointment.

"But I assure you that I'm the brains of the outfit. Suppose you tell me your problem."

Miss Le Fay's eyes moved, taking in his rumpled coat and unknightly features, as though weighing whether to continue would be a waste of time. "Very well," she said. "I have come from London and am endeavouring to locate my sister. I learned that she is here in Camelot with a hedge knight called Sir Logris. I am uncertain where or how she met him. We have never been as close as sisters ought to be. If we had, Corinne would have told me before running off with him. Our parents are touring France and I must find her before they return in two weeks."

Missing person. Sam hated missing persons cases. Usually they were innocent people who didn't want to be found. Still, it was better than spying on cheating spouses. "How'd you learn she was here?"

"I received a letter from Corinne two weeks ago, postmarked Camelot. It said very little except that she was all right. I sent a letter back care of the London Post Office, begging her to come home. I waited a week and no answer came. I cannot say whether she even received my letter, so I decided to come to Camelot myself. I sent a second note saying that I was coming. I should not have, should I?"

Sam shrugged. "It isn't easy to know what to do in these kinds of situations. I take it you haven't found her?"

"No." Miss Le Fay looked down into her lap. "I wrote in my letter that I would take residence at the St. Mark Inn and for Corinne to meet me there. It has been three days and she has not come. Nor has she sent a note. It was horrible, the waiting. Yesterday I left another letter at the post office. I waited there all day and then again this morning, but Corinne failed to call for her mail. Sir Logris, however, did call. I confronted him, but the brute refused to tell me where Corinne was. He said Corinne had no wish to see me. I cannot believe that. We argued and he promised to bring her to my inn this evening if she would come. He said he knew she would not and promised to come himself in her place."

Sam leaned against the back of his chair. God help him but the woman's story moved him. This Logris mook sounded like too many men he had encountered in his life. Some of them cops. He didn't see how he could not take the case. He was about to say so when the clank of metal against stone sounded in the outer office. Then a knight stood in the doorway.

Sam half-expected Sagramore or even Galahad checking up on him, but this was someone new. He was tall, well over six feet, and ruggedly handsome in a Nathan Fillion sort of way. He had coal-black hair and a five o'clock shadow that lent him an air of danger. His coat of arms was the most boring thing about him—three diagonal red stripes against a white background. When he spotted Miss Le Fay, his smile lit up the room.

"Your pardon," he said. "I am Sir Lancelot." He walked over and leaned against Sam's desk, making Miss Le Fay crane her neck to look up at him. "How may my partner and I assist you?"

Sam smiled and nodded, as though he and Lancelot were old friends. He summarized the woman's plight and concluded with, "Miss Le Fay has a meeting with Sir Logris tonight. Maybe he'll bring the sister. Chances are he won't."

Lancelot's smile failed to falter throughout the story. When it ended, he nodded in a self-assured manner. "Should sister Corrine appear, I shall bid the rascal depart, never to darken a Le Fay door again. Should she not appear, I shall thrash the rascal within an inch of his life until he reveals Corinne's whereabouts. Either way, your sister is returned. Problem solved."

The knight's modus operandi was more heavy-handed than Sam was comfortable with, but the words were confident and Sam had the sense that brutality was not uncommon among knights.

"Or," Sam said, "we could follow this Sir Logris character from Miss Le Fay's Inn back to where he's keeping Corrine."

Lancelot lost his smile and looked at Sam as if he were a talking dog. "Perhaps as a matter of last resort, should circumstance prevent my throttling him."

Miss Le Fay reached out a dainty hand and set it lightly on one of Lancelot's massive paws where it rested on the desk. "But you must be careful. I am deathly afraid of this villain, of what he might do."

"Fear not," said Lancelot, taking the small pale fingers between his two rough, manly hands. "I have yet to meet the scoundrel who could best me with a sword or lance."

To be honest, Sam had interpreted the dark-haired beauty's fear as being for her sister's safety rather than the knight's. Le Fay's next words confirmed his thoughts.

"But I want you to know that he is a dangerous man. I honestly believe he would stop at nothing, and would not hesitate to kill Corinne if it would save him."

Lancelot jerked back his head. "Can any man be such a cad?"

Sam had to agree. This tale was getting a little too melodramatic. "Is it possible," Sam suggested, "that this Logris mook has true feelings for your sister? And your sister for him?"

Miss Le Fay's mouth dropped open and a strawberry lip trembled. The lower one. "But he has a wife in London. And three children."

"Ah," Sam said. "That would have been good to know earlier in your story."

"How looks this knight?" Lancelot demanded. He had let go of Le Fay's hand and no longer leaned against the desk.

"He has dark hair," Le Fay said. "And thick, bushy eyebrows. He speaks in a loud, blustery manner and gives the impression of being violent. When I saw him this morning, he wore a light grey hat and a grey tabard emblazoned with a rampant blackfish."

"And he is to find you at your inn at sunset?"

Le Fay nodded.

"I shall be seated in the common room well before sunset," Lancelot said. "You must arrive and sit at a different table. Alone. You will not know me. Sir Logris must meet you there. Do not allow him to find your rooms."

"What of your partner?" Le Fay asked, looking over at Sam.

Lancelot shrugged. "He is not needed for this task."

"That's true," Sam said. "This plan calls for muscle, not brains."

Lancelot nodded while Miss Le Fay turned a light shade of pink. It was no contest which of the two was more intelligent.

"Thank you." Miss Le Fay then opened a cloth purse that was tied to her dress and spilled five ragged-looking silver coins onto the desk. "Will that be enough?"

Sam had no idea, but said, "That will be fine."

"Thank you," Miss Le Fay repeated, rising to her feet. "Thank you so much." Standing, her head reached no higher than the stripes on Lancelot's tabard. She looked up and exchanged deep glances with the tall knight.

Lancelot took her hand and escorted Miss Le Fay out of the office. Then Effie came in, closing the door behind her.

"You heard all that?" Sam asked. "What do you think?"

Effie looked at the five coins. "I think she overpaid you."

"About the story," Sam said.

"Tragic, if true."

Sam nodded. "And Lancelot?"

Effie smiled. "Lancelot to the core. I liked what you said about muscle, not brains."

Sweeping the coins into his coat pocket, Sam smiled. "Looks like I have the night off."

5
A DARK AND STORMY KNIGHT COMES TO A QUICK END

SAM BROWSED THE office shelves as the afternoon wore on, not making head nor tail of anything he found. Mostly it was odd-shaped rocks and pieces of polished glass. Two of the rocks were grey-black and repelled each other when pushed together, like magnets with opposite polarity. One of the glass pieces filtered sunlight into a rainbow that spread across the room. A wide shelf held parts of animals he couldn't identify. Neither the animals nor the parts. A poorly made glass jar contained a clear liquid and what he at first took for a human eye, but the iris seemed odd and the eye maybe a bit too large. Maybe a pig's eye? Closest to the window a pair of polished stone bookends enclosed several volumes so shabby and dusty they might have toured the world in the back of a truck. Sam pulled one out, but the odd lettering it contained was gibberish.

None of what he found looked the least bit magical and Sam would have called Merlin a snake oil salesman if he hadn't seen the man change features before his own eyes. That and haul Sam bodily across time and space. Sam still put odds that he lay shot and dying in an East Hartford alley, that this whole Camelot experience was just confused neurons seeking a happy place. Las Vegas or Hawaii would have been better. Sam told himself that if he did wake up in a Hartford hospital, he'd have a long talk with his neurons.

Dream or not, no one else came knocking at the door and the place began to feel as dismal as his office in East Hartford. Lancelot never returned, and Effie said goodnight well before sundown. Sam hated himself, but before she left, he broke down and asked her about the men's room.

After some confusion about bathhouses and men's gymnasiums, Effie led him to a nearby stairwell that went down to the main level of the castle. The stone ceiling was higher and the corridor several feet wider. Tapestries lined the outside wall, but the light from the thin slits in the wall opposite was inadequate to show them well. Adjacent to the stairwell, a wooden sign above an unassuming door said *Necessarium.* Not much larger than a phone booth, the tiny room contained a stone bench offering a hole through which Sam could see the muddy waters of the moat. Next to the hole stood a stack of clean, coarse towels and a wicker basket containing towels that, from the smell, were less clean. The room's only other feature was a bucket of cold water that may have been clean before Sam arrived, but was not when he left.

It was the Necessarium that convinced Sam Sparrow that he really was in King Arthur's Court, for the sole reason that he could never in his wildest imaginings invent the experience of using such archaic facilities. Like it or not, he had been rescued from certain death by a cranky magician only to find himself stumbling about in the freaking dark ages. He wasn't sure which fate was worse.

After retracing his steps to his office, Sam found on his desk a plate of sliced fruit, meats, an overripe cheese of some kind he didn't recognize, two small loaves of hard bread, and a metal cup filled with wine or vinegar, he couldn't tell which. There were no utensils. Using his fingernails, he tore the bread open and made two ugly, yet tasty, sandwiches. It wasn't the best meal he had eaten in the past month, but it was far from the worst. Maybe the dark ages would be survivable.

Turning his chair and pulling it closer to the window, he piled up a nest of blanket and kicked his feet up onto the edge of his desk. The blanket gave him enough height that Sam could look out over the sprawling city that surrounded Castle

Camelot. He struck his last match and lit the remains of his cigarette, then watched the sun set on an unfamiliar city skyline. Lights appeared in various windows as the sky darkened, lanterns or candles. Sam felt like he was in a Dickens novel.

For the first time since leaving Hartford, Sam looked at his watch, which told him it was five a.m. That felt about right given how tired he was. That and the fact that the sun had been setting when Merlin squirreled him out of Connecticut only to arrive in Camelot at midday. He had no idea what the local time was, but assumed it was still summer and adjusted the hands to say nine p.m.

The watch was a Korean-made Rolex knock-off the Department had given him. Not so much an early retirement gift; more a means of alleviating their guilt for shoving him out the door. The damned thing was not only gold-plated tin with a luminous dial that failed to illuminate, but it couldn't even keep time. It lost or gained up to fifteen minutes a day and Sam was constantly correcting it. The only reason he wore it was as a reminder not to trust anyone.

Rolling his shirtsleeve back over the offending timepiece, Sam cast his gaze once more around the office and noticed it contained nothing remotely resembling a light switch or a lamp, though one of the shelves did support a candle among its curiosities. The ugly lump looked old. It was soft and grey with a wick that had never been lit, possibly part of some collection of Merlin's. Burning it might not be the best decision Sam had ever made, not that he had any matches left. He resolved to ask Effie in the morning about a lamp and matches, and crawled into the narrow alcove cot before it grew too dark to see.

The sleeping alcove—he refused to admit he was sleeping in a closet—blocked from the window as it was, was as dark as a cave. It was all Sam could do to drag the blanket from his chair and throw it haphazardly over where he thought the narrow bed stood. Leaving his trench coat, suit jacket, and shoes by the desk, he climbed into the bed fully dressed, including the holstered semi-automatic on his belt, and cocooned himself in the blanket.

Sam had no idea how long he had slept when he was abruptly awakened.

"Sir? Sir?"

Sam opened his eyes. And was nearly blinded by the light of a small lantern. As his vision adjusted, he discerned a lad of fourteen or so years standing before him. "Sir?" the lad repeated. "Sir Lancelot is dead."

Despite all the weirdness that had happened since the Hartford alley, those were the last words Sam had expected to hear. He glanced at his faux Rolex. Nine twenty-five.

The lad stared at the watch like he was watching a pig giving birth to a cow. "You truly are a magician," the boy whispered.

"You don't know the half of it," Sam said as he rolled out of the blanket fully dressed and squeezed past the youth into his office to slip on the rest of his *mean streets* getup. It had been clear skies a half hour ago, so he left the gumshoes beneath the desk. "What's your name, kid?"

"I am a page, sir," the lad said, watching with wide eyes as Sam grabbed his fedora off the desk and flipped it onto his head.

"Do pages have names?"

"Uh, Robin, sir."

"Well, Robin, take me to the scene of the crime."

The page stared at him like he had sprouted feathers.

"Take me to Sir Lancelot," Sam amended.

This time the lad nodded and sped away.

In the hallway outside his office, Sam nearly collided into Effie who was rushing toward him holding a candle in some kind of holder.

"You heard?" she asked.

Sam nodded, and then said, "Yes." She might not be able to make out his nod in the shadowy corridor.

"Then I shall go see Iva," Effie said. "She may not yet know."

"Iva? Who's that?"

"Lancelot's wife."

Sam blew a burst of air between closed lips. "There's always a wife." He mentally shook his head at Lancelot's ire at a married man running off with Morgan Le Fay's sister, when all the while his own behaviour was not much different.

Then Sam had little time for thought as he chased page Robin and his lantern down the hallway to a wide set of stairs that took him to the main level of the castle, past another

Necessarium, and then a short distance to a broad cross-corridor. The boy turned right, darted past a pair of bored-looking knights, and then they were outside the castle and racing across a wooden drawbridge.

A heavy fog obscured most of what Sam might have seen of the city. That and the total absence of streetlamps, headlights, and neon signs. He could hardly see his own feet never mind Robin's lantern bobbing in the misty gloom just ahead of him. Even so, people and animals brushed past him in the dark while occasional windows glowed ghostlike in the haze. Sam kept his attention on Robin as the page led him down one street after another until they ended up in an alley behind what looked like an inn. The alley was dark and several people stood in the shadows, speaking in soft whispers.

One of the shadowy figures stepped toward Sam through a bank of thinning fog. Robin's lantern revealed him as a knight. "What do you want here? There is naught to see."

"I'm Sam Spade, Merlin's investigator. Sir Galahad sent this page for me." Sam had no idea who had sent Robin, but of the three people he had met so far, the friendly Galahad seemed the better candidate.

The knight squinted at him, taking in his trench coat and fedora. "You must be the Merlin's pie." The armoured man then shook his head. "A bad business is this, to see a knight felled in such a way. Camelot's Third Knight, no less. Sir Galahad is back there." He waved one arm into the darkness.

Sam followed Robin in the general direction the knight had indicated and found another knight. Galahad.

"Greetings, Sam. I thought it prudent that you see what happened before we took Sir Lancelot away. In the event the Merlin questions you regarding this foul incident."

"Nice of you to think of me." Sam could count on one hand the number of times he'd received such a courtesy from fellow officers when he was on the job. His gut told him that Galahad would make an excellent cop. Peering into the darkness, he spotted several lanterns set on the ground a short distance away spaced out in the shape of a body. "What happened?"

Galahad pressed a gauntleted fist against Sam's stomach, just above the kidneys. "A blade entered here. 'Twas not deep, but deadly just the same. Do you wish to look closer?"

"No, you've seen everything I could. Who found him?"

Galahad signalled two other knights who stooped to lift Lancelot and carry him away. Then he turned back to Sam. "A slop boy from the inn. Good eyes, given the dark and the fog. Spends half his evenings out here and saw that the shadows were not right. This is a murder most foul, Mr. Spade. Lancelot's blade was still in its scabbard. He had not even drawn his sword. Also, I discovered several coins in his purse. 'Twas not robbery. Was Sir Lancelot perchance pursuing an investigation, as the Merlin desired?"

Sam let out a heavy sigh. "He was looking into a guy named Sir Logris."

"Logris?" Galahad frowned. "I do not recognize this name."

"He's from London. And a hedge knight, whatever that means. He has a black fish on his shirt."

Galahad snorted. "A landless knight. Little more than a common criminal. For what reason was Sir Lancelot looking into this base knight?"

"Routine," Sam said. Until he knew more of what was going on, anything he told the knights could make things worse rather than better.

Galahad cast Sam an odd look that was visible even in the near dark. "Routine? I am not aware that Sir Lancelot had any routine doings. With men. No. Forgive me. I should not speak ill of the dead. Especially of a knight slain before he could draw his sword. It is a dishonour to all knights for one of us to be killed in such fashion. And Sir Lancelot was the Third Knight."

"That fella back there said the same thing. What's it mean?"

"I thought you knew." Galahad sucked in a deep breath. "Sir Lancelot is, was, the third ranking knight of Camelot, responsible for keeping the peace. It is why he works, worked, in the Merlin's investigations office."

"Saggy called himself the Second Knight," Sam said. He had discarded Sagramore's belated introduction as boasting.

"In charge of castle security," Galahad said, "and deployment of the knights."

"And the First Knight?"

"That is Sir Bors de Ganis."

"What does he do?" Sam asked.

"The First Knight has the King's ear."

"Fine. I thought you Knights of the Round Table were supposed to be equal. The whole point of the table being round."

"That is true," Galahad said. "However, some knights are more equal than others."

Sam snorted. "I'm no stranger to that idea."

Galahad shrugged. "Speaking of the Second Knight, Sir Sagramore will wish to visit you in your offices on the morrow. You had best tell him more of this affair than you have told me." The friendly knight then strode away into the darkness.

Sam looked around and realized that the other knights, Lancelot's corpse, and the lanterns were gone. Only his own page with his small lantern remained.

"Follow me, kid," Sam said.

He left the alley and turned into the street. Sure enough, the wood-framed building behind which Lancelot had been murdered carried a sign displaying a cross and the words *St. Mark Inn*. He marched inside, peered around a room filled with surprised faces, and deduced that the balding jasper wiping glasses and wearing an apron was the innkeeper. "I'm looking for Miss Morgan Le Fay."

The jasper looked Sam up and down. "And who be you, dressed in such odd raiment, that I should answer your questions?"

"I'm the one man who is possibly angrier than the King's Knights about the murder that took place outside your inn."

The man spat onto the floor. "Thou scarest me not."

"Then I'm the one man who, if you don't answer my questions, is going to take the lantern from this page and throw it onto the roof of this inn."

The innkeeper frowned, but let his cool gaze fall to the lantern-wielding boy at Sam's elbow. "If you were to do such a thing, the King would send the Merlin's investigator, Sir Lancelot, to skewer you on the tip of his sword."

"Is that so?" Sam said. "Look. I'm going to tell you two hard things. The first is that the man killed tonight behind your inn was none other than Merlin's investigator, Sir Lancelot."

The aproned jasper's face turned pale.

"The second is that Sir Lancelot has a replacement."

The man's jaw wobbled, but he managed to say, "So soon? Who?"

"Me."

"You?"

"Me."

The balding innkeeper rubbed at his forehead with a corner of his apron and then seemed to make a decision. "In that case, the Lady Le Fay checked herself out a few hours ago."

Sam was not surprised. "Did she say where she was going?"

The innkeeper shook his head. "She failed to say much of anything, which is a pity. She was rather pleasing to the eye."

Sam shook his head and made to leave.

"The night is young yet," the innkeeper said, then smiled. "I would gladly stand the Merlin's investigator an ale."

6
A PROBABLE PATSY

THREE TANKARDS LATER, of the bitterest beer he had ever tasted, Sam allowed a bored page to lead him back to his office alcove bedroom. The fog had cleared, revealing the city that was Camelot in all its glory, but Sam noticed little of it due to the beer-induced fog in his head. Even so, he retained enough of his wits to insist that Robin leave the lantern with him, which was perhaps oracular as moments later there came a pounding on the door.

Two pages holding lanterns stood in the hallway. At first Sam thought Robin had returned with a friend to wreak vengeance for keeping the boy's lantern, but then he saw two knights standing behind the young pages, neither of which was Robin.

"What manner of blade do you carry?" Sir Sagramore demanded.

"None," Sam said, squinting against the bright light of the lanterns. "I told you that a few hours ago. I don't like 'em."

"I see none on your person," the belligerent knight agreed. "Have you one in your rooms?"

Sam sighed. "Come on in and look around. Turn the dump upside down."

"We are not here to trouble you," Galahad said in a much softer voice.

"Then why are you here?" Sam asked. "You told me this visit

would happen in the morning."

"Sir Sagramore did not wish to—"

Sagramore cut Galahad off. "You are to answer our questions, Mr. Spade. Not t'other way round."

Sam waved his hand toward Sagramore's face. "I'll answer anything you want. Tomorrow. Right now, I need some sleep." And some time to figure this out, he told himself. After I sleep off the beer.

Sagramore pushed forward, brushing the two pages aside. "One of our brother knights is dead! It is our solemn duty to see justice done. Willing or no, you shall help us seek justice!"

Galahad laid a gauntleted hand on Sagramore's arm as he glared at Sam with urgent eyes. "Just tell us why Sir Lancelot was in the alley with Sir Logris."

Here it is. Good cop, bad cop. The more things change, the more they stay the same. Sam shrugged. "He was there to meet a dame. Not in the alley. They were to meet inside."

Sagramore snorted. "Lancelot the lecherous. Of course he was. What woman?"

Sam shrugged again. "I couldn't say."

"Was she a client?" Galahad asked.

"I couldn't say."

"I implore you to be forthcoming," Galahad said. "How can we bring Lancelot's killer to justice if you do not tell us what he was involved in?"

Sagramore pressed a metal-gloved finger into Sam's chest. "Where did you go after leaving the St. Mark Inn?"

"I came here," Sam said. "What's it to you?"

The rapacious knight grinned. "Just this: Sir Logris was stabbed to death outside his own inn not twenty minutes after you and Sir Galahad parted ways."

That was unexpected. Sam backed away from the knight's gauntleted finger, walked over to one of the waiting area chairs, and sat. He crossed one leg over the other and leaned back in the chair. "Then I suggest you have a word with the innkeeper at the St. Mark. He was buying me drinks for the past hour. I wasn't kidding when I said I came straight back here after leaving. I arrived two minutes before you did. You can ask Robin."

Sagramore scrunched his face. "Robin?"

"The page Galahad sent for me."

Sagramore finally lowered his finger, but his expression resumed its fierceness. "Innkeepers and pages can be bought for pennies."

"Okay, then," Sam said. "How did I kill Logris? I forget."

"Stabbed in the back four times," the Second Knight said.

"And I suppose there were no witnesses."

"It is miraculous," Sagramore said, "how little people see when they wish to be blind."

"His innkeeper must know something?"

Sagramore scowled. "How is it that you are asking the questions and I am the one answering?"

"Just that Sir Logris has stayed there the past three days," Galahad supplied.

"Alone?"

"Yes, alone."

Sam rubbed his ear. "Did you find out who he was? What his game was?"

"That is what we wish you to tell us," insisted Sagramore.

"Look." Sam shook his head then wished he hadn't. "I sat in a room with Lancelot for all of five minutes. And I've never even seen this Logris character. Why would you think that I have anything to do with either death?"

Sagramore snorted. "All this trouble began when you arrived."

"That may be," Sam said. "But it also began when Merlin left."

7

AN UNLIKELY DUPE

SHOUTED WORDS FROM outside the castle walls forced Sam to shake off the last of his hangover and crawl out of Merlin's alcove. Not literally crawl, thankfully, but he always moved slower after a night of drinking. Back in Hartford, three beers was not a night of drinking; it was just the warm-up. Whatever else one might say about the St. Mark Inn, its beer packed a punch.

The sun was up, barely, and a look out the window revealed pages running up and down the streets waving parchment sheets and shouting at the top of their lungs. "Sir Lancelot murdered. Suspected killer, Sir Logris of London, also murdered. Sir Lancelot and mystery man, Sam Spade, pursued Sir Logris for reasons unknown."

So much for a quiet few days until Merlin returned.

Sam straightened his wrinkled shirt as best he could, donned his shoes, suit jacket, trench coat, and fedora, and then wandered downstairs to the Necessarium. While admittedly overdressed for the trip, he saw his *mean streets* getup as a kind of psychological armour, protecting him from whatever the world decided to throw at him. The only thing missing was his gumshoes, which he didn't feel would be useful inside the castle. A nose plug would have been useful. As would soap. His experience with medieval plumbing was no finer than the first time. After freezing his bare posterior on the cold, stone bench,

45

he decided to ask Effie where he could find additional shirts, pyjamas, a cushion for his chair, and a bathhouse. A laundry was also near the top of his list. He was beginning to like having a secretary.

As he climbed the stairs back to the second floor, Sam found his fingers twitching for a cigarette. He still had some gum in his pocket, but remembered a sign he had seen the previous afternoon. Ambling down the corridor, he paused by a shingle that read *Friar Tuck, Royal Herbalist.* He raised his hand to knock on his neighbour's closed door then thought better and lifted the door's latch. It was a place of business, after all.

The scent inside the doorway almost sent Sam fleeing back into the corridor. It wasn't a bad smell, like the Necessarium or a Hartford alley, but it was a strong one. Like he had snorted tea. Sam tried desperately to breathe through his mouth instead of his nose and eventually found the smells tolerable.

"It takes people that way sometimes," said a youthful voice. "Only the first time, of course. You get used to it."

Sam glanced around the room and saw that it resembled nothing like his outer office. The space was the same size and shape, but that's where any similarity ended. The walls, floor to ceiling, consisted of shelving lined with glass jars. The jars, in turn, were clearly labelled and held liquids and powders of every hue under the sun. Sam examined the nearest few jars. Smyrnium olusatrum, Pimpinella anisum, Eucalyptus olida, Apium graveolens. Either Merlin's translation trick didn't work with herbs, or Friar Tuck was the most pretentious shopkeeper Sam had ever met.

A tall table covered with various plant-filled pots occupied the centre of the room. On the side opposite stood a stool. And on the stool sat a skinny young man dressed collar to toe in sackcloth. At least, Sam assumed such coarse, uncomfortable material must be sackcloth. The youth himself looked about eighteen, with unkempt, curly blond hair and a face full of acne. You'd think that with all the jars in the room, he'd have something to take care of a skin condition.

"You must be Tuck," Sam said. "I expected someone older and more rotund. And with less hair."

The youth stared at him. "I am Friar Tuck, yes. Uh. Why would you expect me to look different?"

"That's not important. What is important is tobacco. Have you heard of it?"

The youth smiled. "Of course. Nicotiana tabacum. I have several varieties. Which would you like?"

Sam grinned. "Which would you recommend?"

"Uhm. I do not use it myself, of course, but I understand Turkish tabacum is quite pleasant." He jumped off his stool and moved toward a shelf. "Will you also be needing a pipe?"

"I roll my own," Sam said.

Friar Tuck froze in mid-movement. "You . . . roll?"

"Also not important. I assume you have matches?"

"Lucifers. Of course." The scrawny youth took a jar filled with wide, dark green leaves from the shelf and set it on the counter. "Tobacco is not much good without Lucifers. Unless you intend to chew it. Some folks do." He reached behind him and retrieved a jar filled with matchsticks. "How much tabacum would you like?"

Sam dug into a pocket of his suit jacket and pulled out one of the five silver coins Morgan Le Fay had given him; the only local currency he had. He flipped the rough coin with his thumb onto the counter, noticing for the first time that it was inscribed with a dragon, or possibly a dog. "How much will this buy?"

The youth stared at it. "A Pendragon? All the tabacum and Lucifers I have. And more."

Sam hummed a bit of a tune—"Yes, We Have No Bananas"–while rubbing his ear. "I don't think I need the whole jar. Can you make change?"

Friar Tuck moved his stare from the coin to Sam's eyes. "Jar? I refer to the two barrels I have in the back. A Pendragon is more than I earn in this shop in a month."

"Right," Sam said. "Then I'll definitely need change."

The youth looked back at the coin and licked his lips. "You are not from around here."

"Do I look like I just stepped off the boat?" Sam asked.

Friar Tuck moved his eyes again, this time examining Sam from his tan fedora to his dark brown dress shoes. He then made his most astute comment thus far. "Yes."

"Got it in one," Sam said. "Look. This is the only local coin I have. Is there maybe a bank around here?"

The friar looked over Sam's shoulder to where the door stood open. Then he spoke in a quiet voice. "I could just give you the tabacum." He licked his lips. "In exchange for a short-term loan, you understand."

"Oh," Sam said. "So *I'm* the bank."

"Shhhhh." The friar held a finger to his lips and then continued in a whisper. "There are banks, of course. Currency exchanges. But without an account they will arrest you for walking in with a Pendragon. They will think you stole it. You do not . . . have an account. Do you?"

"No," Sam admitted. "But I assume you do."

The friar's eyes flew open. "Me? Of course not. I took a vow of poverty. I have no money. No possessions."

"And yet you have a desperate need for a month's income."

The youth looked over Sam's shoulder again. "It is the pages. I fear I owe them a silver penny."

Sam suppressed a chuckle. "They charge that much for a light in the night?"

"A penny, yes," said the friar. "But a copper one. My story is a bit more complex."

"Then I suggest you start from the beginning. The sooner we get this sorted out the sooner I can have a smoke."

The friar chewed on his tongue for a moment and then blurted out, "I have a gambling problem."

"I see," Sam said. "That's not complicated at all. I can fill in the rest, and I'm telling you now that I'm not the kind of bank you're looking for."

The youth waved his hands. "No, no, no. It is nothing like that. My father tried to mend my ways, but I could not help myself. Walking past a dogfight or a turtle race without betting a penny was not in me. The trouble was, I usually won. But my father does not hold with gambling. Says it is not honest work. So he sent me here to Camelot, to St. Stephen's Abbey just outside the city, and I became a friar. Monks are prohibited from gambling. And we have no money." He rubbed the edge of his coarse sleeve between his fingers. "Or clothes. Not a thing in the world to gamble with."

Sam rubbed his ear again. "So now I'm intrigued. How did you end up owing the pages a month's wages?"

"Wages? No, sir. A Pendragon is a good month's business for this shop. The Holy Church owns it, of course. For wages I receive gruel twice a day and a roof over my head."

"Sounds about right," Sam said. "Do go on."

"Friars are not allowed to gamble, but we are allowed to drink if a drink is offered. Page Vaisey is from my hometown, Nottingham. Finest settlement in the East Midlands. Vaisey is something of a bully, and I always thought he did not like me, but last week as I was leaving the castle for the abbey, he stopped me near the main gate and invited me to share mead with some of his mates and reminisce about good old Nottinghamshire.

"To be honest, I had no strong desire to spend time with him, but rarely am I offered mead. I also thought, perhaps, that his page training may have improved Vaisey's character.

"Halfway through my cup, one of Vaisey's sycophants, Page Guy, pulled out a sack of stones. Then he and several of the pages began gambling for copper pennies. Vaisey ignored them, topping off my cup and continuing with news from home. We do not get news in the abbey, you understand.

"The thing is, I had difficulty listening to Vaisey. The stones seemed to draw my eyes. I soon noticed how poorly Guy and the other pages played. A half-roasted rabbit could beat them. Vaisey must have noticed my inattention and asked if I cared to play a round."

"I see where this is going," Sam said.

"Oh?" The friar looked at him. "But I had no pennies with which to play."

Sam chuckled. "This Vaisey character loaned you five pennies."

"Ten. But how did you know?"

"You were sharked," Sam said. "When you joined in, the pages played just as badly and you made out like a bandit."

"You dishonour me with the term, but I understand your meaning. The majority of my winnings were from Page Guy and he did not accept the loss well. He challenged me to a high stakes round."

"And you couldn't help yourself," Sam said.

The friar waved his hands. "I had a pile of pennies and felt I could not lose."

"But you lost the pile and more."

The friar's hand fell to his sides. "Half a Pendragon."

"I thought you said you owed a whole Pendragon."

The youth gritted his teeth. "Interest. Whatever it is they teach pages, Vaisey is now twice the bully he was in Nottinghamshire."

"I have no patience for bullies," Sam said. "Not even ones too young to shave. I'll get this Vaisey character off your back."

The friar's eyes widened. "You will? How?"

"Whatever it takes," Sam said.

Once again, the youth took in Sam's hat, trench coat, and shoes. "Who are you?"

Sam threw a few *hs* into his answer. "Sham Shpade, Private Eye."

"The investigation office next door? You are a knight? I fear the knights owe Vaisey more Pendragons than I do."

"No mere knight," Sam said. "I work for Merlin."

Tuck's jaw dropped open. "The Merlin. Magicians have no patience for fools. They expect a man, or a friar, to make his own bed."

Sam smiled. "I said I work for the magician. I'm not one myself. And I make a business out of helping fools."

"Then I am your best customer, as you will meet no greater fool. But how am I to pay you?"

Sam pulled his tobacco kit out of his coat pocket. "You can start by filling this."

8

ENTER THE BLACK WIDOW

SAM HAD TO admit that the young friar was a whiz with a mortar and pestle. He crushed a double handful of leaves in no time at all and then topped off the pouch with half a jar of loose matches. The fine aroma of freshly crushed tobacco was enough to send Sam hurrying back to his office. He couldn't wait to kick up his heels and roll a smoke or two.

When he opened the outer office door, he found a chipper Lady Euphemia Peregrine sitting at her desk. It was such a splendid sight that it almost hurt Sam to look. If the Necessarium was proof positive that this was not a dream, the world's most perfect secretary was proof it was. Before Sam could give Effie the shopping list he had thought up earlier, the shapely blonde said, "Lady Iva is waiting for you in your office."

"Iva?"

"Sir Lancelot's wife."

Sam let out a heavy sigh. "I guess this meeting was inevitable."

It turned out that Iva was a short, plain woman with mousy brown hair. She looked some years older than Lancelot, maybe five years past her *best before* date. It occurred to Sam that the skirt-chasing knight may have bought his title. Sam left the office door open as Effie had with Miss Morgan Le Fay the previous afternoon. The widow Lancelot remained seated, her gaze studying a bare wall, until Sam sat down.

51

"Did you kill him?" Iva demanded. Her pale green eyes were blotchy from a night of tears and her voice sounded ragged.

"Why would I kill your husband?" Sam asked. "Assuming I *could* kill your husband."

"Well . . . so that you could have me," the widow suggested.

Sam frowned. "Who put that bright idea into your head?"

"Rumour is everywhere," Iva said. "I have been told that you are interested."

"Lady, I've never laid eyes on you before today."

"Yes." Iva sniffed. "I thought it odd as well."

Sam leaned forward in his chair. "I will promise you this. I'll find out who did kill your husband."

"I hope that you do," Iva said. "Lancelot was not much of a man. I know his friends thought different, but they did not know him, not like I did. Still, to be murdered without a chance to draw steel and defend himself . . . It is not right. Especially not for a knight."

Sam rose, indicating that the meeting was over. Iva also stood, and then reached into a colourful bag she kept tied to her waist. "I would like you to hold onto this."

The woman pushed into his hands an amulet, a long loop of glimmering chain links ending in a fistful of silver that clasped a blood-red jewel the size of a quarter. Sam didn't know rubies from glass, but he doubted this was glass. The bought title theory was gaining traction.

"What am I to do with this?" Sam asked.

Iva wrung her hands. "Without Lancelot to protect it, I worry about thieves. This amulet is one of a kind. I would die if it were lost."

Sam tucked the jewellery into the inside pocket of his suit jacket and escorted Iva to the hallway. "I'll let you know what I find out."

When she was gone, Sam motioned Effie to join him in the inner office.

"Well?" said Effie, "how did you and the widow make out?"

"You didn't hear?"

Effie shook her head. "Iva is too soft-spoken. I thought sticking my head through the doorway would be too obvious."

"She thinks I killed Lancelot," Sam said.

"So you could marry her?" Effie laughed. "I did hear that and thought I heard wrong."

"And Saggy thinks I killed Logris, the hedge knight Lancelot was going to bully for the Le Fay dame. Which one do *you* think I killed?"

"Oh," said Effie. "I thought Sir Sagramore was after you for Lancelot's murder. Who did you not kill?"

Sam rubbed two fingers together, itching for that cigarette. "I don't think Saggy cares. Pinning the murders on me would make his day, even though I'm innocent."

Effie pursed her lips. "Perhaps Iva killed her husband so that she would be free for you to marry."

Sam grinned. "You really think that?"

"I know not what I think, but what I know is that Iva was out last night. When I went to tell her that Lancelot had been killed, she pretended she had just risen from bed. But I could see the bed had not been slept in and that she wore a dress beneath her nightgown."

Sam rubbed his ear. "That makes her guilty of something. It doesn't mean she killed her husband."

"Saggy—" Effie swallowed a laugh. "Sir Sagramore cannot really believe that you killed this Sir Logris."

Settling himself into the uncomfortable ladder-back chair, Sam kicked his feet up onto the desk and put his hands behind his head.

The blonde daughter of a duke wagged her head. "There you sit cool as a cucumber. Less than a day in this castle, accused of not one but two murders, and you believe you have all the answers."

"I don't know if I have any answers," Sam said. "But I've a truckload of questions."

Effie reached into a fold of her skirt and handed him a note. "This may be one or the other or both. It arrived while you were with Iva."

Sam unfolded the note. It said to meet Miss Le Fay at the Coronet Inn, checked in under the name Le Blanc.

9

A BAND OF SHARKS

ONE THING SAM Sparrow had always prided himself on was a sense of priority. It was for this reason that he refolded the note, slipped it into his shirt pocket, and removed his tobacco kit from his trench coat. Effie watched with intense curiosity as he rolled a cigarette and then struck one of Tuck's Lucifers against the window ledge and lit it.

"Can I offer you one?" he asked Effie before taking a pull.

"Thank you, no. My father takes a pipe and I can barely breathe when he does. Whatever that is you have smells no better."

Sam placed the unlit end between his lips and took a long, slow inward pull. Then he pulled the cigarette away and blew out a series of smoke rings. "Not my usual brand, but it'll do in a pinch. What can you tell me about the pages' dice games?"

"Dice?" Effie gave him a blank look. "You must mean stones." She sat down in one of the chairs in front of his desk. "There are many rumours regarding the stones. I hear that the pages teach the game to the knights, lending coppers to the losers and demanding double back. It seems to me a dangerous practice. Knights do not take threats lightly."

"But they're not going to challenge kids to duels, either," Sam suggested.

Effie turned her head as though thinking. "A knight would be

55

laughed out of court for suggesting a duel. And if he killed a boy . . . Well, he would find himself lucky just to be clapped in irons."

"And if a knight refused to pay his debt?"

The blonde Maid of Earl drummed perfect fingernails against the top of his desk. "The pages would ensure word got out. A knight of Camelot lives for his reputation. Refusing to make good on a debt ranks high on the list of dishonourable deeds. He could be expelled from court. Or lose his title if the debt is serious enough." She stopped drumming. "What is your interest in stones?"

Sam was saved from answering, and possibly embarrassing their neighbour, by the arrival of a servant bearing breakfast. The man was as short as a page but balding and buttled antlike about the office, placing a plate of incomprehensible, yet aromatic, food onto his desk as well as a tall mug of milk.

"What exactly am I eating?" he asked the little man.

The butler said nothing—he may have been mute—but Effie frowned curiously at the plate of breakfast food. "Poached egg, cranberry salad, grilled tuna, and goat's milk. Is anything amiss?"

"No, no," Sam said. "It's just not what I'm used to. Where's your breakfast?"

Effie was already on her way to the outer office. "I broke my fast with my father before coming to the castle." She smiled. "Better fare than what you are having."

At this the butler gave a soft snort and followed her out.

Sam swung his feet off the desk and sat looking at the lesser fare before him and the unfinished cigarette in his hand. Heaving a sigh, he crushed out the smoke and dug in.

Unlike the finger food he'd had for dinner the day before, breakfast came with a fork. The utensil was crudely made with no pattern embossed in the metal, but at least he didn't have to eat poached egg with his fingers. Sam noted that goat's milk tasted just like cow's milk. After leaving it on the counter for three days.

He had almost grown used to the noises outside his window; it worked as a sort of radio background noise as he ate his breakfast and planned his next steps. Once the food and milk were gone, Sam relit what was left of his cigarette and smoked it until the butt nearly burned his lip. Then he grabbed his hat and headed out the door.

"Off to slay the dragon?" Effie asked as he slid past her desk.

"So to speak," Sam said. "So to speak." He hoped the saying meant something different in Camelot than it did in Hartford.

At the bottom of the stairwell Sam retraced the path page Robin had taken in the night, past the Necessarium, down the wide hallway, and ending at the intersection of two corridors. There he paused to get his first good look at the castle's entranceway. He'd seen it twice before, at night and by lantern light. The first time he'd been in a hurry. The second time he'd been drunk.

The broad entranceway ran maybe fifty feet to where a giant metal grate hung from the ceiling. Sam had seen enough television to know it was called a portcullis and could be lowered to secure the castle. Beyond the portcullis, sunlight gleamed off the wooden drawbridge he remembered running across into the fog. During a siege, it could be pulled up against the lowered portcullis, further adding to the castle's defences. From where he stood, Sam couldn't see any chains, ropes, or winches to work either the grate or the bridge.

An opening on either side of the entranceway might provide access to winch rooms. Sam poked his head into the one on the right and, instead of a winch, found a lounge area filled with ladder-back chairs, carpets, and young boys aged seven to fourteen. Along the far wall stood a row of unlit lanterns. How about that, he'd found by accident exactly what he'd been looking for. He recognized one of the older boys as Robin and waved. Robin ran over and looked at him expectantly.

"Is one of your cohorts named Vaisey?" Sam asked.

Robin presented him with a hand, palm up.

"What's that for?"

"Why, a penny," said the boy.

Sam suppressed a laugh. "You want a penny for pointing out another page?"

"'Tis the price of a page's service, sir."

"Fine," Sam said. He looked out into the room and shouted. "Which one of you is Vaisey?"

All of the boys looked at him, then at each other, and a few of them made whispers. Not one of them volunteered information, however.

"If that's the way you want it," Sam said, "we'll do this the hard way."

He turned away from the pages and walked meaningfully across the broad entranceway and through the opposite opening. This chamber looked identical to what he'd decided to call the page pen, except that there were fewer chairs, no lanterns, and its occupants consisted of a half-dozen knights, none of whom looked over twenty-five. The looks they gave Sam were not friendly.

"Sorry, boys. Wrong room." He stepped back into the entranceway. Damn. The hard way was going to be harder than he thought.

Looking toward the gate, Sam saw two knights ostensibly performing guard duty. Like those inside what Sam figured must be a gatehouse, they seemed young and not particularly friendly. The one had short, dark hair and a scowl; the other curly blond hair, big ears, and an expression Sam could only describe as dim-witted. Both were a bit on the scrawny side. Sam had always assumed that knights would have to pass rigorous testing, like a firefighter. Why did reality always fail to live up to the myth?

And why did disappointment always make Sam itch for a cigarette? Heaving a sigh, he reached into his pants pocket and pulled out a piece of Hubba Bubba. He'd tried any number of types of gum over recent months from Wrigley's Spearmint to Nicorette Cinnamon Surge. None of them did the trick, but at least Hawaiian Punch tasted like something. Peeling open the wrapper, he tossed the pink square of gum between his teeth and chewed.

Sam figured he only had one true vice—smoking. He'd started shortly after his father's arrest, sneaking around backstreets and hiding in the boy's washroom at school. Yeah, it was cliché, but that's what twelve-year-olds did when he was a kid. Once he learned that Humphrey Bogart was an avid smoker, well, that was a green light and he'd started smoking in public at every opportunity. It wasn't until Sam had entered the police academy that he learned that his hero had died of esophageal cancer at age fifty-eight. Cancer had killed Bogart at a relatively young age. By then Sam was a chain-smoker.

Hell, he was probably smoking more than Bogart ever had. For the past ten years he'd been trying to quit. Chewing gum was only his most recent remedy; it worked no better than other things he'd tried.

The gangly knights by the gate were giving him odd looks, probably wondering what he was doing loitering around the castle entrance. Sam tipped his hat at them and then walked back toward the main corridor, turning right instead of left toward his office.

Sam wasn't sure what he was looking for. Truth was, he hadn't expected that finding Vaisey would be a problem. Then again, it was past time he did a little more exploring.

The corridor here seemed more upscale, with banners draped across the ceiling and the occasional suit of armour standing empty, yet at attention. Everything you'd expect in a Disney film. He wondered if Disney Studios might have an inside connection. Maybe Merlin had required a young Walt to cover for him while he attended an opera or went bowling.

The occasional jane or jasper passed Sam coming the other way, each clothed in enough ruffles to house a dozen cats and gawking at him like he was a two-headed dog at a circus. After only a few minutes, a knight with a peacock on his tabard leaned a pike or spear across Sam's path and frowned at the top of his cheeks.

"You cannot be here. Go back the way you came."

"Sure I can be here," Sam said. "Do you have any idea who I am?"

"Of course, I know who you are. You are the Merlin's pie. You still cannot be here."

"I was hoping to say hello to the king," Sam said. "It would be rude not to thank him for his hospitality."

The knight's eyes almost popped out of his head. "His Highness, the King, will summon you if and when he wishes to . . . say hello. Until then, this part of the castle is off limits."

Sam looked over the knight's shoulder and spotted a matronly woman holding up her dress and sweeping across the floor toward a side hall.

"That dame seems in an awful hurry," Sam said. "Is something going on?"

The knight glanced back quickly and then pressed the tip of

his pike—it definitely was a pike, not a spear—against Sam's coat. "That *dame*, as you put it, is the Queen, Lady Guinevere. If you speak her name again without due respect, I shall have no choice but to challenge you at arms."

Sam raised both of his hands, palms forward. "No disrespect intended. If I had known who she was, I would have been more careful with my words. If I can't see the king, how about Galahad? Is he around?"

"*Sir* Galahad," the knight said through clenched teeth, "is not available. I suggest you hire a page to send the good knight a note."

"Fine, I'll do that." Sam backed away and then turned around and sauntered toward the castle entrance. It seemed that knights in Camelot had no greater liking for PIs than cops back home.

Sam could have presented his question to the peacock knight, but his gut told him that the man wasn't really in the mood. He knew Galahad would help him, but finding the castle's one friendly knight would be no easier than finding a certain ruthless page. He decided to give the knights on guard duty a try. What could it hurt?

"Excuse me, sir knight," he said to the dark-haired one who at least looked halfway intelligent. "I was wondering if you could point out Page Vaisey for me."

The knight's scowl transformed into a blank stare.

"The page pen is right over there," Sam added.

The scowl returned and he answered in a whisper. "Why do you want to know?"

"A friend of mine owes him some coin and I'd like to make a payment."

The man's eyes grew three sizes. "I would that I could help, but . . ."

"It's not a difficult question," Sam said.

The knight glanced at his companion, who stared at Sam with wide-eyed stupidity, and then lowered his voice even further. "More difficult than you might imagine."

"I see," Sam said. "Never mind. I'll ask Galahad." When that didn't faze the man, he said, "Or Sagramore."

"Uhm," said the knight. "You may wish to look for the meanest of the lot."

"Okay," Sam said.

"And black." The man's voice was barely audible. "Vaisey wears only black."

"I'm sorry you couldn't help me," Sam said in a loud voice. He tipped his hat and walked back toward the page pen.

Once again, the pages stopped what they were doing when he appeared. Robin left his seat and began walking toward him, maybe with the assumption that Sam was ready to pay a penny.

Sam pulled down the brim of his hat, shadowing his eyes, and scanned the roomful of boys. Several of them looked mean enough, but none was dressed entirely in black.

Robin smiled and extended his palm. Sam reached into his pocket, pulled out his American Silver Eagle dollar, tossed it into the air where it promptly vanished, and then slapped the boy's palm playfully with no real force.

"You win this round," Sam said.

10
A ROSE BY ANY OTHER NAME STILL HAS THORNS

THE KNIGHTS GUARDING the gate paid Sam little notice as he stepped onto the drawbridge. The scowling, dark-haired knight averted his gaze while the blond seemed to be daydreaming. Sam examined the bridge for ropes or chains, but saw none; maybe it wasn't a drawbridge after all. He did notice the massive size of the stonework that made up the castle entrance and, he assumed, much of the main floor. The walls had to be at least twice as thick as the stone that housed the window in his office.

Sam squinted into bright sunlight as he turned to take in the city. The air was warm against his cheeks and a soft, cool breeze carried a host of smells, none of which could be found in Hartford. Perfect weather for finding his way around town. A glance at his junk watch suggested it was sometime between nine and ten in the morning.

After ambling only a few blocks, Sam learned two things. First, that children were like pages and expected you to give them a penny in exchange for directions. And second, that he still didn't have any copper pennies; just those five silver Pendragons Tuck said would get him arrested. That and an American Silver Eagle that he wouldn't spend even if anyone had been interested. As a result, he was sure he saw more of the town than was needful.

His indirect route allowed Sam to learn a third thing, that he was being followed. The mook looked like a knight, but with leather boots instead of steel. He seemed young, younger than the knights in the guardhouse, but had a plain-looking scabbard hooked to his belt and some kind of emblem on his grey vest that was too distant to make out.

Sam Sparrow knew he wasn't much of a detective, but one thing he was good at was losing a tail. Meandering up to a coffee house, he stepped casually inside and, as soon as the door swung shut, raced through the public area, through a door marked *staff only*, past a baffled woman who dropped a pan of steaming water, and out a narrow door into a backstreet of some kind. Turning left, he raced down a dirt and grass path until he spotted a narrow opening between two buildings on his right. After squeezing between the buildings, he crossed a street, dodged a horse-drawn carriage, and then hustled between two buildings on that side. This continued until he was out of breath and more lost than when he began.

It was only as he rested that Sam reflected that the ladies he had startled in the coffeehouse had been dressed head to toe in lace and frills, clothing that seemed bizarre even by dark age standards; it took a moment to realize that the apparel were undergarments. There had also been a distinct absence of coffee. He suspected that the monkey who had been tailing him would provide an interesting report of Sam Spade's doings to his boss.

After an additional hour of hard walking, Sam found the Coronet Inn nestled in a more upscale part of town than the St. Mark. Four floors of bay windows and balconies fronted the street, with more balconies looking out over a partially enclosed courtyard. Flowers in tiny ceramic pots lined most of the walls while a private stable yard and carriage house stood attached to the main building. The innkeeper took one disdainful look at Sam's wrinkled clothes and refused to answer his questions.

Sam considered playing the Merlin's investigator card as he had at the St. Mark, but decided against it. First, a corpse hadn't been found in the street out back. And second, he would rather keep a low profile. As low as he could, given his outlandish appearance. He decided instead to show the innkeeper the note.

The innkeeper scrutinized the slip of paper and puffed air between his lips. Then he grudgingly provided a room number. Sam climbed the stairs to suite 3C and knocked.

Miss Le Fay, or Le Blanc, opened the door and waved him quickly inside. Her hat was absent and her hair, so carefully coiffed the day before, looked almost tousled. Her deep blue eyes shone with a hint of violet, an intriguing colour.

"Come in, Mr. Spade. Oh, last night! Everything is upside down. Poor Sir Lancelot. Logris killed him. I knew he was dangerous. But with Lancelot's reputation I was sure . . ."

"Calm down, Miss Le Fay. Or is it Le Blanc?" Sam led the striking woman by the elbow to a wide, cloth-covered chair with hardwood trim and helped her sit. He then sat in the brocaded, oval-backed chair nearest it. He couldn't help but notice that the chair was nicely padded and briefly considered borrowing it for a few days.

"I—I have a terrible confession to make." Le Fay shook her head and used a hanky to wipe away invisible tears. "That story I told you yesterday; I am afraid it was just that, a story."

"Oh, that." Sam removed his fedora and set it on a side table. "I didn't exactly believe your story, Miss . . . What is your name anyway, Le Fay or Le Blanc?"

"FayBlanc. Bridget FayBlanc."

"Uhm, sure, Miss FayBlanc. I didn't exactly believe your story. It was a little too, how should I put it, made up as it went along? And then there was the money."

"The money?" Le Fay looked at him with large eyes.

"You paid us more than your story was worth, and enough more that we let the lie slide."

"I am not certain what you are saying, Mr. Spade. But tell me, am I to blame for last night?" She dabbed at a dry eye with the hanky.

"Well, you did warn us that Logris was dangerous, though everything else you said was a load of hooey. I didn't believe you, but I suspect Lancelot did. He was thinking yesterday, but it wasn't with his brain. But, no, I wouldn't say that you were at fault."

"Thank you, Mr. Spade. That is . . . if I understand you correctly. But Sir Lancelot was so alive yesterday, so brave, so strong, so handsome, and—"

"Lancelot knew what he was doing," Sam interrupted. "Those are the risks we investigators take. That he took on additional risk was his own decision."

"Was he married?" Le Fay asked. "Are there children?"

"Married, yes. Children, no, at least I don't think so. And I don't think his wife liked him much."

"What a thing to say!"

Sam shrugged. "That's the way it is, and it's too late to do anything about it now. What should be worrying you is that there's a gaggle of knights hanging around my door trying to find out what Lancelot was doing in that alley."

"Mr. Spade, do they know about me?" The young woman's eyes went wide with as much fear as Sam had ever seen.

"Not yet. I've been stalling them."

Le Fay clutched the hanky to her breast. "You are doing that for me?"

"Not really. More out of general principles than anything else." Sam let his face grow pensive. "Look, sister. I can't begin to tell them what's going on until *I* know what's going on. Sure, I could tell them Lancelot got cut open because you told us a tall tale, but there has to be more to the story. I don't see how hanging you out to dry will solve anything. Tell me what's going on and I'll do what I can to protect you."

Le Fay or Le Blanc sprang out of her chair and began pacing the floor. "I cannot tell you. Not yet. Soon." She fell suddenly to her knees in front of him and hugged herself to Sam's calves. "You have to trust me, Mr. Spade. I am so alone and afraid. If you will not help me, I have no one. You are brave. You are strong. Surely, you can spare me some of that strength. Surely. Help me, Mr. Spade. I need help so badly. I have no one else to turn to, only you. Please, help me."

Sam smiled. He couldn't help but notice that FayBlanc, or whatever her name was, used the same adjectives on him that she'd used to flatter Lancelot. Well, except for handsome. She'd called Lancelot handsome. He supposed she was trying not to push it. "Sister, from what I can tell, you don't need much of anyone's help. You're good. It's those violet eyes of yours. And that throb you get in your voice when you say things like, 'Help me, Mr. Spade.'"

Le Fay leaned away from him and filled her mouth with air, plumping out her cheeks, then blew the air out between her lips. "I deserve that. You say I am good, but I am horrible at this. It is my own fault if you cannot believe me when I tell you that my life is in danger."

Sam laughed. "You can ask all you like, sister, but I can't help you. Not if I'm out flapping my arms in the dark. You have to tell me something."

"Such as?"

"What can you tell me about your Sir Logris?"

Le Fay climbed to her feet, stepped over to the window, and looked outside. "I met him in France. We came from Marseille last week. He promised to help me. Then he took advantage of my trust and betrayed me."

That hit Sam too close to home. "Betrayed you? How? Why did you want him shadowed?"

"To learn how far he had gone, of course. Whom he was meeting with behind my back. How to avoid whatever trap he was setting for me."

"Did Logris kill Sir Lancelot?"

"Most certainly." Le Fay spun back toward him. "Mr. Spade, you cannot think that I had anything to do with Sir Lancelot's death?"

"Did you?"

"No!" Le Fay shook her head and began pacing the carpet. "I was still waiting in the common room. When Sir Logris never arrived, Lancelot went outside looking for him."

Sam rubbed his ear. "You picked a nice sort of gentleman to place your trust in."

"I picked the sort who could help me," Le Fay said. "If that had been his true interest."

"How bad a spot are you in, exactly?"

Le Fay's strawberry lips trembled. "I suspect I shall not last the week."

Sam nodded. "Sounds serious. Can you answer one other question?"

"I will try."

"Who killed Sir Logris?"

Le Fay halted her steps and raised a hand to her mouth. "Logris is dead?"

Sam nodded.

The petite woman resumed pacing, her steps moving double-time. Her hands fluttered in the air like birds. "Dead. It—it must have been one of the people he was meeting with behind my back."

"And they are?"

She moved her fingertips to her temple. "I cannot tell you."

Sam threw his hands into the air. "This is ridiculous! You're giving me nothing to go on."

Le Fay stopped pacing again and her entire body slumped. "Will you go to the knights?"

Sam laughed. "Lady, all I have to do is stand still and Sagramore will be looking over my shoulder. It took me twenty minutes to lose the monkey he had following me here."

"You were followed?"

"It's an occupational hazard. Here's a thought. Would you be safe if you were in the custody of the knights?"

Le Fay shook her head. "That would make it easier for those who killed Sir Logris to find me. Oh, it is hopeless. You have been more than patient with me, Mr. Spade. Thank you for what you have done so far. I suppose I shall just have to hope for the best."

"Look," Sam said. "You hold tight. If I find out anything, I'll come back. I'll tap four times on the door. Two hard knocks, followed by two soft. Don't open the door for anyone else."

Miss Le Fay or Le Blanc or FayBlanc sniffed and dabbed at her nose with the hanky. "Thank you, Mr. Spade. I shall do as you ask."

11
JESUS CAME BY WAY OF EGYPT

BY THE TIME Sam found his way through the twisting streets back to Castle Camelot, it was well past noon. He poked his head into the page pen, but still no bully in black.

Outside his office he discovered a poorly dressed man stealing the *Lancelot and Sparrow Investigations* sign from above the door. Sam barely avoided embarrassing himself by spotting a new shingle leaning against the mortared stone wall. *Sam Spade Investigations.* Whoever was in charge of the castle was on the ball. Sam had to wonder why he or she wasn't working as Merlin's investigator.

Effie gave Sam a wide smile as he walked in through the door carrying a padded chair he had borrowed from the Coronet Inn. Though, since the innkeeper had no idea it had left the premises, he supposed *borrowed* might not be the correct word.

"You are filthy with perspiration," Effie noted.

"I feel worse than I look," Sam said.

The chair wasn't really that heavy, made from cedar or a similar lightweight softwood, but it had grown heavier with each step. During the long walk from Le Fay's inn, Sam had altered his grip at least a dozen times to ease stressed muscles that had grown soft since he'd left East Hartford P.D. He'd join a gym when he got back home. Or at least buy a set of hand weights for the office. Assuming he still had an office and could start earning some income. He straightened his back and tried to appear manly as he lugged the chair into his office.

"Lunch is on your desk," Effie called after him.

Sam spent the next few minutes rearranging the furniture. He pushed Lancelot's desk against the far wall and stationed the six ladder-back chairs at convenient places about the room. The padded chair he set directly below the window. Then he slid Merlin's desk the few inches needed to line up with the chair.

Sitting down, he smiled and let out a slow sigh. Then he looked at his lunch plate. Sliced meat, cheese, and a vegetable. He recognized none of them. Just as well that he was still full from breakfast. He'd enjoy a smoke instead.

Sam was just pulling out his tobacco kit when Effie appeared in his doorway. "A gentleman to see you."

Sam gazed longingly at his tobacco pouch before tucking it back into his coat pocket. "I suppose you should send him in." If only business in Hartford had been this brisk.

The *gentleman* had a seedy smile, darkly tanned skin, and something on his head that would have been a turban if it had more cloth. The strands of hair sticking out from underneath the covering were slick and oily. He was short for a man, and carried a narrow walking stick that he seemed not to use for actual walking. Thin yellow gloves covered his hands, and a hunk of god-awful paste jewellery hung from the lapel of a black coat that looked a size too small, as did his off-white pants. The peculiar little man strutted his way to Sam's desk and handed him a small slip of parchment the size and shape of a business card. The name on it said Jesus Cairo. Sam made a leap of faith that the man might be from Egypt.

"Please, Mr. Cairo. Take a seat."

While the gentleman removed his too small coat, revealing a plain, starched white shirt underneath, Effie picked up Sam's untouched lunch plate and took it into the outer office. Jesus leered at her, and then took three quick steps to close the door before returning to drape his coat over the back of a chair on the visitor side of Sam's desk. He then moved the chair slightly, as if positioning it just so, before sitting down.

"Thank you, Mr. Spade," he said in a sibilant, nasal voice.

"So what can I do you for, Mr. Cairo?" Sam couldn't help

but notice that the man stank of cheap cologne.

Cairo tipped his head slightly and began removing his yellow gloves, tugging at one finger after the next. "I understand that your partner recently suffered a tragic end. May I offer condolences?"

"If you feel compelled to," Sam said.

"The city criers imply," continued the strange man, "a possible relationship between that unfortunate occurrence and the demise that same evening of a man known as Sir Logris?"

Sam offered no response, but noticed as Cairo placed his gloves on the desk that thin silver rings inset with paste gems adorned all ten of his fingers. Sam knew the jewellery was junk because it was dull as dirt even with sunshine streaming in through the window.

Cairo smiled. "I ask, Mr. Spade, because I am attempting to recover a certain fowl that has, shall we say, been mislaid. I am thinking that you may be able to assist me."

Sam rubbed his ear. "A fowl?"

"To be precise," said Jesus Cairo, "a chicken. A rare black chicken that I am attempting to recover for its rightful owner. He is offering fifty silver pennies for its recovery. Pendragons, I believe you call them. I am prepared to promise that—how do you say it?—no questions will be asked."

Since the five Pendragons Miss Le Fay had overpaid for services rendered were too valuable to bank, Sam took a shot in the dark. "Fifty pennies is a lot of change."

Cairo's expression never wavered.

"What you are requesting," Sam suggested, "lies outside the purview of this office." When this failed to prompt a reaction, he added, "Though I am not particularly busy at the moment." Again, no reaction. "You mentioned Sir Logris. How is he involved with your missing chicken?"

The door opened and Effie poked her head in. "I am breaking for lunch."

Sam nodded and rolled back his sleeve to glance at his fake Rolex. Twelve forty. Last night's guess at the time hadn't been too bad.

Effie closed the door again and Jesus Cairo was immediately on his feet. From his walking stick he drew a thin, wiry blade. Cairo aimed the business end at Sam and spoke quickly and clearly. "You will clasp your hands together at the back of your neck. I intend to search your offices, Mr. Spade. Do not attempt to prevent me, as I shall certainly cut you if you do."

Sam let his sleeve fall back in place and leisurely placed his hands behind his neck. "Search away. There's precious little to find."

Cairo took one step back and flicked directions with the blade. "Please come to the centre of the room. I must ensure that you are not armed."

Damn. So much for unholstering his gun at an opportune moment and putting a few holes into Jesus. Sam figured he was going to have to do this the hard way.

Rising slowly from his stolen chair, Sam stepped out from behind the desk and inched cautiously toward the middle of the room. Cairo stepped backward, matching him step for step. Then Sam tripped against the leg of one of the visitor chairs. He fell away from Cairo and his pointy blade, but kicked out with his foot, shoving the offending chair into the startled Egyptian's shins. Regaining his balance, Sam picked up a second ladder-back chair with both hands and smashed it over Cairo's head. Jesus dropped like a KO'd cowboy in a saloon brawl. Sam offered a quick prayer to God, thanking Him for high ceilings.

Unlike Hollywood bar fights, none of the struggle damaged the furniture in the slightest. Cairo, however, was down for the count and would take home a rather large goose egg as a souvenir.

Sam immediately went to work doing PI things. He rifled through the peculiar man's clothing and found three sets of travel papers identifying him as a citizen of Egypt, France, and the island nation of Malta. There were also coins of various shapes, sizes, and colours that he assumed were foreign. A narrow leather case held a nail file and a folded piece of paper wrapping what he assumed were candies or breath mints, but smelled like old soap. A clean, if worn, handkerchief filled one pocket. In the last pocket, Sam found a small sheaf of Cairo's business cards.

After putting everything back in its place, Sam sheathed and unsheathed the narrow cane blade several times and whipped it around the room, confirming his belief that he would be killed in moments if he ever engaged in a duel.

Cairo groaned and ran a hand over his head. Then he attempted to smooth his clothes. "Look what you have done to my shirt!"

Since the Egyptian's clothes were only half as rumpled as Sam's own, he found himself unsympathetic. "I'm sorry if you're offended," Sam lied, setting the cane on his desk. "Imagine my own disappointment when I learned that your fifty Pendragon reward was a bunch of stuff and nonsense."

"Not so, Mr. Spade. My offer is genuine." Cairo climbed to his feet, righted the chair he'd been struck with, and sat down. "Do you have the bird here?"

"In my office? No." Sam had no idea whether to believe the man was serious.

"Then why did you risk injury by attacking me?"

Sam leaned against his desk and folded his arms across his chest. "I don't take kindly to being held at sword point."

"I see." Cairo again attempted to straighten his shirt. "You cannot blame me," he suggested, "for attempting to save my employer such a great expense."

"Of course," Sam said. "And just who is your employer?"

"Regretfully, Mr. Spade, I am not at liberty to say."

Sam let out a heavy breath. "I've been getting that a lot lately."

"I am sorry," Cairo said, spreading open his hands, palms up, "but all I can do is offer a sizable reward in exchange for the bird. That is, if you have it or can retrieve it."

"And you're hoping," Sam said. "that I can retrieve your bird without anyone getting killed, robbed, or otherwise run afoul with the law?"

Cairo smiled slightly. "If possible. But as I said earlier, all the rightful owner requires is discretion." Jesus Cairo stood and wiggled his way into his too small coat. "When you are ready to contact me, sir, I am staying at the Belvedere Inn. May our venture result in mutual benefit." He bowed. "May I please have my cane back now?"

Sam grabbed the cane from his desk and handed it to Cairo.

The Egyptian immediately drew the narrow blade. "You will please clasp your hands together at the back of your neck. I intend to search your offices."

"What?" Then Sam laughed. "You may as well. Have at it."

Sam let Cairo do his thing as the Egyptian performed a search of both offices and the sleeping alcove. There were fewer than three places you could hide a chicken, so the entire exercise took less than a minute. Cairo frowned briefly at Sam, gave a quick bow, then left.

When he was gone, Sam rolled a cigarette and lit up.

Moments later, Effie returned to the office. "Did I miss anything exciting?"

12
A LONG LINE OF CHRONICLERS

BEFORE LEAVING HIS office, Sam asked Effie to explain the value of the three foreign coins he had kept from Cairo's pocket.

"You can't spend those here," Effie said. "I'll take them to a moneychanger."

"You have an account?"

Effie flashed him a grin. "Well, my father is a duke." She then gave him a handful of copper pennies from her belt purse. "I'll give you the rest once I'm back from the exchange."

"But how do I know what things cost?" Sam asked.

Effie laughed. "Things cost whatever the seller can get away with."

"Oh, great." Sam hated haggling.

Instead of heading for the stairwell, Sam walked the other way until he found the shingle he was looking for. *Pendragon Jewellers*. He lifted the door latch and went inside.

The place looked much like Friar Tuck's, with shelving all along the walls and a long narrow table in the centre of the room. Shiny rocks, bracelets, chains, and amulets littered the shelves. One small section displayed several rows of rings. Unlike jewellery stores in Hartford, the merchandise wasn't backlit to bring out its quality, though the attempt was made with low, squat candles burning every foot or so along the shelves. However, just like in Connecticut, a musclebound bruiser hefting a heavy short sword stood in the far corner of the room watching for trouble.

Behind the central table, on a tall stool, sat a man dressed in bright velvet robes of purple and gold. He had a tall face with thick black eyebrows and moustache, and greying hair that rose like a brush above a high forehead. His mouth was small and offered only a tight smile. He stood when Sam looked at him.

"I know who you are," the man said. "Sam Spade, Private Instigator."

Sam let the error pass; it was better than being called the Merlin's pie. "You have the better of me," Sam said.

The man bowed slightly. "Thomas Hammett, master gemmologist. At your service." The tight smile grew a bit tighter.

Sam stepped toward him and waved a hand at one of the walls. "This is quite the collection you've got here. Do you do it all yourself?"

Hammett cocked an eye. "By *do it*, I assume you mean do I create everything I sell? By no means." He came around from behind the table, his soft robes swishing with each step. "These," he ran spindly fingers along a shelf set against one of the narrower walls, "are all Hammett originals, designed and crafted by yours truly. The wall opposite," he waved a hand, "are works by other artisans favoured by the court, mostly from the continent. The front wall there," he nodded his head, "are works by local artisans and are generally of lesser quality. Is there something in particular you are looking for?"

Sam smiled. "I suspect that anything you have here is beyond my means."

Hammett pursed his lips. "You are no doubt correct. My clientele consists of ladies and lords of the court and visiting dignitaries. If not to purchase, then why are you here? No, wait!" Hammett raised a long-fingered hand and smiled. "Let me guess. You are here because of my other profession."

That was unexpected. "You could say that," Sam suggested, wheedling for more information. The man did like to talk.

Hammett's narrow smile deepened. "You wish me to document your adventure. I am delighted to do so, of course. There is no better chronicler in the kingdom." The tall man rushed toward him in a flurry of velvet, then halted and spoke in a conspiratorial voice. "To be honest with you, I have already started."

Sam narrowed his eyes.

"I have contacts, you see. At *The Camelot Crier*. Also among the knights and pages." He rushed back to the table and pushed some paper sheets around, at last returning with a fistful of wrinkled paper smeared with ink. "It is all here. Your adventure thus far."

"Uhm, excellent," Sam said. "What do you plan to do with it?"

Hammett turned his head. "Do? Finish it, of course."

"Sure, sure," Sam said. "And then what?"

"And then?" Hammett's gaze flitted about. "Well, I . . . I . . . Were I a bard, I would recite the chronicle in the best inns and before kings. Unfortunately, I have neither the voice nor the temperament of a bard." The jeweller sighed. "I can only dream of the life."

"Why don't you sell your . . . chronicles?" Sam asked.

The man gaped at him. "Sell? Would that I could, but who would buy?"

Sam shrugged. "I don't know. Bards, maybe?"

Hammett grinned at him. "You are having me on. My contacts tell me you do such things. As if a bard could afford to purchase tales. You are familiar with the saying *poorer than a bard*? No? Really? You are a foreigner; I shall educate you. Bards are one step above beggars. And chroniclers one step below, so far as income is concerned. There is no living to be made writing chronicles. Just as playwrights earn a meagre living performing their plays and none from writing them, neither can a chronicler rub two copper pennies together. Unfortunately, my own skills as a bard are wanting, so I have not even that meagre recourse. I am, however, the region's foremost expert on fine jewellery, so this is how I feed and clothe my family."

The biggest nugget Sam took from that lecture was that the man really, really loved to talk. If Sam didn't get down to business, he'd be here all day. He reached into his inside jacket pocket and produced Iva's amulet. "In that case, I'm wondering if you can tell me what this is worth."

Hammett took the silver chain from Sam's hand and frowned at it, paying particular attention to the blood ruby. He then scurried to his table and placed a monocle over his right eye. He turned the amulet this way and that, catching the light from a bright candle that burned near one end of the table. His frown deepened as he took the disk of glass away from his eye.

"Mr. Spade, I do not know what to say. My contacts have informed me that you are a rough man by nature, but thus far have displayed a certain degree of moral fortitude, if not honesty. I must admit that I am shocked, more than shocked, that you would attempt to sell me an item that for generations has been in the family of Iva Lancelot."

"Whoa, whoa, whoa." Sam put up his hands. "I'm not trying to sell you anything. Iva gave me that piece of ice for safekeeping, and I just want to find out if it's the real deal. There's something fishy about the whole setup and I need to figure out what it is."

The gemmologist stared at him and then looked back down at the jewellery. "I can assure that this is the genuine article, Mr. Spade. The ruby is of the right quality, the silver the right weight, and I can see the artisan's mark. If this is a forgery, then it is worth as much as the original."

"Which is?" Sam asked.

"In the neighbourhood of twenty-five Pendragons. Probably slightly less. Amulets are a bit out of fashion this season."

"So not something you'd hand to a complete stranger."

Hammett made a noise in his throat and shook his head. "Mr. Spade, this item is not worth a copper penny without a signed document from Lady Iva indicating the purchaser, date, and agreed upon price. There would need to be witnesses." He handed the amulet back and Sam tucked it inside his jacket. "Mr. Spade, if anyone were to try to sell Lady Iva's amulet in any other way, they would quickly find themselves in a dungeon, or worse. And Lady Iva would never sell it; her relations would disown her."

"What if it were melted down?" Sam asked.

Hammett's face paled and his mouth opened like a fish. "That—that is unthinkable. Who would do such a thing? It would lose half its value. More than half."

Sam had to chuckle. "I can think of a lot of people back home who would. But don't worry yourself, it won't come to that. I'll make sure nothing happens to it. Not here in Camelot, anyway."

The gemmologist looked somewhat mollified, but not entirely.

"Look," Sam said. "Now that I know it's the real deal, I'll be able to figure out why Lancelot's widow gave it to me. You've been a big help."

"I have?" Hammett looked more his regular self. "Well, that is good news. Perhaps in return you would allow me an interview. I—"

"Of course, of course," Sam interrupted. "Just as soon as I figure out what's going on. You'll be the first to know."

Sam backed quickly toward the doorway, his last look at Thomas Hammett that of a tight, yet hopeful, smile. Mentally he kicked himself. He had to stop telling people they'd be the first to know, especially when he had no intention of telling them anything.

13
I'VE BEEN A BAD, BAD GIRL

ONCE AGAIN, SAM took to the streets of Camelot. Before leaving, he poked his head inside the page pen. Once again, no Vaisey. He sincerely doubted the bully was in hiding. Probably out with his toadies extorting protection money from widows and orphans.

Using the copper coins Effie had given him, Sam jumped into an enclosed carriage just outside the castle and managed to talk the driver into taking him to the Coronet Inn for five pennies. From the grin on the man's face, it was probably two pennies too many. The way things were going, Sam would soon have a reputation all over town as the world's biggest chump.

As the horse-drawn enclosure trundled through a crowded market, he told the driver he had changed his mind and wished to go to the St. Mark Inn instead. Moments later he slipped out of the moving carriage and dashed behind a busy stall where bolts of fabric towered in two-foot stacks and hung from every available hold. He watched from a low crouch behind a pile of earth-tone burlap as an open carriage carrying the grey knight who had followed him from the castle rumbled past. As he congratulated himself on once again giving the monkey the slip, a throat cleared. Sam looked up to see the stall keeper glaring at him.

"Do you think the one on the bottom matches my eyes?" Sam asked.

The stall keeper lost part of her glare as she considered the textile in question, which looked no different from the others.

"I'll come back with my wife," Sam said, straightening. "She makes all the important buying decisions." Then he walked quickly away.

As he made his way on foot the rest of the way to Le Fay's inn, the Coronet, he pondered how ditching the carriage driver would only enhance his odd reputation.

"Do you bring news?" the dark-haired beauty asked almost before he got through the door. "Did you manage it so the knights will not need to know about me?"

"The knights won't be onto you for a while," Sam said. A glance around the room revealed flowers that hadn't been there that morning. Le Fay had also gotten her hair done and changed her clothes. She now wore flowing satin the same ice blue as her eyes.

Le Fay's face lit up in a smile. "You are a wonder, wonderful man! This will not earn you trouble, will it?"

"I'm usually up to my neck in trouble," Sam admitted. "Occupational hazard."

Le Fay gestured to a chair, a different one than Sam had taken earlier that morning. Literally. "Please, sit."

Sam made himself comfortable while Le Fay settled herself in a narrow sofa. He found himself gazing at a young woman who exuded innocence, but who he knew was anything but. "You're no stranger to trouble either, are you?" he asked. "I imagine you've had plenty of practice dodging it."

Le Fay looked only slightly scandalized. "Why, I am not sure I know what you mean."

"The ladylike manner," Sam said. "Spending hours on your hair, the elegant clothing with not a seam out of place, the blushing, the coy looks. Like your lies, it's all a façade, isn't it?"

"I admit," said Le Fay, her cheeks reddening, "that I have lived less than a good life. I have been bad. Worse than bad. It is not what I wanted, but it is what life has forced upon me."

"That's good. Because if you were half as innocent as you pretend to be, I'd be wasting my time here."

"Then I shall not be innocent," Le Fay said. "If it is helpful to you."

"It is. By the way, I saw Jesus Cairo today."

Le Fay's eyes widened slightly. "You know him?"

"I do now." Sam smiled.

Le Fay stood and took a step toward an unlit fireplace. "What did he say?"

"About what?" Sam asked.

"About me."

"You? Nothing."

Le Fay turned and looked at him. "Then what did you talk about?"

Sam threw his hand to one side. "He offered me fifty Pendragons for a chicken."

She turned back toward the fireplace. "He what?"

"You heard right. I told him that fifty silver pennies was a lot of change."

"It is." Le Fay turned back toward him. "It is more than I can pay you for your loyalty."

Sam laughed so hard he had to lean forward. "I don't need your money. What I need is the truth. You ask for help and then change your story faster than you change your clothes. If you need help, maybe I can help you, but I have to know what's going on."

Le Fey stood looking at him, her lips moving but with no words coming out.

Sam leaned back in his chair. "I don't care about your secrets, sister, but I can't help you if I don't know the game you're playing. It's your trust I need, not your money."

"Please." Le Fay folded her hands together as if in prayer. Sam feared for a moment that she would fall to her knees, as she had that morning. "Please," she repeated. "Act as though you believe me just a little longer?"

Sam shook his head. "Things are moving fast. I don't know how much longer I can wait."

"Soon," Le Fay said. She sucked on her lower lip, milk over strawberries. "I must speak with Jesus Cairo. Then I can tell you everything."

"Okay. You can see him tonight. I'll leave a message at his inn."

"But not here!" Le Fay almost shouted. "No one must know where I am."

"Fine. My office, then. At sunset."

It was only as Sam left the Coronet Inn that he remembered how dark Camelot got when the sun went down. Maybe not the best time for a friendly meeting.

Paying three pennies this time, Sam took a carriage to the Belvedere Inn. If he had thought the Coronet was upscale, the Belvedere was a small castle. Turrets lined the front façade and a large sign with stylized white letters against a blue background proclaimed its name. Sam entered through a wide double door made from thick oak to find a common room four times larger than the other inns he had visited. People congregated in noisy groups and the place held the air of a carnival. Sam worked his way through the rabble to a wide counter.

"I need to see Jesus Cairo," he said.

The innkeeper, one of several, snapped his fingers and a young boy ran over. The innkeeper whispered into his ear and the boy was off again. He returned a minute later, out of breath, and the innkeeper leaned down to receive a whispered message.

"Mr. Cairo is not available," the man said.

"It's rather important that I see him. Could you give him my name?"

The man frowned. "Unavailable means that he is not in his rooms."

"Oh. How about I leave him a note?"

"That would be acceptable."

Sam ripped a page out of his notebook and scribbled instructions for Jesus. The innkeeper watched with interest as he wrote, and then charged him a penny to deliver the note.

It was midafternoon by the time Sam arrived back at the castle. He saw no sign of the monkey who had tried to follow him twice that day, but there was sign of Page Vaisey.

Tuck's nemesis sat in a well-padded armchair, the only such chair in the page pen, with several minions standing near him or sitting on the floor at his feet. True to the gate knight's whispered description, the boy wore all black, from the soft leather of his shoes to the upturned collar of his shirt. There was nothing about him that wasn't mean. Scruffy black hair. Thick, petulant lips. Eyes as dark as midnight. Even the tattered few whiskers on his chin stuck out like spikes. He looked older than fourteen years, the maximum age for page service according to Effie.

Sam was thankful to note that Robin wasn't numbered among Vaisey's crew, but held himself aloof against one wall with several other boys.

"I am told you were looking for me," Vaisey said in a gruff tenor voice before Sam could speak. "I shall give you a ten count to convince me you are worth my time."

Sam could guess what a ten count was and figured he only needed a three count. "I represent one of your clients who owes you money."

The boy in black nodded. "Go on."

"You might remember him. Dressed in sackcloth. Vow of poverty. Not a penny to his name. Same hometown as you, I understand."

"You are here to pay Tuck's debt?" Vaisey asked.

Sam smiled. "Yes and no."

The underage loan shark snickered. "What is that supposed to mean?"

"It means the whole debt is a scam and he doesn't owe you a dime."

One of the minions spoke up. "A what?"

"Less than a copper penny," Sam said.

The boy in black frowned and waved a hand. "You are no longer worth my time. Go away."

"Happy to leave," Sam said, tipping his hat. "Just delivering the message that you won't see so much as a hand-drawn image of a penny from Tuck."

Vaisey snickered. "I am curious how Abbot Gildas will react to hearing about your friend's problems with drink and gambling."

"Gildas is expecting you," Sam lied. "I've already filled him in on your scam. He mentioned something about speaking with the King regarding Camelot pages trying to corrupt his monks."

When Vaisey's already chilly expression turned ice cold, Sam decided to add gasoline to the fire. "It might be an opportune meeting to bring up corrupting his knights, as well." The hate in the young man's eyes deepened and Sam wondered if he might have taken things too far. "All right, all right." He put his hands in the air. "I'm leaving. Don't shoot the messenger."

He managed to make it down the corridor and up the stairs to his office without a street gang coming after him. He even considered stopping at Friar Tuck's to tell him the good news, but decided to wait. Sam didn't think the pages had any avenue of recourse, but he'd only been in Camelot one full day and didn't doubt that there were still a few surprises in store.

"Here is the balance of the foreigner's money," Effie said, spilling a handful of copper pennies into Sam's hands. "His coins were not worth much."

Sam pocketed little more than a dozen pennies and then handed Effie one of Le Fay's five silver coins. "Next time you're at the bank, why don't you cash that. Expenses in this town aren't cheap."

"I could open you an account," Effie said.

"That's sweet, angel, but let's wait and see. I may not be here that long."

Sam glanced toward the door to the hallway and Effie tightened her lips. She knew something was up. What a woman. She'd make a better partner than Lancelot ever had. Sam hadn't even had to work with the philandering knight to know that.

"I may get some company," Sam said. "If it's a dozen angry pages, you may want to slip away and bring back a few knights."

Effie narrowed her eyes. "You were not playing stones, were you? I had not thought you the type."

"I'm a different kind of gambler entirely," Sam said, tossing off a boyish grin.

After rolling a cigarette, Sam put his feet up on his desk and enjoyed a few peaceful minutes. The minutes turned into hours and Sam found himself glancing too often at his junk watch while a pile of ashes collected on the window ledge. No one dropped by, not page nor knight nor lady in red. It felt just like Hartford.

Eventually Effie came in and said good night.

"How old are you, angel?" Sam asked as his secretary turned to leave. Too late, he realized he had uttered the unutterable question. Frantically, he searched for something to say that might mitigate the damage. I only ask because you seem wise beyond your years? I'm surprised your father lets so young a daughter out of his sight? Shouldn't you still be in school? Each thought that came was worse than the last.

Before Sam could settle on anything, Effie smiled and said, "I am seventeen. Why do you ask?"

Sam spoke the first words that came to mind. "No reason. I'm just no good at judging people's ages. Call it a weakness."

Effie's expression grew solemn. "There are those who feel that a career is no life for a woman, that I should be keeping house and raising two children by now."

"I've never been one to care what other people think," Sam said. "Sometimes it gets me in trouble, but for the most part I do all right. I highly recommend it."

"You are a strange, strange man, Mr. Spade."

"Call me Sam."

"Good night, Sam." Then Effie was gone.

Seventeen! Effie might look like a woman, but she was just a kid. It'd be another four years before a bar in a Hartford would serve her a drink. And people here thought she should have children already?

Sam had to laugh. Effie had called him a strange one? Well, not so strange that he'd rob the cradle.

He'd had to arrest a guy once for shacking up with a fifteen-year-old. The mug was in his thirties and told the court he had no idea how young the girl was. Claimed she'd told him she was twenty-two. His defence lawyer had dressed the girl up to the nines and paraded her in front of the jury. Wouldn't *you* believe she was in her twenties? The jury didn't buy it and neither did the judge. He sentenced the mug to ten years and remanded the girl to child services for mandatory rehabilitation. Sam was sure that if the parents could be found, that they'd be in hot water as well. The world was a sick place sometimes, but it was hard to get sicker than messing with kids. Things might be different here in the dark ages, but kids were kids in any age.

Anyway, seventeen. So much for Sam's aspirations of anything developing with Effie. If she were a few years older or he a lot of years younger, fine. For now, he'd have to settle for harmless flirting.

Turning his pilfered padded chair to face the window, Sam smoked another cigarette and watched the sun settle on the horizon. Then he lit the lantern he'd commandeered from Robin the night before.

14
A GATHERING AFTER DARK

WHEN IT WAS full dark, a knock on the outer office door revealed Miss Morgan Le Fay. She was alone and carried a lantern. A white lace hat adorned her midnight hair and she wore a long red dress the colour of blood. "Mr. Spade! There is a young knight outside the castle watching your office window."

Sam invited her in and placed Le Fay's lantern on Lancelot's desk. He looked out the window but could see nothing in the darkness. "I spotted him earlier this afternoon. He's the same monkey who tailed me this morning."

Le Fay let out a harsh breath. "You are certain he did not follow you to my inn?"

Sam shook his head. "There hasn't been a tail born that I can't shake."

"If you are certain," Le Fay said. "Will you let me deal with Jesus Cairo in my own way?"

"Of course." Sam knew that observing their exchange would tell him more than any question he could ask.

A second knock came at the outer door. Sam opened it to find Cairo in the hallway holding a third lantern and fidgeting like a cat on a hot tin roof. He'd always loved that phrase and was delighted whenever someone's behaviour brought it to mind.

"Mr. Spade!" The Egyptian's nasal voice was painfully shrill. "There is a most disreputable-looking young man watching your window!"

"I saw him." Sam closed the door, took the lantern from Cairo, and set it on Effie's desk. "He must be one of Saggy's men." Sam had no evidence of that, but it was as good an explanation as any.

"Who?"

"Sir Sagramore, Camelot's Second Knight. His monkey has been following me since last night's murders."

Cairo clutched at the lapel of Sam's rumpled trench coat. "Did you lead him to my lodgings?"

Sam brushed the man's hand away. "As I informed Miss Le Fay, no one follows me anywhere. There's not much I can do about my doorstep, however."

He led Cairo to the inner office and the Egyptian bowed formally toward Miss Le Fay. "It is a privilege to see you again, madam."

Le Fay's smile was more a sneer. "You are too kind, Cairo. Mr. Spade said you are willing to pay fifty Pendragons for the chicken. How soon can the money be ready?"

The Egyptian's eyes glittered. "It is ready now."

"I see. You will pay right now in exchange for the bird?"

Cairo paused. "You must excuse me. I did not mean to imply that I have the coins in my pocket. I can get them for you with a few minutes' notice."

Le Fay seemed to think about this. "I do not have the chicken in my pocket either." She smiled. "I can probably get it tomorrow."

A tight frown formed on the Egyptian's lips. "The word *probably* does not fill my soul with confidence. Where is it?"

Le Fay's smile deepened. "Where Sir Logris hid it."

Cairo nodded. "And you know where that is. Why can we not go there now?"

"There are reasons," Le Fay said.

"I see." Cairo's hand tightened on the handle of his cane. "Why are you willing to sell it to me?"

A small pout appeared on Le Fay's lips. "Because I am afraid. After what happened to Sir Lancelot and Sir Logris, I am afraid to touch the filthy thing, except to be rid of it."

Cairo snorted. "Lancelot I am not concerned about, but what exactly did happen to your partner, Sir Logris?"

Le Fay's pout turned into biting her bottom lip. "The fat man."

Cairo's eyes flicked about the room. "He is here? In Camelot?"

"It appears so." Le Fay eyed the Egyptian. "Why the jitters?"

"Foolish woman!" Cairo swung his cane in a small circle and struck the stone floor with it. "The fat man is not one to be trifled with. You could get us all killed."

Sam watched Le Fay's expression grow purple with anger. She stepped forward and slapped the Egyptian across the face. Hard. Cairo's eyes bulged out of his head and he raised a fist in retaliation. Sam leapt forward and pulled down his arm, then glared at him.

Cairo glared back. "This is the second time you have laid hands on me."

"Yeah? Well, you're welcome to a third." Sam then slapped Cairo across the face, twice as hard as Le Fay had.

"You—"

Sam slapped him again.

Cairo raised his fist again.

Sam slapped it away and then slapped Cairo's face a third time. "Look, you. When I slap you, you'll smile and you'll say, 'please sir, can I have another?'" When Cairo gawked at him, Sam slapped him four more times, alternating between palm and backhand, moving so quickly that Cairo had no opportunity to retaliate. Sam would have continued slapping, but was interrupted by a pounding at the outer door.

Cairo widened his eyes and turned toward the sound.

Sam let him go. "You two keep quiet. I'll get rid of whoever it is."

He went through the inner office door, closing it behind him, then opened the outer door to a repeat of last night's ugly experience—two pages with lanterns and two knights with swords.

Sam grinned. "You guys must think I don't sleep. What do you want this time?"

Galahad glanced quickly at Sagramore and said, "We have need to speak with you, Mr. Spade."

Sam nodded. "So speak."

Sagramore growled in his throat. "Must we do it in the hallway?"

Sam shook his head. "I'm not letting you in this time. If you want to visit, come during office hours."

Sagramore growled again. "Do not be absurd. The day is hardly over. It is not yet an hour past sunset."

Sam stepped further out into the hallway. "Office hours are nine to five."

"Come," said Galahad. "You must see reason."

"You would best begin cooperating," Sagramore said. "You sing and dance and fill our ears with excuses, but this cannot continue. At some point the music shall stop."

Sam looked at him. "You know, for a guy who doesn't know a metaphor from a rusty nail, that wasn't half bad."

Sagramore gazed at him quizzically.

"There is talk," Galahad said. "About you and Sir Lancelot's wife."

"There's always talk," Sam said.

"Even the most absurd rumour has its genesis in truth," Sagramore suggested.

Sam shook his head. "Look. I've spent all of two minutes in the same room with the woman."

Galahad continued. "The talk is that Lady Iva sought a divorce from Sir Lancelot that she might clear the way for your advances, but he refused her. Do you deny it?"

Sam couldn't stop himself from laughing. "That's rich. I've been here less than two days and don't plan on being here much longer."

Sagramore took a half step forward. "You failed to answer the question."

"Actually, Saggy, I did answer it. You'd know that if you were paying attention. To put it bluntly, so that even you can understand, I know nothing of Lady Iva. I didn't even know Lancelot was married until after he was dead."

"Humph," said Sagramore. "The talk is that you arranged for Sir Lancelot to be killed."

Sam laughed. "Don't get greedy, Saggy. You can't set me up for killing Logris to avenge Lancelot's death, if you say that I killed Lancelot, too."

The blustery knight sneered. "If you insist there is nothing between you and Lady Iva, then you are a liar."

"Sure. Sure. Is that the big lead that brought you to my door in the middle of the night?"

"It is but evening," Galahad interjected.

Sagramore ignored the junior knight, his eyes brightening. "That is one of them."

Sam cocked a brow. "What's the other?"

The dark knight leaned toward him. "Let us in and we shall tell you."

Sam shook his head. "As far as threats go, that one's pretty lame."

"Please," said Galahad.

Sagramore rested a gauntleted hand on Galahad's shoulder and cast Sam a knowing look. "Very well, Spade. We shall leave. But you should think hard on coming clean the next time we speak."

Sam knew exactly what he meant; Sagramore knew about Iva's amulet.

The two knights turned to leave, but stopped when a shuffling noise sounded from the inner office. Then came more shuffling followed by a piercing male voice yelling, "Help!"

Sagramore laughed. "It appears we are not interrupting your sleep after all."

Sam sighed and opened the door wide.

15
AND IF YOU BELIEVE THIS . . .

THE TWO KNIGHTS pushed their way past Sam, through the outer office, and then slammed open the inner office door. Sam followed at their heels. As there was already plenty of light in the room, the two pages remained in the outer office.

"What is it that transpires here?" demanded Sagramore.

Sam scanned the room and saw Miss Le Fay standing nervously near his desk and Jesus Cairo collapsed on the floor touching a bleeding scalp.

"Look, sir knight," Cairo whined while holding up a hand tinged with blood. "Look what she did!"

Galahad chuckled. "I receive worse injuries just putting on my armour."

"I had to hit him," Le Fay said. "We were alone in here and he tried to attack me. I had to keep him off."

"You odious liar!" Cairo's face turned apoplectic. "I was invited here for honest business, and both of them attempted to rob me. Then, when Mr. Spade went out to speak with you, she said that as soon as he returned they would murder me and dump my body into the castle moat." He waved a frantic hand at the window. "I called for help hoping you would hear and rescue me. Then she hit me with a—"

Sam never learned what Miss Le Fay hit Jesus with in the near-empty room because the dark-haired beauty chose that moment to kick the Egyptian in a delicate place.

"Why not tell them the truth?" she shouted at Cairo's crumpled form over his high-pitched keening.

The two knights quickly pulled the tiny woman away, each of them holding one of Miss Le Fay's arms.

"Well, Galahad?" Sagramore grinned as though he had won a lottery. "It appears that we shall be presenting the gaoler with three guests."

Sam had to think fast. "Hold your horses, boys, everything can be explained."

"Yes," said Sagramore. "There shall be time for explanations in the dungeon."

Sam kept talking. "Miss Le Fay, let me introduce Sir Galahad and Sir Big Saggy Britches Sagramore. Miss Le Fay is my new assistant."

The two knights stared at him.

"I hired Miss Le Fay this morning. To pick up the slack left by Lancelot's absence."

"That is a lie," shrilled Cairo from where he lay crumpled on the floor.

"And this is Mr. Jesus Cairo," Sam said. "An associate of Sir Logris. He came to my office this morning and hired me to find something that Sir Logris was supposed to have in his possession. The whole thing smelled fishy, but I went along with it hoping to find out what Cairo knows about the two murders. Then he pulled a sword on me. Well, that's neither here nor there. Anyway, Miss Le Fay and I discussed the matter and decided to ask him up here for a little heart to heart. Now maybe we were a little rough, but not enough to make him cry."

The two knights continued to stare at him. Then Sagramore frowned at Cairo. "What say you?"

Cairo looked up at Sagramore, then at Galahad, then Sam, and then back at Sagramore. "I—I, there is some truth to what Mr. Spade says, but the way he says it . . ."

"Try telling it in your words," Sam suggested.

"My words?" echoed Cairo.

"Cease this stalling!" Sagramore shouted. "All you must do is raise a complaint that Miss Le Fay injured you with malicious intent, and then I shall throw them into the dungeon."

Sam smiled. "That's good advice, Cairo. Then I'll complain about your actions this morning and the three of us can enjoy each other's company in a six by eight cell for a few days."

"Or weeks," suggested Galahad.

Cairo looked like he was going to faint.

"You need not think about it here," Sagramore said. "Dungeons are consummate environs for contemplation."

Silence permeated the room for several heartbeats. Then Sam laughed.

"Well, boys and girls." Sam offered Cairo a hand and pulled the Egyptian to his feet. "We put one on them nicely." He grinned at Sagramore. "Don't you know when you're being kidded?"

"No need," Sagramore said. "The magistrate shall decide."

Sam made a tsk tsk sound. "That won't go well for you. Wasting the magistrate's time."

"Your meaning?" asked Sagramore.

"You're being kidded," Sam said. "When I heard your knock at the door, I said to Cairo and Le Fay: It's those nosy knights again. They're getting to be a real pain in the caboose. When you hear them begin to leave, one of you cry out and we'll see how far we can string them along."

Galahad shook his head. "That has the ring of a fairy tale."

"The cut on Mr. Cairo's forehead?" demanded Sagramore. "How did it get there?"

"You'll have to ask him," Sam said. "I was in the hallway with you. Maybe he cut himself shaving."

Cairo touched his forehead. "The cut? No. When we pretended to struggle, I fell and hit the corner of the desk."

"Pig feathers," said Galahad.

Sagramore let go of Miss Le Fay's arm and snatched up Cairo's cane. He drew out part of the blade and then thrust it back into its sheath. "We shall arrest you all regardless, for unlawful possession of a sword."

"A sword!" Sam cried. "Now you're reaching. Half the people in the castle have swords. Are you going to throw everyone in the dungeon? Or maybe you can prove that the pig sticker you're holding is the sword Sir Lancelot or Sir Logris was stabbed with."

Sagramore's fist came so fast that Sam couldn't avoid it. It caught him square in the jaw. Another man might have gone down for the count, but Sam had taken a few hits in his life. He knew how to take a punch. All Saggy achieved was to put a nasty kink in Sam's neck.

"Why you . . ." Sam raised his own fist to return the favour, but Galahad's hand was suddenly there holding him back. "It is not worth the trouble it shall cause, Sam."

"I shall be going now," Cairo said, interrupting the altercation. He snatched his cane from Sagramore's left hand and began limping toward the door.

"What's the hurry?" Sam asked.

Cairo paused and looked at him. "There is no hurry. But the night is growing late and our business here is done."

The Egyptian left without either knight stopping him.

"This evening has been a farce," Sagramore said. Then he smiled at his fist. "Though it did have its moments."

As both knights turned to leave, Galahad said, "You play a risky game, Sam. I hope it does not end badly for you."

When they were gone and the office door closed, Sam laughed. Then he scowled and rubbed his jaw. "Like I said, a real pain in the caboose."

Miss Le Fay cast him a puzzled look. "You are the oddest and most unpredictable person I have ever met, Mr. Spade. Do you always carry on so?"

"Only when pushed," Sam admitted. "Well, you've had your chat with Cairo. Now you can chat with me."

"Oh, yes," Le Fay turned to look out the window. Since the sun had long since set, there wasn't much to see.

"You can start any time," Sam said.

"I did not realize it was so late," she said. "I must be going."

Sam moved to block the door. "Oh, no. Not until you've clued me in."

"You are a most insistent man." Le Fay ran one hand down her side, smoothing her dress.

Sam grinned. "As well as odd and unpredictable. So what's this bird Cairo is so hot to get his hands on? This black chicken?"

Le Fay looked at him. "Suppose I do not tell you anything at all about it? What would you do? Something odd and unpredictable?"

"I might." Sam kept any sense of humour from his voice.

Le Fay shrugged. "It is a chicken, much like any other. Only it has black feathers. The breed is raised on the Isle of Malta and the king there has strict rules against allowing them off his island. It is an offence punishable by death."

"That's all very colourful," Sam said. "But there's got to be more to it than black feathers. No bird is worth fifty Pendragons."

"I suppose that is true," Le Fey said. "But I do not know what else there is. What I do know is that we, Sir Logris, Jesus Cairo, and I, were each offered one hundred Pendragons to bring a black chicken to Camelot."

"Each?" Sam asked.

"Our employer set us against each other. He conjectured that if two of us should fail, the third would succeed."

"But you partnered up with Logris, hoping to cut Cairo out of the picture."

Le Fay smiled. "At first we all agreed to split the fee three ways. Then Sir Logris learned that Cairo was going to abscond with the bird once we had it and claim the entire payment for himself. So we decided, as you say, to cut him out of the picture." Her smile vanished. "Then yesterday I discovered Sir Logris was going to do the same as Cairo and leave me with nothing."

"You've seen it, then?" Sam asked. "This black-feathered chicken?"

Le Fay paused. "Sir Logris showed it to me when we arrived in Camelot. For just a few moments."

Sam snorted out his nose. "You're a liar."

Le Fay's cheeks turned pink. "I am. I have always been a liar. I open my mouth and falsehoods come out."

"Is there any truth at all to that canard of yours?"

"Some." Le Fay smiled briefly. "Not much." She shook her head. "I am so tired of fabricating lies. Lies within lies. Honestly, I have lost track of where truth ends and the lies begin."

"Well," Sam said. "You should take a carriage back to your rooms and sleep on it. Maybe a little soul searching will bring you some clarity."

"But . . ." Le Fay stepped toward him and brushed his cheek with a soft hand. "What about that knight outside who is watching this office?"

Sam gently but firmly lifted her hand away; he wasn't about to make the same mistake as his brief partner, Lancelot. "If the monkey follows you, ditch him. Change carriages a couple of times."

"But—"

"He might not be there," Sam continued. "He probably works for Saggy and is only interested in me. Even if he isn't, he could have followed Cairo or was ordered to stay at his post." Sam grabbed Le Fay's lantern off Lancelot's desk and pushed the tiny woman through the inner office door.

"Oh, but," she said. "I thought you and I . . ."

"I'll come by your inn tomorrow if there are any developments," Sam said. Then he closed the outer office door with Miss Bridget Morgan Le FayBlanc, or whatever her name was, safely on the other side.

16

A LITTLE MONKEY BUSINESS

SAM WOKE THE next morning honestly surprised that no one had barged in and disturbed him in the middle of the night. He hoped that meant that no one had been murdered after leaving his office. Part of him mentally kicked himself for not accepting Miss Le Fay's advances. She was a beautiful woman, after all. Well, more than that. She was the most beautiful woman who had ever invited herself to spend the night. If a beautiful woman had been all she was, Sam would have accepted the invitation. Among other things, Miss Le Fay was a pathological liar.

Sam poked his head out the window but saw no sign of the monkey who'd been watching his office the previous evening. He hoped the absence wasn't because he'd dogged Le Fay or Cairo to their respective inns.

He didn't know what to make of the story Le Fay had told him last night. In the end she said it was mostly a lie, but he believed the part about her, Cairo, and Logris being hired by a mysterious employer, them working together, and then turning on each other. He suspected she skipped the part where she planned to cheat the two men and keep the reward for herself. What he didn't believe was that Logris had shown her a chicken. He doubted this Maltese chicken even existed. That she had dissembled knowledge of the chicken's whereabouts in order to wheedle her way into his bed suggested that she had no such knowledge. That she had attempted to wheedle her way into his bed at all suggested that she needed him somehow. Either to find the chicken or to collect the payment.

The missing piece of information was the employer, and Le Fay wasn't ready to give that little tidbit up.

After a trip to the Necessarium and a repeat of yesterday's breakfast, Sam finally remembered to give Effie his shopping list.

"You have acquired a certain fetor," the Lady Peregrine admitted. "I shall move a change of attire to the top of your list. The castle does have a bath house in the basement; I suggest you make that your next stop."

Sam couldn't agree more. He was beginning to feel like a cheese that had sat in the sun too long. Leaving his hat, trench coat, and gumshoes in the office, he walked down to the castle's main floor and poked his head into the page pen. Vaisey wasn't there, but for a copper penny Robin escorted Sam to a stairwell at the rear of the castle, down a flight of stairs, and along a dark hallway that filled with steam the further they walked.

"If you do not mind my speaking, good sir," Robin said as he struck a match and lit the lantern he had brought with him from the page pen, "you have made an enemy in Page Vaisey."

"Occupational hazard," Sam said. "You can't make an omelette without breaking a few eggs."

"An . . . omelette, sir?"

"A lousy metaphor," Sam said. "My bad."

"Vaisey," Robin continued. "He will seek his revenge. Retribution is his middle name."

"Thanks for the warning, kid. I'll keep an eye out."

"But." Robin stopped walking. "Why did you involve yourself? Did Friar Tuck pay you?"

Sam sighed. "Tuck didn't pay me for the same reason he can't pay Vaisey. That vow of poverty gig is for real. Tuck doesn't have a copper penny to his name."

"And yet you risk Page Vaisey's ire. Why?"

"You know, kid. Some wrongs just need to be righted. Vaisey's already got more money than he needs. He doesn't have to go after someone who doesn't have any."

Robin took on a pensive look and mumbled something

about the rich robbing the poor.

Up ahead in the steam-filled hallway, Sam spotted a shadowed entrance. "Thanks, kid, I'll take it from here."

Robin clutched at the sleeve of Sam's rumpled suit jacket. "Nay, good sir. That entrance is for the ladies."

Sam looked again along the hallway and noticed a second entrance further down. "That one?"

The lad nodded.

"How can you tell? I don't see any signs above the doors."

Robin shrugged. "Everyone just knows."

The young page pressed the lantern into Sam's hands and Sam walked down the misty hallway to the unmarked second entrance. These were the first doors in the castle he'd seen without a sign. He couldn't help but wonder if the maintenance people hadn't done it on purpose as a little joke.

The bath itself was uncomplicated. Sam had expected something like he had seen in the movies: seven pools of varying temperature shrouded in steam, towers of towels resting against marble pillars, servants waiting to dry your toes. Maybe that described the women's baths. The men's bath was a slightly oversized tub filled with lukewarm and slightly muddy water. Sam had no idea where the steam came from; maybe the women's baths.

The poor pickings didn't prevent Sam from peeling off his suit jacket, shirt, pants, underwear, socks, and fake Rolex, and climbing in. He set his holstered Smith and Wesson within reach of the tub. You never know. He'd seen a Bond film once where Sean Connery had been ambushed in a bathhouse without his Walther PPK. Bogart would never have made that mistake.

There was soap of sorts, a chunk of sand and wax that took off his outer layer of skin wherever he rubbed it. He did a haphazard job—mostly because it was a bit painful—then climbed out of the cooling water.

Sam hadn't checked for towels and there were none. He contemplated walking naked in the hallway to shake off most of the water, or maybe duck his head into the other entrance to see if women were provided towels. In the end he pulled his wrinkled clothes over damp skin and set out to find the castle courtyard in hopes of drying out in the sunshine.

Sam's clothes had seen better days. They'd been rained on,

dragged a thousand years backward in time, threatened repeatedly with swords, survived a few scuffles—Sam had lost count of how many—been worn and slept in for three days, and were now hanging off wet skin. What they deserved was a good dry cleaning. Unfortunately, dry cleaning wouldn't be invented for a while. They'd have to settle for a stern hand laundering. As soon as Effie found him something to wear while they were away.

As he approached the page pen, Sam pulled a copper penny from his pants pocket, prepared to pay Robin or some other page to show him the way to the courtyard, but then stopped and considered the broad corridor that led to the castle gate. That same passage continued deeper into the castle. "If I were a courtyard?" he mumbled aloud, "where would I be?" Stifling a grin, Sam pocketed the penny, set the lantern down outside the page pen entrance, and then followed the passage deeper into the castle.

The ceiling was high and the passage wide enough for three or four city busses to drive side by side. Despite that, it was darker than other parts of the castle, with no light entering from anywhere except either end of the passage. The floor was also a mess, with dirt and straw filling cracks between stones, and unsightly lumps scattered here and there. The undeniable stench of manure chafed Sam's sinuses as he passed a young boy pushing a broom.

Sam squinted as he left the stone paving and stepped into a grassy yard, though the term *grassy* was generous. The entire courtyard looked like a playing field with hardy grass struggling to survive. Horse stables lined the castle's inner walls to either side. Far on the left stood the smithy he had heard from outside his office. Wooden racks of some kind lined the far wall.

A dozen or more knights loitered about the courtyard, saddling horses or talking among themselves. A few hammered at each other with practice swords. Or had hammered. To a man the knights had stopped what they were doing and now stood gawking at the damp PI wearing a suit jacket, tan pants, and no hat. None of their looks seemed friendly. It reminded Sam of his old precinct in East Hartford.

Shaking his head, Sam retraced his steps back through the

castle, past the gate guards, beneath the raised portcullis, across the drawbridge, and over to the wall where the monkey who had been watching his office had spent much of the previous afternoon and evening. There was no sign of the monkey, but habit made Sam look for cigarette butts and gum wrappers; of course, there were none.

Getting the feel for Camelot town, Sam flagged down an enclosed carriage, tossed the driver three copper pennies, and said Belvedere Inn. It irked Sam that the three conspirators who had complicated his life couldn't conspire to stay at the same hotel. It would have made the whole affair much simpler.

He felt naked without his trench coat and fedora, and regretted not retrieving them before leaving the castle. The suit jacket did a poor job concealing his handgun, though he didn't think that would be a problem in Camelot. Back home, public view of his holster or even its outline could earn him the wrong kind of attention. His Connecticut Concealed Carry Permit didn't require him to actually conceal his weapon, but he preferred to for health reasons. The longer, looser-fitting trench coat did the trick. He'd even ripped open the right pocket seam so he could access the holster on the sly. If needed, he could fire the weapon before anyone realized he had it. Talk about concealed.

His fedora was another matter. Sam didn't feel like a PI without it. He wore his *mean streets* getup as a kind of armour. Today he'd left that armour at home. Maybe that's what put him off his game. He was so focussed on checking behind him for a tail, that he didn't look forward. When the carriage stopped and he peered out through the side window, it wasn't the Belvedere that met his gaze. It wasn't even the right part of town.

"Hey!" he called up to the driver. "This isn't—"

But that was as far as Sam got before strong arms pulled him out into the street.

He fought back. Lord knows he fought back. But there were six hard numbers, big as WWE wrestlers, dragging him away from the carriage. One of them, a rough-looking pug in a torn shirt and with a scar running from ear to chin, laughed. "We was told ter soften yew up a bit." Then he lunged.

At least two hard numbers had a firm grip on Sam's arms. He couldn't reach his semi-automatic, but his legs were free. Using his captors to hold him up, he kicked out with both legs, catching scarface in the midsection. That only made the brute angry. Instead of using his fists, the gorilla leapt in with his feet, one swift kick after another taking Sam in the stomach, groin, and finally the knees. Then a fist found Sam's chest and knocked the wind out of him. The two gorillas holding him up let him drop, and a flurry of feet kicked at him from every side. Instinct made Sam curl up into a ball so that most of the kicks landed on his legs, back, and fists.

At some point the pugs tore his hands away from protecting his face and landed a good punch on his jaw. Sam saw stars. Then it was lights out.

When Sam woke, he was bouncing inside a carriage. A moment later it stopped, and rough hands dragged him once again out into the street. By the time he had his wits about him, the carriage was moving away.

He blinked and looked around. Passersby stared at him, and on the side of a building topped with artificial turrets, the broad sign of the Belvedere Inn swayed in the breeze. Slowly, Sam climbed to his feet, smoothed his hair with his fingers, and then staggered off the dirt road before another carriage could run him down. When he checked his pockets, he was surprised to discover nothing missing. Whether that was criminal courtesy, part of the thugs' orders, or just plain stupidity on their part, Sam had no idea; people in Camelot were more than a little strange.

It had been over a year since Sam had taken a beating like that. Back when he was still a cop. A 405 RED call had sent him to a boarded-up warehouse. His partner juried open a padlocked door and then vanished after Sam went inside. The first blow was a two-by-four to the back and it was downhill from there. He had no idea how many assailants there were, but it felt like a crowd. Eventually his partner showed up and chased them off, but Sam knew the whole deal had been a setup. His complaint to Captain Helliger fell on deaf ears. For all he knew, Helliger had been in on it. Sam had said as much, accusing Helliger, his partner at the time, the dispatcher, and half the cops in the precinct. That had been the final nail in his police career's coffin; plenty of ammunition to get him kicked off the job.

At least this time he knew how many thugs had assailed

him and had a good idea who sent them. He smiled as he figured he had done better than Marlowe when he got pulled into that alley off Hollywood Street and took a pounding from two of Eddie Mars' boys without giving a single good shot in return. Only there was no Harry Jones around to pick him up. Just like in the movie, the thugs made no effort to check his pockets where they might have found a small fortune in Pendragons and a semi-automatic they wouldn't know what to do with. He patted his chest and felt Iva's priceless amulet still in his jacket pocket. He'd thought the safest place for it would be on his person. Now he wasn't so sure.

Checking his watch, Sam saw that it was a little past nine in the morning. Or had been when the junk watch had been broken during the beat down. The plastic crystal was cracked and the second hand had stopped moving. Crappy Korean knockoff. He tore the offending timepiece off his wrist and threw it into the street where the iron shoes of a passing horse smashed it to bits.

Smoothing his suit jacket as best he could, Sam strode into the crowded inn like he owned the place.

"I need to see Jesus Cairo," he said at the front desk.

The innkeeper was different from the previous afternoon, and arched a brow at Sam's bruised face and rumpled attire, but sent the same boy running.

"Mr. Cairo is not available," the innkeeper said when the boy returned.

"Damn," Sam said. "I took a beating for nothing."

The innkeeper arched the other brow. "Shall I summon a surgeon?"

Sam smiled. "This really is a full-service hotel. Thanks, but I'm fine. I'll find someplace to wait."

A number of posh chairs filled out the gargantuan lobby, but all were taken. Even this early in the morning the place was a zoo. Sam really did need to sit down, but would wait. His plan had been to browbeat out of Cairo the name of his employer. And if that didn't work, Sam would use something harder than brows for the beating. Instead, he'd been the one on the receiving end. Well, maybe his bruises would encourage the Egyptian to take him more seriously.

As his gaze wandered the room watching for Cairo to make an appearance, he spotted the monkey who had haunted his office window and tried to tail him from the castle. Since there was no way the grey knight could have followed him here . . . Sam mentally kicked himself. He'd had it all wrong. The monkey didn't work for Sagramore.

Sam strode over to where the young knight slouched against a pillar watching the stairway to the second floor. "Where is he?"

The monkey looked away from the stairs. "Wot?"

"Where is he?" Sam repeated.

"'Oo?" The young knight's pea-green eyes widened as he realized who was accosting him.

"Cairo?"

"I'm just mindin' me own 'ere, mate. Wot do ya fin' you're doin' botherin' me?"

"I'll let you know when I'm bothering you, kid."

The young knight raised his hand and pushed against Sam's chest. "Shove off, ya wanker."

Sam slapped away the monkey's hand. "Your boss is gonna have to talk to me sooner or later. And if it's later, it'll be too late. Tell the fat man I said so." The *fat man* part was a guess, but Sam figured it was a good one.

The young knight sneered. "You're off your 'ead, wanker. I tol' ya ter shove off. Na, shove off."

"It may be crowded in here," Sam said, "but that won't stop me from teaching you a lesson in talking polite."

Before the monkey could come up with a third witty *shove off*, Sam stalked quickly across the common room to where a proper knight wearing gauntlets and steel boots stood observing the crowd. He was maybe an inch shorter than Sam, with chiselled features and a dancing yellow lion on his tabard. Sam had noticed him when he first entered the inn.

"Say," Sam said. "You a friend of Galahad's?"

The lion knight gave him a blank look. "Surely you speak of *Sir* Galahad the Gallant. To that question, I answer a resounding yea. And you are the strange pie the Merlin brought to Court?"

"Yeah, that's him. And yeah, that's me."

The knight frowned. "It is rumoured that you are somehow involved in the death of Sir Lancelot the Amorous."

"I'm pretty sure Sagramore started that rumour. He doesn't like me."

"Sir Sagramore the Ravenous." The lion knight sniffed. "What you suggest is not without possibility."

"Look," Sam said. "See that young knight over there?" He nodded his head toward the monkey who was quick with the *shove offs*. "I'm curious why you let these foreign knights linger about the town."

"City," said the lion knight. "As our king is so fond of saying, *'tis a free city.*"

"Sure," Sam said. "But this mook's been standing there for some time watching the stairs. And he spent all of yesterday afternoon watching the front gates of the castle. My gut tells me he's a foreign spy."

The knight's eyebrows rose with interest and he strode quickly over to where the monkey continued to slouch against the pillar. Sam followed.

"I assume you have business at this inn," the lion knight said. "Please state it."

The monkey looked at him and said nothing.

"Are you so foreign that you cannot speak the King's tongue?"

The monkey curled his upper lip and then walked toward the building's exit. Then he was outside and vanished into the city.

"Curious," said the lion knight.

"I take it he's not one of yours?" Sam asked.

"Ours? He is not even titled. And that two-headed bird on his coat is ridiculous. Only a fool would wear such a thing. I am confident he is little more than a bandit."

"I'm sorry to hear that," Sam said.

The knight cocked a questioning eye.

Sam obliged. "He's been following me around. I didn't think much of it because I thought he was one of Sagramore's hounds. That was a mistake."

"Camelot is a dangerous place for one unfamiliar with the city," the knight said. "The Merlin was a fool for bringing you here."

"You don't hear me arguing." Just then Sam spotted Jesus Cairo strutting his way through the inn's main entrance. "Keep up the good work," he said to the knight. Then he moved to intercept the Egyptian.

"Pah!" said Cairo, not slowing. "It is you."

"We need to talk," Sam said.

Cairo snorted. "I doubt I will survive further talk with you. I spend more time on the floor than on my feet."

"Yeah, about that. Look, Le Fay has us both under a barrel. Of the three of us, only one knows where the bird is, and that isn't you and it isn't me. I had to play it so that Le Fay would talk."

Cairo snorted again. "Your smooth words fail to elicit my sympathy."

Sam smiled. "It's either smooth words or I hit you over the head with a chair again." Then he noticed the Egyptian's haggard look and bruises beneath the eyes. Cairo looked like he *had* just been beaten over the head with a chair. Again. "Did Saggy pick you up?"

"Your two knightly friends caught me up outside your office and offered a tour of the dungeon. During said tour, they spoke with me for several hours. I was permitted to leave the castle only minutes ago."

That was two bad pieces of news in the space of two minutes. Not a good start to the day. "What did they shake out of you?"

"Shake out?" Cairo appeared to take a moment to decide what that question meant. "I corroborated that ridiculous story you told in your office; I felt the fool repeating it."

At least it wasn't three bad pieces of news. "Sorry about the cockamamie tale. A sensible story would have had holes in it even Saggy could find and land us all in the dungeon. And we wouldn't have been let go after a few hours."

"I am less certain on that count."

"Well . . ." Cairo was in no shape for another interrogation. And if the knights hadn't broken him, he was probably a tougher nut to crack than Sam had taken him for. "You'll want to catch some sleep if you've been grilled all night. I've got other fish to fry."

Sam decided not to tell Cairo about the monkey who had been watching his rooms.

17
A PENDRAGON FOR YOUR THOUGHTS

THERE WAS NO sign of Vaisey in the page pen when Sam returned to the castle. Robin was there and Sam got his attention. The page immediately put his palm out. Sam reached into his pants pocket and dropped two silver Pendragons.

The boy stared into his hand. "What?"

"One's for you," Sam said. "The other is for the thugs Vaisey paid to give me a beating this morning. Think you can find them?"

Robin nodded. "But what . . .?"

"Tell them I'd like them to return the favour and then discontinue doing business with the pages. Think they'll go for it?"

Robin nodded again. "They dislike working for a boy, but copper is copper. A Pendragon will convince them to seek clients elsewhere."

"They won't mind bruising up a kid?"

Robin let out a soft snort. "For a Pendragon they would bruise their own grandmother. I dare say they would throw her in front of a horse. But you cannot pay me a whole silver penny. It is too much."

"Consider it a retainer," Sam said.

The boy looked at him. "Why do you not . . . bruise Vaisey yourself? It would be less dear than two Pendragons."

Sam pulled a brief tight smile. "The only thing a bully understands is another bully. Now, I ain't no saint, but beating up kids really isn't in me. I think the lesson will mean a whole lot more coming from his own thugs."

Robin pocketed the two coins. "I will ensure this happens."

"You're a good kid, Robin."

Sam found himself whistling as he climbed the stairs to the second floor, despite the aches ranging from the top of his skull to the toes of his feet. Another soak in the tub after collecting a change of clothes from Effie might be just the ticket. Only now he wondered if that was such a good idea. Leaving his coat and hat behind today hadn't worked out so well.

Sam wasn't the superstitious type, or not the normal kind anyway. Black cats and walking under ladders didn't scare him. Thirteen was just the number that followed twelve. And he only knocked on wood when he wanted someone to answer the door. But wearing a trench coat was like smoking a cigarette. It calmed his nerves. Set his balance. Prepared him for whatever came next out of left field. Then there was the fedora. That hat was his badge of office. At least, in Hartford it was. Sam wasn't sure he could dress up in stockings and a surcoat and still be a PI.

His ambivalence was resolved by a distinct lack of new clothes waiting for him. The only item Effie had ready was a roll of white cloth that after further inspection revealed itself as a bulky nightdress.

"What? No shirts? Pants? Jerkins? Or whatever you call those sleeveless jackets everyone is wearing?"

"The tailor says they will be ready tomorrow morning."

"Tailor? Couldn't you have picked up something in the market?"

Effie smiled, and then chuckled, and then grew serious as she realized that Sam wasn't joking. "The market? Only peasants wear clothing from the market. Men and women of quality require sizing and adjustments. Why did you think I took your exact measurements?"

"Uh, well, truthfully, I thought you were flirting with me."

"Did you now?" The shapely blonde didn't look too horribly upset by the accusation. "If ever I decide to flirt with you, Sam, you will know it."

"Ah, great. Thanks for the warning." That didn't come out at all like he intended.

Effie ignored him. "Someone came by to see you while you were out. Big guy, and not in a pleasing way. Made like he was someone important but he was provincial as dirt. You just missed him." She handed Sam what he now recognized as a medieval business card. The name said *Martin Barth, Esquire.* "He said that he received your message and will try to see you again later."

This was unexpected. Sam figured that Cairo might escape a beating after all. This *big guy* could only be the fat man the monkey worked for.

"Oh, and Miss Le Fay is in your office."

This was also unexpected, and much less welcome than the first surprise. If the fat man had just left, he'd handed Effie his card while Morgan Le Fay was only a closed door away.

"What sort of a mood is she in?" Sam asked.

"Somewhere between frightened and frantic."

"Thanks."

Sam hadn't even reached his desk before Miss Le Fay was up out of her chair and shouting.

"Someone's been in my rooms at the Coronet! It's all upside down! I went downstairs for an early breakfast and returned to find the place a shambles."

"You were supposed to stay in your room," Sam said.

"I did stay inside my inn," Le Fay retorted. "Until my rooms were invaded. Then I came straight here. Did that grey knight outside your window follow you to my inn?"

Sam shook his head. "Of course not. And if the monkey *had* succeeded in tailing me, he would have searched your rooms long before this morning. It might have been Cairo. It wouldn't have been hard for him to follow you home last night. And it's something he would do."

"Cairo?" Sam could see by Le Fay's expression that she agreed with his assessment.

"I found him maybe thirty minutes ago returning to his own rooms. He said he'd spent the night in the castle dungeon keeping company with Galahad and Saggy. That'll be easy enough to verify."

"You saw Jesus Cairo this morning?"

"Yeah."

Le Fay glowered at him. "Why?"

"Because one of you needs to talk and so far you've been less than forthcoming. I'm hoping to have better luck with your friend Cairo. What we need to do right now, however, is tuck you away someplace safe."

The dark-haired beauty continued to glower. "I refuse to go back to the Coronet."

Sam scratched his head. "I've got an idea. Wait right here."

Stepping into the outer office, Sam quietly closed the door. "What does your gut tell you about our Miss Morgan Le Fay?"

Effie gave him a blank look and then looked down at her stomach.

"I mean, do you think she's dangerous?"

"More to herself than others," Effie said, looking up. "I am certain she is at fault for whatever trouble she is in, but I do not believe she has killed anyone."

Sam nodded. "Do you think you can hide her away for a couple of nights?"

"What? You mean at my father's estate?"

"That would be perfect."

The shapely blonde bit her lip. "The Duke might have some thoughts on that. Do you truly believe she is in danger?"

"I'm certain of it."

Effie nodded. "I shall deal with my father then. It is not as though he will object too strongly to having a beautiful woman as a house guest."

"You're an angel." Sam winked and then stepped back into his office, this time leaving the door open. "My secretary has offered to put you up for a few days."

"Your secretary?" Le Fay's eyes grew wide. "Will her hovel have room for a house guest?"

Sam felt more annoyed by the question than he felt he had a right to.

"You'll have to save that question for her father, the Duke."

Le Fay had the decency to blush.

Sam asked Effie to join them. "You'd better go now. Change carriages a couple of times to ensure you're not followed. Effie, come back once you get Miss Le Fay settled. I may still need you today."

Once they were gone, Sam paced the office wondering when lunch would arrive. It had been a productive morning and he'd worked up an appetite.

The knock that came at the door, however, was not lunch. Sam scarce knew what had happened before he found Sir Lancelot the Amorous' widow, Iva, clinging to his arm.

"Please forgive me!" the plain woman pleaded. "It was I who sent those knights to your office last night. I was at my wit's end. A whole day had passed without a convicted murderer hanging from the gibbet. A whole day! And the knights had nowhere to look. It was my hope that you had learned something about my husband's murder, and that you would tell the knights if they confronted you."

Sam pushed the woman away. "So it *was* you spreading rumours that the two of us were having an affair."

"What? Of course not. I am in no position to spread such rumours."

"Not even to one vindictive knight?" Sam asked.

"I—I do not know what you mean."

Sam ground his teeth. "Look. For the last time, I didn't murder your husband. But if you let me finish my investigation, I will learn who did."

"Truth?" Iva asked.

"Truth," Sam said. "By the way, where were you the evening Lancelot was murdered?"

"Me?" The small woman shook with nerves. "I was home in bed."

Sam wagged his head. "No, you weren't. But that's okay; I don't really need to know."

Iva gave him a hard look and then left in a hurry.

Ten minutes later another knock came at the door. Again not lunch. It was a page with a note summoning Sam to a meeting with Martin Barth, Esquire, at the Alexandria Inn. Sam grabbed his hat and trench coat from the desk.

18
ENTER THE FAT MAN

THE ALEXANDRIA WAS not as posh as the Belvedere, but nicer than the Coronet. Three floors of suites occupied the space above the main floor common room and kitchen. The innkeeper glanced at the handwritten note, informed Sam that Mr. Barth occupied suite Twelve-C, then returned to a conversation he was having with a doxy half his age.

While tramping up the stairs, Sam noticed that the suites on the first floor were numbered and ended with -*A*. So he skipped the second floor and ambled down the third-floor hallway until he found a small door sign that said Twelve-C.

He knocked and a familiar mook opened the door. The grey knight with the two-faced bird on his chest glared at him and made just enough space to let Sam pass.

In the suite's equivalent of a living room, Sam found a man who must weigh three hundred pounds sitting in a wide chair and reading several pages of parchment. He wore a white suit from collar to shoes and had a full head of curly white hair with matching beard and a veiny nose. Had he been wearing a red felt suit with white trim, he would have been a dead ringer for Santa Claus. As it was, give him a black string tie and put his photo on a bucket, he'd make a chubby Colonel Sanders.

The man looked up and his eyes went wide, as though he'd been oblivious to the knock at the door and his man's shuffling around. "Mr. Spade!" The fat man didn't get up.

"Mr. Barth, I presume." Sam seated himself opposite the colonel in a chair covered with the ugliest green cloth he'd ever seen.

"You begin well, sir." Barth set down his parchments and poured two drinks from a decanter on the table beside his chair.

The monkey, seeing only two glasses, shrugged and disappeared into a back room.

The glasses were tall. A polite man would say *When* before the liquid passed the halfway mark, but no one had ever called Sam Sparrow polite. Barth tipped the decanter back so that the liquid poured more slowly, but it would still soon reach the top of the glass. The fat man chuckled as he poured, and then said, "I distrust a man who says *When*. He must be careful not to drink too much lest his tongue betray him." With the glass filled to the brim, the fat man set aside the decanter, carefully passed Sam the full glass, and kept the shallow glass for himself.

"Here is to plain speaking," Barth said, raising his glass.

Sam nodded and took the smallest of sips. The liquid looked like Bacardi, but tasted like honey and vinegar.

Barth took a healthier sip and then set his glass on the table. He peered at Sam. "You are a tight-lipped man, I see."

"No," Sam said. "I like to talk as much as the next guy."

Barth nodded. "Very good. I distrust a tight-lipped man. He generally listens more than he should and says nothing of consequence when he speaks. Talking is an art, and like all arts, requires practice. Now, sir. I shall be frank with you. I am a man who likes to talk to a man who likes to talk."

"In that case," Sam said, "let's talk about the black bird."

Barth let out a joyous laugh. "By Jove, sir! You are a marvel. Straight to the point. No droll comments about the weather or the latest fashions at Court. By all means, let us talk about the black bird. First, however, you must answer me one question. Are you here representing the delightful Miss Le Fay?"

Sam shrugged his shoulders. "Well, I guess that depends."

"Depends? Depends on what?" Then Barth's eyes lit up. "Ah! Jesus Cairo!"

"There is Cairo to consider," Sam said.

Barth rubbed his jaw through his beard. "So which do you

represent? Le Fay or Cairo?"

Sam smiled. "It may be more complicated than that."

"Logris is dead. Who else is there?"

"There's me." Sam tapped his chest.

The fat man's face thoroughly beamed. "Why, that is marvellous, sir. I distrust a man who fails to look after his own interests. You are not what I was told to expect, but you are a man I can understand."

"Now that we understand each other," Sam said, "let's talk about the black bird."

"Yes, Mr. Spade. Indeed we must. Have you any concept of what the black bird is worth?"

"Apart from dinner for two? No."

Barth chuckled. "Well, sir, if I told you, you would call me a liar."

"I've been known to call men liars," Sam said, "but at least two people have died so far so I'll probably hold off on any kind of rush to judgment. Go ahead. Put a price on the bird and I'll see if I can swallow it."

Barth pursed his lips. "You have no idea what the bird is, do you? Our Miss Le Fay never confided in you."

"Neither did Cairo, though he did offer me fifty Pendragons for it."

"Fifty! Now I am afraid I shall have to call you a liar, Mr. Spade. Either that or Jesus Cairo lied to you. He has no such pile of pennies to offer."

Sam waved his glass but didn't drink. "Let's assume it was Cairo who lied. Whether or not he has the money, he doesn't have the bird."

"But Miss Le Fay does?"

Sam took a second sip of his drink. The bittersweet taste was beginning to make an impression. "She says she does. But Miss Le Fay says a lot of things that only have a passing relationship with the truth."

Martin Barth pursed his lips and for the first time looked less than joyful. "If Logris is dead and neither Cairo nor Le Fay know where the bird is, then this conversation has become frivolous."

"I thought we were going to speak plainly. You know what the bird is. I know where it is. Together we can help each other."

Barth's expression didn't change. "Well, sir, then if I am to have any confidence in you, you must tell me where the bird is."

Sam slammed his almost full glass of mystery liquor onto the side table, sending a splash of golden liquid sloshing across its varnished surface. "I may not know much about this bird, but what I do know is that you have offered a hundred Pendragons for it. I don't see how telling you its whereabouts for free is going to get me a single penny!"

"Then we are at an impasse," Barth said. "If you expect me to hand you the coins on the mere hope that the information you give me is anything more than a lie, then you have misread me to the fullest."

Sam leapt from his chair, taking care to ensure that his drink tipped over, sending the remaining alcohol washing across the side table, the furniture, and one leg of Martin Barth's immaculate white pants. "Well, you'd better rethink your expectations and rethink them fast! Once I let it be known what I have, other buyers will get interested."

The monkey in the other room must have heard the commotion. The door flew open and he stood watching Sam and the fat man, his hand clutching the hilt of his sword.

Sam looked at the grey knight and reached for the holster beneath his coat. "I told that monkey of yours that if you wanted your bird you'd have to talk to me! And after a half hour of nonsense you've yet to tell me anything. Why are you wasting my time? And another thing: Keep that monkey out of my way while you make up your mind. I'll kill him if you don't!"

"Well, sir," Barth said quietly. "I must say that I did not expect your violent temper."

"I don't mind if you don't like my manners," Sam growled. "They're pretty bad. I grieve over them on long winter evenings." He stalked across the room to the door. "Think it over. You've got until sunset. If we don't have a deal by then, you're out of the running."

Sam slammed the door behind him and then raced to the stairs so that Barth's monkey wouldn't have an opportunity to follow. A smile creased his lips as he stepped out of the Alexandria into the street. If that outburst didn't stir the pot, nothing would.

19
A VISIT TO THE MAGISTRATE

IT WAS WELL past lunchtime as Sam made his way back to Castle Camelot. He was starving. Not only that, but his meeting with the fat man had been a bust. His plan had been to find out more about the bird, but Mr. Martin Barth, Esquire, liked to move his lips without saying anything. That had left Sam no choice but to bluff that he had the bird and apply some pressure to force Barth's hand. The bluff could backfire, of course, with Barth's monkey trying to get the bird's location from him at sword point. But Sam had yet to test his bean-shooter to see if Merlin's magic had worked. The surly knight would make good target practice.

Unfortunately, afternoon didn't look like it was going to fare any better than morning.

"There he is!" Sir Sagramore shouted the moment Sam crossed the drawbridge into the castle.

Two knights Sam had never seen before drew blades and moved to surround him. It wasn't much of a surrounding; Sam could evade two knights. Sagramore also drew his blade to make it three. Other knights from the gatehouse stepped out to see what the commotion was. Sir Galahad wasn't among them.

"What's this all about?" The knights weren't Sam's first choice to test his magic bean-shooter on, but it was out of his hands if Saggy forced the issue.

Sagramore grinned. "The magistrate wishes to ask you a few

questions."

Sam shrugged. "If the fella wants a chat, he didn't need to send such a large welcoming committee."

Sagramore's grin widened. "Most people prefer to avoid chats with the magistrate."

"I'm not most people. Lead on."

The knights escorted Sam through the right-hand corridor where he had been rebuffed the previous day. He tipped his hat as they passed the peacock knight who had turned him around. In addition to tapestries, banners, and suits of armour, the corridor decorations soon included life-sized statues and bigger-than-life paintings. People with long noses clad in lace and frills stood about in twos and threes speaking in soft voices. The hallway felt like a museum.

As they passed an open double door, Sam glanced inside and saw a white-haired old man sitting on what looked like a throne, surrounded by several well-dressed and attentive people. Sam tapped one of his escorts on a padded shoulder. "Hey, is that King Arthur?"

The knight looked at Sam, then into the chamber, and then shook his head. "French ambassador."

Sam couldn't believe he'd been brought back to King Arthur's Court, given an office and space to live inside the castle, yet still hadn't met the once and future King. Fate had some wicked sense of humour.

They passed two doors standing side by side marked *Necessarium*. Apparently the better half afforded a his and hers latrine. Then came a closed door marked *Chapel* followed by a stairwell that seemed to have two sets of stairs, one narrow and the other a bit wider than the stairs by his office. A petite woman, covered head to toe in coarse, off-white cloth and carrying some kind of ceramic jug, stepped out of the narrow stairwell, saw the knights escorting the Merlin's Pie, then stepped hastily back into the stairwell.

Beyond the stairs his escort stopped. An oversized sign announcing *Magisterium* hung above a huge closed door. They stood there for several minutes, saying nothing, and Sam felt his fingers itching for a smoke.

"Say," he asked. "Isn't there supposed to be a room around here with a big, round table? I wouldn't mind taking a peek if all we're gonna do is stand around."

Sagramore glared at him while the other knights shuffled their feet. "We are not a tourist attraction," Saggy snarled.

"Just trying to fill the time," Sam said.

Then the door opened and the escort marched Sam inside.

The room was similar to what he had seen with the French Ambassador. An older man sat on a smallish throne surrounded by several stone-faced, overdressed people.

The old man looked at Sagramore with cold, serious eyes. "This is he?"

"Yes, Your Worship," Sagramore said. "Mr. Sam Spade of Connecticut."

The magistrate's gaze shifted to Sam and swept over him from head to toe, taking in his fedora, wrinkled trench coat, worn shoes, and multiple bruises on his face. He then said something sage and astute, as befitted a magistrate. "He dresses oddly."

"Yes, sir," repeated Sagramore.

"I am not familiar with this kingdom called Connecticut. Where is it?"

"No idea, sir," Sagramore said.

The magistrate frowned. "And he has no title?"

"None, sir."

"Then why am *I* bothering with him? If you believe him guilty, throw him in the dungeon."

"Uh," said Sagramore. "The magician Merlin has some small liking for him."

"I see." The magistrate frowned and then spoke in a louder voice. "You there. Step forward."

"Good day, Your Worship," Sam said. It never hurt to make a good impression; Sam only wished he remembered that more often.

The magistrate eyed him up and down once more. "Those bruises. Did you resist arrest?"

"These?" Sam fingered his face. "I tripped on the stairs, Your Worship. Clumsy me."

The magistrate's eye twitched. "Who killed Sir Logris?"

"I don't know," Sam answered honestly.

"But you could make an excellent guess."

Sam rubbed his ear. "My guess might be excellent or crummy, but Mrs. Spade didn't raise children dippy enough to guess in front of a magistrate, several courtiers, some armed knights, and a spy behind that curtain."

The magistrate's frown deepened and he glanced at the curtain. "Why resist guessing if you have nothing to hide?"

"I'm an open book, Your Worship. But Sir Sagramore here has as much as accused me of murdering Sir Logris and Sir Lancelot both. So I've no choice but to plead the fifth."

A puzzled look crossed the old man's face. "The fifth what?"

"Let me put it another way. As far as I can see, my best chance of clearing myself of Sagramore's accusations is to bring the murderer or murderers in all tied up. And the best chance I have of catching them is by staying away from you lot because you'd only gum up the works." Sam glanced over at the curtain. "Am I going too fast for you?"

"No, sir," a voice mumbled from behind the heavy cloth. "Please continue."

"Right then," Sam said. "From where I'm standing, your knights are too busy chasing their own tails to find a pig in a pigsty. If you decide to throw me in the dungeon, your killers will get away scot-free. Then when Merlin gets back, we'll see what he has to say about it. Merlin gave me this job and I'm going to do it despite your help."

The magistrate stared at Sam for several moments and then said, "I see." He looked at Sagramore with something akin to hate. "Is this your only suspect?"

Sagramore winced. "Mr. Spade is our . . . best suspect."

"Then I suggest you build a better case before coming to me again. Dismissed."

Sam wished he had a camera to snap the look on Sagramore's face. It was priceless. He could make rubber Saggy masks and sell them at Halloween.

The agitated knight said not a word as he muscled Sam out of the courtroom. Sam didn't need the help; his escort almost had to chase after him all of the way back to the gatehouse. He slowed to catch his breath before visiting the page pen. To his surprise, Vaisey's throne was occupied. The boy's sycophants outnumbered the French ambassador's and Camelot's magistrate's combined.

"Looks like we both tripped on the stairs," Sam said to the boy in black. Vaisey sported more shiners than a wannabe boxer. "We should learn to be more careful."

"Shall I teach this fool a sterner lesson?" said one of Vaisey's minions.

Vaisey sneered at the fawning boy. "Shut up, you blithering oaf. I shall deal with this."

The boy in black rose from his cushioned chair, failing to suppress a grunt of pain as he did so. He rubbed his jaw and Sam heard the crack of bones rubbing against each other. The fourteen-year-old stared at Sam with bloodshot eyes. "Do you have any idea who I am?"

"Sure," Sam said. "You're the biggest bully on the block. You think that puts you in charge, but all it really does is put a target on your back." He nodded toward the minion who had spoken. "That one will be gunning for your job one day."

Vaisey looked at his minion. "Guy? He is an incompetent fool. He could not . . . gun for? He is of little import, but I am. My father is the largest landowner in Nottinghamshire!"

"Sorry, kid, I'm not going to play the *my dad is bigger than your dad* game. I'm just here to remind you that what goes around comes around. You lay off me and my friend and I'll lay off you. Got it?"

"You have no idea who you are dealing with," Vaisey shouted. "This is my turf. I am the law around here!"

"Yeah?" Sam said. "Well la di da di da! I just came from a friendly chat with the magistrate and I think he'd beg to differ with you on that point."

Vaisey's expression collapsed into confusion. "La di da?"

"Di da," Sam finished. "I think we're done here." He turned and walked away. Before he was out of hearing distance, he heard Vaisey shouting at his minions. "What are you all looking at, you idiotic buffoons! Go find me some mead!"

20
THE FAT MAN SINGS

SAM DECIDED THAT a late lunch was better than no lunch. Unfortunately, he never got as far as his desk. Barth's monkey stood slouched against the wall outside his office.

"'E wants ter see ya."

"I haven't kept you waiting long, have I?" Sam asked. "I'd hate it if you missed your lunch."

The grey knight sneered. "Keep up the talk and you'll be eatin' steel fer your lunch."

Sam grinned at him. "The chintzier the help, the more tawdry the prattle, huh?"

The monkey stared back, obviously not comprehending a word.

"Well, let's go." Sam turned toward the stairwell. "We don't want to keep the colonel waiting."

Sam followed the grey knight into a carriage and then to Barth's suite at the Alexandria. He kept his hand inside his coat pocket next to his bean-shooter the entire time. Outside the door to Twelve-C, Sam drew the semi-automatic from its holster and pointed it at the monkey, who stared at the weapon in confusion.

"Yeah," Sam said. "I should have expected that." He quickly reversed the gun in his hand so that he held it by the barrel. Then he smashed the heavy grip down onto the monkey's head. It didn't knock him out, but the grey knight lifted both hands to fend off another strike. Sam used his free hand to draw the sword from the young knight's scabbard and then put his bean-shooter away so that he could hold the sword in his strong hand and pretend to know what he was doing with it.

Barth must have heard the commotion, as the fat man opened the door. After taking in the monkey rubbing his head and his man's sword in Sam's hand, Barth smiled and said, "Come in, sir. Come in. Thank you for coming."

Sam stepped through the doorway, handing the monkey's sword to Barth as he slipped past the fat man's enormous bulk. "You shouldn't let him play with this. He might cut himself."

"Why do you have Mordred's sword?" Barth asked.

Mordred, huh? Sam almost laughed. "A one-legged page boy took it away from him; I made him give it back."

Barth exploded into a fit of laughter "By Jove, sir, you are an odd duck." He handed the sword to Mordred and then shooed him back out the door. "Please, have a seat. I am afraid that I owe you an apology, sir."

"Never mind that," Sam said, sitting down in the same ugly green chair he had occupied hours earlier. "Let's talk pennies."

"Indeed, sir."

Barth poured Sam a drink, stopping when the glass was half-full. There was no cockamamie chatter about saying *When* or distrust, and Sam felt that the fat man really might be ready to talk this time.

Barth sank down in his own wide chair and raised a glass he had already been working on to his lips. Sam noticed as he took a small sip of sour honey that the chair had been cleaned and the colonel's pants replaced with an identical pair.

"This will be the most astonishing tale you have ever heard," Barth said. "And I say this knowing that a man of your . . . history . . . will have heard more than his fair share of astonishing tales. What do you know of the Roman Empire's Legion of Jerusalem, later known as the Knights of Rhodes?"

Sam snorted. "Never heard of them."

"Ah," the fat man nodded. "Few people have. After the fall of Rome . . . you have heard that Rome has fallen?"

"Yes."

"Not a complete ignoramus, then." The fat man smiled, as

though confident that Sam would have no idea what ignoramus meant. "After the fall of Rome, the Knights of Rhodes sought refuge by taking over one of the smaller Mediterranean islands—Malta. Do you follow me?"

Sam nodded.

"And at Malta they beat their swords into ploughshares and took up farming. Have you any concept of the extreme immeasurable wealth of Malta's poultry industry?"

"I'm afraid I'll have to claim ignorance on that one as well."

The fat man stiffened slightly. "Yes, well, few people monitor the global state of poultry. To get to the point, Malta is home to a certain breed of chicken that is completely black, skin and feathers. This breed is nowhere else to be found, anywhere, and the Maltese strongly discourage the export of such chickens. Well, sir, what do you think of that?"

"I don't know," Sam said. "I've always held a preference for beef over poultry."

"And eggs, sir?" Barth asked with an undue intensity. "Do you never eat eggs for breakfast?"

"I've been known to scramble the occasional egg."

"Of course," said Barth. "And if I were to tell you that Maltese chickens produce four eggs for every one egg produced by other breeds? That a chicken farmer with one hundred Maltese chickens can take as many eggs to market as a farmer with four hundred common chickens?"

"I'd say that's a lot of eggs," Sam said. "What you're telling me is that you're a chicken farmer. I thought you were a noble."

Barth frowned. "I should have a title. I own land. Lots of land. More land than half the dukes and barons in Britain. More land than King Arthur himself, I dare say. Land swarming with chickens. The sale of eggs lines my pockets and allows me to acquire even more land and more chickens. I could purchase twenty titles."

"Congratulations," Sam said.

Barth waved a hand. "Bah! Titles are for politicians playing games. I do not play games, Mr. Spade. With a brood of Maltese chickens, I could put every chicken farmer in Britain out of business within a few short years. I would control the entire British chicken market. Now do you understand?"

Sam sipped his drink. "A brood? I'm guessing that's a lot."

"A brood begins with one chicken, Mr. Spade. Add one rooster to the equation, and I will soon have as many chickens as I require."

At that moment the door opened and Mordred—Sam still couldn't get over the monkey's name—stepped inside and whispered something in the fat man's ear.

Barth nodded vaguely and then waved Mordred away. "Give us a few minutes to finish our business."

Mordred stepped back outside and closed the door.

"This one chicken," Sam said, hoping not to lose Barth now that he had him on a roll. "You arranged to have it smuggled off the island of Malta."

The fat man leaned forward in his chair. "I could suggest that you are not an ignoramus, Mr. Spade, but that is the natural conclusion anyone would draw. My compliments to you on your mediocrity. Let me top up your drink."

Sam held out his glass. Barth was giving him the information he came for, so he was willing to swallow a few insults. He needed to get the man talking again. "But the chicken never arrived. Your smugglers got greedy."

Barth finished pouring and then sighed and leaned back into his chair. "So it seems."

"And this bird doesn't really belong to any of you, but to a Maltese chicken farmer?"

"Who sold it to me," Barth said.

"Illegally."

The fat man laughed. "Legality is a matter of opinion and perspective. Is it legal for the Maltese to forbid the export of chickens?"

"They seem to think so." Sam took a swallow from his glass.

"And I think they are wrong. There is a saying, Mr. Spade, that I accept as a universal truth, a truth that supersedes the laws of nations and kings. And that truth is this, that possession is nine-tenths of the law. Once I take possession of the bird, it will be mine. And now, sir, before we talk of pennies, when will you be able to produce the bird?"

Sam rubbed his ear. "I can have it for you in a day. Two, if I run into trouble."

Barth nodded. "I grow impatient, but that should be satisfactory." He lifted his glass. "Well, sir, cheers to a fair bargain!"

Sam raised his glass, but before he drank, he said, "And what, exactly, is your idea of a fair bargain?"

"I shall give you fifty Pendragons when you deliver the chicken to me. And another fifty once I have it safely under lock and key."

Sam blinked and shook his head. Martin Barth was smiling at him, but his face looked stretched. His monkey, Mordred, appeared from somewhere and loomed over him. Sam saw a reflection of light against metal and heard Barth say, "Not in here, you fool!" And then, of all people, he saw Jesus Cairo walk up to the fat man, his scrawny legs strutting as the lights went out.

21
SMOKE ON THE WATER

SAM WOKE SOME time later to a mouth that tasted like the Necessarium. He grimaced and forced open his eyes. Utter darkness met his gaze, but he knew he wasn't blind; he'd grown accustomed to the dearth of nighttime light in Camelot compared to Hartford. After stumbling around in the dark, he found a candle resting on a mantle and lit it with one of the matches from his tobacco kit. A search of the suite revealed a narrow counter lined with several small, wooden kegs that smelled of alcohol and a metal ewer half-filled with water. He splashed water on his face and then sampled several of the kegs. All were strong, but none strong enough to wash the wretched taste from his mouth.

The sitting room remained exactly as Sam remembered it, all the way down to an open decanter of mead and two half-filled glasses. Sam sniffed at his glass and wondered how he had missed seeing the fat man spike it. It must have been when he topped up Sam's drink after Mordred whispered in his ear. Barth was a better magician than he was.

Leaving the Alexandria, Sam hired a carriage and asked the driver to take him to the home of the Duke of Earl. It was a lengthy trip, as the Duke's estate was in a ritzy part of town north of the castle and arguably in the countryside. A lone lantern, a poor excuse for headlights, bounced like a drunken bobblehead from a post at the front of the enclosed carriage as the horse-drawn coffin flew over cobbled streets. When the stones gave way to hard dirt, the ride didn't get much smoother.

By the time he arrived, Sam's stomach felt as wretched as his mouth tasted. He gave the driver a penny to wait and staggered up to the large mansion's thick, doublewide doorway. A football-sized hunk of iron, shaped like a lion's face, stood out from the doorframe; the lion's mouth held a thick metal ring. Sam had seen enough novelty doorknockers adorning the entryways of Hartford homes to know how they worked. This one just seemed more elaborate than most, and much heavier. He lifted the ring and slammed it against the lion's chest three times.

A half-minute later a narrow-faced butler opened one side of the double door and glowered at him.

"Sam Spade to see Maid Euphemia Peregrine."

"Do you have an introduction card?" the birdlike man asked.

"I'm all out. It's been that kind of week."

The butler's glower never faltered, but he beckoned Sam inside and directed him to a plush sofa in a waiting area near the door.

A few minutes later Effie rushed into the room. "Sam? Why are you here? Oh, you look awful."

Sam stood up too quickly and swayed on his feet, an after-effect of whatever Barth had slipped into his drink. "I feel awful," he said, "so at least I'm consistent. Listen, I need to speak with Miss Le Fay."

Effie's face darkened. "She is not here."

"What? I told her—"

"She excused herself for a stroll in the garden earlier and never came back. I am reluctant to say this, but I suspect she was not completely honest with you."

Sam heaved a sigh. "Story of my life. I guess I'll see you at the office tomorrow?"

"Of course. But you look as though you should sit. Have you eaten? I know you missed lunch. And your dinner was still sitting cold when I left the office for the day."

Sam's stomach growled at the reminder that he hadn't eaten since breakfast. Effie's offer tempted him, and not just for the chow. The thought of spending time with the tall knockout blonde in a social setting tugged at his gut, maybe more forcefully than his hunger.

"I would," he said. "Gladly. But Le Fay is probably in danger. I'd better go find her."

"Have you any notion where to look?" Effie asked.

"Not a clue."

"Then you should eat."

Sam wiped the palm of his hand across his face. He should eat. And he should treat himself to the company of a gorgeous dame, even if she was too young for him to do anything about it. He wasn't the kind of guy who received invitations often. Or at all. But Jesus Cairo showing up at Barth's door had been a game changer. Sam had no idea what the Egyptian had Mordred say to Barth, but it had been enough for the fat man to mickey Sam's drink and dump him like yesterday's garbage. Something was going down. That Le Fay had disappeared suggested she was somehow involved.

"Call me a sap," Sam said, "but I have to try. If Le Fay is murdered while I'm off sipping wine with an angel, I'll never forgive myself."

"Your heart is too big," Effie said.

Sam laughed. "No one's said that before."

"Then they are not paying attention. I shall not try to stop you, Sam, but I do urge you to take care of yourself." A pause. "Better than you have so far today."

"No worries there," Sam said. "I've met my daily quota of things going wrong. And then some."

Effie waved from the front step of her father's mansion as Sam climbed back into the carriage. "Coronet Inn," he told the driver. It was a long shot, but he had to start somewhere. The driver clucked at his horse and the carriage rolled forward.

Worry ate at Sam as the carriage rumbled along. Had Cairo taken Le Fay hostage? Or had Le Fay decided to work with the Egyptian? Whatever had happened, the fat man felt Sam's services were no longer required. Someone must have the chicken and coins were changing hands, though Sam was fairly certain the hundred Pendragon bounty was a sham. The only payoff rendered would be the pointy end of Mordred's sword.

The carriage turned onto a road that followed the bank of a wide river that cut through the city. Several lantern-lit bridges arched high over the dark waters while small boats drifted with the current.

It was odd seeing so much light in Camelot at night. Buildings, streets, and people offered greater detail than Sam had noticed on his previous nighttime jaunts. Many of the people seemed to be moving along the street in the same direction he was, so he stuck his head outside the carriage and looked forward. About a half mile further on, a bright fire lit the sky. Not a celebratory bonfire or someone burning trash, but a towering blaze.

The driver called back, "Sorry, gov'nor, but we shall have to take another route."

"No," Sam shouted at him. "I need to see what's happening."

The carriage was able to travel another quarter mile before the street became so chock-full of people that it could go no closer.

"Can you wait here for me?" Sam asked.

The driver shook his head. "This mob is just the beginnin', sir. You would never find me again."

Sam passed him two copper pennies, even though he'd paid the rental at the Duke's estate. "For services above and beyond."

The driver accepted the pennies and tipped his hat, then pulled the carriage around and disappeared into the night.

Sam pushed his way through the mass of people, shouting at them with an authority-rich tone he had learned in the police academy and used on the street during his decade on the job. Eventually he arrived at the source of the commotion and was relieved to find that the fire was limited to a ship out on the river. The city itself wasn't in any danger. He watched as a flock of smaller boats manned by people with buckets scooped up river water to douse the larger boat. Cockroaches pissing on a burning garbage bin. The boat hadn't a prayer.

A man with a serious expression and wearing some kind of uniform paced along the riverbank. "Anybody hurt?" Sam asked. "A lady friend of mine went aboard this afternoon. I haven't seen her since. I'm worried."

"No reason for worry," the man said. "The fire started slow. Everyone got off all right."

"Maybe you saw her?" Sam asked. "Five feet tall. Petite. Dark hair. Quite a looker."

"I could not tell you, mister. We see few women on cargo ships, but that is not much of a description. If she came aboard, she got off all right. I cannot say the same for the ship's cargo."

22

AN UNUSUAL BIRD FOR A PIRATE

SAM SPENT ANOTHER few minutes haunting the riverbank, but didn't learn anything new except that harbours in Camelot stank just as bad as harbours in Hartford. Admitting defeat, he pushed his way back through the crowd, hailed a carriage, and handed the driver his last three copper pennies to return him to the castle.

The two young knights who normally guarded the entrance were huddled off to one side playing some kind of gambling game, likely the one Friar Tuck had described. The stones looked like large, six-sided dice with runes carved on them. Copper pennies lay strewn all over the floor. Sam ignored the players and sought out the knights in the gatehouse.

"Who's in charge here?" Sam demanded.

One of the knights with a field of yellow crosses against a purple background on his shirt broke away from the others and glared at him. "I am Sir Percival. What business has the Merlin's pie with the knights of Camelot?"

That again. How did the magician expect him to do his job after making every knight in the castle his enemy?

Sam let out a deep breath. "You don't like me. I get that. I'm just here to report that a cargo ship is burning to ashes in the harbour. Though I can't be the first to tell you, it's been going on for a while now."

"A cargo ship, you say?" Percival turned up one lip. "Why would anyone inform us? There is nought we could do even should we want to."

Sam shook his head. The more things change the more they stay the same.

He crossed the hall to the page pen thinking to collect a lantern so he could find his way up to his office, but Robin grabbed one first and lit it.

"I'm all out of pennies," Sam said.

Robin grinned. "I am on retainer, as you recall."

They walked together down the deserted corridor and as they climbed the stairs, Robin said, "I should not think that anyone has made Vaisey more angry. He yells at his followers. And throws things. More so than usual."

"Well, kid, most bullies can dish it out, but they can't take it. Fact of life."

"Even so," Robin said. "I believe I prefer this Vaisey over the old one. That Pendragon you gave me. I think I shall use it to find additional ways to . . . dish it to him?"

"Sounds like money well spent," Sam said.

Robin led the way into Merlin's office where Sam lit the lantern he had commandeered two nights earlier. Robin said good night and left.

As Effie had mentioned, someone had removed Sam's uneaten lunch and replaced it with a dinner plate of grilled chicken and corn, now gone cold. The food was welcome, but guilt gnawed at Sam for not finding Miss Le Fay. He had told the fat man that Le Fay didn't know where Logris had hidden the black bird, for her own safety as well as for setting up his bluff. But that could have been the one thing she'd told him that wasn't bunkum. It would serve him right if he'd lost his only chance at finding the black bird.

He was still chewing his first bite of cold chicken when there came a sound at the closed outer door. It wasn't a knock so much as a bang. Sam picked up his lantern and went to investigate.

He had hoped to find Le Fay at the door but was instead greeted by an ash-smeared sailor who stank of fish and smoke and fire. He wore a baggy shirt and pants beneath a heavy brown vest open at the front, a tricorn hat that had seen better days, and a leather patch over one eye. Maybe calling him a sailor was being generous. The man looked more the pirate than any Disney character. In his hands he held a wicker cage covered by a heavy red cloth.

Before Sam could say anything, the pirate fell against the doorway. Sam set his lantern on Effie's desk and took the cage before the ailing seaman dropped it. With the cage out of the way, Sam could see that the man's clothes near his stomach were dark with blood.

The pirate's lips moved. "Yew know . . ." He staggered a step forward. "Chicken." Then he collapsed to the floor. Stone dead.

Sam set the cage on the desk next to the lamp and bent to check the man's pulse. That he found none was no surprise. He dragged the seaman further into the outer office then closed the door. A quick search of the pirate's pockets revealed a document identifying him as Captain Jacobi of the cargo ship *Paloma*, hired to bring a hold of tobacco from the Isle of Malta to Britain. Sam didn't have to be a detective to know it was the *Paloma* burning to cinders on the river.

He was still examining the document when a hurried knock echoed on his door.

The knights? Either way, Sam thought it best to hide the wicker cage; he could do nothing about the body. It took only a moment to set the covered cage inside his sleeping alcove and throw his wool blanket over it in such a way that it resembled a pile of laundry. Then he picked up the lantern, cracked open the outer door, and peered into the hallway. Not knights, but a young boy dressed in rags and holding a candle peered back at him.

"Morgan Le Fay begs yahr presence," the boy said. "The lydy say she in danger."

"Where?" Sam demanded.

The boy scrunched his eyes. "She say you pay me a penny."

Sam dug into his coat pocket and pulled out two coins. Both were silver instead of copper, but he gave one to the boy anyway.

The boy gaped at it.

"Well?" Sam said.

"Burlingame, 26 Ancho Avenue," the boy blurted. Then he raced away down the darkened corridor, probably afraid that Sam would take the Pendragon back. The wind of his movements extinguished his candle.

It took Sam mere seconds to retrieve the cage from his alcove and toss his wool blanket back onto the bed before stepping out into a deserted hallway. There was nothing he could do about the dead pirate, but he didn't think he'd left any evidence that the bird had ever been there.

He carried the cage and lantern along the corridor only as far as Friar Tuck's. Certain that Tuck would be long gone, he opened the door to the herbarium. The young friar had lied; the smells that assaulted his nose were as pungent and offensive as they had been the first time.

"Who—who goes there?" asked a soft, worried voice.

"Tuck? Is that you?"

A bedraggled head of dirty blond hair looked up over the table in the centre of the room. "Spade? Why are you breaking into my shop?"

Sam pulled the cage into the room and closed the door. "I'm hardly breaking in. The door isn't locked."

The friar stared at him. "Locked? You do not lock rooms. Only dungeons. And closets for valuables."

"Never mind," Sam said. "What are you doing here? I thought you slept at the abbey."

Tuck swallowed. "I would have to walk past the pages. I—I am hoping they will forget about me."

Sam grinned. "Fat chance of that; they made a big investment in you. But you can stop worrying. I had a little chat with Vaisey."

"You did." Tuck squinted. "Is that a black eye?"

"Shiners are part of the job," Sam said. "Look, if the pages hassle you, just tell them that Abbot Gildas already knows everything and that they've got no leverage."

Tuck's jaw dropped. "You . . . You told the abbot!"

"Of course not, but they don't know that. If the abbot ever does find out, just tell him the truth. The church is all about forgiveness, isn't it?"

"Perhaps in the land you come from," the friar said. "Here it is all about penance."

"Well, I don't think your penance could be much worse than hiding under a table for the rest of your life."

The young friar climbed to his feet and slumped onto his stool. "You may be right about that."

"I need a favour," Sam said.

"Anything. You have done so much to help me. At least, I think you have."

Sam found a clear spot on the table and set down the cage. Then he pulled away the cloth.

Friar Tuck pursed his lips. "A chicken?"

"You'd think so, wouldn't you?" Sam said, looking into the cage for the first time. "But there are people falling all over themselves trying to get their hands on it. I was hoping you could hide it in your back room for a day or two."

The young friar leaned closer. "Never have I seen a chicken with such dark feathers."

The chicken turned its black head to look at the monk, and clucked at him.

"It must be hungry," Tuck said. "There is hardly any seed left in the cage."

"I've never had a pet," Sam said. "I wouldn't know chicken chow from dog chow."

"I have some flax seed somewhere. And maybe some rye."

"Rye?" Sam perked up. "Pour me a glass while you're at it."

Friar Tuck looked at him. "A . . . glass? Are you in need of a laxative?"

"What? No. I thought you meant you had some whiskey."

"Whiskey. I am unfamiliar with that word. What does it cure?"

"Heartache, mostly," Sam said. "But I'm late for an appointment. I'll have to fill you in later."

23
A DAMSEL IN DISTRESS

WITH THE BIRD safely stashed, Sam raced down to the castle entrance, his lantern rattling in front of him. All was quiet in the page pen, with neither Robin nor Vaisey in sight. He found the knights tasked with watching the gate still engrossed in their game; it was no mystery how a dying pirate and a ragged street urchin had entered the castle unchallenged. Sam figured he may have to have a word with the magistrate after all about pages corrupting the knights.

Despite his hurry, Sam entered the gatehouse and called over the knight he had spoken with earlier. "Hey, Percival, about the burning ship we talked about earlier."

"There has been no news," the knight growled.

"Well, I have some for you. The captain of that ship showed up at my door a few minutes ago and dropped dead inside my office."

Percival stared at him. "How could a dying sailor get past the gate guard?"

"You mean the two guys throwing stones on the floor?"

The knight clenched his gauntlets and hammered them together, the noise not unlike a car hitting a guardrail. He headed for the gatehouse doorway, the remaining knights on his heels. "Sir Gawain!" Percival's shout echoed along the corridor. "You and your bloody stones. And Sir Caradoc! I'll have you both back serving as pages!"

Well. Maybe there was no need to bother the magistrate. Sam waited for Percival to take a breath, then interrupted his scolding of Gawain and his big-eared companion, Caradoc. "You let Sagramore know about the stiff in my office. I'll be back as quick as I can."

"You cannot leave!" Percival shouted. "Sir Sagramore will have questions."

"I wouldn't leave," Sam said, "if I wasn't trying to prevent another death."

The knights didn't stop him as Sam fled outside the castle.

A lone closed carriage sat waiting outside the gate. Sam pulled his last coin from his pocket, a Pendragon. Damn. Beneath the carriage driver's expectant gaze, he rifled through all his pockets but succeeded in finding only his American Silver Eagle and one additional coin that had been caught in the folds of his tobacco kit.

"All I've got on me is one copper," he told the driver. "I don't suppose . . ."

The driver was already turning his face away.

"I'm good for it," Sam said.

No response.

"Maybe you have change for a Pendragon?"

The driver laughed.

"It's life or death," Sam said.

"It always is," the driver murmured.

"Fine," Sam said. "Take the Pendragon. But you won't be charging me for the rest of the year. Got it? I've got friends in high places."

But the driver had already turned around and taken the coin.

"Burlingame," Sam said. "26 Ancho Avenue."

The driver gave Sam a huge grin and then clucked his horse into motion.

The address was an odd one and the trip long. Sam guessed that Burlingame must have once been its own town but was now annexed to Camelot. And not a pleasant town, either. The roads had become ruttier, the buildings more squalid, and fewer lights adorned the windows.

Finally, the carriage came to a stop. "Burlingame," the

driver said.

Sam poked his head outside the carriage and then lifted his lantern out as well. The street was dark as death; not a single lamp in a window. He directed his lantern to read the numbers on the sidewalk posts. 24 Ancho. 28 Ancho. There was no 26.

"Are you sure this is the place?" he asked the driver.

"It is the address you gave me," the man answered. He cast a worried glance along the street. "Do you wish to go someplace else?"

Sam looked around; as far as he could see the neighbourhood was a ghost town. Shaking his head, he had the driver return him to Camelot Castle. During the trip he asked himself who could have sent the message and why. Was Le Fay really in trouble? Had he arrived too late? Or had someone else sent the message? That could explain the absence of a written note.

The two gate guards, Sam noted, stood at strict attention. They were not Gawain and his companion, Caradoc. Sam supposed that he had made additional enemies. So what else is new? As he strode through corridor toward the stairwell leading to his office, a woman darted out of one of the many shadowed nooks.

"Thank goodness!" she cried. "I feared you would never come. There was some commotion at the gate. One of the knights was . . . lecturing the others. I was almost turned away."

Sam saw that Miss Le Fay was on the verge of collapse, so he set aside asking her about the message boy and took her elbow to lead her toward the stairs. "Can you make it to my office on your own? Or shall I carry you?"

Le Fay seemed startled by the suggestion. "I—I shall be well when I am someplace I may sit."

Even so, Sam half-carried the young woman up the stairs and down the corridor to his office. It was a good thing she was so petite; she hardly weighed anything. It was a bad thing, however, that holding Le Fay up with one arm and carrying the lantern with the other distracted him from noticing the point of Mordred's sword.

24

YOU ARE PROBABLY WONDERING WHY I ASKED YOU ALL HERE

WITHOUT SAYING A word, sword point digging into Sam's back, Barth's monkey directed them through Effie's reception area and toward the inner office. Sam glanced at where he'd left Captain Jacobi's body and saw only a dark stain on the floor.

Inside the office, Martin Barth, Esquire, lounged in Sam's stolen padded chair, the fat man's generous posterior overflowing the seat's intended design, while Jesus Cairo paced the floor. Mordred took Sam's lantern, slouched over to Lancelot's desk against the wall, and leaned on it, a wide smirk on his face.

Barth grinned at the new arrivals. "Well, now we are all here. Come in! Come in and sit down. Be comfortable. Then we shall talk."

Sam helped Le Fay settle herself into one of the ladder-back chairs and took the one next to her. He eyeballed the fat man. "Can I interpret this visit to mean that you are ready to make the first payment and take the bird off my hands?"

"Well, sir, as to that . . ." Barth pulled a cloth purse from a pocket inside his suit jacket and tossed it to Sam.

Sam opened the purse, held it upside down, and a single silver coin fell into his hand. "One penny? That's not even cab fare. We were talkin' about a lot more change than this."

Barth's grin widened. "Indeed, sir, we were. But a single coin in the hand is worth ten coins promised." The fat man waved one hand about the room. "And there are more of us to be taken care of now."

"That may be," Sam said. "But only one of us has the black bird."

Cairo ceased his pacing and stood in front of Sam. "I should not think it necessary to remind you, Mr. Spade, that while you *may* have the chicken, we certainly have you." He put all too much emphasis on the word *may*.

"I'm trying to not let that worry me," Sam said. Then he flipped the coin into the air with his thumb, caught it, and then opened his fist to reveal an empty hand. "We'll get back to the money later. There's something else we should discuss first." Sam passed his gaze from face to face. "We've got to have a fall guy. Sagramore needs someone he can pin those three murders on."

Cairo canted his head. "Three?"

"I don't know if it was you or the knights who removed the dead sailor from my outer office, but you can bet that Sagramore will find out about it one way or the other."

"We know about Jacobi," Cairo said. "I say two murders because Sir Logris certainly killed your partner."

"Sagramore doesn't see it that way," Sam said. "Two stiffs? Three? Either way the knights are out for blood. We need to give Sagramore—"

"Come now, Mr. Spade," Barth interrupted. "You cannot expect us to believe that a man such as yourself is the least bit afraid of a blustery knight or that you have not the means—"

Sam leapt to his feet, causing Cairo to reel two steps backward. He pointed a finger at the fat man. "Now look here. I'm in this up to my neck. If I can't offer Sagramore a fall guy, that fall guy will be me." He turned his gaze on Mordred. "Let's give them the monkey. He's the one who stabbed Logris in the back."

When no one denied it, Sam continued. "Anyway, he's made to order for the part. Look at him! The poster boy for remorseless killer. I say we give him to the knights."

Barth laughed. "By Jove, sir, you are a rarity. There is no

telling what you will say or do next, but it is bound to astonish."

"Then you agree," Sam said. "The knights will take your man without question—"

"But, my dear sir, what you suggest is ridiculous! You call him my man, but I feel toward Mordred as if he were my own son. Really, I do. But if even for a moment I considered doing what you propose, it would never work. Mordred would simply tell the knights every last detail about all of us."

Sam smiled. "Let him talk his head off. Sagramore doesn't care if he gets the right man. He just wants someone he can point to and say, Look, I did my job. I can guarantee that nobody'll so much as blink, no matter what the monkey says."

"Well?" the fat man looked over at the grey knight. "What do you think of this plan, Mordred? Do you think it will work?"

"Plan stinks," Mordred said, but his eyes were on Sam, not Barth.

Sam sat back down and glanced at Le Fay where she sat slumped in the hard, ladder-back chair. "How are you feeling now, sister? Any better?"

"Much better," Le Fay breathed in a whisper. "But Sam, Barth is dangerous. You toy with him at your peril."

"It's not always easy to know what to do," Sam said. "Sometimes you just have to play it by ear and hope for the best."

Le Fay glanced down at her hands. "I've always found hope overrated."

Sam laughed. "Here's looking at you, kid." He turned to Barth. "Well?"

The fat man tapped his fingers together, looking more uncomfortable than Le Fay. "As you seem serious about this, the least we can do is hear you out. Now, how is it that you can guarantee Mordred would be unable to do us harm?"

"Nothing could be easier," Sam said. "I'll just show the magistrate that if he listens to the monkey's story he'll have a tangled case with everyone pointing fingers at everyone else. But if he agrees with my account of things, he can pin it all on Mordred in the time it takes to tap his gavel three times. I've met the magistrate. He likes things simple."

"That's it!" shouted Mordred. He drew his sword and pointed it at Sam. "Get up on yer feet. I've taken aw the bleedin' ridin' from ya I'm gonna take. Get up and embrace me blade loike a man!"

Sam made no move to rise; he'd already slipped his hand through the split in his coat pocket and unholstered his revolver. Concealed beneath his trench coat, the business end was aimed in Mordred's direction. "Is that what you said to Logris?" Sam asked. "Before you stabbed him in the back? Four times?" Sam then looked at Barth. "You should tell your pet monkey that skewering me before you get your chicken will be bad for business."

"Now, Mordred," Barth said. "The man is correct. We cannot have any of that. You should not attach such importance to words. He is just trying to bait you."

"Tell 'im ter lay off me, then."

Barth turned to Sam. "Your plan is, I am afraid, not at all satisfactory. Let us say no more about it."

Sam shrugged and eased his finger off his weapon's trigger. "All right, then. You've got sentimental reservations. I get that. We could always try plan B. It's not as good as plan A. Plan B never is, but it gets the job done. You want to hear plan B?"

"Most assuredly."

"We give the knights Cairo."

Barth laughed. "Well, by Jove, sir. You are a dog with a bone."

Cairo wasn't laughing. "Suppose we give them you, Mr. Spade," the Egyptian said. "Or Miss Le Fay?"

Sam smiled and wagged his head: "You want the chicken. I have it. It's not going anywhere without a fall guy. As for Miss Le Fay, if you think you can dress her up as a serial killer, I'm willing to discuss it."

Cairo ground his teeth and began drawing that skinny blade from his cane.

"My, my, my!" Sam said, inching the gun beneath his coat away from Mordred and toward Cairo. "Such a lot of swords around town and so few brains . . . put it down, Cairo."

"Come now, gentlemen," Barth said in a loud voice. "Let us keep our discussion friendly lest we forget where our best interests lie and allow emotion to carry us toward an undesirable end."

Cairo slammed the blade back into the cane and leaned down to whisper into Barth's ear.

Sam nodded at Mordred. "Six to one odds they're selling you out, sonny. I hope the blades these cane-edition desperadoes are waving around don't worry you. Think you can take him?"

Mordred growled with anger and moved toward Cairo.

"Mordred!" Barth shouted.

To Sam's surprise, rather than dissuade his man, the master's shout turned the monkey away from his intended target and toward a new one. The fire in Mordred's eyes told Sam that the young man had lost it. Mordred needed to kill someone, and if it wasn't going to be the milquetoast from Egypt, it would be the gumshoe from Connecticut. Le Fay's words had proved prophetic; hope was overrated.

Fortunately, Sam had insurance in the form of a Smith and Wesson semi-automatic revolver hidden beneath his coat. Unfortunately, he'd turned his gun away from Mordred when Cairo began drawing his cane sword; it was now trained on the wrong target. Sometimes even insurance isn't enough.

The room was not a large one, and with two steps Mordred was almost on top of Sam. It would take an enormous amount of luck to re-aim his bean-shooter beneath his coat and get off a solid shot before three feet of steel skewered him. In Sam's experience, luck was even less reliable than hope. He chose instead to leave the gun loose in his pocket and hit the dirt, or in this case, the stone floor.

Twisting away from Le Fay, he dropped, hooked his foot into the legs of his chair, and sent it sliding forward. Mordred's sword swung through air where his shoulder had been and buried itself in the chair's slatted wooden back. In the same motion, Sam rolled to his feet, swivelled around the injured chair, and slammed Mordred's sword arm with his elbow, causing the blade to work free of the chair and fall to the floor. Mordred howled and reached to recover the weapon, but Sam slammed him in the jaw with his fist. Mordred collapsed to the floor atop his sword.

"And a glass jaw to boot," Sam said, breathing hard. "There's our fall guy. Either say 'yes' right now or I'll hand the chicken and the lot of you over to Sagramore and his knights."

The encounter had taken only moments and Cairo still hovered near the fat man's ear. The expression on the Egyptian's and the chicken rancher's face were near identical—a mix of surprise at Mordred's outburst and awe at Sam's cool handling of it.

"I do not like your scheme, sir," Barth said.

"I'm not asking you to like it. That's just the way it is."

Barth sat for a moment and then sighed. "Very well, Mr. Spade. You may have him."

"I won't be able to get the chicken until sunrise," Sam said. "Maybe a bit later."

Barth frowned. "As much as it pains me, I believe it would be best for all concerned if we do not leave one another's company until our business has been transacted."

"I can live with that," Sam said. "The bird will be brought to us here."

Barth's spirits seemed to lift. "Excellent, sir, excellent! In exchange for fifty Pendragons and Mordred, you will deliver the chicken. And then the three of us—" he nodded to Cairo and Le Fay "—shall leave together. Once Mr. Cairo and I have secured passage, I will send Miss Le Fay back here with the remaining fifty Pendragons."

Sam reached over the desk and shook the fat man's hand. Then he righted the damaged chair and sat down. "Now, then. Just so there's no confusion, why did your man stab Logris and why did he burn Captain Jacobi's ship? I need to know everything that happened in case the magistrate wants details."

Barth appeared to weigh the questions before answering. "I shall be candid with you, sir. Sir Logris was Miss Le Fay's ally. Together they sought other bids for the bird in hopes of raising the already generous price. We believed that disposing of him as we did would discourage Miss Le Fay from such activities."

"Ally!" blurted Le Fay. "He was going to cut me out. After I did all the work finding bidders."

Sam waved Le Fay to silence and continued speaking with Barth. "You didn't try to make a deal with Logris before siccing your monkey on him?"

"Indeed, sir, I did. I spoke with him that very afternoon, but he was quite determinedly loyal to Miss Le Fay. So Mordred awaited him at his inn and did what he did."

"Loyal? But I . . ." Le Fay collapsed into silence.

"Okay," Sam said. "What about Jacobi?"

Barth's face strained with anger. "Captain Jacobi's death was entirely Miss Le Fay's doing."

Le Fay continued her silence.

"Tell me what happened," Sam said.

Barth nodded toward the Egyptian. "As you may have surmised, Mr. Cairo contacted me after he left the knights' hospitality this morning. Recent events had inspired him to recognize the mutual advantage of pooling our resources. The *Paloma* was his offering on the table. He heard a crier heralding its arrival and remembered that its captain was something of a pirate. Putting two and two together, he guessed the truth. That Le Fay and Sir Logris had hired Jacobi to deliver the bird to them here in Camelot."

Sam nodded. "At which juncture you decided to slip me a mickey."

"If by mickey you mean that I slipped a tincture of opium into your mead, then yes. There was no need for you in our plan, sir. While you slept the dream of the poppy, Mr. Cairo, Mordred, and I went to call upon Captain Jacobi. We had nearly convinced the captain to our point of view when Miss Le Fay had the misfortune of arriving." Barth glared at the young woman. "We eventually reached a less favourable, yet passable, agreement and set out for a currency exchange office that holds my local accounts, where I was to pay Miss Le Fay and receive the bird."

Le Fay laughed deep in her throat. "That was no currency office we were going to. Hours after dark? And in one of the worst parts of town?"

Sam nodded toward the dark-haired beauty and waved a hand for quiet. "We'll let that sit for a moment." He turned his attention back to Barth. "At what point in this story did you torch the ship?"

"Well, Mr. Spade, that was entirely unintentional and completely unnecessary. Though we, or Mordred at least, were somewhat responsible for the fire. While Mr. Cairo and I conversed with Captain Jacobi in his cabin, Mordred looked about the ship hoping to discover the chicken. His search was no doubt more aggressive than necessary; he must have upset a lantern."

"And the stabbing?"

"You mean Captain Jacobi? Yes, well, as I said, that was

entirely Miss Le Fay's doing. While en route to visit my banker, the young lady took advantage of the confusion surrounding the harbour fire and managed to slip away with Captain Jacobi and the bird. Women are accomplished at such things and it was neatly done. Yes, very neatly done. Yet women are also predictable. We caught up with Miss Le Fay and Captain Jacobi at her inn. I left Mordred to cover the exits and sure enough, while Miss Le Fay busied us at the door of her suite, the captain made his escape through a window and attempted to descend the exterior wall, unsuccessfully as it happened. While the captain pulled himself up off the ground, Mordred jabbed him. But he was too stubborn to die and Mordred had to take care not to harm the chicken. To our dismay, Captain Jacobi escaped under the cover of night.

"After much diligence, we persuaded Miss Le Fay to tell us where she told Captain Jacobi to deliver the chicken. Then, as we discussed our next steps, Miss Le Fay once again managed to escape our hospitality. This accident further limited what we could do. We therefore sent a runner to your office with a message designed to draw you away should you be there. We were confident the runner would arrive before the captain, given his injuries. We then hired a carriage and made our own way here. Imagine our surprise when we found Captain Jacobi's corpse laid out next to your sweet secretary's desk and no chicken in sight."

"You got your timing all wrong," Sam said. "Jacobi arrived before your runner. The excitement on the river may have contributed. You can blame that on your trained monkey as well."

Mordred groaned and started to sit up. Cairo reached down and confiscated the knight's sword before he could reclaim it.

Barth let out a weary breath. "Ah, my dear boy, I am sorry to lose you. I could not be fonder if you were my own son." Then the fat man shrugged. "Sadly, if you lose a son you can easily get another, but there is only one Maltese chicken north of the Mediterranean. I know, it is difficult for young people to understand these things."

Mordred simply stared at him.

"I don't know about the rest of you," Sam said, "but all this talk of murder and fire and escapes is making me thirsty." He looked at Le Fay. "There's a jug of water and some mugs on the table in the outer office."

"You will not be offended if Mr. Cairo provides escort," Barth said. "I would hate for anything to happen to our pretty, young partner."

Once Morgan Le Fay and Cairo were in the outer office, Barth leaned forward in his chair toward Sam. "I wish to offer you a word of advice, Mr. Spade. You will give Miss Le Fay a share of the money, but if you do not give her what she thinks she should have, she will pull her vanishing trick and take all of your Pendragons with her."

"I'll bear that in mind," Sam said.

The two returned with the water and the five of them waited for night to pass. Mordred fidgeted most of that time while Cairo kept himself alert by twiddling the grey knight's sword. Sam felt his fingers twitch and realized he couldn't remember the last time he'd had a smoke. He buried the thought and let his fingers do their thing. It was just him in a room full of killers; he needed a bit of agitation to keep him on his toes.

25

THE MALTESE CHICKEN

As time went by, Sam found himself wishing he still had his cheap Korean watch. The castle was silent as a morgue, and even the frogs in the moat had picked up a case of laryngitis. Wasn't a town crier supposed to call out the hour? Two o'clock and all is well? Or was that the Civil War? How did anyone in this era keep from going insane without knowing what time it was?

The air grew cooler as night settled. Sam retrieved the blanket from the sleeping alcove and wrapped it around Morgan Le Fay's shoulders. He still wore his trench coat to better conceal his Smith and Wesson; that the faux Burberry kept him warm was a bonus. Neither Barth nor Mordred seemed to notice the cold. Cairo paced the room continually, alternately waving Mordred's sword and rubbing his arms through his too-tight coat.

When the lantern light waned and predawn crept through the window, Barth said, "It is almost daylight, Mr. Spade. When can I see my bird?"

"Soon. When Effie gets here." Sam didn't know if he should involve Effie, but figured he had things under control, more or less. And he still had his insurance policy beneath his coat. Part of him hoped that Galahad or even Saggy would intrude first. As it was, no sounds disturbed Sam's office until his secretary arrived and tapped on the inner office door.

"Oh!" Effie said, taking in the crowded room.

"Business is booming," Sam said. "But right now, I need you to get something for me."

"Need I warn you," Barth said, "that if the pretty lady returns with anything other than what we discussed, that I and my colleagues will not support any tale you decide to spin."

"Unlike some people I know," Sam said, "I'm a man of my word."

"I dislike how this looks," Effie said.

Sam let out a soft snort. "You got that right, angel. I need you to do exactly as I ask." Then he leaned in close and whispered into Effie's ear.

The air grew thick after Effie left the office. Moments stretched into minutes and then into what felt like hours. Then Effie returned carrying a cage covered by a heavy cloth and handed it to Sam.

"Thanks, angel," Sam said.

Effie nodded and left the office. Everyone was so focused on the cage that no one moved to stop her.

"That is the proper cloth and cage," Barth said, standing up from his chair. "But does it still contain my bird?"

Sam set the wicker cage on his desk and removed the cloth. A chicken with black feathers, black skin, and golden eyes blinked at them. "You tell me."

"At last," the fat man said as he leaned down and worked the cage's latch. The wicker door swung open and Barth reached in with both hands to remove the chicken. It clucked with irritation and kicked out with its clawed feet. The fat man's smile was a mile wide. "After all this trouble. The first Maltese chicken outside Malta!"

Everyone surrounded the desk, marvelling at the object that had cost three lives and a cargo ship in order to find its way to Sam Spade's office.

Barth nodded and carefully returned the chicken to the cage. "You have fulfilled your part of the bargain, Mr. Spade. A man of odd dress, speech, and manner, but a trustworthy man nonetheless. I—" The flow of words ceased as the fat man stared at his fingers. They were smudged black. "No!"

"It must be smoke," Cairo said. "From the fire."

Barth reached back into the cage. The chicken squawked in

complaint as he plucked a feather and then rubbed it vigorously. The fat man's thick fingers immediately blackened. "It is a fake! An ordinary chicken dyed black!"

Sam turned to Le Fay. "All right, sister. You've had your little joke. Now tell us about it."

The dark-haired beauty took two steps backward. "No, Sam! No! That is the chicken Jacobi brought. Same bird. Same cage. I am sure of it."

Mordred nodded. "I sawr it close. That's the boid Jacobi died tryin' ter escape wif."

Cairo waved Mordred's sword at Barth as he broke into tears. "It is you who bungled it. Your farmer on Malta swindled us. He sent us a fake bird. You . . . you imbecile! You bloated idiot! You stupid fathead, you—"

Barth began laughing and the room fell silent. "Yes, it is Malta's hand. There is no doubting it. What do you suggest we do? Shall we sit here, shedding tears and calling each other names? Or do we return to Malta and try again?"

Cairo blinked away his tears. "You are serious?"

"Why not?" Again the fat man laughed. "The Mediterranean is beautiful this time of year."

"Then yes," Cairo said. "I will go with you."

"Mordred?" Barth looked around and his expression fell.

Sam didn't have to look to know that Mordred had fled the moment no one was looking. "A swell lot of thieves you are."

Barth forced a smile and stepped around from behind the desk. "We have little to boast about, but the world has not come to an end simply because we have encountered a small setback." He looked coldly at Sam. "I am afraid I must ask you to return the penny I paid you."

Sam wagged his head. "I held up my end. You got your chicken. It's your bad luck it wasn't what you wanted. You still owe me ninety-nine Pendragons."

"Come now, Mr. Spade, we have all failed and there is no reason to expect any of us to bear the entire brunt. In short, sir, I must ask you for my coin." Barth pulled a small blade from a hip sheath and held it in front of Sam like a butter knife.

Sam shook his head and reached into his pocket. He tossed the fat man his last copper penny. "That's all you'll get. I'm keeping the silver coin for time and expenses. And before you open your fat mouth again, I'll remind you of how easily I disarmed your cohorts. And if that isn't enough, I've been up all night and may accidentally kill someone rather than disarm them."

Cairo took a step back and threw Mordred's sword onto the floor.

Barth grudgingly put his butter knife away. "Now, sir, we shall say goodbye to you. Unless you care to undertake the Malta expedition with us."

Sam wagged his head.

"No? Frankly, Mr. Spade, I would rather have you along. You are a man of nice judgment and uncanny resources. I feel compelled to remind you that with Mordred running off, you are now without a fall guy."

Sam shrugged. "I'll make out all right. Mordred is pretty recognizable. I doubt he'll get far before Saggy's knights catch him."

Barth puffed up his already compelling chest. "Well, sir, the shortest farewells are the best. Adieu. And to you, Miss Le Fay, I leave the painted chicken in the cage as a memento."

Once the fat man and Cairo had left, Le Fay rushed into Sam's arms. "How did you do it? How could you possibly have switched chickens? Where is the real one?"

Sam gently pushed her away. "Sorry to disappoint you, sister, but that is the real chicken. And by real, I mean it's the one Jacobi brought here before he died. If someone made a switch before that . . ."

"Then Barth had it right; we were deceived on Malta." Le Fay sank into the stolen chair the fat man had occupied and stared into the cage. The chicken stared back at her.

Sam said nothing. A moment later there came a pounding on the outer office door. Sam opened it to find Sagramore, Galahad, and several other knights.

"Did you catch them all?" Sam asked.

Galahad nodded. "A false knight ran into our net first. His tabard bore a two-headed eagle. He fooled no one. Then minutes later came a fat man and an Egyptian. Effie mentioned there may also be a young, dark-haired woman, but when she failed to make an appearance, we decided it best to call on you."

Sam waved the two knights into his office, leaving the others outside for the simple reason that there wasn't room for them.

Sagramore eyed Morgan Le Fay before turning his cold gaze on Sam. "You have given us three men. What do you accuse them of?"

"Listen and listen good," Sam said. "Saggy, if you get lost, Galahad will explain it to you later."

The dark knight growled and tightened his hand into a fist.

"The false knight you caught first. His name is Mordred. He's the one who killed Sir Logris. Then last night he set fire to the ship on the river and killed its captain."

"A ship's captain is dead?" asked Sagramore.

"If you will recall," Galahad said, "Mr. Spade reported this to Sir Percival last evening. He said there was a dead sailor in his office."

Sagramore snorted. "I thought he was having me on. Trying to make me look foolish."

"You don't need any help in that department," Sam said. "And now you'll have to beat out of Mordred where he moved the body to. All he left here was a stain on the floor."

Sagramore's face darkened further.

"The fat man is his boss," Sam continued. "Barth ordered the two murders, but not the burning. Mordred lit up the ship all on his own. Whether that was spite or stupidity, I don't know."

"And the Egyptian?" asked Galahad.

"Another of the fat man's employees. He didn't murder anyone directly that I know of, but he's part of it and his actions helped lead to the two deaths."

Galahad stepped forward and dipped his head to Miss Le Fay. "You must be the young woman Euphemia described. She failed to mention your unequalled comeliness."

Sam turned to consider the reddening of the dark-haired beauty's complexion. "Another of the fat man's victims. Barth and his men chased her for days; I did what I could to protect her."

"Then she has committed no crime?" Galahad asked.

"None that I'm aware of," Sam said, stretching the truth beyond credulity. Le Fay was probably more culpable than Cairo, but at least she'd never threatened him with a sword.

"This is all neat and tidy," Sagramore said. "But I put it to you:

Which of these scoundrels murdered Sir Lancelot?"

"Ah, yes. My partner. That was the trickiest one."

"But you do know who killed him?" Galahad asked.

"I do," Sam admitted. "I also know why."

"My ears itch to hear this tale," Sagramore said.

"And well they should, Saggy, because it is you who killed Sir Lancelot."

The dark knight chuckled. "Once again you poke me in the eye with your vulgar wit."

But Galahad wasn't laughing. "Mr. Spade, how can you make such an accusation? Sir Sagramore is the Second Knight of Camelot."

"It's not difficult," Sam said. "While Lancelot was out chasing skirts, Saggy here was taking care of his lonely wife. Only as Lancelot's behaviour became more scandalous, loneliness turned into acrimony. Iva begged her beau to put an end to Lancelot, but Saggy knew he'd never defeat the Amorous Knight in a fair fight. Then I came along and they had the perfect patsy."

"This tale is outrageous," Sagramore shouted. "How dare you insult not only myself, but Sir Lancelot's widow as well?"

"I'll tell you how I dare," Sam said. "You asked me where I was the hour of Lancelot's death. I'll ask you the same question."

"Well, I was . . . I was . . ."

"I'll tell you where you were. You were in a carriage with the soon-to-be widow following her husband from Camelot Castle to the St. Mark Inn."

"How dare you!"

"The reason Lancelot never drew his sword was because you stopped him from entering the Inn and asked him around back for a quiet word. Maybe you could describe for us the look on your pal's face when you showed him your sword and then punctured his gut."

"This is a fairy tale and I will see you hanged for false accusation!"

"I have proof," Sam said.

"What proof?" Galahad asked.

Sam reached into the inside pocket of his suit jacket and retrieved a silver amulet holding a large red ruby. "Iva gave me this for safekeeping."

Sagramore smiled at the jewellery. "That is only proof of your guilt."

"I had the gemmologist several doors down appraise it. Do you know what it's worth?"

"I have no idea," Sagramore said.

"Twenty-three Pendragons. And change."

Galahad whistled.

"I still fail to see—"

"Iva gave it to me five seconds after meeting me. Do you find that unusual?"

Sagramore said nothing.

"The next thing she did was tell you and Galahad that she and I were an item."

Sagramore continued to say nothing.

"I can only think of two reasons why Mrs. Lancelot would act this way. Either she's loonier than a Canadian dollar coin. Or she was playing her part in setting me up as the fall guy for Lancelot's murder. No, wait, there's a third possibility. Maybe she murdered Lancelot all on her own."

Sagramore sputtered.

Galahad, however, kept his composure. "Sir Lancelot was stabbed with a blade. Lady Iva is but a small woman and he among the greatest knights of the realm in strength and speed."

Sam shook his head. "We already know that Lancelot's killer took him by surprise. Who would be more surprising than his wife?"

Galahad rubbed his chin. "One of those men you gave us tonight, the fat one, had a small, short blade. Easy to conceal and wield up close. A woman could wield such a blade as well as a man."

The sound of steel on steel echoed in the room as Sagramore drew his blade.

"Oh!" sighed Morgan Le Fay, forgotten where she sat behind Sam's desk.

"Lady Iva would nary hurt a mouse," Sagramore cried. "True, she helped me make my case against this knavish investigator, but it is I who defeated the Amorous Knight."

Sam twitched his lip. "I wouldn't call a friendly knife in the gut much of a win."

"Your barbed words end now!" Sagramore cried, raising his sword to strike. At the same time, Sam drew his Smith and Wesson from its holster and took aim at the dark knight's chest.

"I have heard enough," Galahad said.

Sam tried to pull the trigger, but his finger wouldn't move. Sagramore's blade also failed to fall.

Galahad walked slowly around the two of them, and then his face began to age. Moments later it was not Sir Galahad the Gallant who paced the room, but the magician Merlin.

26
PLAY IT AGAIN, SAM

"PUT THAT TOY away," Merlin said. "You have no need of it now."

Sam found that he could move again and slowly slipped the semi-automatic back into its holster. Sagramore, however, may as well have been a statue. Merlin summoned the remaining knights from the outer office to disarm their leader. Then Sagramore swung his arm down at empty space. He blinked when he realized neither his sword nor its target were where they had been a moment earlier.

"I have to say I am surprised," Merlin scolded the Second Knight. "You have brought shame upon all of Camelot."

Sagramore twisted his upper lip. "What I did, I did for love and shall not apologize. It is Lancelot who brought shame upon this kingdom and all who dwell here. I have put paid to the scoundrel's dalliances."

The old magician shook his head. "Lancelot had his faults, yet his indiscretions fell well short of murder. And you would have someone else hang for your crimes."

Sagramore snorted. "A foreigner. Who would miss him?"

"Indeed. Who?" Merlin flicked a hand. "Take him to the dungeon. The magistrate will see justice done."

Obscenities echoed from the hallway as the knights led their once-leader away.

Then Effie entered the office. She must have been waiting in

167

the corridor. It was the duke's daughter who had summoned the knights, the final instruction Sam had whispered in her ear.

"Please escort Miss Le Fay to your father's house," Merlin said to her. "And return the lady here on the morrow."

Effie nodded.

To Le Fay, he said, "Despite Mr. Spade's endorsement, I fear you are not entirely innocent in this affair. But I may have use for you. Perhaps we may benefit each other."

Le Fay curtsied and accompanied Effie out of the office.

The old magician then turned his gaze on Sam. "You surprise me as well, Mr. Spade. I was confident that the trouble brewing in Camelot would come to a boil in my absence, but I never expected you to uncover multiple wrongdoings and bring the perpetrators to justice. I brought you here as a catalyst, not a solution."

"You'll have to forgive me," Sam said, "if I don't thank you for your glowing endorsement. If you felt that way, why bother with me at all? Your mice would have eaten the cheese without me hanging around."

A smile creased the old man's lips. "I needed a witness. Someone to be my eyes and ears. Lancelot would not do. Although a superlative knight, he was not very observant. He failed to notice anything not wearing a skirt. I required someone such as yourself to tell me what occurred in my absence."

"But you weren't absent. You were masquerading as Galahad."

Merlin nodded. "Yes, but all knights have their various duties. As Sir Galahad I spent most of my time in the royal quarter guarding doorways that did not require guarding."

"You could have masqueraded as Lancelot."

The magician shrugged. "If I had done that, I would be dead now. But no, people would see in an instant that I was not the Amorous Knight. Sir Galahad, now. Galahad is quiet and unassuming. Most fail to notice him at all. Still, Sir Lancelot will be missed."

Sam opened his mouth, then froze when he realized what he was going to suggest. Then he said it anyway. "If you need someone to fill Lancelot's vacancy, I know an investigator who might be available."

A huge smile crossed the magician's face. "That is a noble offer. You have proven yourself more than worthy of Lancelot's mantle. I would accept . . ."

"But."

"But a destiny awaits you back in your time."

Sam didn't know what to make of that. He hoped the old magician wasn't referring to a bullet in a dark alley.

"Are you ready to go back?" the magician asked.

"What? Now?"

Merlin cast him a curious look. "Is there somewhat keeping you here?"

"I—ah, I'd like to say goodbye to Effie."

"I shall give Euphemia your regards on the morrow."

"Well," Sam said. "I hope you'll understand me when I say that isn't quite the same."

"I do," Merlin said, nodding. "But it is time."

"What about the chicken?" Sam asked.

Merlin glanced at the cage on the desk. "Ah. The so-called Maltese chicken. Yes. I shall dine on it for breakfast."

"It's not a fake," Sam said.

"Of course not. You had young Friar Tuck douse it in oil of henna even though it was already black as Hades himself. I cannot say that I understand why."

"Just hedging my bets," Sam said. "If I had the real bird, those mugs might have tried to skewer me before I discovered who killed who. As it was, I didn't need the black bird to get the story out of them."

"I see," said Merlin. "Why do anything simply when you can turn it into a circus? I shall give instruction to have the chicken thoroughly cleansed before it is cooked."

"But it's worth a fortune," Sam said.

"No. It is worth a breakfast."

Sam searched for another stalling tactic. "How about Galahad. What happened to him?"

"Ah, that is an interesting story." The old magician grinned. "I sent Sir Galahad the Gallant in search of a MacGuffin."

"A what?"

"A seemingly crucial object that is actually a distracting deception. I sent him in search of the Holy Grail."

"Really?" Sam said. "Christ's cup from the last supper?"

"The same." The magician's grin broadened. "A hopeless quest, but I received word this past evening that Sir Galahad has found it. It is a funny world. A funny world. A funny world."

Sam cracked his jaw, trying to clear the echo in his head. Then everything went dark. And wet. Then his mind cleared and a gunshot rang out. A bullet splintered wood near his ear at the same time that lightning cracked the sky. The alley surrounding him looked all too familiar. Hartford. The stink of mouldy lettuce and stale beer accosted his nostrils. Good old Hartford. It was as if the past three days had never happened.

A voice called from the end of the alley. "Give it up, Sparrow! Time to get what's coming to you."

It was bad enough that Sam's PI business was a joke, but that wasn't even why these jack-fools were out to get him. Two years ago as a cop he'd arrested one of their gang members. Then a month before release, the idiot picked a fight with a rival gang and got himself shivved. Yet somehow that was all Officer Sparrow's fault and these squint-eyed palookas had come gunning for him. Merlin was right. It is a funny world.

"I've reloaded," Sam called out. "You might want to think about leaving."

Laughter echoed down the alley.

Sam shook his head and unholstered his revolver. Then he aimed the barrel between two wooden boxes and fired six shots. After counting to ten he fired six more. Then he listened through the rain to the sound of boots clunking on wet pavement and fading into the distance. Just to be sure, he fired six shots toward the other end of the alley. He waited in the rain for another ten minutes before retrieving his fedora off the damp asphalt and heading home.

27

THE MALTESE FALCON

SAM HEAVED THE heavy desk a little closer to the window and then sat in the chair. The desk was solid oak, an antique Victorian with lockable drawers. The chair was a leather Broderick office recliner. Other than that, they were just like the furniture from his office in Camelot. The new office space had cost him, but Iva's ruby amulet had sold for enough green that he could keep as a souvenir the silver Pendragon the fat man had paid him.

"Effie, could you come in here?"

A tall, shapely blonde sashayed in from the outer office. She had a notepad in one hand and a pen in the other. Her name wasn't really Effie. "What can I get you, Mr. Sparrow?"

Sam laughed. "You can cut the bimbo act; your IQ is higher than mine. That's why I hired you."

Effie also laughed. "I thought we were partners."

"I misspoke," Sam said. "Partners. I wanted to ask if my desk and chair were okay here."

"Fine," Effie said, sitting at a second desk along the opposite wall. "This place is roomy enough for a pool hall."

"How are the interviews coming?"

"I have three good candidates. Are you sure you don't want a say in hiring a receptionist?"

"I wouldn't know what to look for," Sam said.

"Can I ask you something? Why Effie?"

171

Sam let out a deep breath. "You know. Since I was twelve years old I've never been able to trust anyone. Never had a partner I could trust."

"Until someone named Effie?"

"Got it in one, kid."

The blonde gave him a hard look. "You said the nickname was just temporary."

Sam nodded. "Until I know I can trust you. I need to be able to trust my partner."

"Trust is earned, not given." Effie adjusted the embossed brass stand on her desk that displayed her real name—Nora Clark. "We'll both need to earn each other's trust."

"I'm looking forward to it." Sam glanced at his watch—a real Rolex rather than the fake that was crushed in Camelot—and jumped up from his chair. "I'm going to be late."

"Got a hot date?" Effie asked, her mouth twisting in a sly grin.

"Yeah. With Humphrey Bogart. *The Maltese Falcon* is playing at the Plaza."

"I bet you've seen that movie a thousand times," Effie said, her bright green eyes gazing at the movie poster that hung on the wall near his desk.

Sam flipped his fedora onto his head and winked at her. "The odds are in your favour, angel, but you'd lose that bet."

PART 2

THE GRAIL

1
A LADY IN WHITE

HARTFORD, CONNECTICUT. A lousy place to live. A worse place to die.

Sam Sparrow sat hunched over his antique oak desk, poring through the yellow pages listing of Hartford Private Investigators. The list was not a long one. The sole boxed ad, with larger type and a stylized *Sparrow and Clark Investigations* logo, took up most of the space. Of the remaining three numbers, Sam had just called the third. None of the agencies offered a female investigator. His eyes scanned up and down the column and surrounding pages, but found nothing that could help.

Slamming his palm onto the open book, Sam looked over at the other desk in the office. It sat conspicuously empty and a whole lot tidier than his own. Nora Clark had been Sam's partner for coming on six months. He'd stopped calling her Effie after two. A strong woman with a good head on her shoulders, Nora couldn't care less who Sam's father had or hadn't been. In other words, she was the most perfect woman Sam had ever met. That she was also the best detective in Hartford was just icing on the cake. The irony was, because Nora was so capable, she might be dead now, or soon could be.

From the corner of his eye Sam spotted movement. William Morris, his and Nora's secretary, hovered at the inner office door.

"Someone here to see you," William said. "A customer, I

think."

"We're closed," Sam shouted at him. "I told you we're not taking new cases."

William was an excellent secretary. Nora had hired him. He might have been a gentleman's gentleman at his last position. He often took care of things long before Sam or Nora knew they needed taken care of.

"I told her that. She asked me to give you this." William came all the way into the office and set a shiny coin the size of a silver dollar on Sam's desk.

Sam glared at the coin and then pulled one just like it from a suit jacket pocket and set it on the desk beside its twin. He sighed. "Send her in."

William went to the door and spoke into the outer office. "Mr. Sparrow will see you now."

"Close the door on your way out," Sam said.

His secretary cast him a surprised glance. Sam's usual modus operandi was to leave the door open for William to listen in. Not today. William stepped outside and closed the door once the customer had entered.

The woman could have been thirty or fifty or anywhere in between. She had one of those ageless faces. Good bone structure. Milky skin. A cool look. She wore a long, white coat that reached the floor but was free from grime despite three inches of snow and muck outside. It had been a cold and stormy December so far and the weather hadn't improved for the holidays. As the woman sat in a chair opposite Sam's desk, he noticed that her long, straight hair was the same colour as her coat—albino white. As were her eyes; almost white on white, the irises gleamed with a hint of pink, the black dot at the centre standing out in sharp contrast. The woman's narrow brows were also white. Her lips echoed the soft pink of her eyes. Sam didn't think she wore a spot of makeup.

"You are Sam Spade," the woman said, "the Merlin's private investigator."

"And you are well informed," Sam replied. "Though it's Sam Sparrow, not Sam Spade. I assume you have a name as well."

The woman smiled. "My name is not important. I am known as the Lady of the Lake."

Sam nodded and noticed that whatever the Lady wore beneath the coat was also white, and seemed to shimmer. He tapped a finger on the silver Pendragon William had set on his desk. "I'm honoured that you've come to see me. No, honoured's not the right word. I don't know if there is a right word. But the timing is all wrong. I'm in a bit of a crisis right now—"

"Crisis is an appropriate word," the Lady interrupted, "for the business I have brought you. Whatever your other problems, they can wait."

"I don't think you understand," Sam said. "My partner has gone undercover at the Miramar Wellness Retreat, and I've lost contact with her. She could be in danger." He frowned. "Could is maybe too optimistic a word."

"It can wait," the Lady said.

"No, it can't. It's been three days. Three days without a word. I won't abandon my partner."

"Your partner," the Lady said, "is dead."

Sam leapt to his feet. "What do you know?"

If Sam's sudden movement startled the Lady, she didn't show it. "I know many things. I am the Lady of the Lake."

Sam sat down again, slowly. "How did she die?"

"A garrotte." The Lady moved her hands to demonstrate. "Over the head from behind. Like so. And pulled tight. Your Miss Clark struggled, but that only hastened the end. The killer dragged her body into an infrequently used closet. She shall be discovered tomorrow when a maid performs her weekly inventory. It will not be pleasant. Miss Clark was killed the morning after entering the spa and will have had almost four days to putrefy."

"You know quite a bit." Sam had no idea if what the dame said was true or not, but if it was . . .

"I know many things," the Lady repeated. "I also know that you are needed immediately. In Camelot."

"I can't just leave."

"Of course you can. I will send you."

Sam rubbed his ear. "And you'll send me back here when I'm done?"

The Lady nodded. "I or the Merlin."

"I want something if I agree," Sam said.

The Lady sniffed. "I have already given you a Pendragon. That is more than your usual fee."

"Yeah, well, this isn't a usual case."

"Very well," said the Lady. "What it is you want?"

"When you send me back, I want it to be three days ago. Before Nora was murdered. I need to rescue her."

The Lady looked at him. "Is that all?"

"For now—" Sam began, but that was all he got out before lightning blasted him out of his chair.

2
FAMILIAR PLACES; FAMILIAR FACES

SAM OPENED HIS eyes to mortared stone and plain, wooden furniture. Only six months had passed since he'd last seen his old office in Camelot, but he hardly recognized the place. For one thing, there was only one desk. He crawled to it on hands and knees and used a ladder-back chair as an anchor to help him climb to his feet.

He assumed the desk belonged to Merlin; that the old magician hadn't bothered to replace the unfortunate Lancelot. But that failed to explain the vase of purple flowers that adorned one end or the nearly overwhelming scent of perfume. Or the throw rug set beneath the elaborately padded chair set behind the desk. Or the patterned curtains. Or the collection of new knickknacks that lined the shelves and occupied choice real estate on the desk. Yes, it had been six months, but no one redecorates to that extent without first being saved by Jesus. Or Satan.

Sam picked his trench coat and fedora up off the floor. A moment ago they had been hanging on a coat rack in Hartford. His semi-automatic and holster, which had been locked inside a desk drawer, sat beneath the coat.

"The Lady thinks of everything," Sam muttered.

After strapping on his bean-shooter, Sam wrapped himself in his trench coat and flipped his hat onto his head, even though he was indoors. A crisis in Camelot, the Lady had said. He'd need his *mean streets* getup. The only thing missing was his genuine Burberry gumshoes. He hoped the Lady's oversight meant that he was in for sunny weather.

Stepping up to the window, Sam stuck his head out past the richly coloured curtains and saw that the rest of Camelot looked little changed. And smelled little changed. The stable still stood by the moat and a few ducks floated on the murky water. Outside the castle, the city sprawled as it had six months ago with carts, carriages, and townsfolk carrying bundles on their heads. Some kind of black bird soared across the sky crying, "Look at me. Look at me!"

Sam frowned as he realized the city was too unchanged. Six months had gone by and summer hadn't ended. He didn't know if southern England had snow in December, but surely the air would be cooler.

The bird swung back toward the castle and croaked out a laugh.

Sam pulled his head back inside and considered the closed alcove door. The tiny room where he had slept during his previous visit taunted him. Would it, like the rest of the office, be transformed? He decided not to look. He'd left nothing behind, after all. Given Merlin's office's other changes, maybe the old man slept there now. Maybe he slept there right now!

As Sam pondered this thought, one of the shelves on the wall caught his eye. Well, not so much the shelf as a glass oval that was one of the new additions. The size and shape of a chicken's egg, it sat among pieces of oddly-shaped rock and wood he remembered from before. He did not remember the glass egg. From small end to big, it seemed made from a solid, pale-blue glass with no imperfections. Except for a black feather at its centre. The feather was too small for any bird Sam could think of. Well, not any bird. It looked like a chicken feather. Had Merlin encased a Maltese chicken feather in glass? A souvenir?

Sam picked up the egg, which felt lighter than he expected, and slid it into the left pocket of his trench coat next to his tobacco kit. Since he didn't have the answer, he'd settle for the feather.

Having run out of excuses, Sam stepped up to the door

separating the inner and outer office. He didn't know why the prospect of seeing Effie again made him nervous. Sure he'd been attracted to her; what man with a pulse wouldn't be attracted. He was less sure that the attraction was mutual. It could have been, if she ignored that he was several social classes beneath her, from the other side of the world, and inhabited a different millennium. But the real barrier was her age. Seventeen. Sam was many things, but a cradle robber wasn't one of them.

Of course, by now she could be eighteen and legally an adult. Sam smiled. The law was often arbitrary, and rarely more arbitrary than when it concerned kids. Kids don't suddenly grow up on their eighteenth birthday, one day the apple of mom and dad's eye and the next out making their own way in the world. No one knew that better than Sam, who'd lived on his own after his mother had abandoned him at age sixteen. Circumstances had made Sam grow up early. Maybe that's why he felt older than his thirty-one years credited. But if Effie had turned eighteen, maybe this time things could work out. Maybe this time Sam would have a chance. Thirteen years wasn't that big a gap, was it? He had made her laugh, after all; that was always a good sign. Then he'd left without saying goodbye, an act that was pretty much unforgivable in Sam's experience. It didn't matter that he'd had no choice at the time. Thirteen years. Gah! It felt like a lifetime.

Well, even if Effie hated him, it would be good to see her again. He'd missed the medieval blonde bombshell with brains to match. Even so, when he reached for the door latch, his fingers twitched as though craving a cigarette. He didn't know whether to laugh or cry when he found the outer office empty.

Effie's desk looked just as he remembered, uncluttered. Several client chairs still lined the inside wall. Magazines remained conspicuously absent from the table. Sam stretched out one arm and idly pushed apart the few sheets of paper that lay in an ordered stack on one side of Effie's desk. Maybe he could find a clue as to why the Lady of the Lake figured he was needed. A crisis, she'd said.

"Sam!"

Sam nearly jumped out of his skin. He backed away from the desk and turned toward the outer office door. Effie stood there. Not angry, but . . . not Effie-like at all. Something about his one-time secretary was different.

"Ah, hi Effie. You, ah, changed your hair?" Eloquence had never been one of Sam's strong suits.

"When did you get here?" the elegant blonde demanded.

Elegance. That was it. He remembered Effie as playful and flirty. This Effie was more demure. More serious.

"Well?" she said. "I am waiting."

Sam cast her his best smile, and threw in a little chin thrust for good measure. "I just dropped in. It's sure great to see you, angel."

Effie seemed to relax a little. Only a little. "It gladdens me to see you as well, Sam, but how did you get here? It was not the Merlin, was it?"

"That old goat?" Sam felt he was on a roll. "Naw. I've moved up in the world. The Lady of the Lake is my client now. She sent me here to solve a little crisis for her. You, ah, wouldn't know what that crisis is, would you?"

Effie gawped at him.

It occurred to Sam that the flowers and the curtains and the rug in the office all hinted at a feminine occupant. He should have picked up on that immediately. Top PI in Hartford? Really? It was Nora who was the big gun. Sometimes Sam just felt like window dressing.

"Is your name on the door now?" he asked. "Did Merlin give you Lancelot's job after I left?"

"Me? What?" Effie blinked her eyes. "No. Of course not. I am still a clerk. I am just . . . surprised to see you." She turned and poked her head back into the corridor, then closed the door and grabbed his wrist, pulling Sam to the row of visitor chairs. She sat, drawing him down into the chair next to hers. "You should not be here," Effie hissed, her voice a near whisper. "The Lady of the Lake? Who? Never mind. What did she say?"

Sam thought about that. "Actually, she didn't say much of anything except that there was a crisis in Camelot. What do you know?"

"I—" Effie didn't get any further because just then the door swung open to reveal a familiar face.

"You!" said the newcomer.

"You!" said Sam.

"I have an errand to run," said Effie, and the shapely

blonde was out the door before Sam realized she'd let go of his wrist.

"What are you doing here?" The speaker was slim and short, with ice blue eyes and the pale skin of a corpse. Long black hair tied on one side fell across the shoulder of a tight black dress. Red lipstick was the woman's only colour. Not that long ago Sam had thought her the most beautiful woman he had ever seen. He'd been around the block a few times since. Morgan Le Fay looked like she'd seen many more blocks. She'd gotten old.

Something told Sam that being forthcoming with this woman was a mistake. It may have been the scowl in her eyes. Or the fact that she was a pathological liar. It could have been that the last time he'd seen her she'd been at least partly responsible for several deaths and the destruction of a cargo ship.

"I'm looking for work," Sam said. "You wouldn't know of any chickens that require finding, do you?"

Le Fay's answer was as blunt as it was quick. "Get out!"

Sam rose to his feet and spread wide his hands. "Hey, we may not have parted on the best of terms after the chicken fiasco, but that's no reason to get impolite."

A sneer spread across the woman's blood-red lips. "Get out! Please. If I ever see you again, I may be the last thing you see."

"No need to ask twice," Sam said as he shuffled toward the door. "There's nothing wrong with my hearing. But if you're not hiring, do you happen to know if Merlin is in the market for—"

Sam suddenly found himself in the stone hallway with a door slammed in his face. He didn't remember walking through the doorway. Or seeing the door close. He took several steps backward until he could read the shingle that used to say *Sam Spade Investigations. Merlin & Vivian Investigations* now decorated the doorway. He had no idea who Vivian was, but he did know that there was only one desk in the office.

3

A FRIAR GAINS WEIGHT

THE LADY OF the Lake hadn't told Sam what the crisis in Camelot was. He assumed she'd intended for Merlin to provide the particulars. And maybe give him a hand. It was just Sam's dumb luck that Morgan Le Fay was haunting the old magician's office. That was probably why Merlin wasn't there; he was hiding from the woman.

How had Le Fay changed so much in six months! She'd gone from a frightened young woman who'd tried to seduce him in order to gain his dubious help, to an angry harridan who'd threatened to kill him. Well, harridan might be too unkind a word; some women looked older when they're angry. But, why the change? What had he ever done to Morgan Le Fay apart from refusing her advances and saving her from the dungeon?

Effie had changed as well. She had fled from the woman. Sam couldn't remember Lady Euphemia Peregrine backing down from anyone or anything. But it had been six months. Maybe his recollections were at fault, idolizing Effie and making Le Fay more . . . everything. His experiences in Camelot *had* changed his life, after all. Had he Disneyfied his own memories? Making them bigger than they actually were?

These thoughts and more haunted Sam as he wandered along the deserted castle corridor, something he remembered all too well and that felt completely in line with his recollections.

The next shingle down was one he remembered: *Friar Tuck, Royal Herbalist*. The door was closed, as usual. Sam opened it without knocking and nearly fell back into the hallway as the friar's teas from Hell ripped open his sinuses. This memory, too, was all too familiar.

A cheery laugh greeted him and then a sonorous voice sang out: "It takes people that way sometimes. Only the first time, of course. You get used to it."

"Friar Tuck?" Sam gasped, his breath fighting to reach his lungs.

The man behind the wide table grinned and nodded. "At your service. I . . . Wait. Do I know you?"

Sam took in a slow swallow of air. "You *are* Friar Tuck? Aren't you? What happened to you?"

"Ah. Sam Spade! The detective the Merlin brought in who was such a cockup. I mean, who was searching for the missing cock, er, chicken." The friar's face turned red as a tall glass of Pinot Noir, Nora's poison of choice. "What do you mean what happened to me?"

Sam stepped up to the counter and leaned forward so he could see as much of the friar as possible. A burlap robe stretched tightly around an impressive girth. His skinny young friend was now portly as a potbellied pig, well on the way to becoming the corpulent churchman he remembered from Disney. "You've gained weight," Sam said.

The friar looked down and laughed. "Why, so I have. Once you freed me from Vaisey's clutches, I realized that I earn the abbey enough coin in this wretched shop that Abbot Gildas could afford to feed me better. Solid food and the occasional ale. I told him so and eventually he came round to my way of thinking. You have my eternal thanks, Mr. Spade."

"Uhm, sure." Sam knew it was possible to gain weight quickly. Actors sometimes did for roles. He'd also known a few sad cases who succumbed to the sedentary life after a bad accident. That didn't explain how Tuck had lost his acne, was in the process of losing his hair, and looked to be closing in on thirty years of age. "I don't know about eternity," Sam said. "But tell me, how long has it been since Vaisey learned the error of his ways?"

Tuck cast Sam a peculiar look. "Why, it must be five years

since you livened up the castle. No, six. But I fear your success with Vaisey was less than complete. He merely moved on to other modes of villainy. Why, just last week . . .”

But Sam wasn't listening. Six years? For him it had been six months. No wonder Effie looked more . . . elegant. And Le Fay the bitter crone.

"The Merlin!” Sam blurted out. "Can you tell me where he is?”

The Friar ceased describing whatever he had been talking about. "The Merlin? Well, that is the hundred Pendragon question is it not?”

"What about Merlin?” Sam asked.

Again the peculiar look. "Is that not why you are here?”

"I don't know. You tell me. Anything. Just tell me something.”

Tuck scratched his thinning hair. "The Merlin is missing?”

"I take it that's not a question,” Sam said. "You're telling me the old coot has gone AWOL and no one knows where he is.”

The friar's face split into a grin. "It sounds as if you have no need for me to tell you anything.”

"Pretend that I know nothing,” Sam said. "And you won't be far off.”

Tuck nodded slowly. "Very well. The Merlin vanished three days ago without leaving word. Not a problem in and of itself, were it not that the King fell ill around the same time.”

"The King?” Sam asked. "King Arthur?”

"There is only one king,” Tuck said.

"I'm going to need to talk to Effie,” Sam said.

Tuck looked at him. "Who?”

"Lady Euphemia Peregrine.”

"Ah!” The friar's eyes lit up. "The Merlin's clerk. Of course. She is a brilliant woman and works with the Merlin. She may indeed possess clues for you.”

A thought occurred to Sam. "While I've been away, the Lady Peregrine hasn't gotten . . . married, has she?”

"A most curious question,” Tuck answered. "One would think a woman of the Lady Peregrine's age, grace, and rank would have married long ago, yet she claims her work keeps her too busy to contemplate marriage. And now, of course, there is her father.”

"Her father the duke? What about him?”

"Ill, I fear. The Lady Peregrine has been nursing his bedside for well above a year.”

"So you think she may be at her father's mansion?"

"My good friend, you should know that the Lady spends every waking moment by her father's side. When she is not at her desk, of course. Oh!" The friar's eyes widened as though remembering something. "I suggest you avoid seeking the Lady at her office. That woman she works for, Vivian du Lac, is a most intolerable woman. You would be wise to avoid her. Why, she has already demanded that the Merlin's name be removed from the office sign!"

4

KNIGHTS AT THE GATE

THE CASTLE CORRIDORS were cold and drafty, but comfortably familiar with Sam's memory. Despite Friar Tuck's pronouncement, the shingle as he passed his closed once-office door still read *Merlin & Vivian Investigations*. Maybe the poorly dressed man who had been so quick with the new signs six years ago had retired. Or simply knew to keep his distance from this Vivian character that Tuck seemed so afraid of. Merlin sure knew how to pick 'em. First a skirt-chasing knight then an intolerable woman everyone feared.

Vivian. The only Vivian Sam knew was Vivian Rutledge, Philip Marlowe's love interest from *The Big Sleep*. But that Vivian was a sweetheart. And a fictional character. As was the entire cast of Camelot, Sam supposed, though he remembered hearing somewhere that the King Arthur myth supposedly had roots in a real British leader who had fended off an Anglo-Saxon invasion. Bottom line was that it didn't matter. The Lady of the Lake had promised to return him to Hartford in time to save Nora. He just needed to fix some vague crisis first.

Sam found the stairwell where he expected it as well as the Necessarium in its familiar place on the main level of the castle. He wasn't desperate enough to venture inside, so he continued along the corridor. Near the castle entrance he ducked his head into the page pen, purely out of habit, but saw no sign of Robin

189

or Vaisey or any other page he might recognize. Of course, the boys would no longer be boys. Six years had passed, not six months.

The two knights guarding the gate, however, did seem familiar. It was certain they recognized Sam; both their faces twisted in anger and the dark-haired one drew his sword.

"How did you get in here?" the armed knight demanded. Gawain. That was his name. And the one with curly blond hair and big ears was Caradoc. Both looked to have put on some muscle since he'd last seen them, and Caradoc looked less like a half-wit and more like a professional boxer. The two knights stalked toward him across the wide stone floor.

Sam knew potential ugly when he saw it, and the next few moments could definitely get ugly. Making a show of it, he palmed his American Silver Eagle dollar coin and snapped his fingers, making the coin appear as if out of thin air. Since his first visit to Camelot, he'd been practicing his sleight of hand. Caradoc stopped dead, but Gawain advanced the last few steps and stuck the tip of his sword into the skin under Sam's chin.

"Your tricks scare me little," Gawain said. Then he grinned. "There is no Merlin around this time to protect you."

"As I recall," Sam said, doing his best to ignore the blood trickling down his throat, "there was no Merlin around last time, either. I was his replacement. If you don't remove this sword right now, I'll be forced to do something that you'll regret later."

Sam watched as fear and indecision chased each other across the knight's face. Was it a bluff? Could he take the risk? Did Gawain even notice that Sam had his right hand inside his trench coat pocket and was clutching something more dangerous than a Pendragon?

Of course, Sam's circumstance was no better. He had no idea how the castle would react if he plugged the knight. And for all he knew, some of the new muscle beneath that heavy linen coat could be plate armour; a simple ricochet and Sam could plug himself. Gawain looked the type who preferred to ask forgiveness rather than permission. A simple push with his blade and Sam might not have time to pull the trigger. These things look so easy in the movies; why did real life have to be so gummed up?

The stalemate lasted until Caradoc said, "Sir Gawain, mayhap we should let the pie be. Even should the Merlin not return, there may be others who will stand for this man's honour."

Gawain withdrew his blade and thrust it into his scabbard. "Perhaps now is not the time," he sneered at Sam. "But I would watch my back were I you, especially between the shoulders."

Sam slid his semi-automatic back into its holster and pulled out a handkerchief to dab the blood at his throat. "So what's the deal, guys? While people do tend not to like me at first glance, it usually takes a while before they want to kill me."

"He does not even remember," Gawain said, pulling his sword halfway back out of his scabbard.

Caradoc, too, pulled his sword a little way, his big-eared face darkening like thunder. "We would be Knights of the Table long ere now, but for you."

"Six years," Gawain said. "Six years guarding the gate, the meanest task in the castle, because of you."

"Me?" Sam stuffed the handkerchief back into his pocket. "How do you figure that?"

"The stones, man!" said Gawain. "You reported us to Sir Percival for playing stones on duty!"

"Oh, yeah, that was you guys. But it can't be that. There must be other reasons your careers haven't advanced."

"We have been made examples," said Caradoc. "With Sir Lancelot murdered and Sir Sagramore jailed, the King felt we knights were not taking our roles seriously enough."

Gawain snorted. "The King adopted something the Merlin calls a zero-tolerance policy. The rules have been made strict, the penalties severe, and we, the examples, pointed out to other knights so that they might *toe the line*. I believe that is what the Merlin called it."

"Sounds like a royal pain," Sam said. "Listen, I'd love to chat with you about it, but I'm in kind of a hurry." With that he tipped his fedora and stepped quickly beneath the raised portcullis, across the drawbridge, and out into the great city that had grown up around Camelot Castle.

While the knights' story was an all too familiar one, there was nothing Sam could do about it. And he had bigger fish to fry. That Merlin. What a tough old bird.

A half-dozen carriages stood outside the gate. Two drivers

leaned against an enclosed carriage smoking pipes and chatting. The others kicked back in their seats. One appeared to be sleeping. Sam peered up at the sun and figured it must be early afternoon. He went to the first driver in the queue, a waspish man in a black coat with sleeves an inch too short and wearing a bowler hat two sizes too small.

"Take me to the Duke of Earl's place," Sam said as he stepped onto the footplate to climb up into the carriage.

The driver blocked his way and put out his palm.

"Right," Sam said. "Two pennies."

The man snorted. "The Duke's estate is all the way outside the city. The price is four."

Sam couldn't help but laugh. "Inflation is everywhere. Even in Camelot."

The man frowned in confusion but didn't move his hand.

Sam reached into his pocket and found three coins: his American Silver Eagle dollar and the two Pendragons that had been on his desk in Hartford. He palmed a Pendragon and then pulled it from behind the driver's ear. "I don't suppose you have change?"

Greed filled the man's eyes. "For a Pendragon I can take you to the Duke's estate and back."

"I don't think so," Sam said. "For a Pendragon, you can take me to London and back."

"Do you wish to go to London?"

Sam laughed. "I'll get your four pennies from the Duke."

"When pigs fly," responded the man.

"I've never been fond of pork," Sam said. "Or highway robbery." Raising his voice so that all the drivers could hear, he said, "I need to see the Duke of Earl. There's five pennies in it for whoever takes me."

Despite the established tradition of carriages queuing up for the next passenger, all of the drivers rushed toward Sam clamouring for attention.

"The thing is," he added, shouting even louder. "I need change for a Pendragon. Either that, or you get paid when we get there."

The clamour went silent. Sam remembered from his last visit that neither change nor credit and been invented yet. Apparently not in the past six years either.

"Six pennies," he said. "And that's my final offer."

For all the attention the drivers gave him, Sam no longer existed.

He made one last effort, searching faces for the driver he had paid a Pendragon to six months or six years earlier, but it could have been any or none of them. He hated to admit it, but there was some truth to the adage that all taxi drivers looked alike.

There was no way he could walk to the Duke's; even if he could find his way to Effie's father's estate outside the city, walking might take hours. There was no hope but to find someone in the castle who could provide change or, failing that, a loan. Maybe Friar Tuck. The friar no longer appeared penniless and he did owe Sam a favour.

5

THE REAL GALAHAD

"Who goes there?" Sir Gawain demanded at the gate.

"Me," Sam said. "We were chatting five minutes ago."

"I do not recognize you," said Caradoc. "Show us your papers."

"You saw me five minutes ago," Sam said. "I need to get back into the castle."

"No papers, no entrance," Gawain said. A pleased smile creased his lips.

"I'm the Merlin's pie. Suffer the Merlin's wrath if you get in my way."

Caradoc snorted. "Our orders are to allow entry to no one without proper papers. Are you asking us to abandon our orders?"

Sam sighed. "Okay, who can get me proper papers?"

"That would be the magistrate," said Caradoc.

"Terrific. He and I are thick as thieves. Let me pass and I'll go see him."

Gawain sniffed. "The magistrate is busy. Come back later."

"Am I going to have to shoot you anyway?" Sam asked.

The two knights passed each other quizzical looks.

"Look," Sam said. "I don't have time for this. Lives are at stake."

"Whose?" Gawain asked.

"That's a good question. I'm trying to find out."

The two knights just stared at him.

"Fine," Sam said. "Who's in charge of the knights these days?"

"That would be Sir Bors," said Caradoc. "But, ah, the First Knight has not been seen in a while."

"The Second Knight is in charge during his absence," Gawain said.

"How about I have a little chat with him and get you guys a better job?"

"You can do that?" asked Gawain.

I have no idea, Sam told himself. "Most certainly," he said aloud.

The two knights then engaged in an animated, whispered conversation that went on for several minutes.

"If you already have the worst job," Sam threw in, "you can't very well get demoted to a worse one should things go sideways."

That seemed to tip the scale.

"We shall let you enter the castle under the condition that you promise to use your influence to get us both positions at the Round Table," Caradoc said.

"And," added Gawain, "that you deny having left and re-entered the castle. We never saw you."

"I can do that," Sam said. That he referred to Gawain's demand and not Caradoc's, he didn't bother mentioning. He strolled past the knights before they could change their minds.

"You will find the Second Knight in the courtyard," Caradoc called at his back.

"Thanks for the tip."

"The courtyard is straight on through the passage," Gawain added.

"I've been here before," Sam said. The last time he was here that particular passage had been littered with hay and horse berries. It occurred to him that there *was* a job worse than guarding the gate, though maybe it was beneath the dignity of knights.

"Watch the horse berries," Caradoc called after him. "Track them through the castle and the magistrate will have you cleaning the floor stones with your tongue."

But not beneath the dignity of the Merlin's pie, it seemed.

Sam followed the trail of manure through the castle until the horse passage opened up into a grassy yard. Horses nickered from rows of stalls along the nearer walls and a team of young boys mucked out piles of hay. A clang of steel rang through the courtyard, two young knights whacking at each other with swords while a dozen equally young knights shouted encouragement and waved their fists in the air. Most cheered on a flamboyant knight with black hair and the symbol of three gold crowns against a blood-red field on his tabard. His opponent, a blond youth with a white unicorn on a blue background, seemed to be doing all he could just to defend against the blows. His two or three supporters wagged their heads as though the fight were already lost.

"Relent!" the black-haired knight shouted as he rained down blow after blow that pushed the blond down to one knee. "Submit and be done with it!"

There was something about the knight's voice that sounded familiar.

Instead of submitting, the blond gritted his teeth and returned with a sweep of his blade, cutting up under the other youth's sword and knocking it away. He then pressed forward with five quick blows, pushing the black-haired knight several steps backward. The blond's supporters shouted with renewed energy, as did the other spectators. Several additional youths from other parts of the courtyard gathered round to watch.

Sam knew nothing about swords. While the onlookers focused their attention on the blade work, Sam watched the legs and feet. The youths moved much like boxers or street fighters. He wasn't surprised when the black-haired knight moved his torso backward, but stepped forward with one foot, placing it purposefully to trip his opponent.

The blond let out a cry as he stumbled and fell, his sword swing missing its mark completely. His supporters let out a disparaging cry and then fell silent as the black-haired knight followed through with a powerful slice to the blond's arm, sending the other's blade flying.

"Vaisey's done it again!" shouted one of the crowd, confirming Sam's suspicion that the dark knight was none other than the same Page Vaisey who had tormented Friar Tuck and later, when Sam intervened, hired a bunch of thugs to put a beat on him. Now knowing who he was, Sam was not surprised when Vaisey continued to beat at his unarmed opponent, striking his shoulder and back as the blond crumpled to the ground.

"Yield! Yield!" shouted the blond, not that he should have had to. He'd already lost his sword.

A powerful voice shouted, "Enough!" and Vaisey finally relented.

An older knight with grey in his beard strode in among the crowd and, using his own weapon, knocked Vaisey's sword out of his hand. "You may have been King of the Pages, Squire Vaisey, but now you are in my domain. You will not beat a man when he is down."

"I called on Will to relent!" Vaisey shouted. "He refused. What was I to do?"

The older knight levelled his sword with the point under Vaisey's chin, just as Gawain had done to Sam at the gate. "You threaten," the older knight rumbled. "You do not murder. Had these practice swords been real, Squire Scathlocke would be dead or at best crippled for life. You behave as a highwayman instead of a knight."

Practice swords. That explained why the courtyard wasn't knee-deep in blood.

"Will should respect his betters," Vaisey muttered. "He should have yielded."

The older knight pulled away his blade, then turned it suddenly and whacked Vaisey on the shoulder with its flat. "*Squire* Scathlocke is the son of an earl. While you are the bastard of a baron. You have much to learn about respecting your betters. Perhaps cleaning the horse passage will remind you. Go trade that sword for a broom."

Vaisey rubbed his shoulder and stared at the knight. "I am a knight! Knights do not sweep manure."

"You are a squire," the older knight said. "Only five years into your training. It will be two years before you become a knight. *If* you become a knight. You will require my good recommendation before that happens. Now do as I say."

Vaisey spat onto the grass and stalked away, ignoring the looks from his audience.

The older knight sheathed his sword and lowered a hand to help the blond youth up.

"You have done Squire Scathlocke no favours, Sir Ector," a second knight said. "Vaisey will blame young Will for today's embarrassment."

Sam looked critically at this new knight and recognized him despite the passage of six years. Galahad.

Sir Galahad the Gallant continued speaking. "Were you wise you would expel Vaisey of Nottingham with an order never to return to Camelot."

The older knight, Sir Ector, wagged his head. "We cannot expel every squire who displays arrogance or bad judgment. None would be left to us but the Locksley boy. Camelot needs knights, Sir Galahad, especially with the King ill. I am only surprised that our enemies are not already on our doorstep."

Galahad sighed as Ector led the injured blond away.

Sam remembered the unassuming knight as a kind and reasonable man, even if it had been Merlin in disguise. Sam was sure that he could count on the real Galahad as a friend inside the castle. "Sir Galahad, could I speak with you a moment?"

The gallant knight looked at Sam curiously, taking in his tan pants, tan trench coat, and tan fedora. "Who might you be?"

Sam stuck out his hand. "Sam Spade, at your service. I think you were out of town the last time I was here. Looking for a certain yellow cup?"

Galahad looked at Sam's hand just as curiously. "The Merlin spoke of you." His lips split in a grin. "Turned the castle upside-down, I understand. Why are you here?"

"That's a good question," Sam said. "If the Lady of the Lake were here, she could answer it. Unfortunately, she isn't, so I'm trying to solve that one myself."

"I see," Galahad said, which was more than Sam could say. "What is it you wish of me?"

"Well," Sam said, "I was going to ask if you could break a Pendragon, but maybe I should be asking what you know about Merlin's disappearance."

Galahad's eyes went wide. "You suspect I have something to do with the magician's absence?"

"Not at all," Sam said. "I'm just trying to get a feel for the circumstances. What was he up to before he left? Was anything else going on at the time? Do you know of anyone who had a beef with the magician? That sort of thing."

The knight shook his head. "I have already asked myself these questions. I have also spoken with Lady Vivian du Lac, who is looking into the Merlin's disappearance. It is as though he put on his cap and vanished. If you seek more information, I suggest you speak with Lady Vivian. She works from the Merlin's office."

"I've been there," Sam said. "The Lady was out. So I guess I am asking if you can make change."

"Change?"

6

THE LOCKSLEY BOY

WHO KNEW THAT asking for change in Camelot was a grave insult? It wasn't like Sam was panhandling, asking for a handout. He just needed someone to break a Pendragon. Galahad had acted like Sam was trying to ask out his ten-year-old sister. The knight's eyes had grown three sizes, his cheeks turned purple, and his teeth ground together so hard Sam feared they might break. Then Galahad had stalked off.

So it was back to plan A, asking Friar Tuck for change. Or a loan. Sam had reached the entrance to the horse passage when he heard a voice.

"Mr. Spade? That is you, is it not?"

Sam turned to see a young knight, sandy-haired and somewhat dashing in appearance. He wore a yellow shirt with diagonal green splotches that might be treetops seen from above. If Picasso had painted shirts, it would be hanging in a museum somewhere. In addition to a sword at his hip, the young man carried a bow in his hand and a quiver of arrows on his back. Even without seeing up close, Sam could tell that none of the arrows had tips, but ended in a flat nub.

"I was hoping we would meet again," the youth said. "You changed my life. Back when I served as a page."

"Robin?" Sam recognized the strong shape of the jaw and brightness of the eyes. This was the same small boy who had been

201

his only friend among the pages. "You've filled out well."

The youth blushed. "We receive better exercise with squire training than we did as pages. We even get to climb walls and jump rooftop to rooftop."

"Sure. I can see how those skills would be useful, for a squire."

Robin blushed even further. "I have also been learning the bow. Most of the knights believe it an inferior weapon to the sword, fit only for hired mercenaries. What do you think?"

"Me?" Sam knew nothing about swords and even less about bows and arrows. But he'd seen enough Disney movies. "I think you should stick with it. You'll make a name for yourself."

The youth grinned. Then he motioned Sam to one side. "I saw you speaking with Sir Galahad. Are you here to find the Merlin?"

"Yes," Sam said. "At least, I think so."

Robin nodded. "I overheard Sir Galahad suggest that you speak with Lady Vivian. I fear that is not a good idea."

"Oh? Why not? Isn't she the castle's current royal investigator?"

"True." Robin nodded. "But she is not what she seems."

"Okay."

"For one thing, she is not old enough to be Mordred's mother."

"Mordred? You mean that silly foreign knight Galahad—or I should say Merlin—threw into the dungeon after the chicken caper?"

Again, Robin nodded. "There is somewhat amiss with those two. Sir Sagramore would know more. You should speak with him."

"Wasn't Saggy also sent to the hoosegow?"

"Exactly. You shall find Sir Sagramore in the dungeon beneath the castle. Oh, here comes Mordred. Follow my lead."

"Mord—"

"Shush." In a louder voice Robin said, "Oh yes, even leather armour is no defence against a well shot arrow."

A snide voice intruded. "Yer not still sellin' that ba and arra malarkey, are ya, Locksley? Spade. I thought that was ya."

Sam turned to see a man several years older than Robin,

dressed in black and gripping the hilt of his sword. A receding hairline and a missing jaw sandwiched a pair of cruel, cold eyes, while a two-headed bird preened on his tabard. Six years hadn't done Mordred any favours. He was still a monkey.

Sam put on his best smile. "That's right, sunshine. I'm back. Who let you out of the can?"

Mordred grinned and shook his head. "Guards! 'rrest this gezza."

Robin stepped between them. "On what charge?"

Mordred placed a finger on Robin's Picasso shirt and pushed the youth away. "'e besmirched me good name."

"By calling you *sunshine*?" Sam demanded. "That means someone with a sunny disposition."

"It'll do fer na," Mordred said. "I'll fin' me up sum additional charges later."

Two middle-aged knights, with what Sam assumed were real swords, grabbed him, one at each arm. The one on the left was bald and sported a coiled snake on his tabard. The other was something of a giant with shaggy red hair. His coat sported what looked to Sam like a radish.

"Thra 'im in the bloomin' dungeon," Mordred snarled.

Sam looked to Robin. "Can he do this?"

The page-come-squire slumped his shoulders. "Sir Mordred is the Second Knight."

Sam let out a heavy breath. "Oh, that's just great."

7

TWO BIRDS IN A CAGE

SAM HAD MISSED visiting the dungeon during his first visit. All things considered, he wouldn't have minded missing it this visit as well. It wasn't just below ground; it was below moat.

"Mind the steps," baldy said. "It would be a shame indeed, should you slip and crack your skull."

The giant laughed. "Mordred prefers to do the head crackin' 'imself."

"Tell me," Sam said. "Are you guys married?"

"What business is it of yours?" asked the giant.

"Just curious. You got wives? Kids?"

"What if we do?" Baldy glared at him.

"I imagine you've got good insurance, then. In case anything happens to you."

Baldy tightened his grip on Sam's arm. "In sure what?"

"You know," Sam said. "Will your families starve if you accidentally die?"

The giant pushed him forward. "It is you goin' to the dungeon, not us."

"Humour me," Sam said.

The bottom of the stone staircase, like the last several steps, was slick with water and slippery mould. Sam's gumshoes would have felt at home here, but the Lady of the Lake hadn't sent them along with his coat and hat. She must have missed foreseeing the bit where Sam would find himself escorted to the dungeon. The two guards wore heavy boots with thick soles, but even they were having as much trouble keeping their feet from slipping as Sam with his Thorogood Oxford dress shoes.

Sam couldn't help but smile. It would be child's play to stumble and fall, draw his bean-shooter, and introduce these two to the concept of bullets. If Robin thought bows and arrows were swell, wait 'til he discovered guns and bullets. The only thing stopping Sam was the question of going to war with Camelot. Things could easily escalate out of control and innocent people could get hurt. That, and these two were only doing their job, even if they did enjoy the job too much.

"You got a presidential suite down here?" Sam asked. "Something with a hot tub and a nice view of the city?"

"Quit your jabberin'," said the giant.

The basement corridor was dark and stank like a sewer. A single torch burned in a holder on the wall and a dim light in the distance suggested a second torch. Sam's escorts pushed him along the slimy stones until shadows in the wall resolved into vertical bars.

Sam had seen enough police station holding cells to know that Camelot's dungeon wouldn't rate half a star. The place was the Fawlty Towers of incarceration. Within each dank cell sat or stood a prisoner. All men from what Sam could see. Each wore filthy creased clothing and was in dire need of a shave and bath. Some looked like they'd been there awhile. Then he remembered that Saggy was down here somewhere and that Robin had suggested he speak to the disgraced knight.

"All right," Sam said. "You got me. Just don't put me in with that knight-murdering whoreson, Sir Sagramore. You do know he murdered Sir Lancelot? Stabbed him without warning. Right in the gut. You put me near that guy and I'll make your lives miserable. You hear me?"

Baldy twisted his arm. "Do you not ever shut up?"

"We should put 'im in with Sagramore," said the giant. "Serve 'im right."

"And if Sagramore kills him?" baldy asked.

"Then we put 'im next to Sagramore. Someone gets strangled through the bars, no one can blame us."

Sam made a show of struggling. "You pugs will regret this.

I'll complain to the union. That's what I'll do. They'll send you a nasty letter. Signed even. The words will be terse. Terse, do you hear me!"

A cell door opened and Sam allowed himself to be pushed inside. The metal clanged when the door swung shut, and Sam heard rust break free in the lock when baldy turned the key.

Laughter began before the guards even walked away. It came from the next cell, where a great hairy ape lay on a wooden frame built into the back wall of the cell. After the laughter trailed off, a voice croaked from behind all that hair. "I expected to see you down here long ere now. Figured you for dead when you failed to make an appearance. Been keeping your nose clean?"

Sam returned the good cheer with a chuckle of his own. "How ya been, Saggy? You miss me?"

The heap of hair grunted. "Oddly, no. Life has been much quieter without you around causing trouble."

"Yeah, I've heard that line often enough. Listen, Saggy, I came down here to see you for a reason."

"What? You came to see me?" The disgraced knight let out a heavy snort. "Looks to me that you came here not by choice."

Sam pulled out his tobacco kit and rolled a cigarette as he spoke. "Looks can be deceiving. There's trouble upstairs and I need to know what's up with that Mordred character."

"Mordred!" Saggy almost spit the word. "The weasel dares call himself a knight. He is a son of the gutter if ever there was one. No family name. Never properly knighted. That rodent tarnishes our entire class. I almost slit my own throat having to share a dungeon with him. When they hauled him out of here we celebrated." A pause. "You cannot mean Mordred still lives? Did they not hang him from the gibbet?"

"Actually, they gave him your old job."

Silence.

"You still there, Saggy?"

"Mordred is the Second Knight?"

"That's what Robin said when Mordred had those stooges bring me down here."

"And what did you do to deserve such honour?"

"I called Mordred a smiling jailbird."

"Who is Robin?"

"Page Robin, now Squire Robin."

"Ah, yes, your strange wont of learning pages' names."

"Robin said I should ask you about Mordred."

"Me?" grunted Sagramore. "Why?"

"Beats me. Because you spent some time together, maybe. What did he tell you that might be important?"

"Mordred said nothing of import. I bore six years of his yammering, of how his corpulent chicken rancher master had forsaken him and how he was going to murder several people when he escaped this prison, most notably the rancher and yourself. And the fair lady you were working for, Morgan Le Fay."

"I don't know about the chicken rancher," Sam said, "but I saw Le Fay earlier today, very much alive."

Sam took a pull on his cigarette as he watched Saggy shift himself on his cot and stare through the bars. "The rancher was hanged mere days after his arrest," the filthy knight said. "I was told the gibbet broke on the first attempt and a new, sturdier gallows was constructed. The fat man went into his good night. That fact in no way dissuaded Mordred from claiming he would still murder him."

Sam knew the type and figured the fat man's monkey was a good match. "When did Mordred leave the dungeon?"

Sagramore snorted. "A week ago? I lose track of days down here, though it pleases the guards to count for me the years."

Sam breathed out a smoke ring as he rubbed his ear. "So let me get this straight. A few days ago, someone let Mordred out of prison after six years and now he's Second Knight. Around the same time, Merlin goes missing and Arthur falls ill."

Saggy leapt to his feet and clutched at the bars; a great hairy ape in a cage. "The King is ill? And the Merlin is missing?"

"I've been back in Camelot maybe an hour," Sam said. "But that's what I've learned so far."

"It cannot all be coincidence," Sagramore suggested.

Sam laughed. "I don't believe in coincidence."

"There is one thing," Saggy said. "It may be nought. When the guards unlocked his cell, Mordred asked why. The guards replied that his mother wished to see him."

"His mother?"

Saggy laughed. "That is what Mordred said. He behaved as if he had never had a mother. But as I said, it may mean nought." The hairy knight shook his head. "I wish there was ought more I could tell you. I fear that whatever darkness has befallen Camelot, this is but the beginning."

"Well," Sam said, "if that's all you've got then I need to get going. This crisis isn't going to fix itself."

"Get going?" Saggy's fingers tightened around the bars. "You are in the dungeon, my friend. There is nowhere to go."

Sam reached into a pocket of his suit jacket and pulled out a narrow case. "Something I noticed the last time I was in Camelot. You people never search anyone or confiscate their possessions."

The knight shrugged. "Your possessions are your own. And you are unarmed. Had you a sword, they would have taken it; but I have never seen you with a sword."

"And you never will. Swords are not my thing. Hold on to this, will ya?"

Sam passed Saggy his cigarette then opened the case and took out the two largest picks. Flakes of rust rained down onto the wet stones as he worked them in the cell door's lock.

"Is that a key?" Saggy asked.

"Only if you know how to use it," Sam said. The lock turned and he added, "I had an excellent teacher. I hope I can repay her by getting back to Hartford before she's murdered."

"You lead a most interesting life," Saggy said.

Sam put away his picks then gave the door a push; it creaked like a drunken vulture as it swung open.

"Ah," said Saggy. "Perhaps you could . . ."

"I'd love to help," Sam said, "but you're in for murder. I haven't committed a crime, but if I set you free that would no longer be true."

"I understand," said Saggy. "Should you need someone to help you take down that weasel, Mordred, or be there ought I can do to help the King, you know where to find me."

"Well, since you mention it, there is one thing. Do you have cab fare you could loan me?"

8

AS GOOD AS CASH

SAGGY HADN'T A penny, of course; six years of sitting in a sewer did that to a fella. Sam felt bad for him and left him the cigarette. It was the least he could do.

Finding his way out of the dungeon and up the stairs was easier than it should have been. Sam thought he might have to coldcock someone or do some fast-talking, but other than the prisoners, the place was deserted. Then again, he could understand why none of the guards stuck around down below. Between the water, the slime, and the rats, the place had nothing to recommend it. Now that he was above ground, he'd have to be careful. A second run-in with Mordred might not end as happily as the first.

In a perfect world Sam would have gone back to the castle courtyard. He'd once paid Robin a Pendragon retainer for services not yet rendered. If anyone could spot him a dozen pennies it was the page-come-squire. But if Mordred was still there, the upstart monkey would slap him in stronger irons a second time around. Or maybe he'd just use that sword of his. Instead, Sam made his way upstairs to the office of Friar Tuck, Royal Herbalist.

"You are back already?" Tuck asked, incredulous. "How can you be back already? You have scarce had time to ride out to Lady Peregrine's estate."

211

"I ran into a snag." Sam tossed a Pendragon onto the friar's crowded counter. "You don't happen to have change, do you?"

Tuck sighed. "I dream of having change for a Pendragon. The abbot would never let me see that much coin. Perhaps if I accompany you to St. Stephen's Abbey, I could convince Abbot Gildas to exchange coins for you. For a small donation, you understand."

The last thing Sam wanted was to walk to the abbey. From what he remembered the friar telling him, it was almost as far as Effie's father's estate.

"Maybe you could loan me four pennies instead," Sam said, retrieving the silver coin. "Effie knows how to break a Pendragon. She offered to do it before."

The friar cast him a look that suggested he'd rather swallow glass. "The abbot would hang me from the highest bell tower should he find a single penny missing, even for a day." Then his round face brightened. "But I have something better than pennies." Retrieving a small jar from below the counter, Tuck took a square of paper from a small stack and measured out a quantity of a dull, grey-green powder. "Offer this to the driver," he said, folding the paper. "It is *Papaver somniferum*. Five pennies' worth. If he refuses, try the next driver. Most will not refuse."

Sam rubbed his ear. "It's a drug?"

Tuck averted his eyes. "A medicinal herb. Purely recreational. The latest thing. Very popular among the working classes. One of the few they can afford."

"I don't know," Sam said. "I've never pictured myself as a drug dealer."

"If you paid in pennies, they would just buy *Papaver* anyway."

"From you?"

The friar's eyes popped out, just like Wile E. Coyote's when the Road Runner gets the drop on him. "Of course not! I am no drug dealer."

"Then why do you have it?"

"Ahhh, there are certain dwellers in the castle who find edification in emulating the common folk. As a game, you understand. In private. Their game does not extend to purchasing clothing or . . . props . . . from common merchants."

"I see." Sam accepted the packet of powder and tucked it into his pants pocket. He wasn't comfortable with the setup, but what choice did he have? "So what do you know about that foreign mook getting out of the dungeon and being made Second among the knights?"

"You mean Mordred?" Tuck rolled his eyes. "The scoundrel is Lady Vivian's son. I am unsure which is worse, the mother or her get. You will steer clear of both if you know what is good for you."

"Vivian again," Sam said. "I'm going to have to meet this woman."

Tuck stared at him. "If you do, you may wish to be careful what you say?"

"What's that supposed to mean?"

"The woman takes offence easily. And she responds poorly to offence."

"As does her son," Sam said.

The friar smiled. "You have the truth of it."

Another question occurred to Sam. "Look, who's in charge around here anyway? Merlin's gone. The King is ill. Surely there's someone in charge who can deal with things."

Tuck lost his smile. "Sir Bors. But the First Knight has either been ensconced with the King since Arthur fell ill or has gone missing. That leaves Sir Pelleas, the Second Knight before Mordred. The first thing Vivian du Lac did after the Merlin vanished was to banish Pelleas and appoint Mordred in his stead. Officially, Mordred is in charge. But I think he does not so much as comb his moustache without Lady Vivian's blessing."

"And what makes this Vivian so special that anyone cares what she says?"

"Why, she is an enchantress. As powerful as the Merlin. Perhaps more." Tuck leaned in close. "Some whisper that Lady Vivian disposed of the Merlin, even though she was his protégé and then his partner."

That was news. Sam shook his head. "I don't see how I'm going to do any good until I meet this Vivian and take her measure. So my first plan was the right one. Talk to Effie and get the scoop on her boss."

"Effie?"

"Lady Peregrine."

"Ah yes. Lady Peregrine can give you better guidance than I."

Sam thanked Tuck for his advice and the drugs and stepped out into the corridor.

"Sam!"

There, almost walking into him, was Lady Euphemia Peregrine.

"You cannot be here!" Effie said, grabbing his hand and then dragging him down the corridor.

"It's good to see you, too," Sam said, but he didn't mind being pulled along. He thought Effie might take him to some quiet corner of the castle, a linen closet or a shop that had gone out of business. Instead, she took him down the stairs, along the corridor to the castle entrance, past a glowering Gawain and cheerless Caradoc, under the portcullis, across the drawbridge, and into the street. They moved past the queue of carriages almost at a run, and turned left on the first street outside the castle proper.

"Where—" he began, but Effie shushed him. "No talking."

A right turn was followed by a left, then another right and another, and Sam expected to wind up back where they had started. Instead he found himself lost, unable to see the castle above the rooftops.

Effie led him to a building that had few windows and no sign, paused to look over her shoulder, then dragged him inside.

9
WHAT AILS THE KING

THE BUILDING, AS far as Sam could tell, was some kind of warehouse that had seen better days. Dust an inch thick covered the floor while warped and cracked planks hung haphazardly across the lower windows. The only light came in through a few narrow gaps in the walls and three barren windows up near the ceiling. Sam assumed that no one could get in from so high up except maybe Squire Robin with his wall climbing and rooftop leaping training. Though what a burglar might steal was a mystery unless they were after dust. The place was empty. No furniture. No crates. Not even a *condemned building* notice, though the place deserved one.

"Okay," Effie said. "We can talk now."

"I was going to ask where we were going," Sam said, "but now I'll ask where we are."

Effie looked at him and laughed. "For a detective you are not very observant. We are in an empty building."

"Let me rephrase. Why we are. In an empty building, that is."

Effie leaned against one of the walls, which did wonders for her shoulders and hips. Add a cancer stick and she'd be a *Pleasure to Burn* poster for Camel Cigarettes.

While they had first met six months ago, six years had passed in Camelot. That would make the buxom blonde twenty-three years old instead of seventeen. Legal in any state and only eight years younger than Sam. Eight years was peanuts. Common even. What was unthinkable a short while ago now seemed like a good idea. All Sam needed was to pour on the charm. They'd already done the flirting thing, though he remembered Effie once denying it. But she would have been in the same boat, a girl newly grown into womanhood attracted to a man almost twice her age. She would have been confused, frightened even. But that was then. Now she'd brought him somewhere private. He smiled, wondering what the clever doll had in mind.

"Lady Vivian has spies everywhere," Effie said. "If she suspects I have said one word out of place, I will be bird food. Or is it fish food? I can never decide."

Not quite what Sam had hoped for. "You're afraid of your boss?"

A shudder ran through the tall blonde's body. "Everyone is afraid of my boss. You should be, too. If Vivian can vanquish the Merlin and the Second Knight, she can subjugate anyone."

"The Lady of the Lake thinks I can handle her."

"Who?"

"You know, the Lady who gave King Arthur his sword."

Effie arched a brow. "I thought a blacksmith gave the King his sword."

Sam blew air out through his teeth. "Try this, then. How about a tall, leggy albino dame who has a thing for white silk. Oh, and she lives in a lake."

"Did you hit your head or something?"

"You seriously don't know who she is? She has power. Like Merlin. She came to Hartford and sent me here, just like Merlin did six months ago."

"Months? It has been six years."

"For you," Sam said. "For me, I've only been away a few months."

Effie tilted her head. "You are a strange man, Mr. Spade. But you are no liar, so I must believe you. But tell me, if this Lady of the Lake is so powerful, why does she need you? Why does she not rescue the Merlin herself?"

"Because . . ." Sam rubbed his ear. Damn! Why does she need me? "To be honest, I'm not sure that's exactly why she sent me here. She just said that there was some kind of crisis."

Effie nodded. "That is a good word for it. The Merlin gone missing is just the beginning. Lady Vivian running things is much worse. And of course, there is the King."

"What about the King? Tuck said Arthur was ill."

"That may be too simplistic. The King has taken to his bed and barely eats or drinks. Since then there have been all manner of ill happenings. Locusts plague the crops. Calves are stillborn. Chickens have stopped laying eggs."

"No eggs?" Sam couldn't help but smile at that one.

"People have begun behaving oddly as well," Effie said. "Fighting, well, fighting more than usual. I am told the tax collectors are confiscating goods because the people have no coin."

"That reminds me," Sam said. He pulled one of his two Pendragons from his pocket. "Could you get this exchanged for smaller coins? I'm having difficulty paying for things."

Effie stared at the coin. "I . . . well . . . not today. Perhaps not tomorrow. Lady Vivian watches me like a hawk. Oh, I need to get back! I only stepped out to visit the Necessarium. I have to go." And then she was running.

"Wait!" Sam called. "I need you to get me back into the castle." But it was too late. Effie was gone.

Not the reunion Sam had hoped for, but maybe the timing was all wrong. He'd seen people afraid before. As a cop he'd seen more than his fair share of domestic violence. Effie showed all the signs, only the bully was her boss, not family. This Vivian must be some piece of work. It was unfortunate that he couldn't just arrest her, like in the bad old days when he worked for East Hartford PD.

Was Mordred's mother the crisis the Lady of the Lake had gone on about? Sam wasn't sure what he could do about someone more powerful than Merlin. Or was he the Lake Lady's Frodo, someone who might catch Vivian unaware because he's beneath her notice? He sure wished he knew what was going on.

As Sam stepped out from the dark building into the street, his eyes began to water. Was it the sun in his eyes? Or because Effie had called him *Mr. Spade*?

10
SQUIRE DANCE

RETRACING HIS STEPS to the castle was something even a novice detective could accomplish. Getting back *into* the castle was another matter.

"Who goes there?" Sir Caradoc demanded at the gate.

"It's me again," Sam said. "I'm half the traffic you've seen in the past hour."

"Show us your papers," said Gawain.

"Haven't we done this already? I need to get back into the castle."

"No papers, no entrance," said Caradoc. "Unless you have spoken with the Second Knight for us."

"As a matter of fact, I did have a conversation with Mordred." The fact that he knew the Second Knight's name seemed to lend some credibility to the claim.

"And?" asked Gawain.

"And we're still negotiating."

"Not good enough," Caradoc said. "How do we know you are not simply leading us by the nose?"

"I'm a man of my word," Sam said. "If I say I'm speaking with your boss, then I'm speaking with your boss. But I won't be able to continue speaking with him if you don't let me back into the castle."

"And what did Sir Mordred say, exactly?" Gawain demanded.

"My memory isn't what it used to be, but the gist of it is that he needs more time to think about it."

Gawain drew his sword. "Sir Mordred does not think about anything. If there is a man who lives more on the edge of his tongue, I have never met him."

Sam fingered his Smith and Wesson beneath his coat. No one was going to use his neck to measure the sharpness of a blade, not a second time. "Well, that's what Mordred said. He was pretty busy at the time throwing some fool into the dungeon."

"That does sound like Sir Mordred," Caradoc conceded. "But do not expect a kindness from us again unless we see some results."

Sam slipped past the pair without removing his finger from the trigger.

The next part would be even more dangerous. While on his way back to the castle, something Effie had said itched at the back of his brain. Not just Arthur was ill, but the entire land seemed under the weather. Sam was no King Arthur buff, but he remembered seeing a movie or TV show where King Arthur fell ill and the entire land fell ill with him. If he remembered right, that was when Merlin sent Galahad off to find the Holy Grail. Seems the sacred chalice could set things right again. Only Galahad already found the Grail six years ago when the magician sent him on a quest for a MacGuffin so the old coot could take the gallant knight's place. Whether Sam had the facts straight or not, his gut told him that he needed to speak with Galahad again. He'd have to risk the courtyard, after all.

As he ambled through the horse passage, Sam wasn't surprised to see someone other than Vaisey scooping up horse berries. What would surprise him is if he ever saw the deadbeat bullyboy doing an honest day's work.

Near the end of the passage Sam slowed and sidled up against one of the walls. Peering out into the courtyard, he saw several young knights still whacking at each other with dulled swords. The older knight, Sir Ector, had returned from wherever he had gone with the injured blond boy and was yelling at several of the students in turn. Sam failed to see Galahad, but who he was really looking for was Mordred. Well, looking out for. Despite his conversation with the gate guards, he had no interest in a second chat with Vivian's monkey boy.

The kicker was, if he had a penny he could send a page to collect Galahad for him. Being penniless was a phrase Sam had heard often enough on the streets of Hartford. He'd never appreciated it, though, not before coming to Camelot. It was really putting a cramp in his style.

With the coast more or less clear, Sam slipped around the corner and strolled nonchalantly to the nearest horse stall. A mottled brown warhorse glared down at him.

"I'm not here for a ride," he mumbled at it, hoping that would reduce the glare. It didn't. The next stall was empty, so he slipped into it and tried to hide himself in a shadow.

Out on the field, young knights in training continued to dance in pairs, silver blades gleaming in the sunlight. Sam had to admit there was a certain elegance to the back and forth, slash and parry. No armour or shields, just two men with swords. Not a field battle, but an encounter of two enemies. He assumed that in time the exercises would get more complex, with teams of knights warring against each other like the paintball wargames at the Connecticut Police Academy.

Something Sam had learned as a cop was that the most important aspect of fighting is attitude. The slightest hesitation in pulling the trigger could be all that stands between a commendation for bravery and a twenty-one-gun funeral. The second most important aspect is teamwork; that's where Sam's life as a Hartford cop had fallen down. The first partner Sam ever had who watched his back was Nora Clark, and now she was dead. Well, he'd fix that. All he had to do was solve the Lake Lady's crisis and get back home.

Sam was so caught up in his memories that he almost missed noticing Robin as the young man turned with his partner, trading blows. Unlike the desperate practice between Vaisey and the blond boy, these two experimented with different swings and parries, complementing each other when what they did succeeded.

Unfortunately, Vaisey's example was closer to the reality of fighting.

The dance continued as Sam waited for an opportunity to catch Robin's eye. Then Sir Ector shouted an order and everyone stopped what they were doing and moved toward the centre of the courtyard.

"Robin!" Sam hissed. "Robin!"

The youth turned and looked at him, then looked again. Then he split off from the others and joined him in the shadows inside the horse stall.

"How did you escape the dungeon?" Robin asked. "They will kill you if you are caught."

"I need to speak with Galahad," Sam told him.

Robin shook his head. "Galahad will skewer you as quick as any other."

"I'll deal with that problem when it comes up. Is Galahad still here in the practice yard?"

"Somewhere." Robin looked out into the mob of squires and knights that crowded around Sir Ector.

"Could you ask him to meet me at the Royal Herbalist's shop?"

Robin slammed his head around, his eyes wide as dollar coins. "That is next to Lady Vivian's office!"

"You're right. Not the best choice." Sam rubbed his ear. "How about *Pendragon Jewellers*? It's a quarter way around the castle."

"I can tell him," Robin said uncertainly.

"Maybe you shouldn't tell him who he's meeting. Just that it's important. And that he should come alone."

Robin laughed. "Someone wishes to meet you. Secluded place. Come alone. Would you go to such a meeting?"

"I always do. Tell him it concerns the King. That might help."

"Does it?" Robin asked. "Concern the King, I mean."

"Better that you don't know."

11

A MUCH-BELATED INTERVIEW

SAM HAD TO dance almost as well as the squires in order to slip away from the courtyard undetected. Everyone was still gathered around Sir Ector receiving chastisement or encouragement, whichever had been earned, but that meant a full quarter of them were looking in Sam's direction, if not so far. He managed to escape notice by moving slowly from shadow to shadow. That his *mean streets* getup was the same colour as many of the horses may have helped.

The youth cleaning the horse passage was still at it and didn't look to have accomplished much. Sam walked by with the nonchalant gait of someone who wasn't an escaped felon or belittler of knights or whatever Mordred ended up charging him with.

The same strategy got him past the page pen and gatehouse and up the stairs, where he turned in the opposite direction of his old office and made his way briskly along the deserted corridor that followed the curved wall of the castle until he came to *Pendragon Jewellers*. After a quick glance to ensure there was no one about, he slipped inside.

"You!"

Sam figured he was caught. Then he recognized the moustachioed man who had spoken. Six years had left Camelot's master gemmologist practically unchanged: black hair, slightly greying; tall face; small mouth; and a high forehead. If Sam was not mistaken, he even wore the same bright purple velvet robe with gold trim.

"You are the Merlin's private instigator, Sam Spade."

"Got it in one, Hammett." Sam looked around at the shelves of shiny rocks, bracelets, rings, and amulets that lined the room. If Thomas Hammett offered him ten pennies for one piece in the place that might not have been there six years ago, he still wouldn't have cab fare. Even the testosterone-guzzling bruiser who stood in one corner with tree stump arms folded across his chest looked to be the same security gorilla.

"How's business?" Sam asked.

"You," Hammett shouted, "owe me an interview!"

"Uh, yeah, sorry about that. Merlin was in a bit of a hurry to deport me from Camelot."

"Well, you are back now." Hammett's hand reached beneath the counter and came back clutching a fistful of paper sheets. "I have my notes!" he said. "Interviews with witnesses. I even spent a dozen evenings sitting in a chair in that filthy dungeon trying to get an honest word out of Sir Sagramore. The black knight told a different account of the tale every night!"

"Having visited Sir Saggy myself, I feel for you."

"These notes," Hammett said, shaking his fistful of papers, "contain nothing but absurdities and inconsistencies. Your chronicle is a joke!"

"I've often thought so," Sam said.

"Black widows!" Hammett cried. "Dead pirates! Maltese chickens!"

"I'm no writer," Sam said, "but you may want to consider taking some artistic license to smooth things out."

"Smooth things out?" The jeweller's eyes bulged like balloons reminiscent of Homer Simpson. "People want the truth," Hammett shouted. "Why would anyone want to hear a, a, a fiction?"

"It's up to you what you write," Sam said. "All I know is that in the *Barefoot Contessa*, Harry Dawes said that a script has to make sense, but life doesn't. I'm just the poor schmuck who has to live that life."

"Harry Dawes? Who in Hades is Harry Dawes?"

"A fictional character played by Humphrey Bogart. You'd like him."

"The character or the player?"

"Both."

"Well," said Hammett, shaking his head, "what you will have to live with for the next hour is you and I going through each of these notes and you telling me what did or did not happen, what is missing, and why any of it happened."

Sam smiled. "That's why I'm here. I came back for that interview first chance I got. Let's get down to it. Oh, but before we do, let's set the tone by you telling me everything you know about Merlin?"

"The Merlin?"

"Yes."

"Well." Hammett waved his papers in the air. "The magician is missing."

"Yes?"

More paper waving. "That is all. Missing."

"Okay, but any theories about what happened?"

"Happened? Not really. People woke one morning and the Merlin was gone."

Sam took a step toward the rattled jeweller. "I thought you wanted to be a chronicler?"

Hammett frowned. "Do you think I did not ask? No one knows anything."

"Okay. How about the King?"

"The King? King Arthur?"

"Yes."

Hammett began tightening his fist, crushing his papers. "The King is ill."

"Yes?"

"Uh. He fell ill shortly after breakfast."

"On the morning Merlin went missing," Sam suggested.

Hammett glowered at him. "If you already know this, why are you asking me?"

"I don't know anything," Sam said. "I guessed."

"Oh. Well, you guessed correctly."

"And then Lady Vivian canned Sir Pelleas and yanked her son Mordred out of the dungeon to take his place."

Hammett's brows rose. "Is this the same Mordred you put in the dungeon before you left?"

"You didn't know Mordred has been made Second Knight?"

"No one informed me that our new Second Knight came from the dungeon." Hammett uncrushed his stack of papers, leafed through it to find a particular page, and began writing furiously.

Sam growled in his throat. "How is it that I've hardly been here an hour, yet I know more than you do?"

"Because you are a detective," Hammett said. "And I am a jeweller."

"Touché."

"How about this?" Hammett pointed a pen dripping ink at the paper. "It says here that you threatened to kill Mordred and then beat him within an inch of his life."

"I'd say it's an exaggeration," Sam said. "I don't beat people. I hire muscle to do it for me."

Hammett resumed his furious scribbling.

Just then, the door swung open and Sir Galahad stalked into the room. Upon seeing Sam, the sturdy knight drew his sword.

12

A MEDIEVAL CONSPIRACY

"PUT UP YOUR sword and come along quietly," Sir Galahad said.

"I'd do that," Sam said, "if I had a sword."

"But he does have a—" Hammett began.

"Big heart," Sam finished, talking over the wannabe chronicler who Sam was certain was about to mention an anachronistic handgun. "Someone told me that once. Look, Galahad, I asked you here to prove my innocence."

"*You* asked me here?" The knight's sword wavered in his hand. Then he slid it back into his scabbard. "Of course, it was you who slipped Squire Robin that mysterious message; I have heard all about you."

"You have?" interrupted Hammett. "I must interview you for my chronicle."

"Not now," Sam said.

"In what way are you innocent?" Galahad demanded.

"What am I charged with?" Sam asked.

"Why, escaping the confines of the dungeon, of course."

"No," Sam said. "I mean, yes, that. But what was I charged with to put me in the dungeon in the first place?"

Galahad's face flushed red. "Some misdemeanour or other."

"I called Mordred *sunshine*."

"Even so." Galahad thrust out his chin. "The Second Knight sent you to the dungeon, so that is where you must be."

227

"I see," Sam said. "And if I called you *sunshine*, you would have me arrested and sent to the dungeon without even a word before the Magistrate?"

"Do not be absurd."

"And yet you support this Mordred character doing just that."

"He is Second Knight. I must support the position, if not the man."

"Mordred isn't even a real knight. Sir Saggy called him a hedge knight. To me he's just a monkey with a big knife."

"Now you are entering dangerous territory," Galahad said. "A man has a right of challenge for such insults."

"I'd be happy to duel Mordred," Sam said, "but he won't do it. I took his sword away from him six years ago and I could do it again."

Galahad turned his head. "You duelled Mordred six years ago?"

"How do you think he wound up in the dungeon? Your Second Knight murdered two men that I know of and set fire to a ship in the harbour. He's got some nerve sending me to the dungeon simply for calling him *sunshine*."

Galahad looked around the room, probably for a chair to sit on. Finding none, he leaned against the door. "How am I to corroborate your story?"

"That is what I am attempting to do," Hammett said, waving his sheets of paper in the air.

Sam turned and said, "Shut up!" at the same time Galahad did.

"Ask Sagramore," Sam said. "He was there."

Galahad grimaced.

"Sure, Saggy killed Lancelot or is covering for Lancelot's wife, but that's a crime of passion. A love triangle gone bad. I'm convinced that Saggy is otherwise straight as an arrow."

The knight ground his teeth and shook his head. "Since Sir Sagramore has no reason to love you, I can only believe you are telling the truth. Even so, there is nothing I can do. Mordred is the Second Knight and you did escape the dungeon."

Sam rubbed his ear. He had hoped he could turn Galahad, but the man had scruples. Maybe a different angle.

"You've got bigger fish to fry than me," Sam suggested. "Mordred's promotion from jailbird to Second Knight is part of something bigger." He went on to explain the conspiracy theory that he and Hammett had just come up with in a dozen one-word sentences.

"Let me see if I have this," Galahad said. "Lady Vivian disposed of the Merlin, poisoned the King, and made Mordred the Second Knight all in a bid to . . ."

"We have yet to determine that aspect," Hammett said.

"Shut up!" Sam and Galahad said together.

"I think it has something to do with the Holy Grail," Sam said.

Galahad perked up. "The Grail?"

"Think about it. King Arthur falls ill and the entire land begins to fail?"

"No." Galahad shook his head. "I fail to see your reasoning. Certainly, the price of eggs has risen and the tax collectors are having a difficult season . . ."

"It's only been three days," Sam said.

"It is not possible to establish a trend in three days," Hammett suggested. "I know, shut up."

"But Christ's Cup is secure," Galahad said.

"Are you sure?"

"I could take you to see it."

Sam smiled. "That would be swell."

"But you will be arrested before we reach the chapel."

"Right."

"I have an idea," said Hammett. The jeweller shrunk down behind the counter expecting shouts of *shut up*, but instead Sam looked at him, as did Galahad.

"Let's hear it," Sam said. "And I hope it's a good one."

13
THE DINGUS

As far as disguises went, Sam had done better for Halloween when he was ten. In addition to being much too tight, much too long, and much too purple, he had never been fond of velvet, even when worn by someone other than himself. Worse, he'd had to leave his trench coat, suit jacket, and fedora in Hammett's office. But what really stuck in his craw was leaving his Smith & Wesson M&P semi-automatic revolver. There simply wasn't room for it, or its holster, anywhere beneath the almost skin-tight robe. Wearing the holster outside the robe, he may as well have had an *arrest me* sign hanging around his neck. Sam felt half-naked as he walked heel to toe down the castle corridor.

Galahad walked a half-pace ahead, as though not wanting to be seen accompanying someone with such poor fashion sense. Together, more or less, they descended the steps to the main floor and crossed quickly to the royal wing where, during his last visit, Sam had seen numerous nobles as well as visited the magistrate.

There were fewer nobles this time. Maybe that was due to the King being ill, or maybe it was another effect of the land beginning to fail. Whatever the reason, Sam was relieved that no one stopped them.

In the chapel anteroom, Galahad led him into a side chamber that contained a number of art objects: statues, paintings, fancy furniture, and a shoulder-high pedestal that held a golden cup set on a deep blue velvet cloth. A sconce of candles set into the wall above the pedestal had the effect of causing the cup to almost glow.

"Are you sure that dingus is the real deal?" Sam asked. "It looks like something I could buy for a dollar at a garage sale."

Galahad frowned. "It is neither the material nor the craftsmanship that comprises the Grail, but the touch of the Man who blessed its contents."

"Yeah, well, my gut tells me that something ain't right in Denmark."

"What have the Danes to do with anything?"

"That's hard to say," Sam said. "But I think we should let Hammett take a look."

Galahad's jaw fell toward his tabard. "The Grail is hardly a jewel."

"No," Sam agreed. "But Hammett knows things. About craftsmanship, if nothing else. Maybe even who touched what."

"You wish to bring the jeweller here?"

Sam thought for a moment. "Nah, we'd better take it to him." He reached out and grabbed the yellow cup.

"What are you doing?" Galahad shrieked. "You cannot take the Grail from its pedestal."

Sam looked at Galahad and then at the cup. "Looks like I just did."

"One does not simply walk through Castle Camelot clutching the Holy Grail to his bosom!"

"Of course not," Sam said. He grabbed the velvet cloth the Grail had been sitting on, wrapped the cup inside, and tucked it under one arm. "Hey, it kinda matches my outfit."

Galahad gawked at him. "You cannot be serious."

Sam looked down at the lumpy mass under his arm. "I admit it looks suspicious, but I've got a Camelot knight to talk me past anyone who might raise an eyebrow."

"But. I. You." Galahad pointed at Sam's velvet robe and velvet bundle that almost matched. "What could I possibly say?"

"That we're about the King's business and they should keep their comments to themselves. Look, things were quiet enough getting here. Maybe no one will stop us on the way to

Hammett's."

Sam knew he was being optimistic when he said those last words, and maybe even tempting fate. Even so, he had not expected Mordred to confront them in the main corridor.

"Galahad! Wot is this?" He scrunched his eyes at Sam. "'oo is that?"

"I," said the gallant knight. "We. That is." He looked at Sam. "What."

Realizing that Galahad had probably never told a lie in his life, Sam figured it was up to him to talk their way out of this. He dipped his head toward the belligerent monkey, putting all his faith in the fact that a hat made the man and that his *mean streets* hat was back on Hammett's worktable. Mordred hadn't recognized him. Not yet, anyway.

To enhance his disguise, Sam pitched his voice higher and adopted a British accent he remembered from a misspent youth watching reruns of Monty Python. For good measure, he added a lisp. Anything to prevent Mordred from recognizing him. "Abbot Preshley at your dishposhal," he said, "of the Holy Order of Elvish."

"Elvish?" echoed Mordred. "Never 'eard of it."

"We are but a humble order," Sam said, "with a shmall abbey in the vale of Gracheland, far to the north."

"And wot are ya doin' 'ere?" Mordred demanded.

Good question, Sam decided. "A pilgrimage," he said. "For many yearsh we have shaved. Shacrifiched. Oh, the shacrifich. Until I could make the long, difficult journey to Camelot to shee . . . to shee the Grail."

Galahad wavered on his feet and an odd noise escaped his lips.

"The Grail is that way." Mordred pointed a blunt finger back the way they had come.

"Yesh, yesh," Sam said. "We have jusht come from there. The glory, oh the glory of sheeing Chrisht's cup! My eyesh yet burn from the radiench. Your good knight here who found the cup, wash kind enough to eshcort me into itsh preshenche and now returnsh me to Shaint Stephen'sh Abbey sho that I may resht."

"I 'aven't the foggiest wot ya just said," Mordred sneered. "Yer accent is ridiculous. Be gone and good riddance."

Sam bowed again and began walking away.

"Wait," said Mordred. "Wot do ya 'ave there under yer arm?"

Sam froze and then turned back to face the monkey. He moved his shoulder and carefully shifted the velvet-covered Grail into his hands. "Thish? Why, it ish the Good Book. God'sh Holy Word." He held out the bundle toward Mordred. "I have carried God'sh Word from the altar in our shmall Abbey in Gracheland sho that I might bring it into the preshenche of Chrisht'sh Cup. When I return, God'sh Holy Book will be that much more blesshed. Our humble abbey may not hosht a schacred relic like the Holy Grail, but our alter will forever reflect itsh glory."

"Bah!" Mordred turned away. "Yer religious buffoonery is of nah interest ter me. Get ya gone."

Again Sam bowed and began walking away, still holding the Grail in his hands. He didn't want to risk the velvet cloth slipping as he tucked it back beneath his arm.

Mordred's shouting followed him along the corridor. "And ya, Galahad! Don' ya 'ave better things ter do than play nursemaid ter visitin' priests?"

"You are a fool," Galahad said when he caught up to Sam. "You look nothing like an abbot. And what was that language you were speaking? I hardly understood a word."

"I was trying for British," Sam said. "I guess it needs work."

By the time he and Galahad pushed open the door of Camelot Jewellers, Sam was ready to throw Hammett's spare robe back in his face. How did the man move in this getup? Especially on those stairs!

Taking a deep breath, more to calm himself than out of any reverence for the Grail, Sam unwrapped the golden cup and set it on the counter.

Hammett's eyes nearly popped out of his head. "You brought it here?"

"I don't know," Sam said. "You tell us. It could be a fake."

Hammett reached out with a tentative finger and touched the cup. When it didn't bite, he leaned closer and moved his finger along its edge. Then he pulled his monocle from a fold in his robe and set it against his eye.

"Yes." Picking the cup up with both hands, he turned it in all directions, angling it over a thick candle that burned near the centre of the table. "I see. I see." Finally, he set the cup down and removed the monocle. Then he pursed his lips and said nothing.

"Well?" Sam asked.

"There is no craftsman mark," Hammett said.

"Is that unusual?" Galahad asked.

Hammett looked at the knight. "For a cup of this quality? No."

"Anything else?" Sam asked.

"It is made of hammered copper mixed with zinc. You could purchase one just like it in the market for a penny."

"But is it the Grail?" Sam asked.

"I have no ide—wait." The gemmologist's eyes brightened. "Actually, I do have an idea. The Holy Grail is hundreds of years old. This cup." Hammett picked up the chalice and looked at it again. "This cup could have been forged yesterday. There is nary a dent nor blemish on it. No dust. No smudges."

"The Grail is dusted daily," Galahad said. "And no one touches it." He glanced at Sam. "Is supposed to touch it."

"Even so," said Hammett, gently placing the cup back on the table. "Brass tarnishes over time. You could never convince me, or anyone else who knows metals, that this cup is hundreds of years old."

Galahad clenched and unclenched his fists. "The sanctity of the Grail has preserved it from the moment it touched our Lord's hand."

Hammett shook his head.

"The knight has a point," Sam said. "The real Grail has to be special, otherwise it wouldn't be . . . special. Hey!" Sam took the cup from the table and waved it at Galahad. "When you found this, how did you know it was the real thing?"

Galahad's complexion darkened. "There were portents. Lights in the sky. A choir of angel voices. And—and the Grail beckoned."

"I get the sense that you're not telling us everything," Sam said.

The knight frowned and then looked at Hammett and then at the burly guard who stood in the corner of the room. He lowered his voice to a whisper. "Ah, that is, I mean, there is one thing that I have told no one. Not even the King."

"Time to come clean, Galahad."

"The Grail. It, uh, well, it glows in the dark."

"Glows in the dark?"

"Exactly."

Sam rubbed his ear. "Like an LED watch?"

"I know not what you describe," Galahad said. Hammett shrugged in agreement.

"That's not important. Look, all we have to do is douse the lights and see if this thing stands out."

"Douse the lights!" Hammett almost screamed. "Not in here." He waved his arms about the room where dozens of candles lined the shelves to illuminate the hundreds of silver, gold, and gem-studded artifacts. "Do you have any idea how long it takes to light so many candles?"

Sam smiled. "It was a lousy idea anyway. Let's just throw that velvet cloth over it."

The jeweller resumed breathing.

Setting the Grail back on the counter, Sam picked up the blue table cover and draped it over the large cup. Then the three men looked at each other.

"You do it," Sam said to Galahad. "You're the one who knows how it looks when it glows."

"Very well." The knight bent carefully until his knees rested on the floor and his head was at a height with the long table that served as Hammett's store counter and workbench. Then he pulled off one gauntlet and lifted the edge of the cloth with his fingers. He emitted a low growl, and then lifted the cloth higher and thrust his head underneath.

"I see nothing," the knight said, his voice muffled by the cloth. Then he pulled his head out and rose to his feet. "This is not the true Grail." He glowered at Sam. "You say the Danes have done this thing?"

"Let's not rush to judgment," Sam said. "In cases like this the question you have to ask is: Who benefits from the crime?"

Hammett cleared his throat. "This is not unlike Lady Iva's amulet you showed me when you were last here. If someone has stolen the Holy Grail, they cannot sell it. Neither can they show it to anyone without revealing themselves as the thief."

Galahad frowned. "We need look no farther than your Lady Vivian. It is as your conspiracy suggests. Eliminate the magician. Remove the King. And take the Cup." He paused. "Is Vivian a Danish name? It sounds Danish."

"Could be," Sam said, "But we still don't know Vivian's endgame. As Hammett said, stealing the Grail is pointless. It has to be part of the setup, not the prize."

"Perhaps it is as you said," suggested Hammett. "It is the theft of the Grail that makes the King and the land ill, leaving us vulnerable to invasion."

"I said that?" Sam thought about it. "If I didn't, I should have. Tell me, Galahad, what are the three chief motivators of any crime."

"Greed," said Hammett before the knight could speak.

"That is one," Sam agreed.

"Passion," suggested Galahad. "Love. Anger. Pride."

"That's two. And the third?"

Both men gave him blank looks.

"Power," Sam said. "The third chief motivator is power."

Galahad looked at Hammett, who shook his head. "I fail to see it," said the knight.

"Come on." Sam waved his hands. "Power. Those who don't have it want it. Those who do have it want more."

Galahad scratched his neck.

Hammett cleared his throat. "We live in a class system. You are born to power or you are not. One cannot steal power."

"Ah," said Galahad. "You speak of a lord attacking his neighbour to expand his domain. But that is no crime. It is conquest. It is only fitting that a weak lord should lose his domain while a strong lord's domain should increase."

"That may be," Sam said. "But I'm speaking of a sorcerer's apprentice doing away with her teacher and taking all that is his."

"That rings of conquest," suggested Hammett.

Sam sighed. "Or a street kid painting a bird on his shirt and setting himself up as Second Knight."

Galahad's face darkened. "Your endgame is Mordred setting himself up as captain of the knights?"

"Nothing so simple," Sam said. "I suspect Mordred's mother intends to set herself up as Queen."

"Queen?" echoed Galahad. "But Guinevere is Queen. Are you suggesting that Vivian plans to do away with Our Good Lady and wed King Arthur?"

Sam couldn't stop himself from chuckling. "Only in fairy tales, Galahad. Only in fairy tales. That would never work in real life. No, only ruthlessness can take over a country. Vivian intends for Arthur to die and Camelot to almost die with him. Then she will sweep in and promise to fix everything if her son is set on the throne."

Galahad and Hammett both stared at him.

"But," said the knight, "how could she orchestrate such a thing?"

"She already has the first part. Arthur is on his deathbed and the land is dying with him. The only person who could stop her has been disposed of."

"The Merlin," said Hammett.

"Your conspiracy," admitted Galahad. "But how is Lady Vivian to *fix* everything if given the throne?"

Sam snapped up the velvet cloth in one hand and the golden cup in the other. "She'll put the real Grail back. Once restored, the land will recover."

"You know this?" asked Galahad.

"Of course, I—" Sam took a deep breath. "Well, no, I don't know it. But it's the only thing that makes sense. Also, I think I saw it on television somewhere."

Galahad rubbed his chin. "Whether you are right or wrong, what is our next course of action? Do we try to arrest Lady Vivian? Her son is Second Knight. I don't know that we can arrest her."

"Arrest Lady Vivian!" exclaimed Hammett. "How do you arrest an enchantress? Chains will not hold her. And she defeated the Merlin! Or so we believe."

Sam shook his head. "Wouldn't do us any good anyway. So long as she has the real Grail, Vivian holds all the cards."

"Then we quest for the Holy Grail," Galahad said. "I have done it before. I can do it again."

"I think you're right," Sam said. "But first we need to put this one back."

"Back?" Galahad gave him a confused look. "But it is a forgery. Useless."

Sam began wrapping the cup in its cloth. "And if it goes missing, Vivian will know we're onto her. First, we put the fake back. Second, we find the real Grail."

14
A THEFT IN REVERSE

AS HE SET the golden cup back on its pedestal, Sam let out a huge sigh of relief. It couldn't be more than thirty minutes since he had stolen it, but anyone could have noticed its absence in that time and raised the alarm. Galahad reached out and straightened a wrinkle in the cloth.

"Who dares touch the Grail!" demanded a loud voice.

Sam couldn't prevent an involuntary jump. He turned and saw the knight with a peacock on his tabard glaring at Galahad. Then the knight's expression softened. "Oh, Sir Galahad, it is you. As finder of Christ's Cup I suppose you have a right, but I have been ordered to detain any who might approach the Holy Grail."

"Sir Kay?" Galahad turned and stepped in front of Sam, partially obscuring him from view. "Are you not above performing guard duty? And since when is Camelot Castle considered so unsafe that we must place guards in the chapel?"

Kay frowned. "I am here at Sir Mordred's command. It seems a dangerous felon has escaped from the dungeon and is loose in the castle. And a foreign abbot was seen inquiring about the Grail. But you speak truly, Galahad. Guard duty is a task for junior knights. Mordred has the sense of a donkey." He noticed Sam over Galahad's shoulder. "Who is this who accompanies you?"

"A visitor," Galahad said before Sam could speak. "Lord . . .

Lord Pie . . . of Connecticut."

"It is an honour to visit your great city," Sam said, keeping his Monty Python accent but dropping the lisp. He rolled his hand in front of his forehead like he had seen Omar Sharif do in *Lawrence of Arabia.* "Sir Galahad has been kind enough to escort me within the castle. I am most impressed. Oh, and he did not touch the Sacred Cup. He merely straightened the cloth it rests upon."

"That is . . ." Sir Kay seemed lost for words. ". . . good to know. You seem familiar to me, Lord Pie. Have you visited Camelot before?"

"Once," Sam said. "Many years ago when I was a lad. It was my hope to consult the Merlin, but Sir Galahad tells me the magician is away."

"Sadly," said Sir Kay. "That is true."

"Lord Pie," said Galahad, "I must show you the Great Hall next."

Sam ignored him. "Know you where the Merlin has gone?" he asked the peacock knight. "Or when the magician may return?"

"Again," said Sir Kay. "Sadly, no."

Galahad grabbed Sam's velvet sleeve and began pulling. "We are expected in the Lesser Hall in a few minutes. We must not make the Chamberlain wait."

"It is a pleasure to have met you, Sir Kay," Sam said as Galahad pulled him away.

"What do you think you were doing," Galahad hissed when they were out of earshot. "Sir Kay could have recognized you and then where would we be?"

"I was testing my disguise," Sam said. "Maybe this Hammett getup isn't so bad, if only I could move in it."

"Sir Kay is suspicious," Galahad said. "It will gnaw at him and he will want to see you again in order to make sense of it. You need a new disguise."

"Such as?"

Galahad tightened his forehead in thought. "Where do you suggest we look for the Grail?"

"I've already seen Vivian's office," Sam said. "It wasn't there, though I never got a chance to look in her sleeping closet."

"Her what? Lady Vivian has a suite in the main tower. Why would she sleep in her office?"

"It's where I slept when it was my office," Sam said. "There was a trunk and the Grail would fit in it, but that's too obvious."

"Her rooms, perhaps," suggested Galahad.

"She would want to keep it close."

The knight nodded. "There is yet time today before Lady Vivian returns to her rooms. And I know just the disguise."

15
A BETTER DISGUISE

SAM FOLLOWED THE knight to a part of the castle he'd never seen before. Servants scurried everywhere, giving Sam and Galahad surprised, and sometimes nervous, glances. Sam hoped that was due to a noticeable absence of knights, lords, and similar people of higher station, and not because they recognized him as a fugitive from the dungeon. At one point he saw servants carrying baskets of folded cloth that might have been clothing or towels for the Necessarium. A smell of fresh soap permeated the air.

The soap smell soon gave way to baking bread, spices, cheeses, and other food scents. Galahad turned under a wide arch and they were suddenly surrounded by short, bustling women in aprons and poufy hats scurrying about with pots and bowls and trays of plucked chickens and uncooked pies.

"You're going to dress me as a waiter?" Sam asked. He might enjoy that. Bogart played a waiter in *Casablanca*, though to be fair, his character owned the nightclub. But Rick Blaine dressed like a waiter. An upscale waiter. Like a spy might disguise himself. Sam was sure he'd seen Sean Connery wearing the same outfit as James Bond. Was it *Dr. No*? Or *From Russia with Love*? Sam never could keep Bond films straight. But that's who he could be. White shirt. Black jacket. Bow tie. He'd slick down his hair and tuck his semi-automatic into his waistband at his back. Licensed to kill.

"No," Galahad answered. "Our activities demand we miss supper; I thought we would grab a bite now."

Sam snorted a soft chuckle. "Now you mention it, I haven't eaten since breakfast."

Ignoring the tsk tsks and the hand slapping of the cooks, the knight rescued a loaf of hot bread from a pan just come from an oven and a jar of honey from one of the shelves. He set them on a small table at the far end of the kitchen along with a knife that appeared seemingly from nowhere. Sam would have to learn that trick. Galahad broke the bread and smeared it with honey.

One of the cooks, a large woman with beefy arms, waddled up and sniffed at Sam and then at the knight. "This ain't your own private dinin' room, Galahad. Wot do ya fin' you're doin', disruptin' me girls and stealin' food from under me nose?"

"Now, now, Mable," the knight said. "I shall be on duty during supper. You ken how I despise eating while I am tasked with keeping the peace."

"You've always been the most serious of knights," the woman said, shaking her head. "Doin' ovver knights' work for them while they're gamblin' or whorin'. It is ya should be Second Knight, not that wanker Mordred."

"You are too kind, Mable. Listen, I would appreciate it if you and your girls never mentioned I was down here. Or my friend. Mordred might take exception to a knight rubbing elbows with the servants."

The cook peered at Sam with cool eyes. "'e don't belong 'ere. I'll speak wif me girls, but the sooner ya two leef the better. I don't want your Mordred daahhhn 'ere yellin' at me girls. The man's enough ter make an owl spit." And then she waddled away.

Sam swallowed a piece of sweetened bread. "It surprises me after hearing the way you people talk about Mordred that I was arrested for calling him *sunshine*."

"Yes," Galahad said, "but you did that in his presence."

"Well, you've got me there."

"Come," the knight said. "We must find you a suitable costume. The servants are accustomed to seeing me in this part of the castle, but not a visiting lord."

Grabbing a final chunk of bread, Sam followed the knight

into the corridor and down the hall, back toward where he had seen servants carrying laundry. They stopped inside an alcove off the hallway.

The space was a walk-in closet lined floor to ceiling with shelves and cupboards crammed with stacks of clothing. Galahad rifled through a wide closet filled with what Sam at first thought were robes or gowns similar to Hammett's spare robe that he currently wore, except made of starched cotton instead of velvet. He frowned when it dawned on him what these were.

"Women's clothing!"

"Shush!" the knight whispered. "No one must hear us." He pulled out a bulky gown of some kind, gazed at it critically, and then put it back.

"I'm not wearing women's clothing," Sam said.

Galahad pulled out a second gown and held it up against Sam's chest. "Everyone is looking for an escaped man. A serving maid will not receive a second glance. Remove Hammett's robe and put this on."

Sam didn't move. "No one is going to take me for a woman."

"No one looks at servants," Galahad said. "It is either this, or I escort you to the dungeon."

"*I* look at servants," Sam said, but he grudgingly began rolling the purple velvet robe up toward his shoulders. It really was too tight. So tight it got stuck and Galahad had to lever a foot against the wall and yank the slippery cloth over Sam's head.

The bulky maid's gown went on much easier. It was dull white cotton blended with sandpaper or something equally coarse and reached past his ankles to cover his shoes. Galahad gave an appreciative nod and then searched one of the shelves for a sash, settling on a burgundy number that drew Sam's waist in somewhat.

"You need more chest," the knight said.

Sam grabbed a white cotton garment he didn't recognize, wadded it up, and pushed it into the neck of the gown. He did the same with a second garment and maneuvered them around until the sash held them in roughly the right shape for a matronly woman.

"You have done this before," Galahad said.

Sam gave his faux rack a final pat. "I haven't, but I've made a study of the female form."

"I . . . see," the knight said. He plucked something white and poufy from a shelf and began tucking it around the top of Sam's head. He frowned and let out a soft grunt. "It will have to do."

"What is it?" Sam asked.

"A mop cap, meant to keep your hair out of your work."

Sam thought he knew what the knight meant. Most of the female and some of the male servants wore such hats.

"Does this have a snowball's chance in Hell of working?" Sam asked.

"It does not bear close scrutiny," Galahad admitted. "But you look more the maid than you did a lord. Or an abbot. Can you speak in a higher voice without sounding like a discomfited magpie?"

"Let's not get carried away," Sam said.

"Then we are done here." Galahad wadded up Hammett's velvet robe and hid it behind a jumble of slippers that littered the bottom of a closet.

"Shouldn't we return that to the jeweller?"

"Not yet," said the knight. "We must needs avoid that region of the castle; Lady Vivian is wont to occupy her office at this hour. It is, however, a propitious time to visit her rooms in the tower."

"I'm with you there," Sam said.

Galahad cast him a stern look. "You are much too tall. Hunch your back. Further. Good. Keep your head down. It will hide your face and make you appear shorter. Now, follow where I go, walking several paces behind. Speak to no one, even if spoken to; simply nod or shake your head. If any speaking is required, I shall speak, not you. And should you look up, appear fearful, as if at any moment I might shout at you." With that, Galahad strode out into the hallway.

Sam smiled and followed. Looking fearful wouldn't be a problem; he felt like a drag queen strolling the Hartford docks. Alone. At night.

Near the end of the corridor, Galahad paused beside an open doorway and bent down and retrieved a basket of towels that must have been just inside the room. He handed this to Sam before continuing his quick walk along a different passage. When he came to a set of stairs that was much narrower and steeper than others Sam had seen in the castle, Galahad mounted the stairs and went up.

The detective in Sam deduced that these were servant stairs, though the whole concept seemed backward. There were more servants climbing up and down through the castle at any given time than there were upper-class residents or visitors and, more often than not, they carried trays or baskets such as Sam had now. The steeper stairs were harder to manage—it would have been impossible in Hammett's robes—never mind that they were only wide enough for traffic to move one way. Sure enough, at the top of the stairs Sam found a butler who looked nothing like James Bond awaiting his turn to climb down carrying what might have been a jewellery box.

The knight spoke with the man.

"Have you seen a roguish gentleman in the tower?" Galahad asked. "Perhaps a head taller than you and wearing outlandish tan clothing as well as a tan hat?"

"Nay, sir knight. To whom should I speak if I do?"

"Send for any of the knights," Galahad said. "Though we have already searched most of the castle and I suspect the villain has fled."

The butler nodded and slipped down the stairs. Sam kept his face down as though inspecting the contents of his basket.

"Roguish, am I?" Sam whispered. "A villain?"

"Shush!"

Galahad continued up the next set of steps. Then the next, conversing briefly with servants. Sam learned how to stare at the floor and hold up his faux breasts with a basket. There were no lamps or torches in the stairwell, making footing difficult. The corridors accessed by the stairs were bright, however. Each floor offered narrow windows to the courtyard, much as outside Sam's office. Now Vivian's office. In addition, a larger window set near the stairs looked out over the city. Sam figured Robin would find those useful when he was out climbing walls and jumping rooftops.

Finally, Galahad stopped and peered down a hallway. Apparently satisfied, he stepped along the corridor listening briefly at each door. He paused again and beckoned Sam to join him.

"These are the Merlin's rooms. It is a place I might hide the

Grail were I Lady Vivian."

"You'd make a good PI," Sam said.

"It may also be dangerous inside. The Merlin may have left surprises for unwanted visitors."

"So what else is new? After you."

16
THE MERLIN'S NEST

GALAHAD KNOCKED AND Sam waited for a cantankerous voice to demand who was there. When that didn't happen, Galahad knocked again and then silently worked the latch on the door. As Friar Tuck had explained during Sam's last visit, locked doors hadn't been invented yet.

The anteroom of the magician's apartment looked identical to Merlin's outer office, minus Effie's desk and the row of visitor's chairs. The space was the same, but stood completely empty. Not even a speck of lint begrimed the floor.

"Did Merlin's possessions disappear along with the magician?" Sam asked.

Galahad shrugged. "I have never visited these rooms before."

"Then how'd you know where they are?"

"I have committed to memory every nook and corner of the castle public spaces," the knight said. "One never knows when such information will come in useful."

"You got that right." Sam walked through the empty room to what would have been the door of his inner office and pushed it open. "Well, I'll be!"

Late afternoon sunlight crept through the single window to illuminate a giant worktable that stretched the entire length of the room. Despite sturdy construction, the table sagged beneath the weight of rocks, conch shells, wooden racks, and an array of large glass jars filled with glowing liquids, a few of which let off steam or smoke. Sam's eyes were drawn to an empty forty-ounce soda bottle of a variety he hadn't seen since he was a kid and wouldn't be invented for centuries. Near the window a wind chime made from delicate pieces of glass hung from the ceiling. At the far end of the table, a two-foot long model airplane sat suspended in mid-air. A World War I Bristol F.2 Fighter, if Sam was not mistaken. Beneath the table, a jumble of crates crowded each other, each overflowing with paraphernalia too shadowed to make out. One of the crates sported a Sunkist Oranges label.

Along the opposite wall stood seven marble figures about five feet tall. Sam recognized them as chess pieces: a king, queen, two knights, a bishop, and two pawns. The bishop was incomplete, with one side of his head uncut rough stone. A work in progress.

What was conspicuously absent was a bed.

While Galahad poked around the crates beneath the worktable, Sam opened the side door and was not surprised to find a tiny sleeping alcove, complete with narrow bed, wool blanket, and useless pillow. He opened the bedside chest hoping to find the Grail. Its interior was as lint-free as the outer room. Squatting down, Sam searched under the bed. Nothing.

"Are there any clothes under that table?" he asked Galahad.

The knight had finished inspecting the crates. "Nothing recognizably so. No."

"And you're sure this is Merlin's bedchamber?"

Galahad poked the airplane with his finger and watched it twist in a circle. "This is the magician's only apartment in the castle, other than his office. This tower is for castle residents."

Sam rubbed his ear. "Well, there's a bed, more or less. But where are the magician's clothes?"

"Since you mention it," Galahad said, "I have only ever seen the Merlin in his robes of office. I assumed he had a matching wardrobe, just as I have three identical tabards. Perhaps the magician only has the one?"

"I'm not one to judge," Sam said. "The Grail doesn't seem to be here. Let's move on."

17
THE ROOMS OF LADY VIVIAN

GALAHAD LED THE way up an additional flight of servants' stairs and then peered into the corridor from the shadows of the stairwell. "This will involve greater hazard than the Merlin's rooms," he whispered. "'Twould be best I station myself in the corridor and maintain vigil whilst you search for the Grail. Should the Lady Vivian return to her rooms unexpected, I shall speak with a loud voice and occupy her with conversation that you might avail to conceal yourself."

"Why would she return early?" Sam waved a hand at the stair window. "There's still plenty of light."

Galahad cocked his head at a thoughtful angle. "A wise old man came to the castle some years ago. A Welshman, I believe, by name of Murphy. He amused the knights for several days with jests and proverbs regarding ill twists of fate. *If something can go wrong, it will. A problem left unremedied will fester. No plan is foolproof, because fools are ingenious. The more valuable an artifact, the more damage it will sustain in an accident.* He had many others. It was only as the old man stood at the gates bidding farewell that it occurred to me that his proverbs were not jests at all, but sober lessons learned over a long life of tragedy. If Murphy were here now, he would suggest that the one day we choose to break into a woman's rooms is the one day she would choose to return early."

"Right," Sam said. "I think I've met this friend of yours. Too often, actually."

After a second peek into the hallway, Galahad led Sam to a closed door where he knocked and waited for no one to answer. Glancing quickly in both directions, he lifted the latch and motioned Sam inside.

"If you would, madam," he said to Sam in a normal speaking voice, "replace any towels that require replacing." The words were for the benefit of anyone who may have been inside without answering. When there was no response, Galahad gently pushed the door closed.

The layout of Vivian's rooms looked identical to those Merlin had occupied. Sam was beginning to think that Camelot Castle had been designed by Marriot or Hyatt, with cookie cutter suites and offices.

Vivian's sitting area was the same size and shape as the outer office Effie occupied only, instead of a line of ladder-back chairs, it contained a long couch with matching love seat arranged around a low coffee table. There was even a decanter of what looked like water and two empty mugs on the table.

Heavy tapestries draped the walls displaying scenes of wooded countryside, rivers, archers hunting deer, and a field of stones arranged in a circle. Sam wasted no time setting the laundry basket on the floor and searching for the golden cup.

It took less than a minute to look under the coffee table, behind the furniture, under cushions, and behind the tapestries. Not that anything but stones and mortar could fit behind the tapestries.

That left the inner room. Unlike the magician's apartment, the bedroom contained a bed. One of those big canopy jobs with posts that almost touched the ceiling and six acres of sailcloth hanging on all sides. The bed could house a family of five. With room for pets. It also sat high off the floor with several boxes shoved underneath.

The boxes seemed a likely hiding place, so Sam pulled each one out and searched it thoroughly. He found nothing but women's clothing, most of which were black or darker hues of blue or red.

Near the bed stood a writing table covered with sheets of paper. Most were blank, but a few were works in progress.

Sam was tempted to read them—one might mention the Grail—but he decided to leave that for last; if the cup was in the room, he wouldn't need to read about it.

That left the alcove near the window. A full-length mirror sat adjacent to the door. It was the first mirror Sam had seen in Camelot and seemed as fine as any quality mirror one might pick up at Nordstrom. He took a moment to admire his disguise and decided that he was the ugliest maid ever spawned and wouldn't fool Mr. Magoo. Not even on a bad day. What had Galahad been thinking?

Shaking his head, Sam opened the door and found an alcove identical to the one in Merlin's suite and office. Instead of a narrow bed, however, it contained a long rail of hooks upon which hung maybe a thousand pounds of clothing consisting of dresses and coats and long lacy things that Sam assumed were undergarments. Maybe the clothing under the bed had fallen out of fashion or were for a different season. Whatever the case, Lady Vivian's most difficult question each day must be in deciding what to wear.

The real kicker, however, was that Sam now had to admit that he'd been bunking down in Merlin's closet and not a sleeping nook. He supposed that's what happened to closets when you didn't own a wardrobe.

Sam turned and looked back into Vivian's bedroom. There was one additional feature. Next to the single window stood a nightstand. Sam looked at the stand and the bed, and decided that they couldn't be further apart. One couldn't reach the stand without leaving the bed and crossing the room. Maybe that was a means of psychologically making the space seem bigger. The stand's only contents were two glass cups and a tall metal flagon that smelled of wine.

Sam's throat felt suddenly dry. A nip wouldn't hurt. Ignoring the two cups, he lifted the lid from the flagon and raised it to his lips. He'd barely tasted the wine when he heard voices in the hallway. Damn that Murphy anyway.

Looking this way then that, Sam's gaze locked on the space under the bed. If he shuffled some boxes around, he could maybe make a cubby hole to crawl into. Though if Vivian drew wide the canopy, he would easily be spotted from where he now stood by the nightstand. Besides, his gut told him that only the three stooges would hide under a bed.

In the movies, Bogart would steal away through the balcony window. Sam poked his head outside and looked down before remembering how many stairs he had climbed to get here. Even if he did manage to land in the moat, the water would be hard as concrete from this height, though to be honest, it was the Necessarium refuse in the moat that was the bigger deterrent.

The voices became clearer as the outer door opened.

"—must needs secure this region of the castle," Galahad was saying. "This miscreant could be anywhere."

"He will not be in my rooms," an angry female voice said.

"Of course not, good lady. I have merely been watching the corridor in the event this Spade fellow is forced to retreat to these hallways."

"Fine, but you will watch the corridor from the staircase. I will not have knights spying on me."

"Spying? You wound me!"

"I may yet wound you," Vivian snarled even as the door slammed.

Sam timed the slamming of the outer door with his closing of the alcove door, with him inside. The windowless castle closet was claustrophobic given the wall-to-wall clothing, and just as dark as he remembered from sleeping in his office. He had a good memory for some things, including women's voices. That memory plus the voice from the corridor told him that Lady Vivian was just another alias for the ever-deceptive Miss Morgan Le Fay.

18

THE ENCHANTRESS'S CLOSET

EAR AGAINST ALCOVE door, Sam listened as Le Fay puttered about the sitting room. Morgan Le Fay. The pathological liar who had misled him those months or years ago when he had ended up negotiating an exchange for a stolen chicken. And the older version of herself who had chased him from his old office, now her new office, earlier that day. When had the lady in black become an evil enchantress? And when had she become Mordred's mother? As Robin had said, Le Fay was hardly old enough.

From the tap of footsteps on stone, Sam realized Le Fay had entered the inner room. Gingerly, he pressed himself backward among and then behind the wall of clothing. Sudden light entered the alcove as Le Fay yanked open the door. Had she heard him?

The wall of dresses began moving, swaying from side to side.

"Damn! Bloody closet," Le Fay whispered.

Sam could see her now through a gap in the hanging clothes. A hand came toward him as she reached for a white gown and unhooked it from the rail. Sam dared not move; she would be sure to see. It must be his maid's clothing, Sam realized, looking in colour and texture similar enough among the shadows to match part of her own wardrobe, that kept Le Fay blind to his presence.

He watched through the gap Le Fay had left as she turned and tossed the gown onto the bed; she must have drawn back the canopy before opening the closet. He could see clearly beneath the bed and applauded himself for not hiding there. Then Le Fay turned back to the closet and began unhitching her black dress.

If Sam hadn't been nervous as a cornered cat, he might have been entertained. It wasn't everyday he got a closet-eye view of a beautiful woman disrobing. But he remembered suddenly finding himself outside Merlin's office earlier that afternoon. He'd not been paying attention when Le Fay had magicked him into the corridor. The sorcerer's apprentice indeed.

Naked as the day she was born, Morgan Le Fay stepped toward Sam and tossed her dress and underclothes onto the closet floor. Then she turned to admire herself in the mirror.

While the woman's face seemed colder and less inviting after six years, for the rest of her Sam couldn't see much to complain about. Shapely arms and legs, curves in all the right places, skin without blemish. Her breasts were of almost perfect size and sagged only slightly. Not bad for a woman pushing thirty. Sam widened his eyes with amusement as Le Fay raised one hand to cup the opposite breast. When she moved the hand away the breast no longer sagged, but stood firm and proud as an eighteen-year-old's. She cupped the other breast and it too firmed up, but stood a bit higher than its sister. The woman frowned and toyed with both, alternately increasing and shrinking their size, until at last they stood equally firm and high and noticeably larger than when she'd first disrobed.

Le Fay then turned back to the bed and pulled the gown over her head. It was definitely a nightgown, white lace from neck to toe. But night was still hours away. Wasn't it?

She turned back suddenly to face the mirror and, as Sam watched, twirled like a schoolgirl, clearly enjoying the freedom of movement the thin, loose-fitting material allowed and paying close attention to the sway of her fuller breasts beneath the thin cloth. Then she stepped back toward the closet and slammed the door shut, returning Sam to darkness.

Listening carefully and remembering to breathe, Sam heard Le Fay step barefoot across the floor to the writing desk.

It offered the only chair in the room and he could hear the joints creak as she sat. Sam could also hear paper moving and then the nib of a feather pen scratching on paper. Maybe he should have read what was there. Who knew what mischief Le Fay was getting up to with her letters?

Though he'd only been standing still for a few minutes, already Sam's body was beginning to ache. Or maybe it came from standing so rigidly still while Le Fay had used the mirror. Moving one molecule at a time, or so it seemed, Sam leaned back until his shoulders pressed against the closet's stone wall. He then allowed his weight to shift, easing stiff and strained muscles.

Logically, since Le Fay was dressed for bed, she'd have no reason to use the closet again until morning. Sam would have to wait until she fell asleep and then sneak out without waking her. He had no idea if Le Fay was a light sleeper. Did she sleep at all now that she was an enchantress? Or should he stay hidden until she left her rooms in the morning?

Already sore again, Sam began lowering himself down along the wall, sliding against it fraction by fraction. Once his rump touched the floor, Sam shifted sideways, stretching himself out lengthwise against the inside wall, right where the cot had been in Merlin's office. Once positioned, he'd just have to ensure that he didn't fall asleep. Most people snore. Sam knew he was one of them.

Pausing at intervals to ensure that Le Fay was still scratching pen against paper, Sam twisted his body along the floor, careful not to catch on hanging garments and pull them to the ground. Everything was going perfectly until he smacked his head against the wall. He froze.

The writing stopped and silence filled the air. Sam sat there, half lying down, the back of his head throbbing like a nasty hangover. He waited. Waited. And then the scratching resumed. Reaching back his hand, Sam rubbed the back of his head. Then he reached toward the wall. And reached. His shoulder ached and still no wall. Twisting again, Sam felt around with his hand until he found the offending hardness.

At first he thought it was an oversized bowling ball. Smooth, round, and infinitely hard. Exploring further, he determined that it was more of an oblong. Why would Le Fay keep a large stone in her closet? Gripping one end with his hand, he tried to wiggle it.

Heavy, but not unmanageable. He couldn't try with two hands because of how he was twisted against the wall. With a puzzle in need of solving, Sam turned on his hip, trying to right himself so that he was on his knees instead of his back.

A loud knock on the outer door interrupted his surreptitious experiments.

"It's about time," Le Fay murmured.

Sam heard what he thought was the pen being set down, followed by a lid being tapped back onto the ceramic ink jar. Then feet scurried across the floor. A click and swish indicated the outer door opening.

"Greetings, Mother," said a familiar voice.

"Get in here, you fool," said Le Fay.

The door closed, followed by some indistinct noises. Sam thought he heard Le Fay ask Mordred if he had *put down* that nettlesome meddler, Spade. Mordred's response sounded like a dog whining at the door. Le Fay let out a curse. "Should have turned that sharp-tongued interloper into a toad when I had the chance. What in the name of the Goddess is Spade doing here anyway?" The voices grew indistinct again, followed by the creak of joints from the outer room furniture. When the creaking continued, Sam could only imagine what was happening out there. Then decided he'd rather not.

He figured this might be his best, possibly his only chance. Scrambling around onto all fours, he reached out with one hand, pushed aside the wardrobe, and inched open the closet door to let in some light. There, on the floor, in the corner of Morgan Le Fay's closet, lay the Holy Grail. Under glass.

19

PILLOW TALK

SAM BLINKED. WHEN he opened his eyes, the cup was still there, fully encased in glass. Just like the chicken feather he'd pilfered in Vivian's—Le Fay's—office and was now in a pocket of his trench coat beneath Hammett's counter along with his semi-automatic. The cup, of course, was much larger than a chicken feather.

The cushions in the outer room had stopped squeaking, but Sam risked making a little noise. He needed to know if he could lift that much glass. Pushing away the cloth that had covered the Grail before Sam's head and hand had dislodged it, he took hold of the glass casing at either end and lifted. It was like hefting a fifty-pound egg. Doable. Barely. He gently set the weight back on the stone floor.

It was a good news, bad news situation. The good news was that he had found the Holy Grail. The bad news was that he might be dead before he could get it to Galahad. There was only one way out of Le Fay's suite, and that was through an evil enchantress and a bloodthirsty swordsman. He might have been able to accomplish it with his bean-shooter. Sam never went anywhere without his Smith & Wesson, and the one time he didn't have it, that was the time he needed it. Mr. Murphy would be proud.

Running his hands up beneath his borrowed maid's dress, he eventually reached his pants pockets and searched for anything that might help. If he had some matches he might be able to start a fire and escape during the confusion. If he . . . well, the matches were the only thing he could think of. And his matches were in his tobacco kit. In his trench coat. In Hammett's office.

It dawned on him that he hadn't had a smoke since his stint in the dungeon. No wonder he felt so antsy. There was no gum in his pocket either, just an empty wrapper.

As Sam pulled his hand free, however, his fingers brushed across what felt like a packet of sugar. Retrieving the item, he saw it was a folded piece of paper. The drugs Tuck had given him to barter as cab fare.

A mumbled voice from the outer office reached Sam's ears. Mordred. "'aven't ya got summit more comfortable than this couch?"

Knowing his time was up, Sam climbed quickly but quietly to his feet and scrambled out of the closet. The lid of the wine flagon was still open from when he had almost had a taste earlier. Sam quickly unfolded the paper and poured the powdered *Papaver somniferum* into the wine. Then he carefully replaced the lid and quickstepped back into the closet, closing the door behind him. In defiance of Murphy, he made it just in time. Feet on stone greeted his ears.

"Would you like some wine?" Le Fay asked.

"Later," said Mordred, the bloody monkey. "I'd rather taste ya."

"I think that can be arranged," Le Fay murmured.

Sam stood still as a headlight-startled deer as he listened to clothing fall to the floor. Then came the sounds of bodies entwining, lips doing things to other lips and possibly earlobes, then finally the heavy fall of two people crushing a mattress. No noise of springs, however. Bedsprings hadn't been invented yet. Sam took the cover of convenient bed noises to lower himself back to the closet floor.

He had no idea how long he would be there or if an opportunity for escape would present itself. Even if the unlikely couple drank the wine, Sam wasn't sure what the drug would accomplish. A drug favoured by carriage drivers. What did that mean, anyway?

It took only a moment for Sam to realize that the closet

wasn't as dark as it had been. He blinked his eyes to make sure they weren't playing tricks, then looked around until he noticed a faint blue light, barely perceptible, coming from the glass-encased Grail. How about that. It did glow in the dark. Fumbling with his hands, he managed to drape the cloth that had covered the Grail back into position, sinking the closet once again into absolute gloom.

Minutes went by and noises from the canopy bed grew increasingly more identifiable, predictable even. Sam stuck his fingers in his ears, but it didn't help. How long this went on, he had no idea. Few words were spoken. Or whispered. Finally, there came a fast and furious explosion of sound followed by near silence. Then Mordred's voice. "I'll take that wine na."

The cad.

"You cad," Le Fay said, and Sam couldn't help but smile. "If you did not have . . . other qualities, I would throw you out that window."

"Ya kna ya loike it," Mordred said.

"For now." Someone climbed out of the bed; Sam assumed it was Le Fay. "You had best hope that I do not stop liking it."

Feet on stone. A clank of metal. Liquid being poured.

Sam prayed that the *Papaver* was soluble in water and hadn't settled to the bottom of the flagon.

A thud on wood. More feet on stone. Le Fay slipping back onto the bed.

The enchantress and her monkey sipped their wine and shared words that Sam tried to erase from his mind. He'd participated in his fair share of pillow talk over the years, well, maybe less than a fair share, but this took trash talk to a whole new level. There were words Sam didn't recognize. Words he wished he could unhear. Words that, well, *words* couldn't describe. Finally, he heard something he could use.

"'a much longer is the old duffer gonna 'ang on?" Mordred asked.

"What did I tell you about shoptalk in bed?" said Le Fay.

"Yeah, yeah. Sum of the knights are gettin' insubordinate."

"Then you have a choice. You can slap them down. Or you can stop acting like a prat."

Mordred laughed. "That ain't gonna 'appen."

"Then slap them down. Arthur will die when he dies. Then I

shall convince Guinevere to step down."

"'a ya gonna do that?"

This time Le Fay laughed. "If I tell you that, my sweet little bumpkin, you may decide to take the throne for yourself."

"I ain't in this for a throne," Mordred said. "The only prize I want is ya."

"Then show me."

On that cue, the talking portion of pillow talk ended.

Sam had always liked the musical scores and songs from Bogart films. Especially Dooley Wilson's "As Time Goes By" after Rick asks Sam to play it again. But there wasn't a whole lot of it and he could only run "It Had to be You" and Bacall's "And Her Tears Flowed Like Wine" through his head so many times. So when Sam reached *a kiss is just a kiss* for the millionth rendition, he stopped and listened. Soft snoring met his ears. He continued listening until he was sure there were two sets.

The closet door, which Sam remembered being silent the several times it had opened and closed, squeaked like a rusty nail being pulled as he edged it outward. He grimaced, but kept pushing.

With his head stuck out through Le Fay's wall of wardrobe, the bedroom appeared dark as a cave. The sun must have set, with Camelot's typical fog preventing any moon or starlight from entering the window. Breathing between his teeth, Sam felt around in the darkness and slipped away the cloth covering the Grail. Then he gently rolled the giant orb across the closet floor, beneath the hanging clothes, and over Le Fay's discarded dirty laundry. By its faint blue glow, the bed and Mordred's cast-off clothing piled on the floor took vague shape. Sam could see well enough to notice that the canopy had been drawn closed. Modesty couldn't be the reason; maybe it was to keep in warmth or keep out flies and mosquitos.

Now that he was free of the closet, the snoring was louder. If Tuck's drug was half-decent, the villainous duo should be out cold and watching pink elephants dance along the top of white picket fences. Or maybe their drug-induced delusions would be more exotic. This was Mordred and Le Fay, after all. Either way, with luck, they wouldn't wake until morning.

Sam turned to close the closet door, then hesitated. If the hinges squeaked again, it could wake the sleeping beauties. The bigger risk, however, was to leave the closet open. The slightest question in Le Fay's mind concerning the closet would lead to her check on the Grail. With no help for it, Sam pushed the door. The hinges, if anything, squealed rather than squeaked, a pig in distress. Sam bore through it until the door closed.

A snort from the bed startled him, and Sam froze. One of the sleepers had stopped snoring. He waited, wondering if the dim glow from the Grail could be seen from inside the bed curtain. Wondering if he could grab Mordred's sword from its sheath on the floor and manage to do anything besides stab himself with it. Wondering how far he'd get if he grabbed the Grail and made a run for it. Wondering if—. Ah. Wondering if whoever had awoken would fall asleep again. As a second melody of snoring joined the other, he resumed breathing.

Bending his knees, Sam squatted like a weightlifter and hefted the softly glowing, glass-encased Grail up and against his padded chest. He then staggered toward the outer room. Muscles and joints, cramped from having spent the past few hours curled up on the floor, screamed at him. His movements caused all sorts of awkward noises where no noise should be, and Sam's own breath sounded loud in his ears. None of it, however, was as menacing as the squealing of the door as it had closed. Taking one tentative step after another, Sam worked his way across the bedroom, his soft leather Thorogood Oxfords treading soundlessly on the stone floor.

Le Fay, thankfully, had left the door to the sitting room open. Sam paused as his eyes made out the shapes of the furniture he had seen hours earlier. The last thing he needed was to bang his shins against the low table. By the glow from the Grail, he navigated to the cushioned loveseat and set down his burden. He then took a deep, quiet breath and flexed his fingers before fumbling with the suite's door latch.

Again, he hesitated. Had the door squeaked when he'd entered? A good thief would remember. Sam didn't. Not only was he a crappy cop, he was a crappy thief. The jails were full of people just like him. Graveyard plots as well. Maybe he should have aspired to be Rick Blaine instead of Philip Marlow. Managing a nightclub might have required a simpler skillset.

He'd also never have to stick his neck out for nobody, and would avoid getting into these situations. With a chorus of snoring at his back, Sam lifted the latch and inched the door open. It didn't squeak.

Sudden light blinded Sam. He squinted as he poked his head outside, looking left then right down the corridor. He didn't know what he'd expected. Galahad? Mordred's minions? Servants sweeping the hall? As his eyes adjusted, he realized that the empty hallway was actually quite dark, illuminated by a single wall sconce. The human eye was an amazing thing.

As he turned back to collect the Grail, Sam spied the basket of towels he had left against an inside wall. Had neither Le Fay nor Mordred noticed it? It looked untouched. Should he leave it? Take it? It was quite the quandary. If the villains had noticed it, they might question why it went missing. If they hadn't noticed it, they may see the basket in the morning and question why it was there.

Bogart would know what to do. He'd take one look at the situation and see the best way out of it. Like Charlie Allnut in *The African Queen*. Well, maybe Rose was the real hero there, but they had made a good team.

And then it came to him. After wedging most of the towels underneath Le Fay's sofa, Sam hefted the Grail into the basket and draped the remaining three towels over it. It wasn't a perfect disguise—he'd look like a servant delivering a hardboiled dinosaur egg for someone's midnight snack—but if Galahad was right and no one paid attention to servants, he might just get away with it.

20

A FIFTY POUND BASKET

OR NOT. A few steps walk from Le Fay's door confirmed Sam's worst fears. While the upper crust residents this high in Camelot's tower rated an oil lamp in a corridor, that privilege didn't extend to the servants' stairs. And he already knew it didn't extend to the rest of the castle. Sam wasn't sure he could find his way back to Hammett's shop in daylight, never mind wandering without a lantern through the darkened castle.

Had Le Fay or Mordred brought a lamp to her rooms when they arrived? Sam hadn't seen one. Nor had he seen one earlier when he'd been searching. And every minute he stood in the hallway holding fifty pounds of glass in a basket was another minute where someone might come along and ask him a difficult question. Maybe even someone looking for an escaped miscreant. And was the basket getting heavier?

Sam could only think of one solution, though he didn't like it much.

In the absence of daylight, the top of the servants' stairwell looked like the gaping maw to Hell after the eternal fires had gone out. Much darker than they had been that afternoon. Sam had never considered himself the kind of mook who was afraid of the dark. The idea was laughable. But as he peered into the nothingness beyond those first few steps . . . the word *abyss* came to mind, even though he knew the stairs circled down through several flights of Camelot Castle and not into some bottomless void.

It occurred to Sam that he could pull back the cloths that covered the Grail and the Light of Christ would guide his way in the darkness. Sam had never considered himself a religious man either, but he'd take a sop where he could find it. He set the basket down to rearrange its contents and was pleased to see he hadn't imagined the glass egg's soft blue glow in Le Fay's apartment. It wasn't a lot of light, but as he made his way down the steps, it was enough to give him a sense of walls and the twisting of the stairwell.

Subdued light from the opening to the next level down soon competed with and then overpowered that of the Grail. Sam was tempted to continue down to the main floor and through the castle to the stairs leading up to Hammett's office, but knew that if one single soul was about and saw him with a glowing, glass-encased Holy Cup, that his crappy disguise would be the least of his problems. So, instead, he stepped out of the stairwell into the dimly lit corridor and made his way to a door he had visited earlier.

The insides of the magician's rooms were as dark as the stairwell, but Sam was familiar enough with the layout and still had the Grail's glow. Making his way to the small closet in the bedless bedroom, he set the glowing orb inside the empty chest, where it barely fit, and then settled himself into Merlin's narrow cot. He had this to say about the bed—it was more comfortable than the floor of Morgan Le Fay's closet. Whatever the next few hours might bring, he figured lying low in the missing magician's apartment a safer bet than wandering the castle.

Sam didn't know when he had fallen asleep, but he woke with a start and lay frozen, listening. Was it Morgan Le Fay shrieking with rage from higher in the tower that had wakened him? Or just some random noise from the town outside the castle window?

Several heartbeats passed without a fireball turning Merlin's alcove into an oven or an earthquake levelling the tower, so Sam swung his feet to the floor and pushed open the closet door.

The sky outside the window was more white than blue,

with the sun still below the horizon. Sam couldn't remember the last time he'd been awake early enough for predawn in Hartford. He pushed back the sleeve that covered his Rolex. 8:37 a.m. That couldn't be right. Of course, that was Hartford time. His watch was eight hundred billion minutes off. Give or take. Local time was more like five in the morning. Sam hoped Camelot was enough like Hartford that the servants would be up doing blue-collar duties while the hoity-toity got in an extra hour or two of beauty sleep. It did, however, seem a perfect time for smuggling the Grail into Hammett's shop.

Sam took a moment to straighten his disguise; tumbling around in Le Fay's closet and then Merlin's cot had done a number on his bosom. After several attempts to achieve anatomical correctness, he still felt like a bag lady shoplifter with an accordion stuck down her dress. The mirror in Le Fay's bedroom would have come in handy. The witch's magic would have been better. He'd just have to hope the basket against his bosom would hide the major flaws. As a last step, Sam pulled his mop cap closer to his ears, hoping his unfashionably short hair wasn't too obvious.

The lantern in the hallway was dark. Either it had run out of oil or a servant had extinguished it. Dull light seeped along the corridor from the courtyard windows and the larger window set near the servant stairs, leaving long rectangular shadows.

Sam adjusted the Grail's covering before hefting the basket. Had it grown heavier in the night? Or was he psyching himself out with the prospect of hauling it from one end of the castle to the other? He'd considered leaving the basket in Merlin's closet and getting Galahad to do the heavy lifting, but his gut told him that knights were above carrying laundry and that it would draw suspicion. No, this was a job for a servant and Sam was the only one who could pull it off. Was this why the Lady of the Lake had come to Hartford for him? He didn't think it would look that great on a résumé.

Noises echoed from elsewhere in the castle as Sam trundled down the deserted hallway toward the stairs. Clattering. Whispers. Footsteps. It was only a matter of time before his disguise would be tested. Pulling the basket tighter to his chest, he scuttled down the servants' stairwell as quickly as he could.

Two flights down, he paused to let a girl who could be no older than ten exit the stairwell with a pan of steaming hot water. The urchin gaped at Sam's face but said nothing as she slipped by. Sam realized he must have a five o'clock shadow, though by now it could be a fifteen or twenty o'clock shadow. Because of the heavy basket, he couldn't touch his chin for an assessment. Maybe he would have been better disguised as a nun, the kind that wore black veils and kept them pulled down over their faces. On the other hand, a nun shrouding her face while carrying a basket of laundry through the castle might raise undue eyebrows.

As Sam neared Camelot's main level, he found servants everywhere, scuttling like ants and carrying trays and baskets and boxes and even a live chicken. Many of the burdens looked like breakfast, so maybe the nobles were already mobile. Most of the workers were in too big of a hurry to pay Sam any mind, though a few did stop and stare. Sam figured it wouldn't be long before he ranked number one on the servant rumour mill.

Once on the main floor, Sam lowered his face and joined a confusion of servants scurrying in all directions. With hurried steps he made his way through the royal wing, past the gatehouse and page pen, and to the stairs leading up to the retail wing. Several knights strode by, laughing and speaking, expounding with their hands, and giving the servants no notice whatsoever. Then Sam was up the stairs and walking fast toward Hammett's shop. His arms trembled from carrying the glass-encased cup all that distance, but he had only a few dozen steps to go.

"You there! What do you think you are doing?"

The voice came from behind him. Sam toyed with the idea of ignoring it before considering that whoever it was might follow him straight to Hammett's door. He stopped. Turned. Before him stood a butler of some kind with a severe look on his face and a nose that could only be looked down no matter what the man's mood.

The butler managed a deep scowl. "You do not belong in this area. Explain yourself."

Sam put on his best falsetto. "Mary sent me." He figured it was such a common name that there must be many Mary's. Surely this jasper had at least one working for him.

The butler narrowed his eyes and cast Sam an incredulous stare. "Why would Mary do that?"

It was a good question. Sam scrambled for an answer. "The Necessarium," he blurted, then wiggled his basket. "It needs towels."

"And Mary sent you? That lazy ox! You tell her to report to me when you get back. Necessarium towels!"

Sam turned to flee and even made it two steps before the butler spoke again.

"You must be new to the castle. What is your name?"

"Uh, Samonella. Sir."

"Samonella. A beautiful name. Perhaps you will come visit me later. After tea perhaps."

Sam didn't turn around. Whether to avoid the lecherous look he knew must be on the jasper's face or to hide the horror on his own, he didn't know.

"That would be lovely. Sir." He fled even faster.

After the bend of the castle hid him from his admirer, Sam began to sprint. He didn't stop until he was outside *Camelot Jeweller's*. Near collapsing from carrying the bloody basket halfway across the castle, he didn't set it down, but bumped himself several times against the door, using the glass-encased cup as a knocker.

The door opened and Galahad stared at him. When the knight recovered from his shock, he hissed, "Get in here!" and pulled the door shut after Sam.

"Where have you been?" Galahad demanded.

"In Vivian's closet," Sam said, "witnessing for free what some people pay good money for." He allowed gravity to pull the murderously heavy basket onto the floor, letting it settle lightly only at the last moment.

"We were about to mount a rescue," Hammett said. "Well, Sir Galahad was."

"A second rescue," said the knight. "I sent a page earlier this morning to lure Lady Vivian from her rooms, but the boy's knock produced no answer."

"I may have had something to do with that," Sam said. "I spiked her and Mordred's wine."

"Vivian's son was with her?" asked Hammett.

Sam yanked the mop cap off his head and tossed it to the floor, then began extricating himself from the gown. "As to that, I learned a few things last night. First is that Lady Vivian is not Lady Vivian. She's a con artist named Morgan Le Fay."

"A con artist?" asked Galahad.

"A pathological liar with the wit to make a business out of it."

"Le Fay," murmured Hammett. "I know that name. Wasn't she involved with the chicken?"

"That's her. I also learned that Mordred is not her son."

"How did you learn that?" asked Galahad.

"I'd rather not say. Lastly, I learned that Le Fay is waiting for Arthur to die so that she can manipulate the throne away from Queen Guinevere."

"Steal the throne!" shouted Galahad. "How does she intend to do that?"

"She didn't say, but I'm confident she has a plan."

Galahad began pacing the room. "This is a disaster. King Arthur on his deathbed. An artist to assume the throne."

"Con artist," Hammett interjected.

"And we are helpless," Galahad finished.

"Maybe not," Sam said. He had finished shedding his maid disguise and had secured his gun, suit jacket, trench coat, and fedora from Hammett. "We do have this."

Leaning over the basket he had left by the door, Sam pushed aside the covering towels and hefted the glass-encased cup into his hands. He then strode over to Hammett's counter and planted the giant glass egg on the cleared space where the fake Grail had sat the previous afternoon.

"Is that the Grail?" Galahad asked, his expression indecipherable.

"Appears to be. I found it in Morgan Le Fay's closet."

Hammett had retrieved his monocle and was examining the glass. "This is astounding," the jeweller said.

"Yeah. It weighs a ton, too."

"But why," Galahad demanded, "is the Grail encased in diamond?"

"Eh, what?" asked Sam. "I thought it was glass."

"Don't be ridiculous." Galahad waved a hand at the orb. "You can hardly see through glass more than an inch thick; you'd never know there was a cup inside. This material is flawless. And see the bluish tinge? It must be diamond."

"What do you say, Hammett? Have we got the world's largest jewel on your counter? Hammett?"

When the jeweller didn't answer, Sam shifted his gaze from the cup and across the counter. There was no one there. Walking around the long table, he found Hammett on the floor. Unconscious.

"Well," said the knight. "I believe you have your answer."

21

DIAMONDS ARE A
JEWELLER'S BEST FRIEND

SAM SLAPPED HAMMETT across the face. When that failed, he slapped him again, harder. Then harder still. Finally, the man groaned and rolled his head to get it away from Sam's hand.

"Why," asked Galahad, "would Lady Vivian—Lady Le Fay—require a throne when she has an apparently endless supply of diamond?"

"We've already had this discussion," Sam said as he helped Hammett to his feet. "The three Ps. Greed, Passion, and Power."

"Eh," said Hammett. "Greed doesn't start with a P."

"I was never any good at spelling," Sam said. "But you get my drift. Money used to be Le Fay's game. Now she's progressed to passion and power."

"Passion?" asked Hammett.

"Don't ask. Morgan Le Fay wants to be Queen and she's willing to murder anyone who gets in her way."

Galahad nodded. "I understand that, but how is the Grail going to help us?"

"I'm no expert," Sam said, "but I think the King's health is tied to the Grail. If we can remove the cup from its diamond cocoon and get it back on its pedestal, I think maybe the King will recover."

273

The knight snorted.

"That is a lot of *ifs* and *maybes*," Hammett said.

"Even should you be right," suggested Galahad, "will Lady Vivian not simply find another way to murder the King and carry out her plan?"

Hammett nodded. "The knight is correct. The Grail is not the solution. Returning the Merlin to Camelot is. If, God willing, the magician yet lives."

Sam let out a heavy sigh. "Well, that's the million-dollar question, isn't it?"

"Your pardon," said Hammett. "What is a dollar?"

"Something like a Pendragon," Sam said, "but buys less with each passing day."

"Sounds like a currency best avoided," Hammett said.

Sam shrugged. "You'd think. But look, the problems of the world are not my department. I've got a job to do and that job is to solve the crisis here so I can get back to Hartford and save my partner. Galahad and I will focus our attention on finding Merlin. In the meantime, Hammett, you can work on freeing the Grail from the diamond."

"I can what?" The jeweller's hands began trembling. "You want me to cut the diamond! This diamond? Like your dollar, that will reduce its value. This is one of a kind!"

"We must free the Grail!" Galahad insisted.

"Look at it this way," Sam said. "Who do you know who can afford to buy this diamond?"

Hammett puffed out his cheeks, which looked comical on such a narrow face. "What? No one could buy this diamond. Even were it not stolen. From Le Fay or whoever she acquired it from."

"Right, so it's worthless."

"But—"

"Break it up into smaller stones and you can sell them. Earn enough Pendragons to buy a small country."

"But—"

Galahad interrupted. "What if Hammett damages the Grail?"

The jeweller ran trembling fingers across the orb's surface. "Sir Galahad makes a good point. I have never cut a stone like this."

"Then you can practice on this one." Sam pulled from his trench coat pocket the egg he had pilfered from Vivian's office and tossed it to the jeweller. Hammett almost dropped the glass-encased feather as it bounced between the fingers of both hands. His eyes boggled as he stared at it.

"You truly are a magician," Galahad said, also staring at the egg.

"I'd like to say I pulled that egg out of thin air," Sam said. "But the truth is I stole it from Le Fay."

"A diamond this size can be sold," Hammett said. "And the feather inside makes it ten times as valuable. A hundred times." He pushed his monocle against his eye. "Is that a chicken feather? A black chicken feather?"

Sam pulled his tobacco kit from his coat. It was early in the day to light up. He'd been trying to cut down by not smoking before breakfast, but his watch said breakfast was long past. That was good enough for him. "It's up to you if you want to practice or not," he said to Hammett.

As he rolled a cigarette, Sam asked Galahad a question he already knew the answer to. "Any ideas on how to find Merlin?"

The knight shook his head. "Perhaps we could speak with his secretary, Lady Euphemia Peregrine."

"I tried that yesterday," Sam said, striking a match, "though our conversation was a bit rushed. Maybe she'll have something for us now." Sam took a long, sweet pull from the cancer stick and then eyed the door.

"You cannot be thinking of seeing her yourself," Galahad said. "You would be arrested within moments."

"I hope you're not going to suggest a third disguise," Sam said.

The knight chortled. "I was going to suggest that you wait here while I retrieve the Lady Peregrine."

Sam blew out a smoke ring. "I can live with that."

While the knight was gone, Sam leaned against one of the few sections of bare wall and eyed the guard who had stood silent and expressionless throughout two rounds of treasonous conversation.

"You need not worry about him," Hammett said from where he stood at his counter examining the two diamond orbs. "Schultz's family has guarded mine for generations, ever since my great-great-great-grandfather Wilhelm opened a humble artisan shop in Old Saxony and hired Schultz's ancestor as a bodyguard. Our families have been thick as thieves ever since, if you will forgive the expression."

"Even so," Sam said, "What's to prevent Schultzy from talking?"

"We have an understanding," Hammett said.

"What understanding is that?"

"That if castle knights arrive with difficult questions, that Schultz saw nothing, heard nothing, and knows nothing."

The guard smiled.

"If it comes to that," Sam said. "You don't know nothing either. We'll tell them I broke in here and held you at gunpoint. There was nothing you could do about it."

"Gunpoint?" Hammett arched a brow. "I have been meaning to ask you—"

"Remind me to give you a demonstration sometime. You wouldn't want one in your office."

A few minutes later the door opened and Galahad and Effie rushed into the room.

"Sam!" Effie said. "You are still alive!"

22

LADY VIVIAN'S ERRAND

"Did you hear I was dead?" Sam asked.

The tall blonde looked Sam up and down and wagged her head. "What I heard is that you were thrown into the dungeon. You then escaped and every knight in the castle was looking for you. Then this morning Lady Vivian came bursting into the office screaming something about being drugged and knowing it was you, and that she would turn you inside out, scatter your bones to the four winds, and then, after a while, maybe let you die."

"So, she's awake already."

Effie's eyes widened. "You did drug her?"

"I may have added a little flavour enhancement to her wine. Did she say anything about the Grail?"

"The Holy Grail? Why would she?" It was then Effie noticed the diamond-encased chalice on Hammett's counter. "Is that—?"

"—A long story? Yes. You do know that Vivian is really Morgan Le Fay?"

"Of course, I know." Effie turned back to face Sam. "Everyone knows. Lady Le Fay changed her name years ago after she began apprenticing to the Merlin. Something about making a fresh start."

"Well, it would have been swell if someone had informed me."

"Sam, you must leave the castle. If Lady Vivian finds you . . ."

Sam shrugged. "Yeah, well, I can't do anything until I find

277

Merlin. Have you been able to think of anything since yesterday?"

Effie dipped her hand into the pouch she carried at her belt and pulled out a small scroll. "While Lady Vivian was out, I went through her papers looking for anything unusual."

"And you found something?"

Effie gave a noncommittal shrug. "She has been buying a lot of dresses lately. And nightgowns. An ungodly number of nightgowns."

"I think that's legitimate," Sam said.

"And then there is this." Effie rolled out the parchment. "Lady Vivian bought a parcel of property quite a distance outside the city. Just empty land. No buildings. No fields. No one to work the land. It would be difficult to find a poorer investment."

"Really?" Sam rubbed his ear. "It looks like you'll get your wish."

"What wish?"

"I'm leaving the castle."

Galahad shook his head. "Easier said than done. Even should you make it as far as the gate, Sir Gawain and Sir Caradoc will skewer you."

Sam laughed. "Those two I can handle. But you're right. If things get more serious, I may have to shoot my way out."

"You are being ridiculous," Effie said. "I can get you out."

"If you're thinking you could dress me up as a serving maid, that ship has sailed."

"Now you truly are being ridiculous. That is a terrible idea. With Sir Galahad's assistance I shall return momentarily with the means of your escape."

"I trust you, angel. Show me what you've got."

Sam watched as Galahad and Effie left the shop to walk freely about the castle. He rubbed his ear, overcome with the sense that something wasn't right. There was a burning in his belly. Or maybe a little higher. Not a bad burning. A warmth. Like a crackling fire on a cold night. Or a steaming cup of coffee after a fine meal. It took him a moment to put his finger on it, and then he remembered the words he'd just said—I trust you.

Sam couldn't remember the last time he'd said those

words. Maybe he'd never said them. They were true. He did trust Effie. Effie was the first person he had ever trusted. But he guessed he'd never had the chance to tell her. He didn't know that telling her would make a difference. If not for her then for him. It felt good. He'd have to try it again sometime.

A noise from the table drew Sam's attention. He turned to see Hammett with his monocle clenched over one eye and a tiny hammer and chisel in either hand poised over the feather egg. Sweat glistened on his tall forehead and trickled down his cheeks. The man's concentration was so complete that Sam found himself holding his breath.

Hammett must have adjusted the chisel a dozen times before finally giving it a small tap with the hammer. The tap was so light Sam expected nothing to happen, but the egg quietly split into two pieces. After several additional minutes of fussing, the jeweller tapped his chisel a second time, and then there were three pieces.

The door opened and Effie strode in, followed by someone whose arms were so loaded up with coats and dresses that Sam couldn't see who it was until Galahad dumped the whole lot of it onto the floor. Effie rummaged through the stack of clothes until she came up with a long, off-white winter coat that was almost as dark as Sam's tan trench coat.

"Put this on over your coat," she said. "And give me your hat. You will never pass through the castle wearing it."

Sam obliged and then stood like a tree while Effie draped a dress across each shoulder and then piled the remaining clothes across his upraised arms, much as Galahad had been laden. When she was done, Effie said, "Lift your arms higher. We must cover your face. Higher. That should do. Now we should go before your arms fall off."

"I must remain in the castle," Galahad said. "Mordred expects me in the training yard. But you should not go unprotected. I shall send someone out to your carriage."

Before Sam could say anything, the knight was gone.

"We must also leave before Lady Vivian decides she needs me," Effie said, "and sends a page to find me."

Sam followed two steps behind as Effie swept along the hallway toward the stairs. He could barely see where he was going, but guessed that was the point. From what he could tell, the corridor was empty, as usual, but that would change once they neared the gatehouse downstairs.

"Lady Peregrine," said a familiar voice, that of the butler he had run into earlier.

Effie stopped and Sam almost bumped into her. He lifted his armload of clothing higher to hide his face.

"The new maid," said the Butler. "Samonella. Have you seen her?"

"New maid?" asked Effie. "I have seen no one new."

"Pity. We have an appointment later today. I was hoping to learn somewhat about her before then. And this is odd. She was delivering towels to the Necessarium, but that is on the lower floor. She may require a brief tour—"

"I am sorry," Effie interrupted. "I cannot be of help. If you will excuse me. My man here will collapse if we do not reach my carriage soon."

"Of course. A thousand pardons. Ahh, is your office not the other way?"

"I had my winter wardrobe in storage with the dress mistress. I should have taken these things home weeks ago, but Lady Vivian is so demanding."

"Ah, yes, the Lady. Good day to you then."

The butler vanished almost before Sam could blink his eyes. Vivian's name carried weight. Or, if not weight, fear.

At the gate, Sam tensed as the two knights, the same who had been on duty the previous afternoon, moved to block Effie.

Sir Caradoc stepped forward. "Halt. We need to see your papers and inspect your man's burdens."

"That is ridiculous," Effie said. "Since when do you inspect people leaving the castle?"

Gawain spoke up. "Since Sir Mordred left us orders. There is a villain escaped from the dungeon."

"I see. And does this villain look anything like me?"

Caradoc sputtered. "Of course not, my lady, but orders are orders."

Effie let out a heavy sigh. "Very well. Lady Vivian will not be pleased that I am delayed in performing her errand, but I am confident you will be able to explain things to her."

"Wait," said Gawain. "What? Us?"

"You could, of course," Effie continued, "suggest to Lady Vivian that she ask her son to explain your actions. I am confident Sir Mordred will not mind telling his mother that his orders take precedence over hers."

"Lady Peregrine," said Sir Gawain, "I am sure there is no need to—"

Effie turned on her heels. "Come, Simon. We must go ask Lady Vivian to procure you papers and write up an itemized list so that we may refresh the Lady's wardrobe. While she is very busy right now, I am confident Lady Vivian will happily put aside her activities to draw up papers."

"Lady Peregrine," Gawain repeated. "Wait! Delaying you is the furthest thing from what Sir Mordred intended. Please, continue on your way."

"With our blessing," Caradoc added.

Effie turned again. "Well, if you think it is all right. I have no wish to displease your Second Knight."

"More than all right," Sir Gawain insisted. "Please?"

"Very well. Come along, Simon."

Once outside, Sam watched as Effie hired the first carriage in the queue and deftly refused offers to help *Simon* load his burdens into the carriage. "I am paying you to drive," Effie said. "And I am paying Simon to carry laundry."

Sam managed to heave everything onto one of the benches inside the carriage and fall onto the bench alongside it. Anyone watching would see little more than the bottom of his shoes.

"Here comes Galahad's man," Effie whispered. Then she climbed inside onto the opposite bench.

A young man jumped up immediately after Effie and sat on the bench beside her. Robin of Locksley looked into Sam's face and grinned. "It gladdens me to see you still alive, Mr. Spade."

23
A RIDE IN THE COUNTRY

BY THE TIME Sam brought Effie and Robin up to speed, the carriage had left the city and was winding its way through the English countryside. From a basket she had brought, Effie produced Sam's fedora and a simple breakfast of finger sandwiches, fresh fruit, and cheese. Having only eaten a bit of honeyed bread since breakfast the previous day, Sam was famished. He probably ate more than Effie and Robin combined.

"What do you suspect we will find at the property?" Robin asked. "Merlin bound and gagged? Possibly guarded by henchmen?" He reached up and touched the unstrung bow he had tucked into a ledge along the carriage ceiling. "I am eager to shoot unblunted arrows."

"I don't know," Sam said. "I'm hoping it's not an unmarked grave. But it's the only lead we've got."

Robin nodded. "I still cannot believe that Sir Mordred is Lady Vivian's lover and not her son."

Sam snorted. "Six years ago, he was her adversary and she was ready to throw him under a bus for a handful of Pendragons. Morgan Le Fay is not a woman to be trusted."

"The Merlin is a fool," Effie said, her face a thundercloud. She looked at Sam. "You never trusted her. Not completely. You played her game and turned it against her. The Merlin knew she was complicit in murder and larceny, yet he put that aside and made her his apprentice and then his lover. He taught her how to perform magic. Now the Merlin is gone and Vivian is a monster!"

"Don't hold back, angel," Sam said. "Tell us how you really feel."

"Well, she is a monster. She treats people like playthings. Pouts when she fails to get her way. And people have gone missing. Not just the Merlin."

Sam figured Effie had built up a mountain of resentment over the past six years as she regaled Robin and himself with tale after tale of misdeed, indiscretion, and deviltry. By the time she ran out of stories, the driver brought the carriage to a stop at their destination.

After clambering down onto solid ground, Sam stretched as his gaze took in a scene of fields, forests, and a steep hillside. It could have been any wilderness area. "Are you sure this is the right place?" he asked the driver.

The man frowned at him. "The distances are well described in the document." He pointed. "That hill is also marked."

Robin had squatted and was running one hand along the ground. "Another carriage was here," he said. "Recently." He turned his head and looked along the wild grass. "The tracks run toward the hill."

Effie and Robin began walking.

"Will the driver wait?" Sam asked.

The driver cleared his throat. "The Lady has rented my services for the day."

"Right." When Sam caught up to the others, they were examining a rockslide that covered a substantial part of the hill.

"This is recent," Robin said. "See how loose the earth is? And no plants grow between the stones."

"We'll have to dig it out," Sam said.

Robin shook his head. "That could be dangerous. Move the wrong rock and more hill will tumble down from above."

"I fail to see how we have a choice," Effie said. "I shall hire the driver to lend aid."

"Ask him if he has a rope," Sam said. "Maybe we can reduce the danger."

The driver returned with Effie, a long coil of rope hanging

from one shoulder. He looked at Sam. "Of course, I have rope. I would not be much of a carriage driver without rope."

Sam had no idea what a carriage driver might find essential.

The driver eyed the rock fall. "What is your plan?"

Sam pointed at a large rock at the base of the hill that supported other rocks piled above and around it. "We tie the rope around that rock and your horse pulls it free. That should clear a good part of the scree. If more rock comes down, none of us will be near enough to be in danger. With luck, the hillside will break open."

The driver shook his head. "It would be a mistreatment of animals to ask Betsy to do such a thing."

"Mistreat—" Sam was near speechless. "Betsy just pulled a carriage loaded with four people across half of England. I'm sure she can pull a rock off a hill."

Effie sighed. "Would five pennies make Betsy feel better?"

"I am certain it would," the driver said. After collecting the pennies, he began working the end of the rope around a spur of the large rock.

"Here," Robin said. He unsheathed his sword and began spading away dirt and gravel to make space for the rope. "This will be a practice sword when I am done."

It took longer than Sam thought possible to secure the rock, tightening the rope around several spurs that Robin had dug out. The driver unhitched Betsy and tied the other end to her harness. At a word, Betsy stepped forward and pulled the large rock free, bringing a pile of debris with it. Needless to say, behind the freed rocks were more rocks.

"What I wouldn't give right now," Sam said, "for a stick of dynamite."

"Is that a type of shovel?" Robin asked.

Sam rubbed his ear. "Yes."

"Our hands must suffice," Effie said. The tall daughter of a duke was the first to get her hands dirty slinging rocks.

The afternoon wore on as Sam laboured to expose a second and then a third large boulder for Betsy to pull out of the rock fall. Though to be honest, Robin did the lion's share of work and Effie was no slouch either. The carriage driver reluctantly moved a few stones; he must have been allergic to sweat. By the time the sun hung low on the horizon, they'd cleared sufficient rock to reveal a small cave. Fortunately, the cave faced west and the sun shone directly into the opening. Sam and Robin clambered inside while Effie remained a distance away with the driver.

"What do you see?" she called.

"Give us a minute," Sam called back. "There's a lot of rocks."

"I fail to see a tunnel or deeper cavern," Robin said.

"Here," Sam said. "I think." He brushed dust and dirt away from a particularly large rock. "Yes. I've found Merlin."

24

A FATHER'S PERMISSION

"Is he—Is he dead?"

Sam had never heard such concern in Effie's voice before. She must have a real liking for the old coot. "That's a good question. We're going to need that rope again."

It took just short of a miracle to secure the rope in such a way that Betsy could pull Merlin out of the cave without the rope simply sliding off. The driver almost had a heart attack when he saw the magician. Robin just chuckled. Effie didn't know what to make of it. She had seen the diamond-encased chicken feather on Merlin's shelf and the Grail at Hammett's, but that was peanuts compared to a grown man encased in diamond.

"It is a glass coffin," Effie said. "How can the Merlin not be dead?"

"I'd like to get him away from here before we decide one way or another," Sam said.

Robin nodded. "Lady Vivian or her lackeys could return at any time."

"We shall take him to my father's estate." Effie frowned. "Can the four of us lift him onto the roof of the carriage?"

"No," Robin said. "Not even four strong knights could lift that weight."

"So we drag him behind the carriage," Sam suggested.

The driver, who had stayed out of the conversation, shook his head. "Betsy cannot pull the carriage and that great ponderous rock."

"Then we'll walk," Sam said. "The three of us. Will that work?"

The driver nodded. "Perhaps." He looked at the descending sun. "We must depart now if we hope to reach the Duke's estate before dark."

Sam had never been much of a hiker. As a cop he'd walked a beat, but a private eye's life was pretty sedentary. A lot of sitting behind a desk and sitting in cafes and sitting in cars and well, just a lot of sitting. His legs already ached from spending half the day moving rocks. Ached almost as much as his back and arms and hands. They hadn't walked thirty minutes before his feet felt like two huge blisters. His Thorogood Oxfords were an excellent shoe, with a removable shock absorption insert and a non-slip outsole, but they were meant for sidewalks and interior floors, not traipsing about the countryside. His gumshoes wouldn't have helped much. Fortunately, they had to stop now and then to resecure the rope that managed to work itself free no matter how they tied it.

As darkness fell, the driver lit a single lantern and Effie ran ahead. Ten minutes later dusk gave up the ghost and all Sam could see was blackness and a few pinprick stars.

The driver kept Betsy moving, however, either confident in his progress or able to see in the dark a whole lot better than Sam. Another handful of minutes passed. Then several lights bobbed in the darkness before them. The lights came closer, and Sam saw Effie and several of her father's men carrying lanterns. The men took charge of the roped coffin and guided them to a barn where they unhitched and stabled Betsy.

Effie led Sam and Robin into the house where a servant showed them each a room on the upper floor. Sam's room was spacious, with a king-size bed and two windows with real glass. An unlit fireplace stood against one wall and there was a closet as well as a chest of drawers with a mirror and a deep bowl of room temperature water.

The servant left a lantern behind and Sam looked at himself in the mirror. A coal miner looked back at him. There wasn't much he could do about his dusty clothes, but removing his trench coat and suit jacket helped a bit. Sweat stained his wrinkled and dirty shirt, but an inspection of the closet revealed a dark-hued smoking jacket that hid most of the damage. Sam had just finished washing his face in the bowl and running his fingers through his hair when the servant returned announcing dinner.

The Duke was pretty much what Sam expected. A big man with a fleshy face and eyes that cut right through you. No city fop this one. Sam could tell that no amount of blue blood had kept the Duke from chopping down his own trees and furrowing his own fields. He was the block off of which Effie had been chipped. But Sam could see the man was ill. His eyes were sallow and he drooped with a lethargy that didn't seem to fit properly. Except to move between chairs, the Duke spent the entire time sitting. When he did move, it was with the aid of two servants.

The meal consisted of small talk, after which Effie explained to her father some of what was going on. The Duke nodded, his expression serious, but commented little. Squire Robin then regaled them with tales of Nottinghamshire before saying good night after dessert. The talk was excellent. The food wasn't bad either.

When Sam made to follow Robin's cue and excuse himself, the Duke raised his hand and said the most he'd said all evening. "Join me, Mr. Spade, for a glass of port and a smoke by the fire."

By the fire turned out to be some kind of mediaeval man cave, with the smell of tobacco competing with cedar crackling in a wide fireplace. A small window looked out into the darkened night, but Sam sensed that the room would be dark during the day as well. Even in the limited glow from the fireplace he could see that the stonework was black if not dark grey and the wood floor, ceiling, and panelling were stained almost as red as blood. It was a room designed for deep thoughts.

"I see the way you look at my daughter," the old man said as he lit his pipe.

Sam had had the foresight to move his tobacco kit from his trench coat to the smoking jacket. He'd begun rolling a cigarette the moment the Duke brought out his pipe. "Your daughter impresses me, sir. As do you." There were a number of ways this little talk could go. Sam hoped it wouldn't go in a direction that had him fleeing into the night with a load of rock salt in his posterior.

"Euphemia is the apple of my eye," the Duke said. "My only daughter."

Sam lit his cigarette and blew out a smoke ring.

"You are not from around here, are you?"

"No, sir," Sam said. "I'm from about as far out of town as you can get."

The Duke lifted his pipe to his lips, drew deeply, and then puffed out a solid ring of smoke that grew and dissipated as it sailed further from his lips. "Your family," he said. "Well thought of?"

There were a number of ways Sam could answer. Something told him that only the cold truth would suffice. "My father was murdered in prison and my mother skipped town."

The Duke looked at him and blew another smoke ring. "You are a self-made man, then."

Sam rubbed his ear. "About as self-made as it gets."

A third smoke ring.

"Have you ever been married?"

"I thought about it once. Couldn't find anyone who thought the same way."

"But you could support a family?" the Duke asked.

Sam reached into his pants pocket and pulled out one of his two Pendragons. He flipped it through his fingers, rolling it so that it popped up once between each pair of knuckles and then vanished. "I usually have a Pendragon at my disposal."

The Duke drummed his fingers along the arm of his chair. "Euphemia should have married years ago."

"Frankly sir, I am surprised she isn't married."

The Duke nodded. "She does not bring men home. You are the first in a long time."

Sam could only assume that *bringing men home* didn't mean what he thought it meant. He did figure that any kind of response would likely get him in trouble, so he opted for a sip of port. When the liquor tasted exactly how port should taste, he took a second sip.

"It would be a comfort," the Duke continued, "were she to marry before I passed on."

"I'm sure it would," Sam said. "But it might be more useful if you had this conversation with your daughter instead of me."

The old man smiled. "I have lost count of the number of times I have had this conversation with Euphemia."

"I get it," Sam said.

"It would not hurt," the Duke went on, "if you were to court my daughter. You have my permission."

"Ah, thank you, sir. I'm relieved to hear it."

The old man tamped out his pipe and rang a small bell that sat on the table next to his chair. Within seconds, two servants arrived to help the Duke to his feet.

"Good night, Mr. Spade."

25

A TROJAN COFFIN

SAM POLISHED OFF a second glass of port and then eased himself out of his chair. After lugging around the Grail in the morning and mining for Merlin in the afternoon, his body hurt from his toenails to the tips of his hair. He considered ringing the bell to see if two servants would help him to his bed, then chuckled to himself. Unlike the Duke, there was nothing remotely blue about his blood.

As Sam climbed the manor house stairs to the upper floor, he saw no sign of anyone still awake in the house. Deemed a servant, the carriage driver had been sent to a pallet above the barn. That was the last Sam saw of him. Robin was likely fast asleep. That or on the roof practicing his leaping and climbing skills. He hadn't seen Effie since her father invited him for a drink by the fire. He now understood why she had blanched and stormed up the stairs. It wasn't because she hadn't been invited.

Candles rather than lamps lit the hallway, shedding just enough light for Sam to find the way to his room. Inside, the fireplace crackled; one of the servants must have lit it earlier. Sam threw the smoking jacket and his shirt and pants over a chair, then fell onto the bed. He slept the sleep of the damned and woke the next morning as stiff as an over-starched shirt.

His one saving grace was the hot bath the Duke's servants had drawn for him that cooked some of the aches and pains out of his muscles and joints. When he returned to his room, he found his clothes brushed and folded, but not laundered. You can't have everything.

Breakfast consisted of eggs prepared six different ways, three kinds of toast, and several meats Sam didn't recognize. The Duke nodded a greeting, but said little. When it was done, Effie invited Sam to join her outside.

He assumed she wanted the lowdown on last night's talk with her father, but instead the gorgeous blonde said, "I have been thinking on how to smuggle the Merlin back into the castle."

"Wait a minute, angel. We don't know if the magician is even alive."

"And will not," Effie said, "until Hammett frees the Merlin from his diamond cocoon."

Sam rubbed his ear. "You may be right."

Effie took Sam's hand and led him into a small building behind the barn. Woodworking tools covered one wall, and on a bench lay a long wooden crate the size and shape of a coffin. Three iron bars ran beneath the box and stuck out the sides, one at each end and the third under the middle. Sam had seen enough coffins to know this was a six-pallbearer casket.

"Wouldn't it be simpler to bring Hammett out here?" Sam asked.

Effie laughed. "Thomas Hammett? The same Thomas Hammett who in twenty years has rarely left his shop, never mind the castle. You think you can convince him to come out here?"

"Twenty years? Why?"

Effie frowned. "I am not sure. I believe it has something to do with diamonds, drugs, and Denmark. Rumour has it that Hammett was quite adventurous as a young man."

Sam sighed. "If you say so, doll. If we can't bring Hammett to the Merlin, we'll bring the Merlin to Hammett. But how do you intend to get the magician past the gate guards?"

"That is why we require a casket."

Sam watched as the Duke's men carried the casket outside and slid it into the back of a wide cart. That was the easy part. They then pulled the cart into the barn and heaved and grunted until they managed to dump Merlin inside. It was a tight fit. The lid didn't lay quite flat as they nailed it down and a close inspection revealed that it bulged in the middle where wood pressed against diamond.

"Won't the knights want to look inside?" Sam asked.

"They will," Effie said. "I will not let them."

More of the Duke's people arrived, this time with bouquets of flowers that they placed in the cart around the casket as well as on top, arranging them to obscure the lid's slight bulge. Sam noticed the estate staff were dressed in black and the women wore veils over their faces.

"Whose casket is this, anyway?" Sam asked.

"My father's."

"Well, I guess it never hurts to be prepared."

Effie let out a soft sigh. "He will have need of one soon." Then she shook her head. "We need to change."

"Change? Into what?"

"Mourning clothes. You may hide your current attire in the cart beneath the flowers, but you must needs wear black attire like the rest of us."

"I'm all too familiar with funerals," Sam said. "Just point the way."

When Effie asked, the butler reported that Squire Robin's whereabouts were unknown, that he hadn't been seen since breakfast. They found him in a dressing room already buttoning up a formal-looking black coat.

"What do you need to sneak around for?" Sam asked. "It's not your head Mordred's after."

Robin smiled. "It is good practice. One never knows when one may be called upon to infiltrate a castle. Or a manor house."

Sam smiled back, remembering some of the stories he had heard about Robin Hood. "Sure, kid. You never know."

"These should fit you," Effie said, dropping a stack of dark clothing onto a nearby chair. Then she was gone.

Sam changed and agreed the fit wasn't bad. The pants were a little tight at the waist and the shirt a bit short in the sleeves, but after wearing Hammett's robe and the maid getup, he wasn't going to complain. The jacket, though, was a mind-blower. It had wide lapels, buttons the size of quarters, and hung down past his knees. It looked like a duster from Doc Holliday's closet. There was even room for his holster beneath the flaring coattails. "I feel like a cowboy," he said to Robin.

The squire's eyes widened. "Do not let Euphemia hear you say that. You wear the attire of a Lord, not a cowherd."

"I guess it loses something in the translation," Sam said.

As they stepped out of the house, Sam glanced back and saw the Duke of Earl watching from a chair near the front window. The old man gave him a solid nod. Sam only wished he knew what it meant. Was the old man really that desperate to marry off his daughter? If so, Sam would be happy to oblige. He'd never met anyone like Euphemia Peregrine. He just had to figure out how to get hitched in Camelot while at the same time rescue his partner in Hartford.

Effie also made eye contact with her father, sharing with the dying man a look Sam couldn't fathom. Then she turned to Sam. "Let us be away."

The procession left the estate at midmorning, a squadron of horsemen leading the way followed by the cart and then the rented carriage with Effie and three other family members. Sam figured them for the younger brother he had met at dinner and two female cousins who had appeared out of nowhere. Maybe they lived nearby. Several dozen servants followed on foot, Sam among them. His feet were still killing him from yesterday's walk, but he agreed with Effie that the lower his profile the better.

Robin ambled beside him, almost skipping to pass the miles. Initially, the squire tried to engage in conversation, but as Sam's legs flagged and he grew testy, the youth found other ways to amuse himself.

By the time countryside gave way to cobbled streets, Sam was ready to join Merlin in the casket. His legs and back ached and his feet were two bags of burning nerves. He hadn't looked, was afraid to look, but was sure that the soles of his shoes had worn away and he was now leaving a trail of bloody footprints. He was the walking dead. And he still had half the city to go.

He gritted his teeth as the procession wound its way through the suburbs, across a bridge, and into the more urban parts of Camelot where townsfolk began lining the streets. Here and there among the crowds an old man or young boy played mournful notes on piped instruments. Even more numerous were women with covered faces who wailed with such ferocity you'd think the Duke was their son. Most of the spectators just looked on with expressionless faces.

Robin sidled up to Sam. "Funeral processions for the nobility are common enough, but the lower classes never tire of them."

"Maybe it warms their hearts," Sam suggested, "to see that death plays no favourites."

The squire nodded. "We all bleed red."

The crowds thickened as the sun dipped lower in the sky and Sam believed that surely, surely it would set before they reached the castle. But as the procession neared the gate, the sun stood well above the horizon. Apparently, when one walked endlessly without a break, one could retard time.

When the procession reached the drawbridge, the horses parted and came to a halt to either side. The cart with the casket rolled ahead and then stopped at the foot of the bridge. The carriage pulled up beside it. The mourners marching with Sam crowded around as best they could while curious city residents swarmed in behind them.

Sam watched as the carriage door opened and Effie, dressed head to toe in black lace, stepped down. The mob remained hushed as she crossed over the moat, her close relatives a few steps behind.

"Halt! Who goes there?" Sir Gawain demanded.

Sam had to restrain himself from walking up and slapping the idiot knight upside the head.

"You know who I am," said Effie. "You must let us pass."

"Let you pass?" Sir Caradoc roared. "A less intelligent knight might believe you were invading the castle."

Sam could almost see Effie's eyes widen behind the black lace.

"Invasion! This is a funeral procession. My dear father has died."

"The Duke!" said Gawain. "My deepest sympathies, Miss Peregrine. I always liked your father."

"We have not seen him in some time," Caradoc said.

"The Duke has been ill!" Gawain admonished his partner. "Of course, we have not seen him."

Effie cleared her throat. "We have been in procession all day. I must get my father to the Great Hall where he may lie in state."

"Of course," said Gawain. "Please carry on."

"We must not," said Caradoc. "We are required to inspect everyone. And everything."

Effie put her hands on her hips. "We have eighty persons in our procession. How long will this take?"

"I—I am not sure," Caradoc admitted. "We have never inspected a funeral procession."

"Then why do so now?" demanded Effie.

Gawain's face darkened. "We are searching for an escaped felon. We told you that yesterday when you left the castle."

"And you expect this malefactor to break back into the castle?" she demanded. "Your felon is in London by now. Or France. Why would he be in our procession?"

Caradoc fidgeted with his sword. "Ahhh—"

Effie stamped her foot. "Get out of my way. My father grows riper with each minute we stand here."

Gawain nodded and stepped aside. Caradoc continued his fluster dance for a few moments, then joined him.

Effie turned to look back at the procession. Seeing her nod, the horsemen dismounted. Half the men took the reins from their neighbours to lead the horses to the stables in the courtyard. The other half moved to escort the cart on foot. In no time at all Sam was walking again, following the cart into the castle. He moved near the centre of the walking mourners, keeping his head down and avoiding the eyes of the two knights on guard.

Once inside, he saw that all bedlam had broken out. Several of the horsemen had led their mounts toward the royal wing rather than continuing straight toward the horse passage that led to the stalls in the courtyard. Knights from the gatehouse scrambled to prevent them, but were obstructed by a group of the Duke's staff who somehow managed to get in the way of one knight after another. In the middle of it all, Sir Kay, peacock tabard in full bloom, stood screaming at Effie, somehow blaming her for the chaos—which was true—while her relatives stood by with their hands to their faces, wailing louder than the professional mourners in the street.

In the midst of this confusion, the cart, surrounded by mourners from the procession, had stopped and the dismounted horsemen were hauling the casket off and straining to hold its weight. Sam grabbed Robin's arm and pulled the squire along as they joined a small party of mourners that followed the casket, obscuring it from view, as the Duke's men carried it along the corridor to the staircase to the second floor.

Coffins had never been designed to traverse stairs, especially a coffin that was essentially filled with rocks. Several of the men stood at the bottom end of the crate, pushing it upwards as the six men on the poles concentrated on just keeping it in the air.

From the main hallway, Sam heard increased commotion as horses were turned around and now tramped among the gate knights, mourners, and curious castle residents.

"Hurry," Sam whispered, more to himself than to the straining men.

At last they were up the stairs and racing down the corridor as quickly as the sweating men could move. Sam ran ahead and opened the door to Hammett's shop, relieved that neither Vivian nor anyone else had discovered them in the hallway.

The casket couldn't fit through the door with its carry poles in place, so the Duke's men lowered it to the corridor's stone floor and used a hammer to remove the lid. Though the men were exhausted, Sam pressed them to empty the casket as quickly as they could, which was easier said than done. In the end they had to remove the carry poles, heave the casket in through the door, and then tip it on its side so that the Merlin rolled out, turning over once before coming to rest face up.

Replacing the lid took only moments. Then the Duke's men were racing back down the corridor. They had to get the empty casket back to the cart before someone enforced order at the gate and realized it was missing.

Hammett, exhausted and wild haired, his hands raw and blistered, stared down at the jewel-encased magician. "You did it, Mr. Spade. Of course, you did. You just had to go and find another bloody diamond!"

26

HAMMETT'S LITTLE HELPER

SAM LOWERED HIS gaze from the jeweller's down-in-the-mouth expression to the countertop. A grin split his face as he took in a mountain range of button-sized diamonds surrounding a plain yellow chalice. "You've been busy."

"You have no idea," Hammett said. "I thought I would never say this, but I am sick of diamonds. Galahad has confirmed this is the genuine Grail, by the way."

"He did that trick with a cloth covering the cup?"

Hammett nodded. "I tried it myself. Fascinating. The Grail glows like a giant firefly."

"Really?" Sam rubbed his ear. "It was dimmer than a dying flashlight when it was encased in diamond."

The jeweller picked up one of the transparent stones and peered at it. "Perhaps that is the purpose of the diamond. Anything locked inside would be preserved from the elements. One might even say *frozen in time*."

"I'll leave the science stuff to you experts," Sam said.

"Galahad meant to swap the Grail with the sham cup in the chapel," Hammett said, "but Mordred sent him a page bearing instructions to perform guard duty in the buttery. A punishment of some kind. Apparently, Lady Vivian is displeased with your knight."

Robin let out a low whistle. "I fear the buttery is but the

beginning of Sir Galahad's punishments. Lady Vivian's displeasure knows no bounds."

Sam stepped over to the counter and flicked a fingernail at the yellow cup. It made a modest *ting* noise. "Well, there's not much we can do for Galahad right now. The dingus, however, might be fine right here. Maybe all it needs is to be free of the diamond. Either way, what we really need is to get Merlin released from that rock so he can deal with Le Fay."

"The Merlin is alive?" Hammett asked.

Sam picked up a handful of diamonds and slipped them into his pants pocket. "You said it yourself. Preserved by the elements. Frozen in time. I don't think I've ever worked a case with so many questions and so few answers."

Hammett stared at the giant gemstone on the floor of his shop. "How would the magician get himself encased in diamond?"

"I imagine the same way as the feather and the Grail. I'm pretty sure Merlin is responsible for the feather. I think we can credit Morgan Le Fay with the other two."

"Well, yes. But." The jeweller scrunched his eyes. "Why did you bring the Merlin here? That was foolhardy. Much easier if you had taken it someplace safe and I had joined you."

"Effie said you haven't left your office in twenty years."

Hammett shrugged. "I have had no reason to leave." He waved a ragged hand at the magician. "This looks reason enough."

"Well, what's done is done. How soon do you think you can get him out?"

Hammett frowned and shook both raw hands in front of Sam's face. "I have been chipping away at the chalice for almost as long as you have been gone. It may take several days to free the magician. With my hands like this, it may take weeks."

"We don't have weeks," Sam said. "Or days. We may not have hours. What if several of us grab a hammer?"

The jeweller's eyes grew like plates. "It takes years of training to cut a diamond. There is not a soul within miles who could do this besides myself. If you—"

"Then I suggest you start at his head," Sam said, "and work your way down."

"But my hands!"

"You'll have more than your hands to worry about if we're discovered. Now get moving."

Turning away from the jeweller, Sam grabbed Robin's arm and took the squire aside. "I need you to go to the Royal Herbalist and ask Friar Tuck to come back with you."

"Tuck? That fellow Vaisey tried to extort?"

"That's him. Tuck has a few tricks up his sleeve. Maybe he knows something that could help us."

Robin nodded and hurried out the door.

Sam turned back to Hammett. The jeweller was on his knees next to the magician, moving his tiny chisel left and right, looking for the right place to make his first tap.

"The clock's ticking," Sam said.

Hammett growled. "One wrong tap and I may split the magician's head rather than the diamond."

"Even so," Sam said. "We made quite a stir at the main gate. There's bound to be some fallout."

The door opened and Effie stepped inside, still shrouded in black. "We managed to convey the casket into the Great Hall without too many people wondering why it seemed to disappear and then reappear. My father's men guard it now. The casket will remain sealed until the King's Chamberlain arranges a state viewing. Once that happens, our deception will be discovered."

"When might the viewing happen?" Sam asked.

"As early as tomorrow morning."

"I heard," Hammett grumbled before Sam could say anything.

"I must go find Lady Vivian," Effie said. "I disappeared yesterday and it is only a matter of time before she learns I have returned and how I returned. I must need allay any suspicions she may have."

"Be careful, angel."

Effie laughed. "I have spent years being careful around Lady Vivian."

Almost as soon as the shapely blonde had left, the door opened again. Robin entered followed by Friar Tuck. The churchman stared at the jumble of diamonds on the counter. "Is that the Holy Grail?" Then he saw Merlin on the floor with Hammett taking a chisel to his face. "Oh my!"

Once he composed himself, the friar said, "Mr. Spade, I thought things were loopy the last time you were here. This . . . I have no words."

"We've got a problem," Sam said. "And there's no time to waste. We don't know if Merlin is alive or dead, but if we don't get him out of that diamond prison in the next few hours, I can almost guarantee that for the rest of us, living won't be an option. Have you got anything in that tea shop of yours that could help?"

"Help?" Tuck asked.

"Maybe something that dissolves diamond?"

Hammett choked from where he worked on the floor. "Nothing dissolves diamond. Diamond is the hardest substance in the world. Were it not crystalline in nature, even my chisels would be useless."

"The jeweller is correct," Tuck said.

"How about you?" Sam asked. "Are you any good with a chisel?"

"No one," Hammett said, "is touching my chisels. The only one qualified to do this is me. So let me get on with it."

"Maybe you have something for his hands," Sam said, not giving up. "He's been at this for hours and his fingers are raw. Maybe a lotion? Or a pain reliever?"

Tuck rubbed his chin. "I may have something in my shop that could help."

"I shall accompany you," Robin said.

The two were gone only a few minutes.

"Drink this," Tuck said, passing a flagon to Hammett.

The jeweller sniffed at it. "What is it? Wine?"

"Yes," Robin said. "I tried it myself. Quite refreshing."

"Perhaps a taste," Hammett said. "You do not want me doing this while intoxicated." The jeweller lifted the flagon and took a swallow. Then a second.

Tuck took the flagon back and led Sam across the room.

"Okay," Sam said. "What's really in there?"

"Wine," the friar said. "I simply added a few crushed coca leaves. You will not have heard of coca; it is very expensive and not very popular, but the herb aids with focus and precision. Some of the knights use it in the lanes during tournaments. Hammett should be able to work much faster while it is in his system."

"I'll take your word for it," Sam said, glancing at the jeweller. It might be his imagination, but Hammett's pupils looked dilated and it was taking him less time to place his chisel.

Robin also seemed a little too energetic, pacing across a small section of the floor and looking everywhere with his eyes.

"Say, Robin," Sam said. "Some of those candles look to be running low. Maybe you could refresh those that need it."

"Good idea," Robin said, a wide grin splitting his face. "I love candles. Anything to do with fire, actually. Nothing beats a roaring fire in the hearth. The way the flames dance and the wood crackles and sparks fly up into the chimney. Have you ever wondered where those sparks go and what they do when they get there? Maybe they—"

"There is a box of candles behind the counter," Hammett interrupted, not slowing in his work. "Has anyone ever told you how candles are made? First you have to—"

Sam tuned the two men out as they delivered their words with increasing speed and intensity. Any suspicion that the herb *coca* was cocaine and not chocolate needed no further confirmation. Sam had never tried the stuff himself, but had heard tales of various cops in Vice giving it a whirl as a means of gaining an edge. None of them had stuck with it; too many lousy side effects. As Hammett chipped away at the magician at an ever-faster pace and Robin scurried about the room replacing candles that didn't need replacing, Sam wondered how many leaves were a few.

Minutes passed like hours and Sam walked several times to the door before stopping himself. He didn't dare show his face in the castle. But Effie should have been back by now, hadn't she?

"Tuck," he said finally. "Could you walk back to your shop and swing past Vivian's office. If the door's open, maybe you'll be able to see if Effie is inside and if she's all right."

"Effie?"

"Lady Peregrine," Sam said.

"Ah, yes. You believe the good lady in danger?"

"She went to report to Vivian to make certain her boss isn't on to us."

"Of course," Tuck said and was gone.

More time passed and Tuck did not return. Robin ran out of candles and joined Sam pacing the floor, nattering into his ear something about the transcendence of the bow over the sword.

Finally, Sam had enough. "I can't just stand here and do nothing."

"I am with you," Robin announced. He drew his sword, blunted and battered from digging through the rock fall. He stared at it with glassy, startled eyes, and then muttered something unintelligible and sheathed it. Possibly his words were a lament that his bow was still in the carriage.

Leaving Hammett talking to himself while he worked, Sam stepped into the castle corridor with Robin hot on his heels. The corridor was eerily quiet after all the traffic through Hammett's door and the endless pacing, chattering, and chipping at Merlin's diamond coffin. Sam hushed Robin's cocaine-induced mumbling and they launched themselves toward Effie's office.

They had almost reached Vivian's door when a man entered the corridor from the stairs and pointed a finger. "You!"

It was the long-nosed butler. What was with this man? On his previous visit, Sam couldn't find servant nor mouse in this hallway, and now this jasper seemed to live here.

"You do not belong in this corridor," the butler said. "What are you doing here?"

"Seeking services," Robin said. "This is a public corridor."

"Do you not know there is a madman on the loose? No one is allowed free movement in the castle without authorization."

"What?" said Robin. "I have never heard such a thing. Who—"

"It comes straight from the knights," said the butler.

"But I am a knight." Robin rested his hand on the pommel of his sword and struck a manly pose. "Well, a squire."

The butler snorted. "You do not look like a squire."

Robin looked down at himself. Sam looked as well and then at his own attire, only then remembering that his *mean streets* getup was still in the Duke's cart.

"We are dressed for the funeral," Robin said. "The—"

"The Duke of Earl?" asked the butler.

Robbin nodded vigorously.

"A wonderful man," the butler said. "Been ill for months, of course. His passing comes as no surprise, bless his soul. But you still cannot be wandering the castle."

"Because of the madman," Sam said.

"Yes." The butler looked at Sam closely and then shook his head.

"We've lost track of the Lady Euphemia Peregrine," Sam said. "Do you know if she's in her office?"

The butler's eyes went wide. "I would be surprised if she were anywhere other than the Great Hall with everyone else. The viewing is about to begin."

27

THE VIEWING OF THE DUKE OF EARL

SAM HAD NEVER seen so much traffic in the castle. Once he and Robin reached the main level, they were almost overrun by servants scurrying through the hallway with armloads of fabric, baskets overflowing with flowers, and wooden casks almost too heavy to carry. At the castle gate, guests poured in from the city and were herded by pages to the royal wing that Sam now knew housed the magistrate chamber, the chapel, and the Lesser and Greater Halls. There was no sign of Gawain and Caradoc trying to search the townsfolk for papers. Indeed, many of the squires and younger knights looked to have been roped into page duty.

Through the open portcullis above the mob's heads, Sam saw twilight deepening to purple.

"Evening is a deplorable time for a viewing," Robin said. "The viewing itself shall be cut short and guests will be required to travel home in the dark. Many who should come will not even have heard of the viewing until after it is over."

Sam hissed into Robin's ear. "There can't be a viewing. The coffin is empty."

Robin jerked. "Yes. Yes, you are right. We must disrupt it. I know. A fire. We shall set the Great Hall on fire!"

"Isn't the castle mostly stone?" Sam asked. "When was the last time you had a fire here."

"Well," Robin admitted, "we have never had a fire. Nothing

larger than oil catching flame in the kitchen. Perhaps we could burn the coffin."

"That'll be good for about two minutes," Sam said. By this time, they were nearing the crowded Great Hall. "Let's go in and see what's what. Maybe a better plan will make itself obvious."

"We must go to the courtyard first," Robin said. "I must arm myself with a sharper sword. Just in case."

Seeing that arguing the point with the squire in his current state might not get much traction, Sam followed him back to the castle entrance and turned into the horse passage. The practice yard was deserted, which was just as well as any of the knights might just stick a sword through Sam rather than chat first. The sky was now a deep purple, but there was still sufficient light to find the weapons rack. Robin grabbed a replacement sword and then gazed wistfully at a bow and sheaf of arrows.

"I can't see that being much use in a crowded room," Sam said.

"No, but it should be. I swear to you, Sam Spade, that I shall practice with the bow until I am the best bowman in Britain. Then it shall be child's play to enter a crowded hall and steal the crown, or save the damsel, or, or whatever circumstances call for. With only a bow."

"Sounds like a plan, but let's concentrate on saving today's damsel in distress."

"Oh?" asked Robin. "Which one?"

"Effie, of course."

"Euphemia. Right, right."

As they left the courtyard, Sam paused by the Duke's cart that had been rolled there after the casket had been carried to the Great Hall. He brushed aside some of the flowers until he could see his trench coat and fedora. He felt naked without them, but knew they would only get him into trouble at this point. At least he had his Smith and Wesson.

The corridor was even more crowded as they again made their way to the Great Hall. With the fall of night, servants scurried along the walls and waited with impatience for mourners to move out of the way so they could light a lantern or candle before racing off to the next one.

The Great Hall was already wall-to-wall with people; Sam and Robin had to squeeze themselves past shoulders and elbows.

"A normal viewing lasts most of a day," Robin said, "with friends, family, and admirers coming and going. This." He waved his hands. "This is a circus. Who would arrange such a farce?"

"I think we know the answer to that." Sam nodded his chin toward the front of the hall where the wooden coffin rested upon a low pedestal. Behind the casket stood a row of chairs in which sat Effie, her three close family members, and two others: Morgan Le Fay and Mordred.

The enchantress and her lover looked anything but serene. Both were dressed in black, but not for mourning. Mordred always dressed in black or grey and Le Fay favoured dark colours. A pompous old goat who Sam decided must be the King's Chamberlain stood at one end of the casket surveying the room. His expression suggested he had just eaten a grapefruit; whether that was for the crowd or for Le Fay rushing the viewing, Sam had no idea.

"If I had my bow," Robin said. "I could shoot the Chamberlain. That would delay the proceedings."

"Why not shoot Morgan Le Fay?" Sam asked.

"One cannot shoot a lady!"

"Okay, then Mordred."

"You suggest I murder my superior?"

Sam laughed. "It happens with disturbing frequency where I come from."

A soft sigh escaped Robin's lips. "Either way, I do not have my bow. And if I did, I would look rather conspicuous."

"I've got something better than a bow," Sam said. "But let's see what happens first."

Minutes passed as additional townspeople tried to squeeze into the Great Hall. Sam and Robin insinuated themselves through the masses, mostly by means of Sam tromping on people's feet, until they were almost sitting on top of the casket. Sam made eye contact with Effie and thought he saw a forced smile beneath her lace veil.

Then the Chamberlain stamped his staff against the floor for silence, which was slow to spread throughout the hall.

"We are gathered here," he shouted, straining his ancient voice to permeate the hall. "We are gathered here to bid farewell to our beloved kinsman, the Duke of Earl."

The pompous goat went on to recount various exploits carried out by Effie's father, drawing from the crowd laughter, tears, and cheers. Sam watched Effie sit through it all knowing that her father was still very much alive, if ill, at his estate, and that the casket contained little more than a fresh pine scent. When the Chamberlain reached the end of his speech, two men rose from their seats and prepared to lift the casket's lid for the viewing.

Sam tightened his hand on the grip of his Smith & Wesson where it sat in its holster beneath his borrowed duster. He didn't yet know who he would shoot first, Le Fay or Mordred, but he figured that once the empty coffin was revealed, all Hell was going to break loose.

Hammers pulled nails and the lid came up, turned in the air by the two men and set on its side against the back of the casket. Gasps rose throughout the room, but none louder than from Morgan Le Fay, who leapt to her feet and shook a fist at the box. Then she froze, still as a statue. Mordred had also stood and was reaching for his sword. But reaching was as far as he got; the faux knight also froze. Then the old man lying in the box sat up, causing a riot to break out in the hall.

And why not a riot, for the old man was not only not dead, he was not the Duke of Earl. The greybeard who rose from the coffin to face the gathered people of Camelot was none other than Merlin the Magician!

28

THE PREDILECTIONS OF
MAID EUPHEMIA PEREGRINE

"IT APPEARS," ROBIN shouted over the uproar, "that Hammett succeeded in releasing a portion of the magician sufficient to allow him to free himself from the diamond."

Sam could have said something about stating the obvious, but was so relieved he hadn't had to shoot up the room that he let it go.

Through the confusion he saw Effie speaking with her father's retainers. Soon they were pushing through the masses telling everyone that the Duke was not dead at all, but was safely ensconced on his estate and that this charade was contrived to entrap Lady Vivian and her son, who had conspired against the King. Even so, no one exhibited any inclination to leave the Great Hall until Galahad, Ector, and several other knights began forcing them out with the brunt of large shields.

Sam managed to avoid the evacuation by shouldering his way to Effie's side. Robin, however, vanished into the crowd. It was probably just as well.

"Ah, it is you," Merlin said upon seeing him, "Sam Sparrow." The old magician frowned. "I suppose I have you to thank for my timely rescue."

"Some mutual friends helped out," Sam said.

"I shall be sure to thank them, but how did you get here?"

"The Lady of the Lake hired me."

"Blast. Now I owe that old cow a favour."

"Old?" Sam rubbed his ear. "She was quite the looker when she came into my office."

The old man harrumphed. "She is that, but the Enchantress of Avalon is much older than I am. What did she promise you?"

"That you would send me back three days before I left."

Merlin rubbed his bearded chin. "Tricky."

"And," Sam said.

"And?"

"That when you send me back, that I would be a woman for a day."

The old man's eyes nearly popped out of his head. Effie also gave Sam a most peculiar look before being pulled away by an irate relative.

"I have to help someone," Sam explained. "The only way I can do it is as a woman."

The Lady of the Lake never promised any such thing, but it occurred to Sam that, even going back to Hartford before his partner Nora died, breaking into the women's-only spa to prevent the murder would be, as Merlin had just said, tricky. He didn't think putting on a maid's outfit with fake bosoms would work as well in Hartford as it had in Camelot.

"Trickier," was all Merlin said.

Sam had no idea why it would be trickier. He had seen Merlin disguise himself as a ten-year-old boy and as Galahad, and watched Le Fay adjust her . . . form . . . in front of a mirror. Maybe altering gender was not something magicians did. Like making change for a Pendragon.

Merlin finally lowered his hand from his beard and wagged a gnarled finger. "Very well. But it will have to wait while I settle some other accounts."

"Take all the time you need." Sam was in no hurry for a replay of the sudden departure he'd experienced last time. So long as he arrived early enough to save Nora, he had all the time in the world.

As Merlin turned to consider the two frozen villains, Effie escaped her relative and grabbed Sam's hand. She had thrown the black lace veil back over her hair and her eyes looked a bit wild. She led him a few steps away. "We need to talk."

With the crisis averted, Sam wondered if maybe now he and Effie would have time to address unspoken words, words that should have been spoken yesterday when they ran into each other in her office, or later in that abandoned building, or even this morning at her father's estate. Sam couldn't deny there was something between them, but like shy teenagers they had avoided the subject, making jokes and flirting in roundabout ways. But right now, she needed to talk. He could tell it was serious talk. Maybe talk regarding the conversation he'd had with Effie's father. Was it too much to hope that Euphemia Peregrine was finally ready to settle down? And that she might settle for a man like Sam Sparrow?

Effie stared Sam straight in the eye. "What is this about asking the Merlin to change you into a woman? What do you know?"

"What do I know?" This wasn't exactly the talk he'd been hoping for.

"Do not play coy with me, Mr. Spade. I know that you harbour an interest. You did the last time you were here and you do now."

That was more like it. "Who wouldn't be interested, angel? You've got everything going for you. Looks. Brains. Heart. You're the real deal, kid. The only thing that surprises me is that you're still on the market. I can only assume that you haven't met your match."

Sam knew the words he wanted Effie to say next. He'd dreamed them often enough. A pipe dream for the past six months with Effie centuries dead while at the same time too young for him. A desperate dream for the past two days when he had returned to find a more mature, yet still single Effie. Especially after the encouraging words from her father. He knew the words he wanted to hear: *I have been waiting for you, Sam. You are my match.*

Effie gazed deeply into his eyes. "I cannot get married, Sam. My feelings do not go that way. As you have apparently figured out. Damn you for being such a good detective. But even should the Merlin change you into a woman, I cannot promise that I will have feelings for you. The heart is a capricious thing."

"The heart is a—" Sam repeated. "Effie, what are you saying?"

She gave him a startled look. "That my heart does not run toward men. But you know that. You asked the Merlin to—" Effie's cheeks turned as red as Morgan Le Fay's lips. Then she fled from the room.

"I see you still have a way with the ladies," Merlin said, turning back toward him. The old man was grinning like Alice's Cheshire cat.

"Story of my life," Sam said, though none of those stories had kicked him in the gut as hard as this one. He peered past the magician and saw that Le Fay and Mordred were now encased in diamond, still standing in the outraged poses they'd been frozen into. It seemed like a good time to change the subject. "What about those two?"

The old man glanced over his shoulder. "They shall remain as they are, reminders to us all to be wary." Then he snorted. "I am the last who should berate you regarding women. I made a mistake taking Vivian—Morgan—as my mistress and teaching her magic. She had me completely fooled."

Sam nodded. "That's her nature." He tried to envision the magician and Le Fay in her canopy bed and immediately regretted it. Maybe that's why she'd found Mordred so . . . refreshing. She'd been six years with the old man.

Merlin huffed out a breath of air. "I suppose I shall send you back now. Three days, you say?"

"Around the time Morgan Le Fay did," Sam waved a hand at the two diamond statues, "that to you. But I can't leave yet."

"Why not?"

"I still need to sort things out with Effie."

The magician harrumphed. "I fail to see how speaking further with Lady Peregrine will help. Your complete misreading of her circumstances has left her unsettled and I fear anything further you might say would only throw salt in the wound."

"You knew about Effie's . . . predilections?"

Merlin grinned. "It does not take a detective to know that our Euphemia is sweet on the ladies."

That was a matter of opinion, but Sam wasn't going to argue the point. "Okay, but what about King Arthur? He's still ill, and the land with him."

"Is he?" Merlin waved his fingers and the golden cup rose

up out of the pine coffin and into the magician's hand. "Arthur's recovery began the moment our jeweller friend freed the Holy Grail from diamond, just as I recovered when released. Camelot shall be fruitful again now that all is set right. Safe journey, Sam Sparrow."

"What?" Sam said. "Don't forget to—"

29

A FRICTION OF FEMME FATALES

"—MAKE ME A woman," Sam finished. But the magician was no longer there. Or rather, Sam was no longer there. Instead he stood in a familiar darkened office with the lights of East Hartford shining in through the window.

Sam set a new land speed record racing through the outer office, out the *Sparrow and Clark Investigations* door, and down the hall to the small restroom shared by the six second-floor business offices. A small mirror hung above the sink. Sam stared into it. He didn't know what he'd expected, but the raven-haired beauty who stared back at him wasn't it. It wasn't even a version of himself. It was Morgan Le Fay from six years ago.

But that hardly mattered. What was important was that Merlin had remembered that he needed to be a woman for a day. At least, he hoped it would only be a day; he wasn't sure a permanent change suited his personality.

All Sam needed now was some appropriate clothing; he still wore the black duster and pants borrowed from Effie's estate, now several sizes too large for his slight frame. His expression in the mirror sagged at the realization he'd left his *mean streets* getup in the cart that had carried the casket.

"I loved that Burberry coat," he said in Morgan Le Fay's voice. Then he stamped his foot. "My tobacco kit is in that coat!"

Sam's violet-blue eyes widened in the mirror. "The date!"

A quick glance at his Rolex, which hung limp on his elegant, narrow wrist, revealed the time as 9:37 p.m. two days after the Lady of the Lake's visit. Of course, it did. If only Merlin's time travel trick synchronized watches.

Dashing back into his office, Sam went to William's desk and hammered on the space bar of his secretary's computer. It was the only computer in the office. Sam and Nora were gumshoes in the true sense of the word. They did their work by pounding pavement. Anything more complex than a phone call they tasked to William.

The computer eventually woke up and Sam's gaze darted to the bottom right corner of the display. The clock on the task bar said it was six-twenty a.m. and the date . . . the morning after Nora checked into the Miramar. The morning Nora dies.

Sam hurtled himself into the inner office and dug his car keys out of his desk. With luck, he could still get there before Nora was murdered. With luck. Murphy had better be taking a holiday.

But he couldn't go dressed like this. The Miramar had standards. Men's pants, shirt, and cowboy duster wouldn't do, no matter what era they came from or how badly they fit. Rushing to the closet, he ignored the rain slicker and two spare Brooks Brothers shirts and examined the spare clothing Nora kept in the office.

The dress was a bit loose around the shoulders—Le Fay was a petite woman while Nora was statuesque, though in a very feminine way—and hung further below his knees than was fashionable. He took the dress off again and tried on one of Nora's bras—who keeps bras in an office closet?—as he bounced around too much with just the dress. He wished he could do what Morgan Le Fay had done in the mirror, reshaping and resizing her bust to fit her mood.

For shoes he chose a pair that looked dressy, but were flat without heels. He knew he would never pass muster on heels. The shoes were too big and shifted around as he walked, but it was the best he could do.

Lastly, he threw on a fur-lined winter coat. He suspected it wasn't real fur, but couldn't tell the difference. He didn't waste time trying on hats. His shoulder-length raven hair looked fine as far as he was concerned. He needed to get to the

Miramar.

A sigh of relief left his lips when he found his Volvo S60 sitting in its narrow stall marked *Reserved for Sam Sparrow*. He couldn't remember where he or his car had been that cold December morning just a few days earlier. With a little thinking he'd have it, but there was no time for thinking. What was called for was action. Slush coated the windshield, so he dug the scraper out of the back seat and attempted to wipe the window clean without getting any dirty snow on Nora's fur coat or shoes. When the windows were *good enough*, he jumped into the car and headed down Pitkin Street.

Sam cursed as he realized that he couldn't speed, run a light, or break any other traffic laws that the situation might call for. If the police pulled him over, he'd look nothing like his driver's license. He'd wind up in jail and miss his chance to save Nora. He cursed again as early rush hour traffic turned his clear sailing into stop and go gridlock. He'd never get there in time!

Keeping calm and humming Dooley Wilson, Sam inched his way through traffic until he hit the suburbs and quieter streets, then he was racing past the city limits, along a rural road that cut through acreages with big houses and even bigger lawns, and finally pulled into the spacious parking lot of the Miramar Wellness Retreat.

The car clock read 7:48. The sun had been up for thirty minutes and Sam could see activity through several of the health spa's windows.

He parked in the vacant stall closest to the main entrance and raced along the icy pavement and up the steps without bothering to lock the car.

Inside the Miramar he found a cheerful woman sitting behind some kind of curved reception desk. A nametag on her starched white shirt identified her as Patty Green, Receptionist. "Welcome to the Miramar. Are you checking in?"

"No." It took no effort at all to sound like Morgan Le Fay. No speaking falsetto and faking an accent. With the soul of British faux nobility Sam said, "I'm here to see someone. Nora Clark."

Patty's face lost its cheer. "Oh, I'm afraid we don't allow visitors outside of teatime. Our guests have a schedule."

"It's an emergency," Sam said. His mind raced for a workable ploy. "Her business partner has been in an accident. He may not survive the day."

"How awful," Patty said. "I'll make sure she gets the message."

Sam stood speechless for a moment. She'd make sure Nora got the message? What kind of dumb onions did this place hire? "That's not good enough," Sam said, raising his voice. "I need to see Nora immediately. Her partner gave me important information to deliver. Life or death, he said."

The skin around Patty's eyes tightened. "Which is it? Her partner's in the hospital or you have information from him?"

"Both." Sam gripped the edge of the counter. "An attempt was made on his life while he tried to get word to Nora. He passed the message to me to deliver. A private message. You understand?"

The woman frowned. "And you are?"

Sam's mouth fell open. So much for workable plans.

"I'm, ah, her partner's sister, Samonella Sparrow."

The receptionist raised an eyebrow. "Salmonella?"

"I get that all the time," Sam said. "Our parents' sense of humour leaves something to be desired. But, please, call Nora to your desk or tell me where she is. I'll give her my brother's message and then get back to the hospital. I wouldn't have left his side if the information hadn't been so important."

"Well, I don't know."

Sam slammed a fist on the countertop. "Listen you, it's more than your job's worth to make me angry. So just tell me where Nora is before I give you something you really don't want to know about!"

The woman's jaw dropped and her eyes boggled. Then her eyes glanced down at a sheet of lined paper.

Sam reached across the counter and snatched it up. He ran his gaze along the columns. There was Nora's name. Beside eight a.m. it said hot sauna. Sam looked up at the wall clock. 7:55.

"Where's the sauna?" he shouted.

"I'm going to call security," Patty said.

"Never mind, I'll find it myself." Then Sam was running down a wide corridor.

Small signs with arrows littered the walls. Yoga. Zen Garden. Massage. Finally, he saw one that said *sauna* and followed the arrow into a section of the building that felt humid and included other signs that said lap pool, therapy pool, and whirlpool.

Racing into the sauna, he peered through the steam and saw several women of various ages and states of undress. None were Nora. She hadn't arrived yet. Or maybe she never would.

Back in the hallway, Sam retraced his steps to where women might approach the sauna from any of three directions. A closet stood to one side, the kind with horizontal slats. Sam opened it and saw there was enough space between the door and the shelves for a person to stand and watch the hallway. He closed himself inside, then wondered if he had chosen the same closet where the killer would stash Nora's body. He hoped so. That meant he still had time.

Sam wasn't convinced that he needed to hide, but it felt like a good idea. Especially if the murderer tailed Nora to the sauna. Well, never mind the murderer. How was he going to explain to Nora who he was and how he knew her life was in danger? He didn't have long to think about it. Peering out between two wooden slats, he spotted Nora walking sedately along the corridor. Alive. Nora was still alive.

His partner wore a white terrycloth robe that covered her from chin to ankle. She'd tied her blonde hair in a tight bun and wore no makeup. Sam couldn't remember ever seeing Nora without makeup. She looked just fine without it.

He was about to reveal himself and try to explain the situation, when he spotted a second woman, also wrapped chin to foot in a robe, following a few paces behind. Sam recognized her. The hair was all wrong, but she was the spitting image of their client, Miss Dorothy Wynant. What was she doing here?

Dorothy Wynant had hired Sparrow and Clark Investigations to determine who had murdered her father, Clyde Wynant. Initially misidentified by the police as a derelict named Rosengreen, the elderly family patriarch had been found a few months earlier in one of Club Miramar's gardens with his head smashed in and wearing a suit of clothes three sizes too large for him. After wasting several days looking into the background of the wrong man, the police made no progress in finding Clyde Wynant's killer.

Wynant was an inventor and something of a scoundrel, well

known among Hartford's movers and shakers, few of whom failed to have motive, means, and opportunity. The lengthy suspect list was too well placed to be touched by any kind of meaningful investigation, so the police had tossed the case into their cold file. Not to be daunted, Miss Wynant had hired Nora and Sam because, unlike the police, they weren't afraid to step on hoity-toity toes.

So why was Wynant here? As if things weren't complicated enough? Sam's fingers itched for a cigarette, of all the lousy timing. He clenched his fists and tried to order his thoughts. Talking to Nora was no longer an option. He'd need a plan B. He'd have to follow both women into the sauna and see what played out. All he needed was a robe.

While neither woman would recognize Sam disguised as a femme fatale con artist hundreds of years dead, Nora would be sure to recognize the clothes from her office closet and wonder what they were doing in Miramar's sauna. Maybe the closet stored a robe. Or some towels. Sam didn't think he could turn around to check until after the two women walked past. What was Wynant doing here?

In the moments Sam had taken to revise his plan, Nora walked past the closet and Miss Wynant approached not far behind. Sam watched as their client reached into a pocket of her robe and pulled out something long and thin—a wire with handles at either end. A garrotte! The daughter was the killer? That was unexpected.

As Wynant passed in front of the closet, Sam heaved the door open, knocking the petite woman sideways. Dorothy turned to face him, her expression one of startled anger, but Sam had already pulled his semi-automatic from where he'd stashed it in the fur coat's pocket. A gun trumps a garrotte any day.

Wynant stared at the gun barrel, her garrotte stretched tight between her hands.

"I'd rather not have to kill you, Miss Wynant," Sam said. "Why don't you drop your little toy."

"What's going on here?" Nora was looking back at them from where she had stopped in the corridor.

Sam held his bean-shooter steady and never took his eyes off their client. "You may not recognize Miss Dorothy Wynant with the wig or dye job, whichever it is, but she's here to kill you."

"I do recognize my client," Nora said. "As well as that coat you're wearing. But I don't recognize you?"

"Your partner sent me," Sam said.

"He did, did he?"

"Yes. He received information suggesting you might be in danger and asked me to check on you."

"He asked you to check on me." Nora's tone was anything but appreciative.

Sam sighed. *Try to do a good deed and this is what you get.* "He didn't know the danger was your client."

Miramar security chose that moment to arrive, followed by an irate Receptionist Patty.

"Freeze!" one of the uniformed women shouted, aiming her own weapon at Sam. *Well, of course the Miramar would have female security.*

"I'm a licensed PI," Sam said, "thwarting a murder. It's Miss Wynant here you need to take into custody."

"You're the one with the gun," the guard said.

"Yeah? Well, that toy Wynant is holding so tightly is a garrotte. Take that away and I'll gladly hand over my weapon."

"Wynant?" asked Patty. The words left her lips slowly, indicating she recognized the belatedly revealed name of the corpse found earlier on the property. "We have no one here registered by that name."

Nora stepped in. "I'm Nora Clark and I am registered here. And I *do* recognize the name and the woman. She must have used an alias. Apparently, that garrotte was intended for me."

30
A NIGHT ON THE TOWN

"I'M SORRY YOUR spa weekend was cut short," Sam said. They were back at the office where Sam had spent the past hour trying to explain to his partner why he was now five foot nothing and female. The Q and A had gotten pretty intense at one point.

"Forget my weekend," Nora said. "You're a freaking woman!"

"So you do believe me." Sam leaned back in his Broderick recliner. His shoeless feet occupied his desk and a half-empty glass of Bogart's Real English Gin sat near his hand. Also on the desk sat two silver Pendragons and a pile of rough-cut diamonds. It surprised Sam that anyone could believe his story, but Nora Clark was no dumb onion.

His partner shook her head. "Never mind that you know too much about me that only Sam could know, your habits speak for themselves. What are you going to do about the police?"

The police had been none too happy with Sam's hollow explanations and lack of ID. If Wynant hadn't broken down during questioning and confessed to attempted murder, he'd still be humming "Old Man River" in one of East Hartford City Jail's air-conditioned guest rooms. Then there was the matter of carrying a weapon without a license. They were holding his Smith & Wesson hostage until he returned tomorrow with promised ID and license.

Sam took a sip of gin juice. "At six-fifteen tomorrow morning

I should be my old self again."

Nora snorted. "They're still expecting Samonella Sparrow to show up. Couldn't you have picked a better name?"

"Best I could do under the circumstances. But now they'll get Sam Sparrow. It's my gun and I can prove it, if they haven't figured that out already. I'll say I was in disguise."

"Right. They'll believe the woman they interviewed today was really an older, taller man in disguise."

"I'll pass a lie detector test."

"Okay, okay. But Wynant never explained why she tried to kill me."

"That's easy," Sam said. "We're too close to solving her father's murder. Closer than she expected us to get."

"Close? I thought all we'd done is eliminate everyone on the suspect list. All right. I'll bite. Who did murder Clyde Wynant?"

"Again easy. His daughter did. Why else would she try to kill you?"

"But she also hired us?"

Sam shrugged. "She didn't know how good we were." Setting his feet back on the floor, he leaned forward in his recliner. "Clyde Wynant was not a nice man. I don't know what made Dorothy Wynant angry enough to murder her own father, but we both know through our investigation that he treated his family no better than he did his business partners. What Dorothy didn't count on was the old man's estate being tied up until his murder was solved. When the police dropped his case in the cold file, she hired us to move things along."

Nora tried to speak but Sam waved her down.

"I know what you're going to say. As the murderer, she wouldn't want the murder solved. But that's where she was smart. Her old man had no end of enemies, any one of whom could have pulled the trigger. She figured we'd help the D.A. set one of them up. Winning a high-profile case is a career maker and she knew no one was breaking down our door. When, instead of pointing a finger, we shortened the suspect list, she got antsy. She couldn't risk us discovering the real killer." Sam paused. "She did get away with killing you the first time around. And no doubt would have left me behind a hedge or under some floorboards a few days later. As a killer she was getting pretty good at the trade."

"It's a great theory," Nora said. "But we still have to prove it. We have nothing connecting Dorothy to her father's death. And I don't think time travel is going to make a good argument in court."

"Tomorrow's another day," Sam said. "This one's mostly shot. What say you and I go out on the town?"

"Out on the town? We never go out on the town."

Sam downed the remains of his gin and jumped out of his chair. "Then it's high time we did. Besides, I'm not feeling much like myself tonight." He stretched his lean arms and thrust out his chest. "Might be kinda of fun to turn some heads. Flaunt 'em if you got 'em!"

Nora chuckled and rose from her own desk chair. "I'll get my coat. My other coat. Sam, just when I think I've figured you out, you surprise me all over again."

Sam flashed his partner a wide grin. "I can live with that."

THE END

ABOUT THE AUTHOR

RANDY MCCHARLES is a full-time author of speculative and crime fiction.

He is the recipient of several Aurora Awards, and in 2013 his short story "Ghost-B-Gone Incorporated" won the House of Anansi 7-day Ghost Story Contest.

Randy's most recent publications include *A Connecticut Gumshoe in King Arthur's Court* from Tyche Books, five novels in the Peter Galloway private detective series, the 2017 Aurora Award shortlisted novel *The Day of the Demon*, and the 2016 Aurora Award shortlisted novel *Much Ado about Macbeth*, also from Tyche Books.

In addition to writing, Randy organizes various literary events including the award-winning When Words Collide Festival for Readers and Writers.